MW01196807

SARAH A. PARKER

# TO FLAME A WILD FLOWER

A CRYSTAL
BLOOM
NOVEL

Copyright © 2023 by Sarah A. Parker
*All rights reserved.*

No part of this book may be reproduced in any form or by any
electronic or mechanical means, including information storage and
retrieval systems, without written permission from the author, except
for the use of brief quotations in a book review.

iii

FOR THOSE WHO DANCE
WITH GHOSTS AND FORGET
TO FACE THE SUN.
I SEE YOU.

# GLOSSARY

**Stony Stem** — *Orlaith's tower at Castle Noir.*

**Bitten Bay** — *The bay at the bottom of the cliff below Castle Noir.*

**Safety Line** — *The line Orlaith hasn't stepped over since she came to Castle Noir when she was a child. It surrounds the estate—running the forest boundary and cutting through the bay.*

**The Tangle** — *The unutilized labyrinth of corridors in the center of Castle Noir that Orlaith used to travel around in a more efficient manner. These corridors are typically without windows.*

**Sprouts** — *The greenhouse at Castle Noir.*

**Dark zones** — *Places Orlaith has yet to explore in Castle Noir.*

**The Den** — *Rhordyn's personal chambers in Castle Noir.*

**The Keep** — *The big polished doors guarded by Jasken. One of Orlaith's dark zones in Castle Noir.*

**The Plank** — *The tree that has fallen across the selkie pond and is often used for Orlaith's training at Castle Noir.*

**Spines** — *The giant library at Castle Noir.*

**The Safe** — *The small door where Orlaith placed her offering every night at Castle Noir.*

**Whispers** — *The dark, abandoned passageway Orlaith has turned into a mural at Castle Noir.*

**The Grave** — *The storage room where Orlaith discovered Te Bruk o' Avalanste at Castle Noir.*

**Puddles** — *The communal bathing chambers/thermal springs at Castle Noir.*

**Hell Hole** — *The room where Baze often trains Orlaith at Castle Noir.*

**Caspun** — *A rare bulb Orlaith relies on to calm her attacks brought on by her nightmares and sharp sounds.*

**Exothryl/exo** — *The contraband drug Orlaith used to take in the morning to counteract the effects of overdosing on caspun every night to ensure a good sleep.*

**Conclave** — *A meeting that consists of all the Masters and Mistresses from across the continent.*

**Tribunal** — *The monthly gathering where citizens get to voice their woes with their High/Low Master.*

**Fryst** — *Northern Territory.*

**Rouste** — *Eastern Territory.*

**Bahari** — *Southern Territory.*

**Ocruth** — *Western Territory.*

**Arrin** — *Central Territory that was destroyed during The Great Purge.*

**Lychnis** — *The crystal island.*

**Mount Ether** — *Home to the Prophet Maars.*

**Reidlyn Alps** — *The mountains that block the border between Fryst, Ocruth, and Rouste.*

**The Stretch** — *The band of barren land at the base of Reidlyn Alps that is riddled with Vruk traps.*

**Parith** — *The capital of Bahari.*

**River Norse** — *The river that flows through the continent. The main trade route.*

**Quoth Point** — *The only area on the western shore that is not a cliff. Territory battles have been fought here in the past.*

**The Great Purge** — *The event that wiped out the Unseelie.*

**The Blight** — *The spreading sickness.*

**Candescence/candy** — *Ground Aeshlian thorns, sometimes diluted with powdered sugar.*

**Whelve** — *The obsidian stone rings scattered across the continent that offer refuge from the Vruk.*

**Te Bruk o' Avalanste** — *The Book of Making.*

**Valish** — *The ancient language.*

**Shulák** — *Faith dedicated to the words the Prophet carves into the stones at Mount Ether.*

**Moal** — *People who work the Vruk traps on The Stretch.*

**Forgery** — *The place where cuplas are forged.*

**Mala** — *The afterlife.*

**High Septum** — *The leader of the Shulák.*

**Shadow's Hand** — *The Aeshlian the Shulák are hunting—the one they believe will bring about the end of the world.*

**Ether Trial** — *Bahari/Shulák tradition. A trial where a Master/ Mistress/High Master/High Mistress coupling into a seat of power must prove their worth to the Gods by climbing out of The Bowl, mimicking the creatures that spilled from the crater lake at Mount Ether at the dawn of time.*

**Impurists** — *Those the Shulák have branded as Soiled Souls in need of redemption for them to make it into Mala—the afterlife.*

**Gray Guards** — *Shulák militia.*

**Liquid Bane** — *A deadly poison made from seeds of a bane bush.*

**Senka Seed** — *A potent antidote for liquid bane.*

**Mail Tree** — *The sprite message depot.*

**Sprite Warren** — *the underground tunnel network the sprites use to get around. Often, these tunnels have exits near mail trees.*

**The End** — *The void between life and death.*

**Krah** — *Leather winged, meat-eating creatures with long tails and feathery plumage. They are tied to omens of impending death.*

**Endagh Ath Mahn** — *The Sword of End.*

**Coupling Ceremony** — *The 'coming together' ceremony for two people choosing to spend their life together. Different in each territory.*

*18 years ago*

# PROLOGUE

*Orlaith*

*If I make myself small, nobody will know I'm here.*

I shuffle closer to the wall, hugging my knees, the mattress a roof over my head that smells like feathers and straw. My teeth chatter, eyelids trying to shut, like when I need to sleep. Little puffs of white come out when I breathe.

The cold inside my chest is so big and heavy. But I like this cold—it feels slow and quiet. Better than my dreams that are hot and hurting.

This cold feels like it has an end. Somewhere.

Perhaps if I reach it, I'll remember who I am?

My memories … they're a splat of black. A scribbled drawing that makes no sense.

*I think I'm missing something important—*

The door creaks open, but I'm too sleepy to turn toward the sound of footsteps stomping into the room.

"Where did you say she was?"

My heart does this jumpy thing that makes me feel sick.

*I don't know that voice.*

It's not from my nightmares; not one of the voices that whispers at me. It's not the voice from that night when my memories began—the deep voice that said I was *safe*, but that I've never heard again.

"Under the bed. My arms aren't long enough to reach her, and the damn thing is bolted to the floor."

*I know that voice.* The woman who gives me warm cuddles at night and tells me everything's going to be okay.

She says I need more sunshine. That it'll make me feel better.

But I like the dark.

More tears slip down my cheeks as bare feet move around the bed. I watch each step, tucking into a tighter ball. Another shiver, and I rest my head on my knees, breathing cold air all over them.

I squeeze my eyes shut …

*If I can't see you, you can't see me.*

"Orlaith?"

They keep using that name.

*Not me.*

*Not me.*

*Not me.*

I'm someone else. Someone happy … I think. But I don't know where my giggles went.

*What is this big blackness I can't stop slipping into?*

Something tugs at my shift, and I'm dragged along the floor, clawing at the boards. I scream bigger than I ever have, but my sound doesn't come. It never does.

*I think it fell down that hole, too.*

I'm pulled into the sunlight that makes my eyes hurt;

pulled against a warm chest that smells like flowers and wood, wrapped in big arms I bleed with my teeth and nails.

*They got me—*

I thrash and claw and kick, desperate to get back under the bed.

To *hide*.

"It's okay," the woman says from beside the door, over and over. "His name is Baze. He's here to help."

Her face scrunches up, and she turns away. The smell of her sadness fills the room.

The arms tighten until my strength goes. Until I stop fighting and trying to make my scared sound that always hurts my throat.

The man places his hands on my cheek and arm, and a warmth fills me that makes my teeth chatter less. Makes me feel less sleepy.

"I know the hurt is loud, but it won't always be." He holds my hands, like they're butterflies caught in a warm hug. "One day it'll stop screaming at you. It'll become nothing more than a *whisper*."

It's the whispers that scare me most. There's so many of them, and they're always there, speaking to each other.

Speaking to *me*.

Maybe I should let that huge hole in my chest gobble them up. Maybe the horrible dreams would stop. The ones where I hear those same voices but from real people that always end up burnt in the dirt with wide eyes that won't blink.

"Small seeds grow into big, strong things." He blows heated air onto my hands. "But they need sunlight and warmth to set their roots in the soil. And like it or not ... you can't get that under the bed."

I thread my fingers through my hair. Fisting it. Tugging at the roots. Images blooming on the backs of my lids in rapid succession:

The burrow. The small rank cells and their withered inhabitants.

The Aeshlian—chained beneath a single beam of light.

A cut in my palm. A trail of blood.

Rhordyn stepping amongst a pack of Irilak, validating Cainon's condemning accusations.

*I saved lives,* I tell myself, hammering the words into my brain until it's ripe and swollen.

*I saved lives ...*

Then why does it feel so *wrong?*

My face crumbles, silent sobs racking through me ...

*Not real. Just a horrible nightmare.*

"Wake up."

My voice is broken glass. It's a tree splintered at the base, now strewn across the ground with flames licking its spindly branches.

It's regret. Sorrow. Grief.

It's the feeling that I've ripped something vital from my chest, leaving a deep web of holes where the roots were sown. Where they came out bloody and snapped in places.

Oily perusals scribe across me from all angles, making my skin prickle.

I lift my head, the waterfall's thunderous heave a constant roar in my ears. A cluster of Irilak are loosely gathered around me, watching, nesting beside vine-strangled trees like black vapors spilling from the gnarled trunks. Ghoulish spectators to my violent unraveling.

*He was warm ...*

I flinch.

A nightmare. A terrible, devastating nightmare where I heard terrible truths and did terrible things.

"Wake up."

I slap myself. Again, and again, cheek flaming from the brutal assault. When that doesn't work, I reach behind my arm and pinch an inch of flesh.

*Hard.*

The pain doesn't help. It doesn't bring me a sense of relief.

*Doesn't wake me up.*

A few Irilak move closer, stretching from one pocket of shadow to another like dark taffy.

"Wake up."

I release the latch of my necklace. Feel the stone, conch, and chain slip down my front and thump into my lap. I ease my shirt off my right shoulder and skate my fingers over the risen, barky blemish growing from my skin, sobbing when my hand brushes a clutch of silky protrusions.

My eyes squeeze shut, brow crunching as I breathe deep.

Hold until my lungs burn.

I reach beneath my shirt and pull my dagger from the makeshift sheath bound around my waist.

My eyes pop open.

"Wake up," I growl, glancing down at my shoulder.

Three crystal blooms bare themselves to me, like iridescent swirls dipped in a sky full of sparkles, the biggest the size of a plum. I grab the smallest one first—no larger than a thimble—bunching its healthy cluster of petals before I set my dagger against the black stem.

"Wake up."

I slice.

Fierce, fiery pain snaps through my collarbone, snatching my breath, filling my eyes with tears quick to spill down my cheeks.

This horrid reality doesn't dissolve. I don't wake in sweaty sheets with a scream splintering my throat.

I let the hardening bloom fall from my hand and grab another. Tilt the head.

"Wake up."

Another blow of pain flays me, pouring fire through my veins as I heave breath into my staggering lungs. I don't wait for the pain to ebb before I snatch the biggest bloom, gather the petals, and set the blade against its thick, woody stem.

"*Wake up!*" I snarl, and *slice*—once, twice, three times before I finally sever the head, releasing a tortured wail as more tears spill. The bloom tumbles from my fingers. Thumps to the soil.

Still, this nightmare continues to pin me down with its crushing might.

"Please wake up …"

A blow of humid air dusts the side of my face from the waterfall's spray, and my gaze drifts to the right. To the ledge *he* fell over, the frothy nether that swallowed him in a misty gulp lit by a beam of sunlight breaking through the canopy, creating prisms of color that are almost *inviting*.

I stare, mesmerized by the lure of their intoxicating beauty. Like a soft *hello. Come look at me. Touch me.*

*Play with me.*

A strange yearning fills me, and I become bluntly aware

that this is one of those horrific nightmares where the only way to jerk awake and escape ... is to fall.

To follow him.

Relief surges through my veins, and I let the blade slip from my hand, necklace clattering to the dirt as I push to a stand. I step closer to the ledge, into the spill of sunlight that bathes my skin with its lustrous warmth, caressed by another flurry of misty wind.

I imagine somebody whispering for me to wake up, becoming more insistent, buffeting me with a demand, then *screaming*. Imagine somebody shaking me so hard I jolt back to the now, nestled in a bed of inky sheets in a room that's all curved edges and sun-soaked windows, packed full of a botanical scent.

Those oily perusals scribble across my skin in erratic motions ...

Another step forward.

The tips of my toes tingle, the sensation traveling through the arches of my feet, up my legs and spine, making me shiver. My hair—a tangle of thick, iridescent ropes—is tossed around my shoulders by the thunderous, billowing spray rushing up to meet me.

*Don't cry ...*

"Wake up," I whisper, the words lost against the roaring might of the water heaving over the edge.

My eyes drift shut, and I tease my toes farther forward—

The jarring squawk of a krah crackles down from above, followed by a shrill squeal.

I whip around, attention delving through the jungle's gloomy guts to where a sprite is spiraling toward the ground, propelled by its single wing hanging at an odd angle. Another chases, half the size and making twice the sound.

There's a soft thump as the injured one plunges into the underbrush, chased more delicately by the child—stealing nervous glances at her surroundings before she flutters beneath a silver-blue leaf in the same vicinity.

Irilak stretch from their darker pockets of shade, curling around tree trunks and waxy-looking shrubs, sniffing in the direction of the fallen meal. A rattling symphony shakes the silence, and my heart dives, thoughts churning.

Like a tidal pool gushing full of inky water, the Irilak converge on the helpless sprites.

Something inside me *snaps*.

*"Stop!"*

The voice that tears up my throat is not my own, but a hundred others wrestling free with the force of shattered glass. It's anger, fear, sorrow. It's all my heartache and hurt honed into sharp bits that cut.

The Irilak crouch, cower, *hide*—squeals of fear ripping free, some condensing into puddles of black, others stretching to blend with the trunks of lanky trees.

Silence follows, stark and so hollow it feels as if my heart is the only one beating in the world. The Irilak's collective attention scrawls across my face. My arm.

My outstretched hand.

Looking down, my guts drop.

Splits web across my skin, barely containing the black, bulging matter that singes the edges of my frayed flesh like a silent threat to release.

To slash and saw and *slay*.

Again, I look at the Irilak, each one jolting away from my sweeping gaze.

*I almost spilled myself. Almost killed them all.*

A sick feeling takes root inside my chest ...

"I— I didn't mean to."

They twitch in unison, like they're dodging the blow of my words.

I step forward; they flinch again.

Icy shame douses me from head to toe, and I scrunch my hand into a trembling ball.

They're ... *scared* of me.

These predators that suckle the wet life from anything that steps into their domain—that *feed* on fear—are afraid of this thing beneath my flesh.

Of *me*.

"I'm sorry," I plead, my heart lodged so high in my throat it's hard to speak past. "I didn't mean it."

*Any of it.*

I grip the tether of darkness flowing through my veins, feeling it singe my soul as it thrashes against me like a fish on a line, finally giving in to my firm and persistent tug. I reel it in, in long, deep drags, until it's a slithering knot coiled within the chasm beneath my ribs.

The splits in my skin knit together, leaving scratchy lines all over, but I don't stop reeling. Don't stop apologizing.

*Don't cry.*

My internal fingers tangle with the thorny vines of loose emotion that tore up my throat, pulling them back inside one sawing drag at a time. "*I'm so sorry,*" I rasp, unwrapping them from around my ribs and rotting heart, leaving a trail of ravaged flesh I know will never heal.

I gather all the hurt and the sorrow and the pain into a single barbed ball, then pluck little beads of luster from the branches of my veins—squishing them flat. Smoothing them. Wielding them into a crystal shell around the knot of prickly pain.

I don't want to hurt anymore.

To *feel*.

I want nothing—blissful, empty nothing that doesn't coax me to think about the horrible thing I did. Because this isn't a nightmare at all.

It's real.

Fissures crackle across the surface of the dome, so I add another layer. Another.

*Another.*

I keep plucking, dimming my insides one pinched bead at a time. Keep squishing, smoothing, applying—until the crystal is thick and sparkling, that ball of emotion stuffed down deep and locked away.

My next breath pours into me unburdened, blown out on a shuddered sigh. I blink, freeing the warm tears that had gathered in my eyes, feeling heavy but light. Hollow but full. Broken but whole.

Nothing.

*This is better ...*

My gaze drops to my dagger and chain and the three bloody blooms in the grass—the large one too big and bulky to tuck into my pocket. I dig a hole in the ground and bury it, patting the soil before I carefully gather the others. I secure my necklace around my neck, succumbing to the tight gulp of my fake exterior as I stab the dagger into the makeshift sheath bound around my waist.

Looking at the blood on my hands, I frown, stretching my fingers, scrunching them up ...

Hairline cracks weave through the dome.

"Shit," I mutter, squishing more beads of light, bogging up the gaps. Unfortunately, it's no magic fix-all. I just have to ... keep plucking and squishing and bogging. Forever.

*I can do that.*

The underbrush crunches and pops beneath my bare feet as I walk toward the spot where the sprites fell. Every step, every *breath,* tracked by countless pairs of eyes.

The Irilak drift backward in the wake of my approach, maintaining a healthy distance. I kneel, drawing on the heady scent of damp soil and decaying vegetation, brushing through soft, flimsy foliage to reveal the sprites—the smaller one with tear-stricken cheeks and twigs in her fire-red hair.

She looks up at me, dragging on the other's torn garb, trying to haul her toward a tiny scrap of light filtering through the canopy. *"Ge ni ve lashea te nithe ae nah! Ge ni ve lashea te nithe ae nah!"*

Something, something, chase, worry ... *cake?* Or is it eat?

Hmm.

*Too bad I flunked sprite linguistics.*

I look at the larger one face down in the dirt, her hair the same bright red. Perhaps they're mother and child? She's even wearing a similar dark shift, but in place of her left wing is a frayed nub, a clear liquid leaking from the wispy sever.

Another sharp caw pierces through the canopy, and I peer up, squinting toward a single blade of light and the dark shape circling, circling ...

13

*"Ge ni ve lash te nithe ae na!"*

"It's okay," I murmur, gently sweeping the injured sprite into my sore palm that bears a wound I refuse to acknowledge, tucking her close to my chest. The younger one flutters up until she's hovering near my face, her wide eyes steeped in emotions that make more cracks appear in that crystal dome—cracks I bog with another layer of light plucked from my dimming insides.

My next blink feels heavier than the last.

"Where do I take her?"

She looks around at the Irilak still cowering in the shadows.

"They won't hurt us." I don't know why I'm so certain—as certain as I am that I never want to feel again.

Ever.

Nothing is everything I never knew I needed. The ability to skate along the surface of my conscious mind, lift my feet and move forward. To continue down this pulseless, soundless void.

It's ... *safe.*

With a pained glance at her mother, the sprite waves her little hand—a gesture for me to follow.

The Irilak cleave a path for us as I trail her through the jungle, every step away from that heaving waterfall feeling like a string is tethered to my ribs, stretching.

*Stretching.*

I tune into the injured sprite's shuddered breaths, timing my own to match their pattering beat.

*Rescue this life. Make her safe.*

A task. A tiny, quivering task. Something for me to focus on.

A faint beacon in this shadowy pall.

# CHAPTER

*Cainon*

## 2

"I don't care if you have to go out there and slaughter the beasts yourself, Grimsley. We're down to the dregs," I say, staring at him from beneath my brows—exuding an air of nonchalance when I feel the fucking opposite.

Grimsley's perched on the edge of his seat before my desk, not one strand of hair out of place, features so long and sharp he looks like a well-tended rat kid scooped from the gutter, then dressed up real nice.

"I'm aware, High Master." Sweat dapples his brow, the pungent waft of it curdling my guts. "We're doing everything we can."

"If you were, we wouldn't be in this predicament."

His gaze drops, and mine spears over his shoulder to the clock on the mantle.

*It's almost time.*

I cross my ankles, bouncing my foot to the frantic beat of his heart. "If our oil stores don't return to a healthy level soon, I'll be forced to make an example of somebody. Now get the fuck out," I say, scrunching my nose.

He shoves up, bows, and strides toward the door—every step stiff, as though he's trying not to run.

"Oh, and Grimsley?"

He turns, those beady eyes latching onto me. "Yes, Master?"

"If we run out of oil, your family will be the first to lose their rations."

His face takes on a sickly pall before he dips his head, shuffles backward toward the exit, and leaves, clicking the door shut behind him.

My rage boils, gaze drifting to the pile of scrolls stacked on a tray on the edge of my desk. I whip my arm out, sending them flying, the tray clattering to the floor.

I stare at the mess and sigh.

A knock echoes through the spacious room.

"Enter."

A string of servants trail through my office, heads bowed, each carrying various delicacies I ordered for the morning tea: a stack of scones, fruit drizzled in honey, mulberry tea, asparagus rolls. Only the best ingredients—imported from all over the continent.

The servants step onto the balcony where a table has been prepared, and I stand and charge around the desk, intercepting the woman carrying a bowl of clotted cream. "Clean up that mess over there," I mutter, dragging my finger through the cream and shoving it in my mouth—the hint of vanilla instantly warming my mood.

The cook added *just* the right amount. At least somebody can do their fucking job right.

The girl scurries off to gather the scrolls while I step out onto the balcony, bowl in hand. "Leave it," I holler at the servants trying to find places for all the plates, bowls, and utensils, and failing miserably.

They scatter, pouring inside, out of my sight.

I set down the cream, rearranging everything until it's presented just right. Nodding to myself, I move toward the balustrade, my fifth-floor vantage point providing a panoramic view of the city.

I watch a stout barge emerge from the Norse, stacked with cubes of glass, sitting so low it's a miracle water doesn't slosh over the sides. It drifts past a whaling ship that's the opposite; perched much higher than it should be for a returning vessel, despite its filthy patchwork sail— tribute to a long and tiresome journey.

*Fucking hell.*

Casting my gaze on Parith glittering in the morning sunlight, I scour the square buildings like I'm walking the streets.

Searching them.

I tap my finger against the rail to ease my fraying patience.

She should be back by now, on her knees, begging for my forgiveness. She'll see how easy it can be once she gives herself to me completely. I'll prove to her that I'm *better* than him—that I'm everything she's ever dreamed of—and she will love me for it.

*Truly* love me.

Footsteps approach from behind, and my doorman clears his throat. "High Master, the High Septum is here to see you."

My heart skips a beat. "Send her in. Make sure I have no more interruptions until she leaves."

He dips his head and scampers off, and I turn my attention to the table of refreshments, smooth the gray tablecloth draped across the stone, then restraighten the plates, bowls, and utensils. Shuffling footsteps approach, and I frown, spinning to see the High Septum limping onto my balcony, the folds of her gray robe ruffling in the light wind.

Scenting blood, I hurry forward and take her arm. "Heira, what have you done to yourself?"

She looks up at me from beneath the shadow of her hood, passing me a tight smile that etches lines at the corners of her purple star-burst eyes. "I've taken to wearing a metal spur around my thigh until I hunt down Shadow's Hand. I want to *feel* the passing of each day, as everyone will surely feel the consequences if I do not succeed."

I swallow my urge to tell her I think that's a fucking terrible idea.

"I'm certain the Gods note your servitude," I bite out instead, escorting her toward one of the two chairs set around the square table, dashing a napkin over her knees. I take the other seat, rolling my sleeves. "Refreshment?"

"Tea, please." She sweeps back her hood, pulling long, loose, golden locks over her shoulder, the tangled length shot through with silver streaks that bounce the sunlight—a salute to her age that her relatively smooth skin does well at concealing.

My fingers itch to brush it.

*Braid it.*

To tame it into something less wild and unruly.

"And a scone," she continues, eyeing up the bowl lumped with a swirl of cream. "Oh, Cainon. *Clotted cream?* I haven't been able to get my hands on any for months."

I offer an indulgent smile. "Only the best for you. I had the cook fold vanilla through it. I know it's your favorite."

She pats my cheek, eyes aglitter. "You're too good to me."

"Never."

She pulls the ornate soft-bristle hairbrush from the folds of her cloak, then sets it on the table between us, letting her hand rest upon the handle. My heart pounds as I pour her tea and prepare two plates of scones capped with a dollop of cream, gaze nipping at the brush.

Her hand.

With a knowing glint in her eye, she lets it go, then looks out across the ocean rumpled by the warm breeze, giving me an unhindered view of her tousled locks. She tips her face to the sun—the skies clear but for a few slow-moving tufts of clouds. "The Gods blessed us with a beautiful day." Opening an eye, she asks, "Would you not usually spend it offshore?"

"Not today." I set the scone before her, glancing at the brush again. "Too much on my mind. Are the preparations in order for the coupling ceremony? I'm looking forward to seeing which creature Orlaith chose."

"From what I understand, yes." She lifts a brow. "And with the clearing of the skies, I believe the Gods favor this union."

*Hopefully.*

I stir a cube of sugar through my tea. "Have you picked the Impurists?"

"Indeed," she says tightly. "My daughter would have had the great honor, but she opted to take her oath before the stones. I shipped her off this morning."

The punch of pride is potent in her tone.

Dragging my spoon along the cup's lip, I look up. "Oh?"

"Finally, after all these years. She even had the third eye carved," she boasts, gesturing to the raw mark between her eyes with a flick of her hand. "I had mine deepened at the same time."

With a slight tilt of my head, I offer her a small smile, looking at her scone that's yet to be touched—the cream beginning to yellow and melt from the sun's fierce heat. Clearing my throat, I pluck a grape from the bowl of fruit and toss it in my mouth, relishing the way it pops beneath my piercing teeth. "Why the sudden change?"

Gael never struck me as one to follow her mother's footsteps, and their strained relationship never threatened me before.

But *now* ...

"I did not question her turn to faith—simply welcomed it with open arms. She'll spend some time atoning at the Glass Palace, strengthening her body and mind. I'm hoping she will join me in the hunt for Shadow's Hand."

I nod, watching that cream drip, drip, fucking *drip* ...

"Well, I hope we still get to enjoy our monthly morning teas?" I ask, struggling to keep the jealousy bubbling in my chest from seeping into my tone. Counting two visible tangles—not to mention the few loose strands frolicking around her face like a fucking *taunt*.

She offers me a comforting smile, reaching out to set her hand on mine. "I'm not going anywhere."

21

Relief nuzzles into my chest.

She finally picks up her scone and takes a healthy bite, humming her appreciation as she chews. "I'm sorry I missed the last." She sets it down and draws a sip of tea, tucking a loose tendril behind her ear. I grind my teeth, itching to take the brush and pull it through those golden locks. "I journeyed to Mount Ether to speak with Maars myself."

I drop my fucking scone, eyes blowing wide. "You should have *warned* me! I would have provided you with a congregation of escorts!"

She looks at me from beneath raised brows. "Who would have gotten in my way?"

I bite down on the inside of my cheek, drawing a deep breath through my nose and blowing it out. "How did it go?"

"Well. I took him a goat and watched him feast upon its warm heart," she says with such savagery I can almost picture her standing there with the organ in her hand, blood dribbling down her arm. "He told me my daughter would come face to face with the one we seek." Chin lifted, a fierceness ignites her eyes. "We're getting close, Cainon. I can *feel* it."

I give her a tight nod.

I want to believe her, but after so many years, those words feel more myth than reality. A false sense of comfort, no doubt, but my mind is elsewhere lately.

I sip my tea, scouring her messy locks, the brush, before staring over the balustrade at the barge piled with blocks of glass that glimmer in the sunlight. It drifts toward the bay's narrow mouth bracketed by twin towers of blue stone, each burdened with a massive cog that winds the thick iron chain draped across the ocean floor. Turns it into a hull-shredder when pulled taut.

Yes, the shallow banks crouched beneath the waves are perilous in rough weather, but the chain is worth far more than just a warning for when the chop is up. It protects Parith from an ocean-borne attack almost as effectively as Ocruth's famous cliffs.

"Are you happy with the latest shipment?"

"Very. The clarity is impeccable. That's the last of it being ferried to Kilth," I say, gesturing toward the barge. "All going to plan, it will be shipped off the continent by the next full moon."

The logs I receive in exchange will add greatly to the production of my fleet, and it didn't cost me a single Baharian tree.

"Our understanding works well for both of us," she says, bouncing her brows, and I hum my agreement.

"To sacrifices."

She nods, and I sip the steaming liquid, gaze drawn back to the city's blocky skyline. I bite down on another grape.

"Now, what about the news you promised in your scroll?"

"Of course." Swallowing my mouthful, I nip a glance at the brush, then clear my throat and dust off my hands, savoring the moment.

Gorging on it like the feast it is.

"It's too early to say for sure, but ... I may have found a way to knock him off the board. For good."

"Do you mean—"

I smirk.

Heira's eyes widen, hand stabbing across the table to grip my own. "Oh, my boy. You have done *well!*"

The praise, the tone, the look on her face—

I'm infused with a spill of rapture that makes my blood surge. "As soon as I become Master Consort of Ocruth, you'll have unchecked access to scour Vateshram Forest for Shadow's Hand. You'll also have access to the unlimited resources you desperately need to support your swelling militia."

"Wonderful," she gushes, squeezing my hand, wielding a smile so big my chest inflates with pride.

"I'm so glad you're happy …"

"I'm more than just *happy.*" She nods to the brush, and I reach for it—the movement slow and controlled.

*Savored.*

I ease around the table and gather her hair. Pull it over her shoulder.

The length tumbles down her spine, and I slide the bristles through her flaxen strands one exquisite sweep at a time, taming them into a river of silk—a motion that does similar things to my messy insides.

Tames that savage voice in my head.

"Long have we knelt to the stones," she preaches while I brush. "Felt those words as if they were carved into the very flesh of our hearts. We have been true servants to the Gods, and they will reward us."

My hands flex around the handle.

I should have told her the bad news first, but this hair … the knots …

Her hand whips back, snatching my wrist, halting my movement midstroke. She turns, looking at me over her shoulder. "You're anxious. I can feel it in the way you're brushing."

I sigh—long and deep. "I have something … *controversial* I need to speak with you about."

"Nothing leaves this balcony, you know that." She sweeps her hair over her shoulder, out of my reach, and I tighten my grip on the brush. "I would *never* hurt you."

My hand loosens, the words soothing old wounds that may have stopped bleeding long ago but still boast scars that remind me of things I wish I could forget. Most of the time.

Other times, I'm glad I remember. That the hurt burns within me like the blaze of a fiery poker stabbed through my chest.

I clear my throat and reclaim my seat, setting the brush back on the table—bunching my hands into balls that I rest on my bouncing knees. "Orlaith …"

Heira tilts her head to the side. "What about her?"

Sweat prickles the back of my neck as I gather the poisonous words. "I want to keep her, if not publicly, then *personally*," I say, pausing. "*However* this unfolds."

"Hold on …" Stark realization widens her eyes, disapproval thick in her tone. "Is the girl not *intact*?"

"I believe she is but can't be sure."

Her eyes become slits. "There are *checks* one of the Brothers could perform—"

"No," I snap. "No checks."

*Nobody touches her but me.*

Heira grits her teeth so hard I hear them grind against each other. "Let me understand this correctly, my boy. You are requesting that we do not seek to understand the reasons why the Gods remit their favor should she fail the trial, and that we do not *punish* her accordingly?"

I nod.

She draws deep, shoving back against her chair. "This is *blasphemy*."

"I know."

But there's something inside me—a hungry certainty I can't shake, sown since the day I first looked in those orchid eyes.

Orlaith is *more* than just a political pawn to me. I don't want to let her go. If the Gods find her unworthy of being my High Mistress, I'll have her in a different way.

*Any* way.

"Should she fail," Heira chastises, "the Gods will still expect blood to be spilled. They will not let this slide without punishment. Without an equal dose of *atonement*."

"So long as there's something left of her for me to tuck away."

Heira lifts her chin, looking at me down the line of her nose. "A public whipping. And a lifetime sheathed in a metal spur. You'll also have to keep her out of the public eye so they believe the Gods have taken their due."

"A sacrifice I'm willing to make."

Silence stretches, and I can feel her thoughts churning in the whirl of wind between us. In the way she looks at me as though she's worried Jakar might rip the sky apart and turn me to glass this very second. "The Gods will also expect extra donations to the cause. *Healthy* ones."

"Of course. They can be taken from the islands. I have an influx of refugees, and drownings are common with the

26

high seas and rough weather. Especially at bay. It'll be easy to explain to the mourning parents."

Her eyes soften. "So be it, but you're making a grave mistake."

Probably, but I want Orlaith. Want the fire she ignites in me.

The fearless gleam in her eyes.

Want her to look at me the way she looks at *him*. For her to fall in love with the way I fucking *consume* her.

My tongue tingles, and I swallow.

Heira's gaze turns contemplative. "This was supposed to be political, but you've transfixed on the girl …"

I shrug, plucking another grape from the bowl and tossing it in my mouth, bursting it between my teeth. "Maybe."

She releases a deep sigh, scouring me with a look that picks me apart. "Careful, my boy. Big feelings can wound. They can stab you in the chest while you're sleeping. You know that better than most."

I lift my cup and stare out across the city again.

*Yes, I do.*

# CHAPTER 3

*Orlaith*

The jungle opens into a verdant clearing drenched in sunlight and the smell of young grass, a lone tree at the center, long forgotten—as though the wild half swallowed it many moons ago. Its thick, bleached trunk is knotted and gnarled and pocked with gloomy holes no bigger than my fist, its branches strung with little rusted lanterns, the glass panes tarnished or smashed.

*A mail tree.*

We draw closer, moving beneath a stretch of pale branches that bear no leaves, and I'm led to the other side that's cushioned by a dense shrub dusted in wee blue flowers that look like painted stars.

The sprite darts around the bush, then hovers, reminding me of the tiny nectar-eating birds that fluttered about the gardens at Castle Noir. She wiggles her fingers, gesturing for me to follow, then threads between the foliage and disappears.

*Huh.*

I glance over my shoulder at the Irilak nesting in the dense jungle shadows, watching, making my skin prickle. At least they don't look so scared of me anymore.

The injured sprite quivers against me, and I tuck her closer to my warmth.

*Rescue this life.*

*Make her safe.*

I nudge some branches aside, revealing a small cleft in the tree's trunk, its edges smooth. Tucking the sprite closer to my chest, I crouch and poke my head in, contorting my body as I wrestle past the bush, its twiggy fingers ripping at my clothes.

Sliding one leg into the cleft, I wriggle through to find myself in a tight cavity, dappled light filtering past the bush's foliage. "Is this place common knowledge, or ..."

The sprite hovering inside the entrance rattles off a string of unfamiliar words, then beckons me with a wave of her hand.

"Silly question," I mutter, and clamber over a maze of gnarled roots to follow her down a hollow, the air rich with the smell of damp soil.

The faint drone of beating wings fills the space, and I frown.

Hugging the wounded one, I maneuver through the tenuous ladder of knots and thick, twisting sinews as we descend into the gloom. The sprite flutters around me, waving her hands, tattling away even though we both know I have no idea what she's saying until, finally, I step onto more sturdy ground.

Crouching, I see we're in some kind of warren.

Sinuous roots intertwine to line the entire space, pocked

with small cavities holding worms that glow from their bulbous bums, casting the tunnel in a soft, golden light. Sprites come and go, some carrying scrolls, others sparkly jewels, stones, or other knickknacks. Some moving so fast they're nothing but dusty blurs; others halting mid-flight to look at me with big, curious eyes. Some even settle on my shoulder and touch my hair, the side of my face, making trilling sounds that shiver through me.

I peel back my hand and check the injured sprite, the tremoring bundle whimpering with every exhale. Her clothes and hair are now smudged with Rhordyn's blood—a vision that jolts me to the core.

*Rescue this life.*

*Make her safe.*

The young sprite waves me forward, her bright-red hair an easy-to-follow beacon in the fluttering commotion.

I take tentative steps, careful not to tread on any of the fat, glowing worms tucked amongst the pockets of dirt as I follow the sprite along another low passage, passing many small tunnels stemming from random heights along the way. Finally, we turn down a larger one that leads us into a domed hive swarming with sprites and their sharp riot of chatter.

Their chittering conversations come to an abrupt halt the moment we enter, sprites settling onto roots, legs swinging, while others stretch over the edge and peer down at me.

I ease my hand away from my chest to reveal the injured one curled in my palm, quivering.

Silence for a beat, and then a diverse clutch of them flutter down, stealing tentative glances at me as they ease her into their arms and carry her inside the darkened hollow between two large roots—the young sprite garnishing my cheek with a soft kiss before she follows.

*Gone.*

A lonely heaviness settles upon my chest like a boulder, and I stretch my empty hands, feeling the flaky residue of *his* blood.

My hammering heart swipes at that crystal dome, and I flinch, knees threatening to buckle as cracks weave across the surface. I scramble to gather those little beads of luster, squishing them down.

*I saved lives,* I internally scream, bogging up the holes. *I saved lives—*

The hairs on the back of my neck lift, and I turn, wavering, seeing a pale, hazy smudge hovering before me.

Frowning, I maintain my balance and raise my arm like a perch.

The sprite lands on my forearm, crowned in a nest of fluffy white hair, a black pin pierced through the sharp tip of her ear. She's gripping a black spider by its bum with both hands, assessing me with big, gloomy eyes while it claws at her arms.

Her gaze narrows on the blood staining my hand, and her head ticks to the side. She looks at me with an intensity that makes me blink. "Has te ... nah ve heilth neh?"

"I can't speak sprite," I admit, and she raises her fluffy brows, glancing at my hand again before she lifts the spider and stuffs its head into her mouth, crunching down.

A quiver rakes across my skin, and I cringe inwardly as she swallows, biting into its abdomen with a juicy *pop* that sends brown liquid slugging down her chin. She tilts her head the other way, offering me the remaining torso and eight curled legs that seem to have given up their fight.

My gut knots.

I shake my head. "Looks"—*terrible*—"so good. But no, it's okay. I, ahh … ate earlier. Had a whole bowl of them, in fact."

Her eyes widen, and she looks me up and down like I'm some sort of deity, then stuffs the rest in her mouth. With a few spindly legs still protruding from her lips, she waves at me to follow, bobbing ahead in a blur.

*If she takes me spider hunting, I'm fucked.*

I clamber after the sprite, passing through passage after passage, finally turning into a cramped tunnel heavy with the familiar smells of braised meat, wine, and woodsmoke.

*We must be near Parith's market square.*

She hovers before my face, babbling, indicating with an excited wave toward a trail of tangled vines and roots that appear to meander skyward.

I nod my understanding and thank her with a smile. In a blink, she's gone, leaving me alone but for the fat worms and my whisking thoughts that keep trying to tunnel toward that crystal dome.

Toward everything it's keeping contained.

Drawing a shuddered breath, I reach into my pocket and pull out the smaller bloom now entirely calcified, albeit a little chipped in places from being stuffed in my pocket while I crawled through a labyrinth of tunnels.

Hairline fractures crackle across the dome, and I pluck and squish and smooth those little luster beads, bogging up the gaps. A cold blast seeps through my veins, and I wobble, gripping hold of a root to steady myself.

Dropping my chin to my chest, I swallow thickly, tightening my bloody hand around the bloom, the hardened petals digging into the raw wound made by that shard of glass.

A lump forms in my throat as I realize what I have to do.

My arms take most of the damage as I shove through a thorny bush cushioning the base of Parith's mail tree. I stumble into an opening sheltered by leafy branches that stretch far and wide, strung with strings of lanterns that emit a golden glow—what I now realize is likely from the worms that have been stuffed inside the glassy coffins.

The blue-stone fence that wraps around the tree gives it a healthy berth, providing protection from the people bartering, laughing, and singing just on the other side.

*Market square.*

I creep around the gnarly trunk and step into the wooden booth by the tree's base, the air above me rife with the soft hum of beating wings. The fluttering commotion slows, and a sea of tiny faces peer out of gloomy holes, peeking down at me from their frail perches.

A slew of oily guilt pumps through me.

Do the sprites know what I did? Do they whisper amongst themselves about the girl who saved one of their own? How strange, when her hands were covered in the blood of another.

*Murderer.*

I pull my gaze from their curious stares and shove the thorny thought deep, burying it beside the crystal dome.

Dragging a trembling breath, I open the wooden latch

on the mailing box, take one of the tiny slips of parchment from the stack, and lean in close to scrawl my message upon it with a sharpened stick of coal—the paper too fine and thin for words so hard and heavy. After rolling it into a tight scroll, I scratch a name on it, fasten it with twine, then reach for the long string, its length garnished with golden bells that jingle when I give it a firm tug. "I have a message for somebody …"

Silence ensues—the awkward, hungry kind, as though they're waiting for me to confess.

*I just murdered the Western High Master.*

Part of me wants to scream it so I can remove some of the crippling weight stashed inside my chest.

Finally, a sprite flutters down, landing on the table in a flurry of long, ruddy hair and wings the color of autumn leaves. She looks at the name and nods, takes the scroll, then slides it into the holster tucked between her wings, her movements slowing when she notices my cupla.

Clearing my throat, I shove it farther up my arm and dig into my pocket. I pinch the smallest bloom and pull it out, extending it toward her.

Her eyes widen as she looks at it, then at me, then *above*. I do the same, seeing every sprite in the tree hanging over the edge of branches or out the lips of their hollows, gazes locked on the tiny crystal bloom.

My skin nettles.

The sprite bounces onto my hand, picks up the bloom, gives me a shy curtsey, then darts into the air in a flutter of tawny tones, disappearing through the branches with my grief strapped to her back …

It's a wonder she can fly at all.

# CHAPTER

*Orlaith*

## 4

I hurry through crowded streets, the afternoon air warm and sticky, rich with smells of roasting meat, sweet smoke, and salty brine. The cobbles are hot beneath my feet, saturated in sunshine hammering down from a near-cloudless sky.

I stick to the shadows where I can, away from the searing heat. From the glare of the sun upon my skin.

My soul.

I finally find a fountain set within the side of a building and plunge my hands into the cold water, digging my thumbs into my palms and scrubbing hard. *He* swirls down the drain in lazy turns, and a lump forms in my throat.

"I saved lives," I murmur as more cracks weave across the crystal dome, and I pluck and squish and smooth and bog, then smear a layer of light upon the shield. The world seems to tip, ice shooting through my veins, and I waver, planting my weight against a lofty street lantern, teeth chattering.

*Breathe ...*
*Breathe ...*
*Breathe ...*

Blinks heavy, I glance over my shoulder at a merchant's cart tucked against the far wall. A swirl of people fawn over the various goods laid out on tables, but my attention's drawn to a wooden rack crammed with clothes, snagging on a velvet cloak the color of blueberries.

I wobble forward.

Easing it off the hanger, I caress the material—thick and buttery.

Heavy.

I check the price on the label, then extend my coins to the young, weary-looking merchant, murmuring a thank you as I drape the garment across my shoulders. I huddle amongst it, sweep the deep hood over my head, and relish the comforting gloom.

The security of being *hidden*.

Then I walk, letting my feet carry the weight my heart is too numb to bear, every step nothing more than a distraction.

I'm barely aware of the men, the women, the children jostling around me, their chatter buzzing in my ears like flies. Barely hear the booming voice of a guard shouting through a cone before a huddle of people, saying words like oil shortage, restrictions, and conserve our resources.

I barely notice the sun setting, the sky dashed with ribbons of purple, peach, and blood red by the time a familiar building dawns in my peripheral, its rocky wall lit by the blazing glow of an overhead streetlamp.

My feet still. So does my heart.

Slowly, my gaze climbs three stories up the masonry work—the very same path I clambered down yesterday while smothered in Rhordyn's scent, the ugly threat I spat in his face chasing me like a rockslide.

My chest tightens at the sight of his window. Closed. Empty.

I look away so fast my head spins, plucking more light from my dimming insides and reinforcing that crystal dome, using the wall as a crutch while I battle the responding wave of lethargy that chills me to the bone.

*It seems to be getting worse ...*

Clamping my jaw shut to contain my chattering teeth, I edge around the building, regaining some sense of composure by the time I reach the front door that's capped with an awning, its lip pierced with a swaying sign.

I grasp the tarnished handle and pull.

Struck with a puff of warm air rich with the smell of baked bread, I step into a room swollen with gruff, black-haired men bearing dark eyes and olive skin. Their collective baritone tackles me, and the door claps shut as I lean against it, taking in the sea of blood-red merchants' cloaks haphazardly worn, boasting peeks of dark territorial garb beneath.

"Shit," I mutter, gaze dropping to the floor as I make sure my cupla's hidden, sucking air that suddenly feels too thick.

Ocruth men.

*Rhordyn's* men.

The ones he was smuggling into Bahari, ready to sail the ships the moment they were secured. The ones loyal to *him*—who answer to *him*.

They'd kill me in a blink if they knew what I've done.

Stab me through the chest. Burst my heart. Watch the light bleed from my eyes, their victorious chants tainting the air along with the smell of my traitorous blood.

I frown, realizing I find a small comfort in the knowledge that if I scream my transgressions to the ceiling—right here, right now—Rhordyn's men will dish me the same fate I dished him. Part of me even … *wants* to. Like some morose itch begging to be scratched.

The door at my back shoves open, catapulting me between two bar tables surrounded by men whose heads swivel in my direction. The chatter dims, and a dark sea of eyes burn into me.

I tug my hood lower, straightening.

Aware of my bare and filthy feet, I beeline toward a couple of empty mismatched stools on the left end of the bar, dragging one back, the wooden legs scraping along the stained and dented floorboards. I slouch forward on the seat, leaning all my weight against the smooth slab of mahogany, inwardly cursing the persistent stares that prickle my skin.

A woman with a long, messy side braid the color of corn approaches me in a spill of blue fabric, an apron tied around her waist. She offers me a tight smile, but there's wariness in her raised brow as she appraises my shrouded face. "Can I get you anything?"

I dig my hand into my pocket, pausing when I collide with the lump of caspun I always keep close—finger brushing its leathery skin once ... twice ...

A cold sweat breaks across my nape.

I nudge the caspun aside, pluck three coins, then slide them across the bar, hand trembling when I gesture to the man seated a few spaces away from me. "Whatever he has."

She looks at the glass—half the size of his head and filled with a black liquid capped with white froth.

Big enough and dangerous enough to warm my insides.

With a curious sweep of my garb and a tight nod, she takes my coins and makes for the shelved wall holding a scattering of empty mugs. I look to the back wall lined with a mirror that's mottled in places, noting my reflection.

Or more to the point, my *absence* of one.

My hood is pushed so far forward there's nothing but a scoop of blackness in place of my face, resembling the shadows I spent all my life learning to cling to. My gaze drifts sideways to the sea of men—almost every one of them stealing looks in my direction.

I drop my stare to the bar.

A glass of water lands before me with a thump, liquid sloshing over the sides. "I didn't ask for water," I say, making a move to hand it back when a bowl of something steaming and fragrant lands before me. "I *certainly* didn't ask for—"

"No. *However ...*"

The voice knocks me off guard—deeper than that of the barmaid and with a cynical lilt.

Slowly, I look at the woman now claiming the stool beside me.

Her long hair is dreaded, the stark-white tresses twisted at her temples and bound in a half-up, half-down style that contrasts her dark skin and boasts her severe features: pale gray eyes, sharp nose, high cheekbones. The scar that runs from the corner of her mouth and up her cheek reminds me of the man I gave myself to—a thought that might strike somewhere tender if I weren't so blissfully numb.

She's familiar, but the memory of where or when I've seen her is hard to pinpoint.

"Who are you?"

"Cindra," she tells me, and I wait for her to elaborate.

She doesn't.

"However?" I prompt, watching her ease the merchant's cloak off her shoulders, revealing Ocruth garb—pants and a shirt, the sleeves of which are rolled to her elbows. A leather vest tapers to her plump curves, Ocruth's sword-through-a-crescent-moon sigil pinned to her lapel.

She drapes the cloak upon the bar and leans back, digging through the pocket of her tight pants. "You'll need to consume both if you want *this*." She slams a brass key on the bar, then intercepts the barmaid, taking what I suppose is my original frothy order and downing the liquid in three drags.

I should be pissed. Probably would be. Except there's the faintest hint of a leathery musk nipped with frost ...

My gaze drops to the key again, clings to it as I draw

deep, realizing Rhordyn's touched that key. Held that key. *Used* that key.

*Does it open the door to his room?*

My fingers itch to reach out and snatch it. To cradle it close to my broken chest.

I swallow, curling my sweaty hands into fists, stretching them out again.

I thought my feet led me to this inn, but I was wrong. It was my bruised and battered heart. The part of me that wants to be surrounded by *him*. Tasting him in the air I breathe.

The part of me that almost took that final step over the cliff and chased him through the doors of death.

"What's that?" I feign past the lump in my throat.

"Don't ask questions you already know the answer to, *Mistress*."

My heart falters, then gallops ahead.

I meet her steady appraisal, her eyes cast with a knowing glint.

Slowly, I slide my gaze past her to the men perched around tables, shoveling chowder and bread, guzzling ale, throwing the occasional look in my direction.

*They all know who I am.*

Bile claws up my throat. Threatens to choke me.

*Murderer.*

"I could always climb through the window," I grind out through gritted teeth.

"You'd have to smash it, and in doing so, piss off Mr. Graves." She tilts her head, the motion almost predatory. "Thirty years he spent pillaging copper pipes from the city's underbelly to fulfill his lifelong dream of becoming an innkeeper, and glass is not cheap. Do you really want to cost him a month's earnings to replace a windowpane just to avoid eating his wife's famous chowder?"

"Even if I was hungry, it's not your concern."

"Quite the opposite. It's *my* job to make sure everyone's heartily fed, and I take my orders seriously. I can hear your stomach howling from here."

"Who—" I suck a jagged breath, willing my hammering heart to slow. "Who gave your orders?"

"Who do you think?" She gives me a knowing look, then turns to her own bowl. Grabbing the wooden spoon, she blows on a chunk of fish she digs from the broth, devouring it with gusto while more fractures crackle across my dome.

The tapered tip of a wiggling vine peeks through one of the hairline clefts.

If she knew what I've done—that he's gone—I doubt she would be treating me with such hospitality.

What if I told her what he was? The things he's done? That I *saved* lives?

*Your monster.*

I close my eyes and rummage through my gloomy insides—plucking, squishing, smoothing those little beads of light. Jamming luster into the cracks. My blood turns slow and slushy, plagued with ice fractals that make me clench my jaw; make my muscles twitch.

Opening my eyes, I stare at the chowder. The hot curls of steam lifting off it.

It seems like an easy trade, but my roiling insides tell me otherwise.

I could snatch the key and sprint toward the stairwell at my back. There's a good chance I'm swifter on my feet—

As though reading my thoughts, Cindra sets her hand atop the key and slides it close to her chest, guarding it with her body.

Something surges inside me, fierce and feral, erupting with teeth-gnashing violence. I consider the consequences of demanding she hand me the key by the point of my dagger, stealing another quick look around the room. At the men, no doubt concealing weapons.

I sense tension in their glances, as though they're assessing the violent path of my thoughts.

If she's their overseer, as I suspect ... I'd put up a good fight, but it'd be a stupid one.

Cindra spoons a prawn into her mouth and tears a round of bread in two, lumping half beside my bowl, then using hers to mop some broth.

I frown.

Breaking a loaf to share is a sign of respect in most territories. It would be a bit rude if I threatened to stab her now.

With a resigned sigh, I plant my elbows on the table and curl over my bowl, grabbing the spoon with my sliced hand. I eat my fill of the hearty meal, a fullness that does nothing to feed the hollow in my chest; the void like a chapped wasteland with the absence of my caged emotions.

Stealing peeks of the key tucked in the protective shield of her arms, I guzzle the entire mug of water in one long tip. I thump the mug on the bar, scrape the remaining chowder up, and scoop it into my mouth, then drop the spoon in the bowl and extend my hand.

Staring at the back wall, I wait, fingers curling around

the key the moment it's placed in my palm. I shove off the stool and stalk toward the stairwell.

"Orlaith." My name is served with the confident precision of someone far too familiar with it.

With one foot on the first step, I look over my shoulder at the woman—her back to the bar, one elbow resting on top, sharp eyes searching the shadow within my hood.

She lifts her other hand to display my dagger hanging loosely from her fingers.

My heart vaults, and I dash forward, catching curious glares from some of the other patrons. As my fingers grasp the handle, Cindra pulls me to her and hisses in my ear— five sharp words that prickle my skin.

"You look better in *black*."

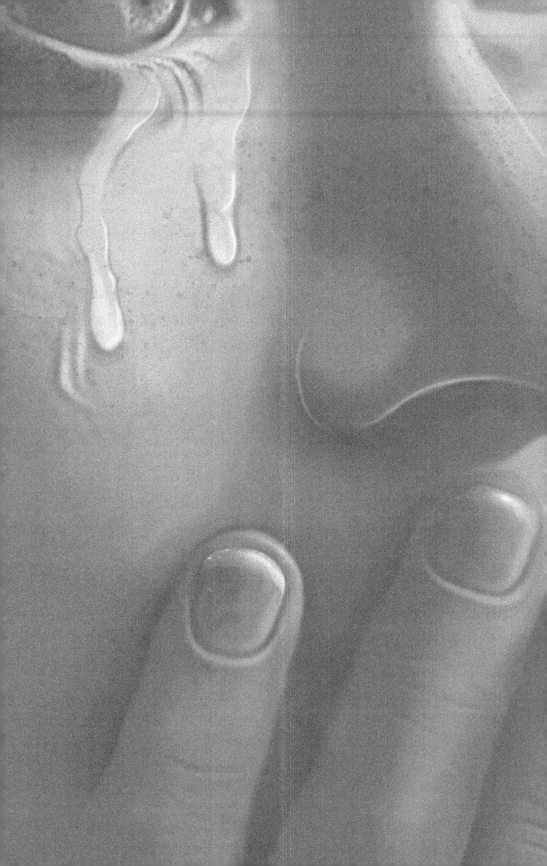

# CHAPTER 5

*Orlaith*

I stand before his door, clutching his key with the same hand that clenched around the shard of glass that tore through my flesh and bled me.

Drew him to me.

The same hand that gripped the hilt of that talon and slammed it through his chest.

More fractures, and I scramble to patch them up, planting my head on the door as I breathe through chattering teeth ...

*Don't think.*

I shove the key into the lock and clunk the bolt aside. Pushing the door inward, I step forward, struck by the flood of *him* that pours into my lungs like a stormy deluge.

He's an icy wind that gushes down my throat and soothes the ravaged path. He's heavy drops of rain that dump upon the sizzling ember of my self-hatred. He's a lightning bolt of *life*—electrifying my heart and forcing it to beat faster.

Faster.

*Faster.*

Clawing at my throat, I fold my weight against the door, slamming it shut behind me as I gulp breath like I'm parched. Like this is the first time I've come up for air since he slipped from my grasp with unsaid words trapped within his split chest.

My gasping finally calms to slow, deliberate breaths, and I take in the room, heart pounding.

The stone walls appear flat in the dull light, a stark contrast to his city map, the attention to detail making it seem lifelike. The desk to my right is still littered with bits of rock and his half-finished sketch—

I rip my gaze away. Look at the bed.

His sword lays across the end, as though he made the conscious decision to leave it before he followed me into the woods. Other than that, the crumples in the sheets have not shifted since I fell backward onto them. Since he lowered his weight upon me and ground his body against my aching parts.

Since he told me to show him my damage.

No—not told.

*Asked.*

Instead of talking, I sharpened that damage into a curved weapon and punched it through his chest.

My knees give way, and I collapse into a pile of knotted limbs, fingers reaching for my neck, clawing.

*Clawing.*

He may have been a monster hewn from a dark and bloody era, he may have been a murderer once upon a time, but he was *my* monster.

*Mine.*

"*I saved lives,*" I chant, hunting for dwindling beads of light. I smear them across that protective shell, my lids so heavy it's a battle to keep them open. A shiver wraps around my ribs and shakes, shakes, *shakes*—

Clutching my middle, I slump to the side, stare diving beneath the bed, landing on a black parcel half the length of my forearm.

My gaze rakes the shape of it, its placement. The exact position as my hiding place in Stony Stem.

My heart lurches.

This package—it's intended for *me*.

Part of me wants to dive across the floor, snatch it up, unravel it. The rest of me is frightened of what I might see, conscious of the crystal dome inside my chest that's growing more fragile by the second. Like the churning, sawing, slithering emotions trapped beneath are wearing it down.

*You did this.*

*You fucking did this.*

I reach out. Pause.

Snarling, I shove forward on my hands and knees, flattening against the floor as I wiggle beneath the bed and grab the parcel. I edge back, rocking onto my knees and holding it in my palm, gasping at the unbalanced weight of it. Top-heavy.

Familiar.

Heart thundering, I loosen the twine and unravel the cloth. It falls to the floor, a small scroll landing beside it, leaving my diamond pickaxe resting upon my trembling hand.

My eyes flame with unshed tears that distort my vision.
*He got it back.*

I touch my lips to the handle and breathe deep, picking up the faint residue of *him* spliced with layers upon layers of me.

A sob breaks free, and I bite down on my fist, squeezing the handle so hard my knuckles turn white.

He *has* been speaking ... I just haven't been *listening*.

The bluebell heads ...

The sheath ...

*This* ...

Trinkets of affection passed to me with silent hope I slashed and stabbed.

I set the pickaxe on the floor, retrieve the scroll, unravel it ... whimpering as I look upon the splayed masterpiece. The beautiful disaster he's stained upon the parchment one delicate stroke at a time.

I'd know that cobbled hall anywhere, the curve of it almost calling for me to fall into its length and break myself against the stares of the many people lining one side.

*Whispers.*

And there—huddled in a ball on the ground, face tipped, gaze cast on the wall—is me. Unmistakably me. Like I just fell into the paper in a tangle of wrought limbs and tear-stained cheeks.

He was there that day, watching me from the darkness. He saw me disassemble myself as I finally looked upon the eyes of the brother I lost.

He saw the worst parts of me. My weakness.

My ugly secret.

He saw the full, unguarded horror of my monstrous

mistake. My horrendous confession—unwittingly given from a guilty subconscious that was overflowing with all the lives I'd taken.

He saw *me* ... yet he still came to Bahari. Stood before me and absorbed my blows. Tried to sponge my pain and stop me from hurting myself.

Me?

I took one look at his monster and murdered him.

A deep, agonized moan tears me up from the inside out. The parchment falls from my hand, curling in on itself as I tip forward, hands assaulting the floor.

*Simple, Milaje. I refuse to live in a world where you don't exist.*

The crystal dome inside me shatters with a strident *pop* that rattles my teeth, sharp splinters lodging into my heart and lungs and bones. Another guttural sob as those thorny vines erupt with vicious, slashing vengeance, slicing me to ribbons. They saw up my throat, paralyzing me.

*Don't cry ...*

Face crumpling, my mouth falls open with a silent scream, the echo of his words a barbed blow to what's left of my unguarded heart.

I buckle, fold around the hurt, scramble to collect those thorny vines with torn and bloody hands, a feeble attempt to contain their sawing rampage.

It's useless.

There's too many broken bits. Too many cutting thorns.

Too many mistakes and unsaid words sitting on my chest like a jagged, unscalable mountain.

Digging through my pocket in jerky, trembling motions, I pry out the caspun root.

I don't want to hurt anymore.

I just want to sleep.

*Don't cry. Don't cry. Don't cry. Don't cry. Don't cry—*

I shove the caspun between my teeth and crack off a chunk, letting the remaining piece fall to the floor. Chewing through the crunchy, bitter-tasting flesh, I tear off my cloak and crawl toward the neatly folded black shirt sitting atop the side table.

Gripping my tunic front with both hands, I cleave it apart, popping buttons, my tender shoulder throbbing in my haste to undress myself until I'm naked but for my underwear.

Cold.

Alone.

*My fault.*

I pull Rhordyn's top on, dousing myself in *him.*

*He had something to show me ...*

Perhaps it was his *own* damage? But he didn't get the chance because mine chewed him to pieces.

Because I thrust that talon forward.

I'm attacked by the sight of him falling, the talon lodged deep within his chest—

A shuddering breath, and I grope at his top, crunching it in my fists. I'll never be able to go back to that terrible, terrible moment and make a different choice. We'll never experience the beauty without all the pain.

I'll never be able to look him in the eye and tell him I *hear* his silent words.

*Don't cry—*

I grab the caspun and take another bitter bite, haul myself onto the mattress, body growing heavy as I crawl across the sheets and fall against his pillow. The chill strikes my marrow and seeps through my flesh, turning my exhales milky.

Slow.

It feels like *him* wrapped around me, pebbling my skin.

I nuzzle his pillow, gulping breath.

I don't want to run anymore. To push him away.

*Hurt him, or myself.*

I want to pull him so close that all sense loses shape, our mistakes a bony battlefield to build our castle upon. One that's not pretty or extravagant, but deep and dark and a little bit broken.

*Too late.*

 Another crunchy bite. Another bitter swallow.

Tugging his blankets over my head, I tuck into a tighter ball, my laden lids drifting shut as my mind dunks into that inky pool of sleep, consumed by a chilly embrace that feels like home.

# CHAPTER 6

*Orlaith*

*I*'m without anguish, sorrow, regret. I'm without the
shades of right and wrong and the gray
smudge in between.
*Without the warm dawn of hope or the cold drop of fear.*
*I'm without fingers to tangle with truths that no longer*
*matter. Without hands that hold and caress and hurt.*
*Without the substance left to snap.*
*I'm without breath to fill lungs that no longer exist.*
*Without tight skin to keep me contained.*
*Without blood to drip. To spill or drain or splat or stain.*
*To gift.*
*I'm without ...*

*Him.*

*Weight no longer pins me down, roots pulling from soil*
*that falls away as I tumble with dewdrop stars floating*
*on a sea of black ink. I dart through an ebony forest that*
*seems to stretch for eternity, racing small globes of light*
*that whiz between trunks.*

*The trees bear no leaves, no life, but I can feel their violent pulse through whatever's left of me as I zoom past a place I might recognize. A castle that's black like the gloomy trees, the sky, the soil, its walls choppy in places—as though unfinished.*

*I want to go there, but I'm at the mercy of the pull.*

*The terrain slopes, and then I'm plummeting toward a glittering iris that pours into a fathomless pupil.*

*I slow.*

*The eye looks at me. Assesses me.*

*A layered voice whispers in slithering tones, reeling me toward the hungry darkness. Two echoing words caw like a krah through the midnight murk and speak my hollow, condemning truth ...*

Burning hands grip me by the shoulders and shake, shake, *shake*—wrenching me away from that seeing end. I reach, fingers stretching, pleading for it to swallow me ...

*Dissolve* me.

For it to scatter me into a trillion insignificant pieces.

I'm shoved inside a body that's icy and hostile. That feels too much all at once, abrading my hollow heart.

"Orlaith ... *fuck*—"

A soft voice. Concerned.

"Wake up—"

*Angry.*

"—*what have you done?*"
*Terrible, terrible things that weigh too much.*
*Terrible things I can't undo.*

Another stiff shake tosses my head around. My chin smacks against my chest, and a burst of red explodes across the backs of my lids as I bite my tongue that's cold and clumsy, tasting blood.

Eyes prying open, I take in the blurry profile of a woman with familiar shape ...

Colors ...

Smells ...

Butter and spice, cut with the sharp scent of fierce, erupting emotions that battle the musk of *him*.

Hands too warm and small and *not his*.

Because he's gone.

Because I ...

I ...

"I don't want to feel."

The words flow without shape or heart or the will to sink their roots into soil. Without the petals of hope, happiness, sadness, grief ...

Empty as my empty heart—confirmed by a mighty, unfathomable entity. Cawed words that call me now.

I blink away, open my eyes on the empty, the cold, the end.

Peer into that fathomless pupil.

I drift closer ...

Closer ...

"*You are without*"

Something hard collides with my face, smacking me into my too-tight skin—crammed into all the nooks and crannies. "*Don't you dare die.*"

I'm rolled across a sea of soft blankets I want to wither amongst. Ice clogs my veins as hands slide beneath my knees and back, and I'm tucked against a warm chest, lifted, floating ...

Floating away from the smell of *him*.

I mumble.

Groan.

*Plead.*

"*Geis ta ne vale—es tin nah!*"

The string of sharp, crooked words lump upon me, the curled edges rolling off Zali's tongue like a gentle pat after a scalding smack.

*Guess she got my note. Meaning she knows I—*

I whimper, warm mist settling upon my cheeks and hands. Gurgling, splashing sounds erupt around me, echoing, coaxing the image of a frothy waterfall to etch upon the back of my lids.

Again, I'm standing on the edge of that cliff, watching *him* disappear through the pillow of mist, falling from my life in devastating detail.

I can see the pain in the flat pools of his eyes, his outstretched hands an invitation for me to fall with him.

One tiny step. One tiny plunge.

One deep dive into our ever after that never was, before an inky nothing pours into my lungs and snuffs out my flame—

I'm folded forward against something hard and cold. My jaw is pried open, fingers probing so far down my throat my stomach spasms. Bile saws up my throat in a lumpy, splattering pour of acid and half-digested caspun.

"That's it. Get it all out."

Again, her fingers gore deep. Again, my throat blazes with fiery wrath until I'm so empty the only thing left for me to spew is my aching guts.

I'm lugged back, head flopping, and then I'm lifted.

Floating again.

Scalding water hammers my chest and smothers me in a boiling spill, waging war with my frosty skin.

A scream rips up my throat.

I try to squirm, buck, flee—but my limbs are cast in ice. "*S-stop ...*"

I'm certain my flesh is blistering. Will it slip off my bones in bloody drips that swirl down the drain and disappear forever?

*Don't cry—*

My raspy scream echoes off the walls, and I reach up, tangling my fingers with the long, sodden streaks of Zali's hair. "Pl-please ... t-too ... *hot*—"

"If I don't heat you up, you'll die."

The words fade into a soft, distant echo as I'm reeled toward that inky endless ... head tipping ... arm dropping to the stone ...

Another slap tosses my head sideways so fast the world tips on its axis.

"*Stay awake.*"

Her voice attacks me like a swinging hammer, and I

open my eyes. Sketch the blurred shape of Zali's face—her eyes twin swirls of rusty resolution.

She eases me onto the stone floor, my head in her lap, then reaches sideways and digs through something that rustles about. Water continues to pound me as her fingers thread between my lips and crank my jaw. Something is shoved beneath my tongue before my teeth are allowed to snap shut, the gooey substance softening.

Melting.

A familiar taste glides across my tastebuds, tugging the strings of my conscious mind ...

*Exothryl.*

"Swallow," Zali orders, and the milky sheen glides down my throat, planting a seed of warmth inside my gut.

*Why is she trying to help me?*

"I k-killed ... your ... promised ..."

"And now you're stuck with me," she murmurs. "Hopefully my superior communication skills will save me from getting stabbed in the heart."

I groan, and my lids yield to the downward tug. Again, my lips are pried open, the underside of my tongue burdened by another chalky node.

Water continues to stomp my chest, thawing me from the outside while warmth takes root within—planting an ember in my barely beating heart. Stirring my pulse.

My mind.

Even so, the pull to follow him is fierce. If I were to tuck into a ball, I'm certain gravity would roll me toward a swift end. Like I'm tethered to him, my soul seeking his.

I slam the lid on that thorny thought and drag my eyes open, squinting through the drizzles of water.

Frowning, Zali studies me, her hair a curtain around her face, lips a thin line, as if she's biting down on words threatening to spew forth. Like another slap to the face, it occurs to me that I'm stripped bare—all my weaknesses on display for this woman who is so put together. So poised, perfect, strong.

I've never felt so raw. So vulnerable.

So fucking lost.

"I just wanted to sleep," I croak, and her palm collides with my face again. My head tosses sideways, cheek blooming with a slap of pain.

"Stop that," I slur, upper lip threatening to peel back.

She grabs my chin and jerks my face to the side, forcing me to look at her. "Don't make it so easy for them," she hisses, waving the half-chomped lump of caspun in my face.

"You don't make any sense," I groan, closing my eyes against the water's relentless spray. Against the swirl of wrath, disappointment, and concern staining her eyes.

She cares. For me.

I don't know what to do with that. How to handle it. It's easier to ... not. Because I hurt people who care.

Every. Single. Time.

"I make perfect sense," she grits out, and I'm lugged into a sitting position, swaying like a bloom in the breeze. Water batters my back and seeps through my heavy length of hair, my shoulders bowed forward, blinks slow and deep as I take in our surroundings.

We're in Rhordyn's washroom, amidst a sea of smoggy steam heavy with the leathery, frosty scent of *him*. Of *us* crushed together. Crammed into each other's atmospheres. Before my damage devoured him.

Before I killed the man I love.

Zali's sodden, bright-red cape drags along the floor like a trail of blood as she walks to the corner of the room, drops the bitten stump of caspun into the latrine, and pulls the chain.

My heart plummets so fast I almost rock forward and face-plant the stone. "What are you *doing?*"

"Welcome to your reckoning," she bites out.

"I *needed* that!"

She glares at me so hard I'm forced to drop my gaze. Probably not the right choice of words considering the state she just found me in.

She strides toward me and kneels, and I look up in time to see her hand crank back. I snatch her wrist a second before her palm can collide with my cheek again.

Her eyes widen, darken, like pots of honey flamed over a bed of hot coals as I use my grip to pull her so close her breath is blasting me—the water streaming over her head, her hair the deep, dusky shade of red wine now that it's plastered to her cheeks.

"*Don't.*"

Her lips slash into a wicked smile. "There she is."

I snarl.

She stands, scrubbing her face with her hands. "Did you tell anyone else?"

"No ..."

"That's something," she murmurs, then sits on her heels and stares down all my broken bits like she's not afraid to cut herself on them. Her gaze lands on my eyes, and the divot between her brows deepens. "You need sunshine."

A thousand other versions of the same proclamation

pick at me from the past. Mersi, Baze, and eventually, *him* ...

I frown, still swaying with a tide of my own. "You don't know what I need."

*Nobody does.*

"Your *kind* needs sunlight to survive," she growls, forcing me to look.

To *see*.

My mouth falls open, heart vaulting.

*She knows what I am.*

"*You ... How—*"

"It's why Rhordyn had you housed in the northern tower all these years. It got the most of it."

"He *told* you?"

"Because I can be *trusted*," she declares. "Because I'm an *ally*, not an enemy."

My vision goes hazy.

Rhordyn trusted Zali with my hidden identity. Trusted Baze.

*Didn't trust me.*

I was so mad at Baze for knowing. For keeping it from me. Was so mad at Rhordyn for the same that I let it rot my perception of him. Let all that mad boil into a thick, potent, deadly poison.

Now I'm seeing it from a different angle—one absent of the hurt and heartbreak and those feelings of betrayal that bubbled to the surface the moment he unlatched the necklace from around my neck.

A question bulbs in my chest, roots curling around my ribs as the shoot begins to spike up my throat—

What am I *missing*?

Zali looks at the ground, seeming to consider, then at me. "Are you *certain* you got him in the heart?"

The words stake through me, jerking me back to the now, and I flinch at the memory of how it felt to wield that talon as it slid through his chest.

The underside of my tongue prickles with the urge to vomit again.

"Yes," I force through the bars of my teeth.

"Was he wearing anything around his neck?" she asks, her voice lifted with something akin to hope. "A rope of some sort?"

A vision flashes in my mind's eye—of Rhordyn. Bleeding. Battling for air his lungs wouldn't pull. Of a leather thread draped around his neck, tethered to something hidden beneath his shirt.

I shove the image away, heart bouncing around in a rib cage that suddenly feels too small.

Too tight.

"Yes."

Her face pales, and she curses, eyes swirling pools of pained calculation. "What now?" she croaks, crucifying me with a glassy stare.

"What do you mean?"

"Ocruth is yours."

The words slide through me like a sword, stopping my heart's ferocious rally.

My mouth opens, closes, opens again. "N-no ..."

"You're his ward, Orlaith. He had no children. No family."

*No.*

*No-no-no ...*

"But you're his *promised*—"

"A political pairing that was far from *sealed*." She pulls Rhordyn's cupla from her pocket and waves it at my face. "This doesn't mean shit for my people now."

"I—I don't want this ... I don't fucking want *any* of this!"

"Too late."

Two small words that shackle me, adding to a thousand *too-late* cuffs already wrapped around my arms and legs. Weighing me down.

Rhordyn showed me what I really am. Kissed me like I was his salvation. Told me he would try harder.

*Too late.*

*Too late.*

*Too late.*

He said he'd show me the worst of it ...

*Too late.*

Somebody had already shown me the worst and staked his death in the soil of my malnourished heart. And now that we're here—now that he's gone—there's a voice bellowing in my ears, telling me I was wrong.

That I should have taken notice of the gray smudge between Rhordyn's black and white. That I should have waited just a little longer. Listened to the words I snuffed on his tongue when I plunged that talon through his heart.

I flinch.

*Too late ...*

# CHAPTER 7

*Baze*

Doused in the heady smell of my own sweat and vomit, I cup my hands against the window and peer through it, scouring the Inn's murky innards. All the wall sconces are blown out except one behind the bar, casting a rinse of warm light over a broad man bent over the till, stacking coins and scribbling on a piece of parchment.

Sniffing, I edge around the building beneath the heavy shroud of a silent night, noting the Closed sign on the door before I grab the tarnished handle anyway, giving it a yank.

I feel the man's abrasive gaze as I weave between tall tables laden with upside-down stools, lifting one off the bar and thumping it on the floor. I sit heavily, inhaling the smell of beeswax mixed with the rich musk of ale, hard liquor, and sugarcane smoke.

"We're closed, son."

"I know," I murmur, pushing back my hood. I reach into the folds of my cloak and retrieve a pouch of coins, sliding a gold drab across the bar. "I'll have a bottle of whiskey."

Looking up through my hair, I note the deep gouge between Graves's heavy brows. His fair hair is pulled back in a low bun, his neatly trimmed beard a stark contrast to his cruddy apron—testament to a hard day's work.

He tilts his head to the side, eyes narrowing. "I recognize you ..."

"Don't."

He watches me with shrewd regard. "Are you going to cause me any trouble?" he asks, his voice a gruff rumble.

Brows lifting, I hold his powdery stare. "Not if you get me that whiskey."

With a low grunt, he retrieves a bottle of amber liquid off the back shelf, as well as a glass, and lumps both before me amongst a litter of pale ring stains. Noting a single black line—almost impossible to see—stitched through the collar of his midnight-blue shirt, I nudge the gold drab toward him, then pull out another and add it to the pile.

I sense his rising confusion in the tightening of the air between us as I pop the cork, wrapping my hand around the bottle. Heavy.

*Cold.*

Desperate to rinse away the sour taste of vomit, I ignore the glass and draw straight from the source. The cool burn slips down my throat, charring some of the tension—the unsaid words—that have been choking me since Zali received Orlaith's sprite.

I drain a quarter of the contents, the chained screams inside my chest softening with each drugging swallow. Hissing through my teeth, I slam the bottle on the bar and dig through my pocket, pulling out a small, corked jar and placing it before him.

Graves sucks a sharp breath and stumbles back, steadying himself against the shelves as he looks upon the morbid, bloody contents: two crystal thorns, the roots still wet from where they were torn from flesh.

"I'm looking to sell those," I say, tipping my bottle toward the jar. "I was wondering if you were aware of the street rules around these parts?"

Eyes wide, he swallows, his complexion now a pasty shade of gray.

Tension cuts the air as silence prevails. Hardly surprising. Loose lips sink ships—a lesson most street rats learn the hard way. But I've got time. And patience.

Lots of fucking patience.

"C'mon, Graves," I say through a smirk, "I know you grew up in the undercity."

His complexion pales further as I wait, and wait. Drain more of the bottle and fucking *wait*.

*Maybe I'm not so patient after all.*

Finally, he fills his chest, then clears his throat, nipping a glance at the thorns. "Madame Strings is the woman you're after."

*I thought as much.*

"Word is she lost her parents young and traveled the continent many times, though she looks naught over two and five," he says, a knowing shadow darkening his eyes. "Doesn't add up to me."

I gobble the information, glancing at the thorns, heart thundering along at a ferocious pace …

*She must use.*

*Regularly.*

"She's in with those gray robes," he says, taking the

cloth draped over his shoulder and using it to dab his dappled brow. "You know the ones."

Oh, I fucking do.

"And how do I find this ... *Madame Strings?*" I ask, trying to hide the fierce hunger clawing up my throat. Revenge is a meal I'm determined to feast on—the only thing powerful enough to keep my mind occupied.

To keep it off *him.*

*Her.*

*This fucking place.*

"She's pretty hard to nail down. It's a big city, and she's not always here ... though based on murmurings I've heard, I believe she's currently this side of the wall. If you were to chance it, you might find her around one of the campfires in the city's heart, telling tales to children and dishing out sweets."

Meaning I'll have to hunt her down like a dog.

*If the shoe fits.*

Graves watches me closely while I drain the rest of the bottle, then slam it on the bar, pocket the jar, and slide off my stool rather than push it back across the floorboards. Old habits, or whatever.

I'm halfway to the door when Graves's voice chases me. "She has *runners.*"

I stop and turn. "Runners?"

"Men who coax kids into trying candy while force-feeding them whispered words of a *brighter* future, free from the horrors chipped upon the stones. Talk on the street is that some of these kids are disappearing. For good."

The blood drains from my face so fast my head spins, forcing me to grip hold of a nearby table. Or perhaps the bottle of alcohol just hit me all at once. Either way, I feel like I'm going to throw up for the fifth time since the sun sank, and all over Graves's freshly mopped floorboards.

"There was a bloke in here not three days ago boasting about a meeting with Madame Strings. Something to do with replacing a runner who contracted the Blight." He raises his bushy brows, gaze steady. "But you didn't hear it from me."

"When?"

"Not tomorrow night but the next, if my ears served me well. And they usually do."

I stretch my hands, then bunch them up, that monstrous rage sitting inside my chest surging to savage life. "Do you know where he lives?"

With a clipped nod, Graves reaches for a stack of parchment beside the till, and I approach as he scratches something upon the top sheet with a sharpened piece of coal. "You'll want to ditch that black cloak, son," he says, looking at me from beneath his brows while he folds the parchment and slides it across the bar.

"I'm good," I mumble, then pocket the note and flick up my hood. "This one's important to me."

He releases a deep sigh.

"Wait here," he grumbles. Muttering something about a death wish, he disappears through the back door that swings to a creaking halt behind him.

I glance down at myself, frowning.

Clearing my throat, I unclip the cloak, then reluctantly drape it across the bar, still rubbing the material between my fingers when Graves returns—a thick, Bahari-blue velvet bundle in his arms. "I only have a winter one, but it'll do."

"My balls are sweaty just looking at it."

He makes a sound somewhere between a chuff and a grunt. "I'll look after your other one until you return."

"I appreciate that," I mutter, reaching for the cloak, but he holds tight.

I meet his cutting stare riddled with warning. "You take care now, you hear?"

My skin erupts in a blast of goose bumps.

He gives me a tight nod, then lets go, picks up the rubbish bin, and carries it out back, leaving me alone with the hungry silence.

Dragging my gaze across my black cloak, I resist the urge to snatch it, gritting my teeth as I wrap the blue one around my shoulders, then head for the door, about to shove it open when I catch a whiff of wildflowers pinched with a hint of spice.

My heart jumps into my throat so fast I choke on a breath.

*Laith* ...

Head whipping around, I power toward the staircase, bunched fists swinging at my sides, kicking to a stop the moment my boot hits the bottom step. Breath labors in and out of my aching lungs, and a fresh swirl of nausea whisks my guts as I try to picture how I'll greet her.

What I'll say.

Whether I'll wrap her in my arms, tell her it's going to be okay, even though it's not, and squeeze her until she stops fighting me.

Fighting *herself*.

Or if I'll cut my instincts loose and charge her until she slams against the wall, then rally upon her with all my wrath, sorrow, and bitter disappointment. Let her see the fierce side of our nature in its full, unguarded glory.

Fuck knows she needs it.

Another beat, and I swallow the growl trying to erupt, looking at my boots.

If I go up there, I'll tell her truths that'll cut to the bone. I'll spit them like shrapnel because I'm not feeling nice right now.

I'm feeling wrought and raw and mad at the world—mad at *her*. Maybe even a wee bit drunk. And she deserves better than that. She may have made a devastating mistake, but I still fucking love her.

Snarling, I punch the wall, storm toward the exit, and charge into the night.

# CHAPTER
*Orlaith*
## 8

A large candelabra douses the room in a warm glow and the smell of softening beeswax. The springs of the swivel chair squeak as I kick back and forth, tucked amongst a fluffy throw, gaze cast on the drawing spread across Rhordyn's desk.

I trace the slants of the streets etched on the paper with poised precision. Study each shadowed line.

I can't bring myself to look at his bed again. That morning was packed full of so much potential. I could feel it prickling my skin, kissing my lips with phantom hope, pouring into my lungs with every breath. I could taste it in the fruit he fed me; in the water he left on the bedside table.

It was in the casual way he'd dressed, like he was paring back one of his many hard layers, giving me a glimpse of a softer side.

He was *trying*.

And I ...

I was too lost to *see*.

Zali drags her spoon along the bottom of her bowl, and I catch another hint of chowder in the air. A chill scurries through my veins, and I tuck deeper into the throw, swallowing, my tongue still stained with the acrid residue of my own regurgitated serving.

"We need a plan," she says, setting her empty bowl on the floor beneath the window she's leaning beside, pulling the curtain back to peer out on the gloomy street below. A simple, dark blue tunic and black leather pants cling to her shapely curves, her sodden cloak hanging on a hook beside the door.

"We?" I croak, and she looks at me, dropping the curtain, her eyes sparkling like amber jewels in the flickering candlelight.

"You and me. *We*."

I frown. "I ... You don't *hate* me?"

A brow hikes up as she crosses her arms and leans against the wall. "Do you *want* me to?"

I stab my stare at the drawing again.

*Yes.*

Rhordyn was close to getting the ships her people so desperately need, and I killed him. Killed hundreds, maybe thousands of her people with that one faithless strike.

But that tiny, two-letter word sits inside me like a rib notched into its rightful place. Like an antidote I wasn't aware I needed until this moment.

*We ...*

I need her hate. Deserve it. But I think ...

I think I want her friendship *more*.

"You've taken out the most formidable man on the continent." I look up, catching Zali's blunt stare. "Cainon has the advantage, and his father was always one step ahead. I doubt the apple fell far from the tree. Whatever grand tapestry he's been weaving before your eyes, you need to assume it's laced with the threads of his own motivation to gain political traction."

I think back to the conversation we had in the Unseelie burrow, then flinch away from the poisonous thought.

Was I really *that* naïve?

Has he been using me as a pawn this entire time, wielding me into his own personal assassin?

Hot, noxious shame flares my cheeks, chasing away the remaining drabs of my caspun-induced chill.

"The Vruk raids are getting worse, and Rhordyn was one of the few actively cutting them down," Zali continues, making bile blaze up my throat. "Without him, there will be more casualties, more villages wiped out across Ocruth and Rouste. So what's our plan?"

"We still need the ships ..."

"Yes." She shoves off the wall and begins to pace the room, her black knee-high boots clapping against the floorboards with each restless step. "I take it Rhordyn didn't work out where they're docked?"

"Not that I'm aware. Can't you send a sprite out there to hunt for them?"

"No," she murmurs, then plants her hands on her hips and tosses her stare at the ceiling. "The winds are too steep."

Letting the blanket drape down my shoulders, I reach forward and pluck the parchment off the table. I open the desk drawer, find a pottle of glue, and use the stubby brush attached to the lid's underside to swipe across the back of Rhordyn's drawing.

Casting my gaze on the map that dominates the wall, I trace the streets like the threads of my thoughts—knotting, intertwining, clashing. Following the steps I took to get here.

From the moment I boarded that ship, I fumbled through the world like a newborn foal. I fed on freedoms that went against the grain of everything I'd hoped to achieve. I was sightless, gullible, *impulsive*.

I promised so much and gave so little, then I tried to bow out.

No wonder Zali slapped me so hard.

I'm a selfish person with no shoes and no sense of the world, leaving a trail of destruction, self-detonating because my own actions *hurt*.

My stomach roils, the vision before me becoming smudged from unshed tears.

This mirror ... It's relentless. *Sickening*.

Sobering.

I look at the drawing again—unfinished, just like the story of *us*. A tear streaks down my cheek as I set the parchment on the wall in its rightful place and pat down the edges.

Living a cloistered life has led me to be so easily swayed, whether by Rhordyn's silence or Cainon's noise. But it's time I learned to think for myself.

It's time I grew up.

Another chill slips through me, making my teeth chatter, but I clamp them down, dash the tear from my cheek, and continue to trace the streets—a skeletal web beneath the busy world above.

I stretch my instincts, trying to see if any of them ache when I give them a firm tug.

There is no voice telling me to run. Nothing screams for me to turn my back and take the easy route. Instead, something's niggling at me. Urging my gaze to chase the tunnel that dips beneath the palace before threading across the bay.

"I need to go back," I murmur, wondering if that's the tunnel I'll eventually break into once I crack through the wall in the tapestry hall. "Keep Cainon occupied while you continue Rhordyn's hunt for the ships. There's a bunch of men downstairs he smuggled into the city who can sail them once they've been secured—"

"Orlaith, no."

I spin my chair, clashing with Zali's wary stare. "Are you in a rush to get back to your territory? If you need to go, that's fine. I can come up with another plan."

Her eyes harden. "My regent is more than capable of watching over my people while I work to secure their future. That's not my concern."

I'm pushing tendrils of hair off my face when her gaze drifts to the burn on the inside of my wrist, now a popped, weeping wound of angry, raised flesh.

I smother it with my hand.

"I made a promise," I bite out. "I have to follow through. It's the only way we can secure the ships without inciting a territory war we both know will cost Rouste and Ocruth dearly."

She stalks forward, slamming her hand on the desk. "You're willing to give yourself to a man who bartered to possess you? *Really?*"

My cheeks flame.

She shakes her head, upper lip trembling, eyes glazed with unshed emotion. "No," she snarls. "Get your teeth out. Bring him to his fucking knees if you have to. *Anything* is better than going back to that man and offering yourself on a golden platter. Pretending to be *his* when we both know you're not."

The words stab that raw, tender wound, making me want to buckle around it.

*Don't cry.*

"You said Ocruth is mine," I rasp. "That implies it's mine to protect in any way I see fit."

A clipped nod. "Correct. But you're in a boa den, Orlaith. You're one wrong move away from getting *bitten.*"

She slams the statement down like a stake, making me flinch.

"By coupling with you, he automatically becomes your consort. Then he's one *unforeseen casualty* away from having full control of Ocruth."

The unsaid word lumps between us like a tombstone.

*Me.*

"Not to mention governing over fifty percent of the continent's land mass, the largest fleet in all five seas, and the largest army these lands have ever seen. The majority of Rhordyn's militia are currently stationed at Quoth Point. If they were to suddenly answer to Cainon, they're a wave of deadly force painfully close to *my* borders. *My* people."

"I don't intend on sealing our coupling," I admit, hewing my messy, selfish truth from where I'd tucked it away. "I'll climb out of that stupid bowl and complete the ceremony *as promised. I'll buy you time to find the ships. To seize them before he has a chance to bed me and realize he's not the first ..."*

*Zali blinks, all the color dropping from her cheeks. She straightens, and a lengthy silence ensues, battered only by the churn of breaths as we hold each other's stare, unblinking.*

*"Who?"*

*"I didn't catch his name," I say, and something glazes her widening eyes—a look that suggests she's starting to realize the vast scope of my self-destruction. Unfortunately, this grave I've dug for myself is so deep, the only way out is to dig down and pray I emerge on the other side.*

*Her eyes soften the slightest amount. "Orlaith, this is a suicide mission. If Rhordyn knew—"*

*"Rhordyn's not here," I blurt, chest heaving with the smoky residue of words still blazing between us. I don't want to think about Rhordyn. Thoughts of him make my spine as weak as my broken heart, and I can't afford to be weak right now.*

*Zali lifts her chin, and again, her eyes glaze with something I can't quite put my finger on. "As your political ally, I can't support this." I open my mouth to speak, but she cuts me off. "Assuming Cainon's aware that Rhordyn and I were yet to seal our coupling, there's no saying he wouldn't murder you the moment he finds out Rhordyn's gone. Ocruth would fall into a vicious civil war as its* Low Masters and Mistresses battle for the silver throne. A territory at war with itself is *vulnerable,* and Cainon's recent plays prove he's suspiciously trigger-happy."

*Fuck. She's right.*

*There would be a bloodbath over Rhordyn's seat of power.*

I swallow the rising lump in my throat as she stabs her finger at the tabletop. "We *must* keep Rhordyn's death a secret until we've found somewhere else to pin the blame. Until you're safely out of this territory and at no risk of being slain for the sake of your inherited throne."

"So ... what are you suggesting?"

"Rest, drink, eat," she's quick to respond—three pelted words that itch my restless soul. "Keep out of sight until I've done some digging and we've had a chance to thoroughly think this through. Stand in front of that window when the sun comes up and get some damn sunlight because you look like death warmed up."

"That sounds an awful lot like my life at Castle Noir."

"Then it should be easy," she quips, a sparkle in her eye.

I drop her gaze and draw deep, feet tingling with a restlessness I can't shake. The need to shove forward and move.

To *atone.*

I glance at the window. Release a shuddering breath.

Zali's right. We need time to think this through.

"Okay," I finally concede, the word poison on my lips. Because it's not okay—not at all. I'm utterly responsible, yet helpless to fix anything. The feeling clings to me like a sticky goo I can't scrub off.

Relief softens Zali's brow, but my mind continues to swirl so fast my gut cramps, thoughts tunneling to places I don't want to look.

Don't want to see.

*Don't cry—*

"There's a woman downstairs with white hair who seemed to be in charge. Cindra. She made me eat the chowder," I rasp, barely able to stop myself from dashing to the latrine and having another go. "She might be able to help us."

"I'll have a talk with her when I leave you to sleep. She's a Warrior General of Ocruth and one of Rhordyn's trusted few. She was keeping contact with Baze as we made our way south."

My heart lurches, and I'm forced to grip the desk to steady myself. "You've seen Baze?"

The words come out choked.

"Yes." She tips an empty wooden rubbish bin upside down and sits on it, back to the wall, legs crossed at the ankle as she works her long, damp hair into a strawberry braid. "He was with me until we reached the border and I met two of my most trusted escorts. I left him at the outpost staring down a barrel of wine." Her brief pause gives me a chance to swallow the thickening lump in my throat as she flicks me a knowing stare from beneath heavy lashes. "I ordered him to stay out of Bahari."

An image flashes in the forefront of my mind of Cainon trussed up against the wall in Stony Stem, held in place by a dagger pressed to his throat, a drip of blood bubbling at its tip.

*I should have your head for that, boy.*

That slither of scalding darkness coiled inside me

unravels like a loosening knot, and a shiver crawls up my spine one vertebra at a time.

"Good."

# CHAPTER

*Orlaith*

## 9

I listen to Zali's footsteps fade until there is nothing but silence—the kind that sits heavily on my chest, making it thump harder.

*Harder.*

Slowly, I lift my gaze to the bed cast in candlelight. To the sheathed sword nesting amongst the rumpled sheets.

A sudden ache tightens my throat, and I swallow, stand, caped in the fall of my fluffy, frazzled hair as I ease around the desk and stop just shy of the bed.

I study the sheath, the intricate detail swirled across it only visible when the light touches it just right, like wisps of smoke kissed their shadows upon the surface. The sword's hilt is dominated by an inky stone not unlike the heavy one hanging against my chest ... The same bottomless black. The same infinite pull that makes me feel as though I'm falling into a seeing end—

I blink, slamming my palm against the bed's end post to

stop my sudden sway, feet tingling, like I was just standing on the perilous crux of a deadly plummet.

Heart thundering, I reach out, hesitation bunching my hand before I force my fingers to unfurl and grip the hilt. I gasp as a sudden jolt locks my bones and shocks my heart into a brief pause.

A wave of trepidation punches down my throat.

I suck a sawtooth breath, brow furrowed. Shaking my head, I pull.

The sword whispers free, the sable length glinting in the flickering candlelight—such a deep shade of black that I'm again reminded of the darkness I tumbled through while I was falling toward that glittering iris.

I lift it high enough for me to study, and my arm shakes with the heft of it, as though the sword is laden with the life I took. With every drop of blood I spilled from *his* chest. With the crushing weight of my regret.

My hand tightens, the backs of my eyes stinging with unshed tears. Suddenly, the thought of not bearing this burden feels *selfish*.

I ease the sword back into the sheath and study the leather strap I've seen bound across Rhordyn's chest, gaze darting to my dagger sitting on the side table.

I edge around the bed and snatch it up.

Smoothing the leather across the wood, I set the tip of my blade much higher than the rest of the holes and punch through the thick material.

Zali told me to rest and hide until we form a sturdy plan, but the thought of climbing into that bed and falling asleep shrouded in *his* scent is a luxury I don't deserve. And sitting still—swiveling in Rhordyn's chair while I stare at that unfinished map—is quicksand. I'll do nothing but slip into the gullies of my mind and steep in my mistakes. Dig my toes into the dirt of a thousand what-ifs.

*No.*

I need to go. To roll like a tumbleweed blown in a stiff wind. To move my feet and distract my thoughts from churning in the wrong direction.

I drape my cloak upon my shoulders, then thread the strap across my chest and secure the buckle between my breasts, shouldering the sword's heft. Hands bunching into fists so tight they shake, I look to the floor, my vision obscured by puddled tears.

*Just roll like a tumbleweed until I find somewhere to ground myself. To ease this restless energy.*

*Dirt makes everything better.*

I lift my head and glance toward the window; at the moon peeping through the gap in the drapes. The sun will be up in a few hours, and the city will blink awake. I can absolutely be back by then, hidden away from prying eyes like Zali suggested.

I dash my hand across my cheek and grab the leather satchel resting against the desk, then tuck it full of Rhordyn's shirt, my diamond pickaxe, and the drawing he did—hesitant to leave them for even a few hours while I expel my restless energy. I chug a glass of water, secure my dagger to my thigh with strips of material fashioned into a sheath, and move toward the window, cracking it open.

I crouch on the sill, drawing deep gulps of air as I look down upon the city's sleepy stillness. A wispy blur of white darts close enough for me to feel puffs of air kiss my cheek—a familiar, comforting presence that soothes the plowing thump of my heart.

The sprite doesn't still long enough for me to make out her shape and confirm my suspicions. She zips off like a star shooting through the alleyway, dragging my gaze north toward the wall that hugs the city tight.

My curiosity thrashes, gnawing at her restraints.

From the moment Rhordyn became a presence around Castle Noir, he tried to get me to step outside my comfort zone. My Safety Line.

To *live*.

Until recently.

*Don't climb the wall that borders the city. It's dangerous.*

He placed the warning upon my chest, and I felt stomped. I bucked it off and threw my own words, sharpened into barbs aimed to maim.

I didn't give enough attention to the break in his pattern. His contradicting desire to keep me in this city he obviously disliked. Which begs the question ...

*What's on the other side?*

# CHAPTER 10

*Orlaith*

The moon drenches the city in a stark luminescence that fails to seep into the clefts between lofty buildings. I weave along these paths, tracing that charcoal map now etched into the folds of my brain.

The alleyways become tighter with every turn, the thick, puddled shadows making it hard to see the odd slumbering lumps tucked against the walls, their faces shrouded within the frayed hoods of their patched cloaks. I pull my own hood farther down, ensuring my face is cast in blackness.

A layer of mist swirls underfoot as I ease onto a wider street, the end barricaded by the steep wall—a foreboding presence holding the city in its illuminated embrace. Blazing turrets line the top, reaching for the blackened sky like the points of a gilded crown.

I drag my hand along the wall and follow its gentle curve, edging between buildings nesting close, until I find one that leaves *just* enough room for me to work with—a four-story structure with a flat roof that's half the height of the mammoth wall encompassing the city.

Tucking my satchel, sword, and cloak behind a wooden crate, I peer upward. The grooves between the rocks are like hairline fractures, but my toes are nimble.

So are my fingers.

I press my hands against the adjacent structures, using the force to hoist myself up so I'm suspended between the two, enabling me to ease up the empty space in a spider-like shuffle. I make quick work of the four stories, though every breath burns by the time I'm edging onto the roof, shaking out my hands and feet as I look up at the abrupt terrain I still have left to scale—this time *without* the backbone of the adjacent building to brace my ascent.

Easing my toes off the roof's lip, I tip forward and stamp both hands upon the stone, finding a frail cleft to delve the tips of my fingers into. I do the same with my right foot, then drag a deep breath, swing my left foot forward, and dig my toes into a groove, shifting my weight to the wall.

Heart pounding, I locate the next feeble divot just above my head and *push.*

Reach, pull, repeat.

The wind tousles my hair about my face and threatens to peel me off.

Yank me down.

There is no pump of thrill. No blood-zapping excitement. That part of me fell off the cliff with *him,* leaving this heavy sense of impending relief sitting on my chest like a boulder—ready to lug me toward a swift and sudden death the moment I let my guard down.

Refusing to look that thought in the eye, I keep moving.

Keep climbing.

My thighs and calves and shoulders burn by the time

I slap my hand upon the top of the wall, face contorting with a silent snarl as I push all my strength into my arm and *shove*. Throwing my weight forward the moment my ribs scrape against the honed edge, I swing my other arm out and snatch a metal peg impaled in the stone.

Legs dangling, I haul myself onto the smooth, flat surface drenched in firelight by two blazing turrets. I roll onto my back and toss out my arms, one hand hanging over the lip while the wind weaves between my throbbing fingers. Gulping sea breeze, I stare at the winking stars that look almost close enough to touch, sweat trickling down my face ...

*Fuck.*

I tip my head sideways, frowning when I realize I could roll five times before tumbling off the other side.

Another cooling gulp of air, and I ease onto all fours, crawl toward the outer edge, then peek over the side.

My gaze plummets in symphony with my guts.

I'm not sure what I expected to see, but it certainly wasn't ... *this*.

The cramped city has *nothing* on this stout band of civilization squashed into the broad gully between the wall I'm standing on and another—running parallel with this larger one as far as I can see both ways. Like the bands of a rainbow, but far less pretty.

Small ramshackle dwellings appear to have been crudely constructed with all the broken bits the rest of Parith had no use for; patched roofs held haphazardly together with uneven planks of wood. Between some of the dwellings are strings draped with frayed material and ragged clothes ruffled by the slight breeze.

There's an eerie, sad silence disturbed only by the bellowing roar of the flaming turrets and a forlorn wail coming from somewhere below ...

Skin prickling, I cast my gaze along the outermost wall, following its path into the distance left and right—perhaps protecting its inhabitants from the outside world. From the Vruk attacks that will eventually make it this far south.

That *have* made it this far south.

But the wall over there ... it's shorter, lined with stumpy turrets that cast it in weak, rusty light. From my perch I can see that it's thin, crumbling in places, as though whoever is housed in those derelict dwellings are considered less than those inhabiting the city side.

Another keening wail echoes through the stagnant air, followed by a gurgling cough, and I frown.

*Who are the people down there? Why are they isolated from the rest of the city?*

I notice a pail and coiled rope tethered to another metal peg much closer to the northern edge. Lips pursed, I inch closer and peek inside the bucket, noting the oily sheen as I choke on the rank smell of rendered lard.

It must be what they use to haul up replacement oil—fuel for the blazing turrets.

I use my blade to slice the bucket free, then tuck the dagger away and give the rope a tug, checking it will hold my weight before I gather the length and toss it over the side. The end *thwacks* against the wall about four feet from the ground.

Heart pounding hard and fast, I grip hold of the rope and turn, blowing a shuddered breath as I edge backward down the wall one blind-footed shuffle at a time—dropping farther from the quenching sea breeze. Deeper into the stagnant stench of sour milk, dirt, and something foul that coats the back of my throat.

A faint drone gets louder … *louder* …

Drawing closer to the soft *thwap* of the rope slapping against the wall with my descent, I glance over my shoulder, drag a breath, and drop.

A swarm of flies lifts off the ground as I land in a crouch, dirt blowing up my calves. I use my collar to barricade some of the rotten stench clogging my lungs, flies landing on my arms and face, tickling my skin. I slap them away, straighten, then spin and take in my surroundings.

Shadows spill off cramped shacks too small to house anything more than a whelping dog. I turn my attention down a crooked path that weaves between them, illuminated by the firelight pouring from above.

I frown, noticing what appears to be a child's wooden rattle discarded in the dirt. Pausing, I crouch, reaching out to touch it—

Movement catches my eye.

I look to the right, squinting into the shadows.

Reeling back, my heart skips a beat at the murky outlines of people lumped on the ground, spilling from their crooked doorways.

Big people. Small people. Big people *cradling* much smaller people.

They're huddled together, perhaps seeking comfort from each other. And it's silent … No wheezing exhales. No whispers. Even the tragic wailing has ceased.

Something latches onto my left hand and grips tight.

My breath snags, head swiveling, an itch flaring across my clavicle.

A man eases from the shadows, his face pocked with craters of decay riddled with maggots grubbing at his weeping flesh.

A scream lodges in my throat as eyes that might have been blue once wobble around sightlessly, his pupils blown so wide there's only a frail ring of color left, fringed with dark dents to match his hollow cheeks. "Help m-me ..." he rasps through pallid, cracked lips, flashing nubs of decaying teeth. "P-please ..."

Blight.

He has the *Blight*.

He releases a gurgling cough, and I stumble back a step, another, gasping the stagnant air—tripping on cracks in the dirt while prying my hand free, gaze darting from him to the many people now groaning to consciousness. Lifting their heads. Easing from the shadows.

Looking in my direction with tragic, vacant stares.

This isn't just another ring of the city. It's a *graveyard*. It's the place the sick have been sent to be forgotten about.

To *die*.

*Rhordyn was right. I shouldn't have come.*

"I'm so sorry," I rasp through a thickening throat, clambering toward the wall. I snatch the rope and haul myself up one frantic pull at a time, arms burning, hands straining. I'm halfway up when I realize the rope is jolting beneath me.

One glance down, and my heart plummets into the pit of my rotting conscience.

A young, black-haired woman is attempting to climb

the rope. Other than her hands being riddled with weeping lesions, she appears healthy—her face luminous, almost beautiful. As though the sickness has only just begun to nibble at her.

Like it's yet to sit down and truly *feast*.

A wave of deep sadness sweeps through me.

By the light of the blazing turrets, I can see the desperation in her gaze. Her desire to *live*.

The backs of my eyes burn as realization stakes me through the chest.

If I let her climb free of this macabre pen, she'll spread sickness throughout the city. She'll kill hundreds, maybe *thousands* of people.

With a pained groan, she hauls herself closer ... closer ... while others hobble and crawl across the hard-packed dirt, coughing and spluttering, edging toward the rope as though it's the dangled key to their salvation.

All I can see is the painting of Zane's older sister—the tiny child who bore the same love heart birthmark on her thigh as I do.

*Viola.*

All I can smell is her mother's tears as Gunthar recounted the young girl's death. The same vicious death now clawing up this rope, threatening to take more lives.

To *spread*.

Cainon's voice cuts through my foggy thoughts like a blade ...

*Sacrifices.*

I close my eyes, biting down on a scream threatening to charge through my teeth as my thorny emotions spike, slash, and *saw*. I reach for the sheath wrapped around my thigh—hating myself. Hating the fact that *Cainon's* my voice of reason in this fucked-up moment.

Wrestling my bucking conscience, I pull my dagger free and drop my hand to the taut stretch of rope beneath me, releasing a mangled sound.

I force myself to catch the girl's wide-eyed stare as I set my blade against the coarse fibers.

"I'm sorry," I whisper.

She stills, her mouth falling open. I squeeze my eyes shut and run the blade through the rope in one hard, clean swipe.

I feel the weight fall from the end of the line. Hear her too-short scream ... the meaty *thump* that cuts it off.

"*I'm so sorry,*" I sob, refusing to look at the scene below, the words ash on my tongue. Because it doesn't matter what I say, how I feel, it won't unbreak her body. Won't save these people from their suffering.

From being a human wall that buffers Cainon's treasured city from any army that would dare break through.

Rhordyn was so desperate to quell the deadly wave attacking his territory, while Cainon's busy wielding his as a *weapon*. Lacking the empathy to give them a comfortable end when his city is steeped in gold.

Fury slashes at my ribs. Devastating, destructive fury that saws me to shreds from the inside out.

My wild, unruly emotions ... they're just as savage as my caustic blackness.

Just as deadly.

And right now, they're frothing for me to bring Cainon to his fucking *knees*—just like Zali said.

Except that's not what we agreed upon.

My face contorts, and I tip it to the sky, fiery rage billowing up my throat in a raspy scream I pour upon the stars.

I pluck beads of luster from my dim and dusky insides, molding them into a small stack of crystal domes I use to catch my hate, my hurt, my sorrow. Separately, I button each wrestling emotion against my ravaged insides, then pluck the petals of my morality, too—stuffing them beneath a fourth dome. Sealed away like a sparkly mushroom patch.

A heavy calm settles upon me as my scream tapers. Still, I study the stars while chilling cries and gurgled moans echo from below, the souls of the dead rising up to haunt me, dragging their ghostly fingers across my pebbling skin.

*Sacrifices.*

I think I'm finally starting to understand.

# CHAPTER

*Orlaith*

## 11

I land heavily upon the stone back on the safe side of the wall and shake out my hands, glancing up at the lightening sky.

*I need to get back.*

My domes quake, like everything tucked beneath them disagrees. The one containing my rage rattles the most—hairline fissures crackling through the sparkly surface.

I bog up the gaps, paint them each in another layer of light, and stumble a step toward my stuff tucked beside the wall.

After securing Rhordyn's sword down my spine, I heft the satchel over my shoulder and begin moving down the tight alleyway.

Two broad-shouldered men dressed in the decorated garb of a palace guard ease around the corner, cutting off the exit—each heavy-booted step echoing off the wall, stoning the silence.

I slow at the sight of the gold-tipped spears strapped

to their backs. At the surly looks on their clean-shaven faces—barely visible in the dull light.

Perhaps they're just … out for a stroll. Fully armed. At four in the morning.

*Doubtful.*

If they see me with Rhordyn's sword, I'm fucked. There will be questions that all point in the same damning direction.

That I killed the western High Master.

I backstep, almost tripping over my feet as I spin, bursting out of the opposite exit just before two more charging guards have a chance to box me in. I dodge them, ducking a swoop of snatching hands that skim the top of my head.

*Crap—crap—crap—*

I sprint down the street, my heart a drum in my chest. Commanding bellows and boots pounding the cobbles draw people to their windows and out their front doors.

Muddying the situation even further.

I sidestep toward a dark alley, stumble for traction as my feet slip on the slick cobblestones. Slamming my hand down to steady myself, I throw a glance over my shoulder to see a stampede of gold-plated guards gushing down the street, whisking the smog.

Coming straight for me.

Where the hell did they even *come* from? Shouldn't they be sleeping?

I charge down the alley, dashing wet laundry out of my way, leaping over fallen bins and puddles of piss while I muddle over my predicament.

This changes things …

I really, *really* have to get back to Zali so we can formulate a new plan now that Cainon has set his dogs on me.

Exploding free of the alley, I dart down another that's almost too thin for me to fit through. Cutting a glance behind me, I see a guard trying to follow, but his inflated chest plate makes it impossible for him to jiggle sideways like I am; trying to prevent them from getting a good look at the sword strapped to my back.

I pick up my pace, biting my bottom lip in concentration as I *jiggle*.

*Jiggle.*

*Jiggle.*

I bust through a bush into a small cobbled courtyard to see a ring of armed guards standing shoulder to shoulder.

My heart lurches.

Their arms are crossed, expressions stern, standing so close I can pick apart their scents from the smell of piss and mildew.

Churning breath, I nudge the bush aside to look back down the alley. One of the smaller guards has removed his chest plate and is shimmying along faster than I did, blocking my only out.

My domes oscillate, thorny vines of emotion scraping at their undersides, producing an ear-splitting *screech*.

I hiss a breath through gritted teeth, looking at the shield of guards again. Each of the men cut shrewd glances at the sword strapped to my back.

A few of them even frown.

I can see it in their eyes. They're wondering why I'm

wearing the Western High Master's sword. If they were to run a bag check, they'd also find Rhordyn's shirt.

Icky, oily unease floods my chest, clogging my lungs and making it hard to draw breath into my starved lungs.

Zali made the implications of Cainon discovering Rhordyn's fate *very* clear. But there's no way around that now that I'm surrounded by a wall of Cainon's men who look ready to drag me back to the palace.

Wearing Rhordyn's sword.

*Shit.*

If I don't admit the terrible thing I did to *acquire* said sword, there's no way Cainon will reignite our agreement. He explicitly told me that so long as Rhordyn was still *sniffing around* there would be no coupling.

It's the only line I have to reel him in and secure those ships … A poisonous risk I now have no choice but to swallow and hope for the best.

"Gentlemen," I rasp, lifting my chin, scanning my austere crowd. "You're up early."

"We need you to come with us to the palace," one guard announces in a gruff voice, dropping his hand to rest on the hilt of a golden dagger sheathed at his hip.

My skin nettles, fingers twitching to reach back.

To snatch the hefty blade threaded down my spine.

I frown, finding a thorny weed of rage hiding between my ribs. I rip the errant thing out and stuff it beneath my anger dome, squishing deviant tendrils that try to claw free as I pin it back in place. I smooth another lustrous layer upon each dome, wavering from a surge of chill that bites all the way to my bones.

"That's an awful l-long w-walk," I fudge out between chattering teeth. "I'm pretty spent from my morning j-jog."

*And I desperately need to speak with Zali.*

One of the guards raises a brow. I cringe inwardly, recognizing him as one of the men who escorted me back to Cainon after I spent the night comatose in Rhordyn's bed. I'm sure this is getting old for him, too.

"How ab-bout we pretend you never saw me, and we all just ... part ways? I'll meet you back there after I've had a n-nap."

"If you resist, we've been instructed to carry you there, kicking and screaming."

I chomp down on a curse.

Boxed in by a swarm of towering men, I'm escorted through the labyrinth of streets, the light growing less murky by the second. Zali will be awake soon. When she finds me gone, she's going to think the worst ...

*Fuck.*

I should have leashed my restless energy and stayed in Rhordyn's room. Now I'm tending a sparkly patch of domed emotion, plucking rogue weeds that keep slipping through the cracks while I'm escorted back to the palace by Cainon's tight-faced guards.

Things really took a turn for the worse.

Given the new circumstances, I'm left with one option ... and it goes against the grain of my tender, aching heart.

My soul.

*I won't think about that right now.*

*Can't.*

A wispy white blur snags my attention, and my heart

leaps into my throat, hope pooling through my chest. I don't dare turn my head as my gaze chases the little sprite frolicking about us at lightning speed, like a bee bopping about on the hunt for troves of pollen.

*Please be the sprite that saw me leave Graves Inn ...*

"All I wanted was a bit of fresh air," I blurt, receiving sideways looks from the guards. "Oh well. It's a lovely morning for a stroll to the palace with such *spritely* chaperones."

One of them clears his throat. "Are you okay, Mistress?"

"I'm fine!" I yell in the most upbeat voice I can conjure, stomping through a puddle of something putrid that slops up my calves. I grit my teeth. "Perfectly fine."

The two guards behind me whisper between themselves, voices so low they probably think I can't hear them pondering over my withering sanity.

Whether or not Cainon's promised to a dud.

"Though I do wish I had a chance to tell Cindra I won't be meeting her for breakfast," I continue, praying the sprite understands my bizarre ramblings and passes my message on. That it gets down the line to Zali—her name too explosive to throw around in front of Cainon's guards.

"Guess I'll get in contact with her later." I dodge another puddle that looks suspiciously like the contents of somebody's emptied chamber pot. "I'm sure she'll understand."

The sprite darts off in the direction of Graves Inn, and I breathe a sigh of relief.

We round a corner, a quenching blow of sea breeze ruffling my hood, and I catch a glimpse of the lapis lazuli palace glimmering in the morning light. My skin prickles at the thought of what I'm about to do …

Fall to my knees before Cainon and beg to reignite our coupling.

A grieving sprout pokes above the surface of my aching heart and crawls up my spine, delicate tendrils curling around my ribs and anchoring it in place. Floret unfurling, it tips its head to me and bares a flush of silver petals that make the backs of my eyes sting.

It looks like a grayslade.

I snip it at the stem, untangle its twining length, and stuff its coiled corpse beneath a dome where I don't have to look at it.

Wooden rowboats pock the ocean, fishermen stooped in their bows with glistening lines threaded deep. The salty air is baked with the smell of fish guts, the gentle slap of water on rock echoing off the underside of the bridge as we draw closer to the looming palace.

I'm no longer marveled by its beauty. By the gold trim that glints in the sun or the massive, buffed blocks of rich, blue stone I'd never seen before I stepped upon these shores.

All I can see are those shacks barely holding together. All I can smell is the putrid taint of rotting things still clinging to the back of my throat.

How many men, women, *children* from Ocruth and Rouste are making the perilous trip to Parith in the hopes of finding refuge behind its impenetrable wall, only to end up in that Blight-infested band?

Gulls squawk, scrapping over some tossed offal, and I'm reminded of the woman who fell too fast.

Screamed too short.

Cracks pop across the surface of my many crystal domes, and my hands bunch into balls that shake.

*Don't think. Just do.*

I pluck at the dimming forest inside myself, squishing beads of luster. Lids growing heavy as I bog up the holes.

*Walk in.*

*Tell him I was wrong, silly, naïve. Play the little broken girl he crossed paths with in that hallway at Castle Noir.*

*Get down on my knees and beg him to take me back— to keep me safe.*

Play it fucking *safe.*

The tangerine sun lifts above a tuft of low-hanging cloud, spilling rays across the glossy ocean. They cut through the bridge railing and plunge into the scoop of my hood, dousing my cheeks in a warmth that seeps beneath my skin, drips upon my chapped veins, and lubricates my insides with a surge of liquid warmth.

More lustrous beads bloom.

I'm led into the palace's blocky shadow before I can quench my thirst, and two more guards peel from their posts, their heavy-booted steps thumping after us in perfect unison. A swarm of armed guards slot into place before the golden gate that towers over us like bared teeth.

I frown.

Isn't he ... *expecting* me?

One guard clears his throat and strides forward, gold-tipped spear peeking over his shoulder. "I'm sorry, Mistress. I must conduct a weapon search before you enter the palace.

I'll start with your sword," he says, reaching out his hand. "Orders from the High Master."

A jagged cleft forms in the dome containing my rage, spilling a thick, thorny vine that saws up my throat. An icy calm settles upon me, sharpening my mind, my perception, and the words sitting upon my tongue like thorns.

My head banks to the side, and I hold his stare, unblinking. "You'll have to pry it from my lifeless corpse."

His eyes widen, mouth falls open with some semblance of a word squeaking out while my fingers itch to unravel. While I frantically rummage through my insides, *plucking …*

*Try it,* I almost scream.

*Squishing …*

*Try it!*

*Bogging up the hole.*

The rogue emotion snips off like a blown candle flame, and my heavy lids flutter as I waver, mellowing. Like I've just been dropped in a bowl of oil.

I clear my throat, pull the sword from its sheath, and lay it upon the ground. I do the same with my charred dagger, then force myself to step back.

The man casts me another nervous glance, then drops to a crouch and examines the weapons. Another guard moves closer, lifts my left arm, and begins to pat me down.

My skin bristles, and I cast my mind somewhere else as he brushes along my forearm … my shoulder … my back …

*Play it safe.*

*Play it safe.*

*Play it sa—*

"Let her through."

The deep, booming words echo from beyond the gate.

My gaze threads through the men, through the golden bars, and down the throat of the domed entryway to the broad-shouldered man with his arms crossed, a stern look bunching his brow.

*Kolden—alive and healthy.*

His bold blue eyes scrape across me. "I'll check her over."

Relief plunges into my chest.

The man with his hand uncomfortably close to my waist steps back, and I crouch to retrieve both weapons, sliding them into place.

A guard inside the courtyard cranks the lever.

The gate lifts, the barricading men step aside, and I move through the short tunnel, holding Kolden's eye contact until I'm standing right before him.

He frowns. "Your lips are blue. And you're pale."

"I'm fine."

The muscle in his jaw bounces.

"Apologies," he says, and I nod.

He drops to a kneel and pretends to pat down both legs—all hidden by the fall of my cape. Surprise blossoms inside my chest as he rises and continues the ruse to my waist and hips, a stern look on his face.

The faintest smile touches my lips.

"All clear," he bellows over my shoulder, and I lift a brow.

He spins, steps close, then matches me stride for stride. We spill into the courtyard lit by bowls of blazing oil, our footsteps a harrowing echo. "I'd hoped you would evade the hunting party," he rumbles low, setting his hand between my shoulder blades to guide me toward the grand entryway on the right.

Frowning, I look sidelong at my former guard. His gaze is cast ahead, the muscle in his jaw popped and prominent. "Sick of seeing me around, are you?"

"Quite the opposite, I'm afraid."

I whip my stare to the twin doors as footmen haul them wide.

*Play it safe.*

# CHAPTER 12

*Orlaith*

I'm ushered through the central lobby where several servants are using long poles to light the sconces, then up the sweeping staircase and down the hall that leads to my quarters. I pause, ease the bag off my shoulder, and tuck it into a large, golden urn balanced atop a thin table pushed against the wall.

"*What are you doing?*" Kolden hisses, scanning our surroundings.

I fit the lid back into place, knowing *exactly* how this impending conversation will go if Cainon discovers I have Rhordyn's shirt tucked in a bag I stole from his room.

"Playing it safe," I mutter, urging us forward. I'd stuff the sword in there too if the guards hadn't already seen it.

We enter the small lobby that leads to my room, coming to stop before the door opposite my suite; one I've never passed through. Kolden knocks three times, and a doorman answers, keeping his head bowed as I enter a vast space adorned with velvet chaises and plush rugs. Kolden follows me through, and I stop, turning. "Thank you. That will be all."

His eyes harden, hands flexing into fists at his sides. Gaze spearing behind me, he steps close. "Be careful," he grinds into my ear before he ushers the doorman out, closing me in the room.

Alone.

Relief filters into my lungs.

I don't want Kolden to see this exchange. For him to watch me crumble myself down into a shape that fits Cainon's perfect perception of who he believes I should be.

I make for the only other exit—a set of double doors on the far wall. Pulling them open, I step into a room that boasts big, square windows that look out across the bridge.

A lapis lazuli dining table dominates the space, capped with a glazed hog nesting on a bed of braised tomatoes, boiled eggs, and potatoes stung with the scent of lemon. The table is set with enough food and seats for eight people, though only one is occupied.

Cainon sits at the head like a bronze statue, one leg draped across the arm of his seat while he sips from a golden goblet, scorching me with his heated gaze. His face is sun-brushed, hair tied back in a loose knot, his deep blue shirt rolled to the elbows, the Bahari sigil pinned to his chest.

He looks at Rhordyn's sword before our stares collide like boulders hurled together, splintering those domes— the sound cracking through me like a thunderous warning.

"Good morning, petal. I've missed you," he says, the corner of his mouth kicking up, like a cat that got the cream. "I was so pleased to see my guards escorting you over the bridge, especially after the way our last conversation ended. I've been worried about you. I know those truths were hard to swallow."

*Play it safe.*

I scream it to myself while scrambling through my insides, sweeping through my veins, hunting those beads of luster—finding seven ... ten ... *thirteen* tiny ones glimmering in the dim.

*Not enough.*

I gather them up, squish them down, and bog only the worst cracks, keeping hold of what's left and tucking it somewhere safe.

"Come." Black dots distort my vision of him glancing again at Rhordyn's sword, before he gestures toward the chunks of meat piled on his plate. "You're just in time for us to break our fasts together."

My steps feel heavy as I move through the room, unbuckle Rhordyn's sword, and gently rest it upon the polished stone floor. I drop into the seat at the table's opposite end, not bothering to flick my hood back.

I stare at the hog. At the pear perched between its lifeless jaws.

At its charred and scored flesh.

Cainon kicks his leg off the arm of his chair and sits straight. "You're very quiet, petal. Is everything okay?"

*No.*

I feel like his puppet—strings strung to my arms, legs, and heart. The blood of the man I love dripping from my hands.

"Perhaps your silence has something to do with that

sword on the ground? Is there something you need to get off your chest?"

Another splintering sound, and I almost whimper, using what's left of my remaining luster to bog the cleft in the dome containing my ravenous rage—though it still leaves it eggshell thin. The furious might sawing beneath it grinding it down from the inside out.

Wavering, I swallow thickly, catching the furrow between Cainon's brows while soiled truths gather on my tongue, threatening to choke my airway if I don't set them free.

His frown deepens, stare *digging*.

I squeeze my hand into a ball; the one with a cut that dripped a trail of blood.

That led—

"Did you ... *do* something, Orlaith?"

*Yes.*

*I killed the man I love.*

"How did you obtain the Western High Master's sword?"

I barely hear the words, deafened by the sound of those crystal domes popping—one by one—caving to the internal pressure swelling beneath their frail shape. To the sprouting, *vining* emotions that fill my chest with drowning sorrow and a crippling stab of pain. With a flush of gray morality and a twist of thorny rage that shreds my chest, threads up my throat, and coils on my tongue like a sitting serpent.

I draw a shuddered breath, blow it out.

Feel like the world's rocking beneath me.

"Did you kill Rhordyn?"

*Rhordyn ...*

His name flutters through me like a silver-winged butterfly, seeking somewhere to land. Perhaps a pretty flower to perch atop of.

But there's just a graveyard of crystal splinters and thorny vines waiting to *pierce*.

*I'm sorry ...*

"Did you?"

The two short words come to me like a distant tug—repeating—and I realize my eyes have closed. I snap them open, waiting for the black dots to fade as I reach down, absorbing the hollow thump that pulses through me when I lift Rhordyn's sword off the floor and set it upon the table.

The chill slugging through my veins is no longer jarring me. But *one* with me.

"Yes," I admit, tears slipping down my cheeks as I study the weapon ...

*I'm sorry.*

*I'm sorry.*

*I'm sorry.*

"I did."

There's a beat of pause while a teeth-gnashing scream threatens to spear up my throat. While I try to remember what it is I have to do ...

*Tell Cainon I was wrong, silly, and naïve. Play the little broken girl he crossed paths with in that hallway at Castle Noir.*

*Get down on my knees and beg him to take me back.*

My thorny rage coils around those safe, submissive thoughts, constricts the life out of them, then feasts on

110

their remains while Zali's stronger, *fiercer* words slither down and watch the carnage unfold—ready to strike.

*Anything is better than going back to that man and offering yourself on a golden platter. Pretending to be his when we both know you're not.*

"*How,* Orlaith?"

*Fuck this.*

I hook Cainon's darkening gaze as my upper lip peels back to expose the venomous rage within, more tears puddling my lower lids. "You told me *exactly* how."

A brief pause, his stare *digging.*

"And you're *certain* you hit his heart?"

*Too* certain. Cainon wielded the perfect weapon.

*Me.*

Shoving to a stand, I stalk past several empty seats before I pause beside the hog, picturing Cainon laid out on this table with that pear between his teeth. I whip my dagger from its sheath and slam it down, unable to suppress a flinch as it cleaves through flesh and bone, plunging into the hollow that used to house its beating heart.

Cainon's throat works, and I hold his harrowed stare, wondering if he's regretting his decision to couple with me.

"Silly question, it seems."

I don't answer.

Landing a kill strike to the heart was one of the first lessons Baze taught me. But when he scooped me up and told me that small seeds grow into big, strong things, I doubt he knew I'd grow into a caustic weed that would use that heart-impaling strike on someone who meant so much to him.

*To me.*

Cainon's gaze flicks to my dagger still hilt-deep in the hog, behind me to Rhordyn's sword, back to my eyes. He cants his head. "You think I'm going to hurt you?"

"I think you know Ocruth is mine."

Silence as both his brows lift—all the confirmation I need.

I lurch the blade free and stalk back to my seat, slouching down, legs wide as I flip the dagger—the metal hot and slick with the rich, fragrant juice of the cooked beast. My hollow belly churns at the smell, and I wonder if food will ever appeal to me again.

"You took down a monster, Orlaith."

*My* monster.

A surge of raw emotion slashes my unguarded heart, and it's an effort to keep my face smooth as my entire body threatens to fold around the hurt.

*Don't cry—*

"You should be *rejoicing*. You rescued countless people from a fate worse than death and cleared the path for us to continue our courtship. The Gods will be pleased, and I have no doubt you'll climb from The Bowl next time you try. Then there will be *nothing* standing in the way of us bringing our great territories together."

It feels as though he chose each word from a vast collection of leftovers that weren't perfect enough to make the cut.

"Except my conscience," I say, flipping the blade again. Watching it dance for me while Cainon's gaze carves across my face.

"Why don't you put the dagger down, Orlaith? Look me in the eye so we can hold a proper conversation."

*Look me in the eye so I can weave my words into a web and sting you with fragments of truth. Make you pliable enough to mold to my will.*

I harden my regard and do as he asked, shredding the silence with my own words before he has the chance to wield his. "I intended to come in here and beg for you to take me back. Now, I realize I don't have the stomach for it."

A frown shadows his brow. "I don't understand your meaning."

"Beyond your wall is a city's worth of sick people rotting. Slowly. *Painfully.*"

His head kicks back, arms folding over his broad chest. "Would you rather me blow them all up?" he asks indignantly.

*Asshole.*

"No. I'd rather you give them a *choice*. Drop a pallet of liquid bane into the mosh. Stop using their disadvantage to your advantage."

He plants his fists on the table, leans forward, and looks at me like I've got sauce on my face. "I know you're new to this, but a bleeding heart does *nothing* to stack the stones of a great territory. Something you need to move past since you'll soon be sharing my throne."

I bristle all the way to my toes. "You'll have to *solder* me to it."

He cocks a brow, the corner of his mouth curling into a salacious smile as he steals a glance at my cupla. "I'm good at that."

*Yes you fucking are.*

Holding his stare, I flick my dagger into a spin, catching

the honed tip between my thumb and forefinger. "And I'm good with a knife."

A familiar flash of thrill ignites his eyes, making my cheeks flame. "Clearly. But if I'm to be perfectly honest, that *excites* me."

I stab it into the makeshift sheath, but his smile only grows.

He picks up a goblet and drains the contents with the remaining drabs of my patience, wiping his mouth with the back of his arm as he clonks the empty chalice down.

Watching me.

I break his stare. Let my gaze roam across the hog and platter of eggs, potatoes, and tomatoes it's nesting on—all Ocruth produce shipped down the great river that weaves through the continent before spilling out here in Parith. I spent *years* creeping around Castle Noir, listening to conversations not meant for my ears. Bahari produces nothing more than sugar, seafood, and a shit ton of gold that buys almost everything it can't pillage from the sea ...

*Get your teeth out. Bring him to his fucking knees if you have to.*

Zali's words bolster me, and I lift my chin, forcing myself to hold his stare. "While your territory might glimmer in the sun, it's codependent. Vulnerable."

That smile finally falls off his face. "Vulnerable, you say?"

The words seem to writhe across the table, coil in my lap, and hiss at me.

I nod. "You'll send the ships to Ocruth. Now. Or I'll stop all trade with Bahari and prevent any barges from sailing farther south of the border. You currently have an oil shortage, do you not?"

His eyes bulge the slightest amount, and he looks at me as though he's seeing me for the first time.

A beat of silence.

Another.

"That's not all."

"Do go on," he bites out, and I picture him backed against the wall with my dagger poised at his throat while I scream at him like he screamed at me—his face pocked with the same weepy, maggot-infested lesions currently gnawing on his people.

Zali's people.

Rhordyn's people.

"In addition to *gifting* your ships to the cause, you'll reopen the vast network of underground tunnels beneath your capital. You will use this *extra space* to offer refuge to anyone rushing to your border—a small price to pay."

His pupils blow so wide his eyes are more black than blue, and there's a slight paling to his brassy complexion.

I feel my heart race. Feel it come to *life*.

*Rhordyn was right ... Cainon's hiding something down there.*

"You'll do all this or not only will I cease trade, but I'll instruct Ocruth's army stationed at Quoth Point to carve a path through your precious jungle, leaving Parith more vulnerable to Vruk already threading through your defenscs. Your people will lose faith in your ability to protect them, and you'll be forced to flee to the islands and give up land I'll happily accept because frankly, after what I've seen beyond the city wall, I'm now *convinced* you view everyone but yourself as sacrificial pawns."

I snap my teeth together, relaxing my upper lip that had curled with my spitting rage.

"Threats …" he murmurs, and I shrug.

"If that's what you want to call it."

"I didn't know you had it in you."

I ignore the swipe and hold his gaze. Watch his mind churn within the depth of his eyes.

This is all one big fucked-up political game. I see that now. I believe Rhordyn tried to tell me it once in his own brutish way—I was just too busy cowering to listen. Too busy pouring my energy into the circles I spun.

Now I've got *too much* energy. Responsibility. Regret. Too many unbridled thoughts and emotions smashing around inside my head. My heart.

*Too much to atone for.*

"I don't *want* a war, Cainon. And I don't want your land. Not really. I just want those ships so I can secure Ocruth."

*For* him.

*So I can finish what he started and make his people safe.*

"You're starting to sound like Rhordyn," he says, gaze dragging down my body, up again. "Though I dare say, a more delectable version."

I sigh and shove to my feet, grip Rhordyn's sword, then swing it over my back and buckle it between my breasts. "I'll give you time to consider your options," I say, before striding toward the door.

"And what about Zali?"

The words are pelted at me, stilling my feet.

That slithering darkness tucked inside me wiggles.

Slowly, I spin, looking at him down the line of my shoulder. "What *about* Zali?"

He tips his head to the side, brow bunched. "What do you plan to do about her, of course?"

I chew on his words, not wanting to admit that I have no idea what he's talking about, but in the end, ignorance will get me nowhere.

I realize that now.

"I don't understand," I admit, pushing the words past the clamp of my teeth.

Cainon releases a deep sigh and wanders around the table, pausing by the hog, prying the pear from its maw. "Lyra!" he belts out, leaning against the stone, inspecting every side of the bright-green fruit.

Movement catches my eye, and I look up to see one of the palace servants step through a door on the far wall—a long lighting stick clutched in her white-knuckled fist. The woman is parchment pale, shoulders curled, her eyes shaded by the forward tip of her head. Her simple blue tunic sways around her slender legs as she shuffles toward the table.

I notice the tracks of sweat lining her temples. Dappling her forehead.

She's *nervous.*

A lump of dread rises in my throat, and I move forward a step.

Another.

Lyra stops a few long strides away from Cainon, head bowed. He continues to inspect his pear, pulling a small dagger from the inside of his boot. "Have you been listening to our conversation, Lyra?"

"N-no, Master. I w-wasn't—"

He stabs his blade at her face, making her flinch. "*Don't lie to me,*" he belts out, the words blasting off the walls.

Breath whooshes out of me as a whimper escapes her lips.

I steal another few steps, the pads of my fingers skimming the hilt of my dagger.

"Did you hear my promised admit to murdering the High Master of Ocruth?"

*Silence.*

"Yes or no, Lyra."

She shoots me a nervous glance, swallows, then nods. "Y-yes, Master. I did."

"Right. Thank you for your honesty." She curtseys deep and begins to shuffle backward, but Cainon halts her with a sharp look. "Stay right there," he says, carving off a slice of pear and biting into it, looking at me sideways. "Once word gets out that you killed Zali's promised, her Masters and Mistresses will expect her to challenge you to a duel."

This sinking feeling plunges through me as I recall Zali's stern warning: *We must keep Rhordyn's death a secret until we've found somewhere else to pin the blame.*

The words hold a different weight now that I'm sitting here, choking on the sharp tang of Lyra's fear.

"To the *death,*" Cainon adds, plunging the last word through me like a spear.

My knees threaten to buckle.

"Zali's land is mostly sand. Hard to carve out reliable bunkers. By blurring the line between their borders, Rhordyn was offering refuge to many who will otherwise perish in the surge of Vruk attacks. You've cheated them out of extra resources, extra land and revenue. Extra *safety*.

If Zali doesn't challenge you for the right to claim Ocruth, she will be seen as *weak,* and it'll only be a matter of time before she's usurped."

The blood drains from my face, gaze darting to Lyra who's shriveling by the second.

*Fuck.*

I open my mouth, but nothing comes out—my tongue pinned to its roof, heart pumping so hard and fast my head spins.

*Never show your hand unless you know exactly what you're up against.*

Rhordyn's words strike me like an axe swung from the past—another sound piece of advice I let ricochet off my stony regard. Too blinded by my own rage and the lovesick dance swirling inside me.

The realization sours my insides, making my cheeks tingle, mind scrambling as I weigh my options.

A cold sweat gathers across the back of my neck ...

"You really are selfish," I bite out, and his eyes soften.

"Open your heart to me and I'll prove you wrong."

My hand tightens around the hilt of my dagger, stare darting between Cainon and Lyra, but instinct stops me from whipping out the blade. Flinging it at his head.

His confident stance, the way he carves off another piece of pear and bites down on the crispy shard, winking at me ... it all tells me he'd have the stealth to dodge it. Then I'd be without a dagger, bearing no other weapon but a close-combat sword I've never used before.

"Seems we're at an impasse." Another crispy bite. Another languid chew. "We can keep his death a secret for now, and I'll take care of your little ... *problem* so you can claim it as an accident," he proclaims, waving the pointy end of his dagger at the trembling woman cowering in his shadow. "Though I will require insurance to keep *my* mouth shut." He looks straight at me. "You."

*No.*

"All of you. Once we're officially coupled, you'll be under *my* protection, which will eliminate most of our issues. And if you're a good girl, I'll garnish the deal with some ships. But first you'll have to prove yourself by completing the trial. I'm sure you'll understand that I, too, have lost trust."

My gaze darts between him and Lyra, trickles of sweat beading my brow.

He's got me backed against a wall of spears primed to slide between my ribs.

Based on the assumption that I make it out of The Bowl, there are only three possible outcomes to this political shitshow:

One, he'll couple with me, bed me, burn me at the stake once I don't bleed for him, then claim Ocruth as his.

Two, if I'm pliable—let him use and abuse my body and political stance—he might let me live, though I doubt he'll be very forgiving once a portion of his fleet disappears without his consent. Because there's no fucking way he's willingly giving me those ships.

I see that now.

And the final option, the one that leaves Cainon just as far from getting his claws into Rhordyn's territory as he was before I stupidly accepted his cupla, I take the duel, sacrifice myself, and leave Zali in charge of Rouste *and* Ocruth—an easy sway of power since Rhordyn's people have already accepted her. Lyra won't die, and Zali can implement the trade halt. Starve Cainon out until he's forced to yield the ships.

Rhordyn trusted her.

I trust her.

"Cat got your tongue, petal?"

I blink, lift my chin, and turn my attention back to Cainon. "I'll take the *fucking* duel."

He sighs, long and deep. "There you go again, pushing me away."

His arm whips out.

There's the short whistle of metal splitting air before a meaty thud makes me jolt. Slowly, I let my gaze drag to the dagger now protruding from Lyra's chest, amidst a blossom of red blooming on her tunic. She lifts her head, looks right at me, then opens her mouth, spilling a ribbon of blood that pours down her chin.

Her lighting pole clatters to the floor, and she crumples into a heap at the same moment my knees smack the stone.

I taste the metallic perfume of her blood in the air as I draw a shuddered breath, hands clapping upon my mouth in a failed attempt to stop the violent scream that rips up my throat.

*He killed her.*

*He—*

Cainon whips a napkin off the table, flicking it open. He strides toward his motionless servant and rolls her onto her back. "Look what you made me do," he mutters, exposing me to her vacant, wide-eyed stare.

I force myself to watch him pull the dagger from her chest. Endure the wet sound of it slipping free before he wipes the sharp on the dark-blue napkin that gobbles up the red.

"I appreciate the fact that you're trying for the sake of your new responsibility, but all you're really doing is hurting more people." He looks at me from beneath folded brows. "If you were better prepared for the outside world, you wouldn't be constantly making such costly mistakes."

He walks toward me and threads his hands beneath my arms, hauling me up like a strung puppet—my body a shell folding to his whim. He sets me in my seat, then uses the blade he just pulled from Lyra's chest to carve a hunk of meat from the hog, piling it on a spare plate. "But it's okay, you have *me* now." He places the meal before me, and my guts cramp.

Easing down my hood, he sweeps my hair over the back of my chair and runs his fingers through the length, separating it into three long sections. "You will never cut this, do you understand?"

I don't answer.

He weaves it into a braid that tugs at my roots, my head jerking with each forceful twist while I stare at the puddle blooming beneath Lyra's lifeless body.

"I know we're off to a rough start, but I'm certain we can overcome *anything* together."

A shiver runs the length of my spine ...

*And I'm certain he's delusional.*

He yanks my braid so hard my head whips back.

I'm forced to look up at his features pinched with an unreadable expression. "Would it be so hard? To love me?"

I squeeze my eyes shut.

He clears his throat, releases my hair, and walks back to his seat.

I stare at the blank wall. Feel like I'm pinned against it.

His chair grinds along the floor, utensils scraping together as he carves into his meal while I choke on the musk of Lyra's blood.

For a moment, I consider ripping off my necklace. Letting my ugly spill. Until I picture the palace heavy with the reek of fiery death, blackened halls full of the charred remains of men and women who were nothing but innocent bystanders.

"I will give it to them, petal."

"What?" I rasp.

He stuffs a chunk of meat in his mouth, chewing, one cheek bulging as he says, "The liquid bane. None will take it. The sickness only has a ninety percent mortality rate. Most cling to that sliver of hope with clenched and shaking fists until they draw their last breath." He shrugs, drowning his mouthful with a guzzle of red wine that bleeds down his chin. "Take your time to mourn, then pick yourself up, plant that dazzling smile on your face, and *try*."

# CHAPTER
*Baze*
## 13

I sit with my back to the bars, legs spread, the laces of my boots so loose they're gaping. A blazing lantern rests between my thighs, as well as a bottle of whiskey. On a sigh, I raise the bottle and tip it to my lips, drawing a deep gulp that does nothing to warm my insides or smooth my pebbled skin.

The thick, dark-blue cloak Graves lent me is heavy upon my shoulders but appreciated here, where the cold bores all the way to your bones.

Shafts of sunlight shoot down through holes in the ceiling, failing to reach the back corners of the small cell. I steal nervous glances at the pockets of dark, making sure they're not shifting.

Slithering out to smother me.

Flipping open a fold-up shaving blade, I snap it back into place. Repeat the process again, and again, drawing another glug of whiskey, marinating in the reek of dust, death, and fear steeped within the stone. The lumpy, shit-stained mattress. The single sheet half-eaten by moths.

This place used to feel so fucking big.

Now the walls feel tight, like they're crowding me.

*Choking* me.

I flip the blade again, scouring my prisoner with a virulent gaze.

His hands are tied to the armrests of a worn, wooden chair, the ample folds of his gray robe concealing a *very* dense body. He may live in a shit part of town, but he's certainly not eating like a pauper—wearing bricks of muscle that almost broke my back lugging him all the way down here.

I'm nothing if not dedicated.

Deep breaths saw through his gaping mouth that's leaking a string of drool. A snort, then a gravelly moan. He lifts that big, bare, bulbous head off his shoulder, bloodshot eyes landing on me, squinting. The welt on his temple from when I snuck up behind him and knocked him out cold is raised and angry looking.

"Morning, beautiful."

His eyes widen, gaze dropping to the blade, breathing patterns rallying into a fierce, panicked rhythm as he takes in our cramped confines—no doubt coming to terms with his prickly predicament. Stare digging between the bars at my back, he makes a choked sound as he takes in the sights across the hall. The long-forgotten corpse still clinging to the bars, mouth caught in an eternal scream.

I draw another glug, the chair scraping and bumping against the ground in his effort to wrestle free of his restraints.

"*Help!*" He screams, shrill and desperate.

Again.

*Again.*

"It's no use," I mutter once he stops to gulp air, his head dappled with beads of sweat. "Nobody can hear you."

"W-who are you?" he croaks. "What do you want from me?"

Snapping the shaving blade back into place, I roll the jar of thorns across the filthy cobbled floor. It comes to a halt by his feet, and though he pales, a glimmer of hope ignites his eyes.

"You w-want candy?" he rasps. "I-I can get you some! My cousin organized a meeting for me and Madame Strings. Tomorrow. I'm to be her new runner for the city's west."

"So I've heard," I mutter, sweeping my hair off my face and pushing to my feet. Wobbling toward the wall, my boots scuff against the chalky sheen that coats the ground. Powdered remnants of the burrow's ancient inhabitants.

I drag my finger down a groove etched into the stone, one for each person who was carried out dead. "And how did you prove yourself *worthy* of this meeting?"

"Th-there are many young children about the city in need of direction and stability. In need of *hope* that the world will not end in shadows. I-I purchased a jar of Candescence I used to bring over *twenty* children to the temple doors—each with minds opened by their first taste."

My gut knots, and I swallow the bitter spill of disgust rising in my throat.

"And what happens to these children?" I ask, running my finger through another jagged groove.

Another.

"They're brought into the open arms of the Shulák, of course. Some are taken to the land without shadow. To the great Glass Temple," he proclaims, and I whip my head around, eyes narrowed. His are glazed, expression wistful. "A place many of us only *dream* of seeing."

*Glass ...*

*Without shadow ...*

This place—it must be in *Arrin.*

I clear my throat, casting my gaze through the bars to the beams of light piercing down from above. Even now, they look so beautiful—so *transcendent*—that the backs of my eyes sting.

There was once a time when those beams of light were so, so far away. When a dimness seeped through me, little by little, day by day.

When those shadows drew closer.

*Closer.*

"It's bright here in the middle of the day. But at night ... the shadows *dance.*" I spin, flipping the blade open, then shut again, making him jump. "They creep and crawl and slither along. They *sing*—a rattling tune that makes you quiver."

I pocket my blade and approach, stopping close enough that his rancid breath stains the back of my throat. Lips pulled into a feral sneer, I squeeze my hand into a ball, force myself to release it, heart racing as I grip my ring and nudge it past my knuckle.

Let it clatter to the ground.

A heaviness settles upon my shoulders, like my feet are suddenly nailed to the stone. My spine wants to curl, my limbs want to fold. It's an effort not to tuck into a ball and shuffle to the brightest part of the room as my fake skin loosens its barbed-wire grip on my true self.

His mouth drops open, eyes widen with unbridled fear. The hair hanging before my eyes goes from auburn to iridescent, and the air ripens with the reek of his piss.

This place seems to do that to people.

"You ... *You're*—"

"Unfortunate, I know. We both are, I guess, given your current predicament."

He pales.

I pinch one of the thorns lining my right ear, drawing a tight breath before I rip it free. The side of my face ignites in a deep, tear-inducing pain that seeps into my jaw, making even my teeth ache with the relentless blaze. A warm wetness slips down the side of my neck, and I blink, freeing the tears that had gathered in my eyes.

Sniffing, I weigh the bloody thorn in my palm; so fine and delicate at the tip, stumpy at the base, the long, pronged roots making up its majority.

I lift my gaze, stabbing him with a hard stare. "Did you know that every time one of these is ripped free, it feels like the entire ear is torn off?"

He shakes his head with vigor, like he thinks that'll absolve him. "N-no. I— I had n-no idea!"

Such a terrible lie. There's no way he thought it felt *good.*

"Shocking, right?" I set the thorn down and kneel at his side, reach into my pocket, and pull out a pair of pliers. His eyes bulge, fingers twitching to bunch despite his binds as I pinch his right thumbnail between the metal jaws and clamp down. I flash him a smile. "It feels a bit like this."

Jerking my arm back, I *yank*.

He screams so loud his voice cracks, hand trembling, blood splattering across the floor. His face crumbles, chest heaving, guttural sobs bubbling past his lips.

"Thankfully, our thorns grow back faster than fingernails," I say through a twisted laugh that holds no humor, tossing the bloody pliers aside.

*Much, much faster.*

Perhaps I would feel bad about that, but the drugging numb of alcohol softens every sharp edge.

The world seems to rock beneath me, and I stumble onto my arse, landing so heavily my brain rattles. Deciding this is rather a decent spot to sit, I reach back and grip my dwindling bottle of whiskey.

"I'll let you in on a little secret." I drag a long glug, then tip the bottle toward the man, raising my brows as I swallow. "I know the one you seek," I say on a hissed breath. "The one you believe will bring about the world's end."

His jagged moans whittle, eyes almost popping out of his head, and I note the deep shade of blue wrapped around the inky pupils. Far from the perfect match to mine, but beggars can't be choosers.

"The one you use to justify this *sick* behavior," I spit, flicking my thorn in his face.

He flinches.

"She might do it, too." I bank my head to the side, trying to narrow my double vision. "She might just end us all. But perhaps that's *exactly* what we deserve."

Again, his face crumbles, more sobs erupting from his twisted mouth, like he thinks the sound will save him. He'll quickly learn it's a waste of air. Waste of tears.

Waste of hope.

Perhaps I'd deal in mercy if it'd ever lined my pockets. But all they've done is take, take, fucking *take*.

"Here's what's going to happen," I mutter, leaning so I can dig through my pocket for the shaving blade, snapping it open. I lift it, sliding the honed edge across my scalp, severing clumps of iridescent hair that rain upon my shoulders and tumble to the floor. "You'll tell me where you're set to meet this *Madame Strings* ..."

Another shave.

"What's expected of you ..."

*Another.*

"Anything else you can possibly think up. And with each tidbit of information, I'll give you one of those," I say, gesturing to the basket beside me brimming with tall, plain candles and a shard of flint. "Precious flame you'll need when the sun sinks and those shadows start to *sing.*"

# CHAPTER

*Zali*

## 14

Seated in Graves's large desk chair, facing away from our company, I stare at the wooden shelf half-crammed with books, tracing the whorls of grain in the wood that reminds me of Rouste's rolling dunes.

I can almost smell the sun-scorched sand. Can almost taste the sweet, watery fruit of a prickly pine bursting between my teeth. A perfect, calming distraction that stops me from spinning my chair.

Taking the lead despite the risks.

"Look, lady, I have no idea where his fleet is stored." Captain Rowell's ragged voice rumbles. "If I did, I'd steal a ship, collect me family, and get the fuck outta this Blight-infested shithole. And I'm not the only one who feels that way."

"How many others do you think ... feel that way?" Cindra asks from beside me, propped against the wall—arms crossed over her chest, her red merchant's cloak hanging skewed over her curvy frame, the long, dreaded lengths of her hair bound into a tidy braid.

"Fair few. I know a handful of whaling crews 'bout ready to throw in the barrel. Some of 'em have teenage sons who know the way of the seas."

I do the math.

We smuggled sixty-seven members of Rhordyn's militia down the Norse. Most whaling ships have a crew of around thirty to forty able-bodied men.

If Rowell pulls through ... we might have enough.

"And you have access to your ship stored at the city dock?" Cindra asks.

Rowell chuffs a humorless laugh. "Aye. I have access to that ol' heap o' whale shit. They keep us coming back for more. Filling the bellies o' the oil beast."

"This could work," Cindra muses, flicking me a look.

I nod.

"Yuh ... *friend*," Rowell grumbles, pausing.

I can feel his attention boring into the back of my cloaked head, frustrated I have to keep my back to him. But I can't be seen conspiring to milk Cainon's population and resources. Certainly not before we have all the pieces on the board.

"Can they guarantee the protection of me family? Of me entire *crews'* family?"

"Yes. They can also guarantee the protection of anybody else you might be able to recruit. Preferably crewmen who are familiar with sailing rough seas and can keep their mouths firmly shut."

"They'll be requirin' somethin' to solidify their faith in

yuh," Rowell says. "Me men have been mighty burnt of late, and most of 'em are strugglin' to feed their young."

I reach into the pocket of my red cloak and pull out a pouch heavy with topaz beads, most no bigger than the tip of my pinkie finger, though still large enough to feed a family for a couple of years in most corners of the continent.

Tugging my hood low, I hand the bag to Cindra, who lumps it on the desk.

There's the sound of loosening strings before, *"Fuckin' 'ell ..."*

"Each recruit will receive one bead upon pledge," Cindra states. "A *second* upon reaching the destination. Straight from your ... *benefactors* personal vault. You, Captain Rowell, will receive an entire pouch should you gather us enough able-bodied sailors to man at least forty ships."

Again, I feel Rowell's attention bore into the back of my head while I continue to trace those woody dunes.

He clears his throat. "And once we reach Ocruth, what assurance do we have that our families will be safe from the Vruks?"

A sandstorm stews in my chest, and I almost spin. Tell him we *are* the assurance. That without those ships, we're all fucked—be it now or in a few years' time. I can tell by the hard look in Cindra's pale gray eyes that she's biting back similar words.

"Castle Noir is widely known to be the safest place on the continent," she says, her voice crisp and cold. "You will each have residence within the castle walls until the threat has ceased."

"And that's *theirs* to offer?" Rowell asks, and there's a

lilt to his tone that makes me wonder if he's worked out who I am.

"Yes," Cindra states.

There's a long, drawn-out inhale before, "Very well, then."

I nibble my relief, crunch my teeth on it, then spit it back out. When I lived in The Vein, dressed in sand and bruises and my own scrappy rage, there was always a bigger, badder shadow just around the corner. Always another battle to be won.

Nothing's changed.

You're not on top unless you're a God, and even *they* can fall.

I hand Cindra a small scroll, which she passes to Rowell.

"Here's everything you need to know about what we require of you. Prepare your family. And if you speak of this to anyone who could jeopardize the mission, I'll boil your balls."

My brows bump up, stare sliding sideways, taking in Cindra's perfectly serene profile. I have to hand it to the woman, I don't think I could've delivered that line with such a straight face.

"Fuckin' 'ell, lady. That won't be necessary." There's the sound of Rowell's chair scraping across the ground, then his departing steps. The door squeaks open, snips shut.

I spin my chair, stare raking across the top of Graves's wooden desk. He let us use his office, which was kind— and only cost me three topaz beads. Gotta respect a man who's willing to look a High Mistress in the eye and barter.

"I like Rowell," Cindra says. "I think he'll come through."

"Can't imagine why he wouldn't." I smile wryly. "Think he got the message loud and clear."

She flashes me a grin. "Aim for the soft spot. Never fails." Her smile fades, and she moves around the desk, settling in Rowell's seat. She leans forward, hands clasped before her. "What are we doing about Orlaith?"

I think of the sprite that came zipping up to Cindra right before our meeting, chittering a rambled message that could have only come from one person's mouth. I didn't even bother to check her room to confirm.

I suck a breath, lips pursed. Blow it out slow.

"She wants the ships as much as I do, and there's nothing we can do until we locate them. Once we have some coordinates we can devise a plan." I shrug. "So long as she keeps in contact—and keeps her lips shut about Rhordyn—everything should be okay. We pour our focus into getting what we came for, then snag her on the way out. The rest we can figure out later."

"So we're just ... leaving her to it?"

I raise a brow, looking at Cindra. "You're thinking of her as the kid you've seen scuttling around the castle. A liability."

"Hard not to after what she's done."

"There's a strength in her that needs time to hatch, and she's not going to do that with me breathing down her neck," I say, toying with my braid.

Now that I really think about it, she was more of a danger to herself sitting in that room upstairs with nothing to do but think. Surrounded by Rhordyn's things and clothes and smell.

No wonder she climbed out the window. I would have done the same.

"Then how are we going to find these ships?" Cindra asks, frowning. "Stow on a barge?"

I shake my head. "Too risky. I've planted a sprite on Cainon's ship. With the escort of a sail, I figure the little thing should be able to track a path and make it back to relay it safely."

"That's—"

"Useless if he doesn't set sail before the coupling ceremony," I mutter, "I know."

There's no plan without a backup plan. You're dune cat chow if you put all your boa eggs in one basket.

Cindra's eyes harden as she nods. "Then we better devise a plan B."

I flick a lopsided smile at her.

*I like this woman.*

# CHAPTER 15

*Orlaith*

*Try.*
  *Try.*
    *Try.*

I internally chant the word every time my chisel cleaves into the stone with the force of my savage determination, chipping off chunks that collect in the small hole I've dug into the wall.

My hair is still wet from spending most of the day trying to scramble out of The Bowl—getting fleeting sips of sunlight every time the clouds broke—my guts sore from violent bursts of vomiting between my failed attempts.

The tapestry is a heavy weight upon my back, the air thick and musty and drawn through my gritted teeth, residue of my exertion dripping down my temples.

The blisters on my palms have long since popped, sweat and dust and bits of stone aggravating the tender, weepy flesh of the deep cut in my palm as I *stab*.

*Try.*

*Try.*

*Try.*

My hand slips.

A blaze of sting sears my knuckles as I grate them across the ravaged stone. Hissing, I whip my hand back and shake it out, the chisel thumping into my lap. I shuffle around and lean against the wall.

Using my sleeve to wipe my face, I give the tapestry a shove with my leg, allowing fresh air to waft into the tight space with a rush of golden light from my lantern sitting just beyond the hole. Drawing deep, relieved breaths, my gaze coasts across the back of it. Across the swirling lines of pale thread and jagged black stitches that look angry enough to transcend the material.

I frown.

The woven threads bear no resemblance to the image on the front.

I untangle my bunched limbs and cleave free of the tight space, a litter of stone shards scattering onto the ground with my chisel as I ease past the heavy weave.

Standing in the dim, dusty hallway, I lift my lantern and study the tapestry mounted with a rod of wood, the ends strung with a single length of rope hooked over a nail. I set my lantern aside, grab the bottom border, and walk backward, lifting it away from the wall before I flip the thing, eyes widening when it thumps back into place with the back matter facing forward.

I stumble a step, hand whipping up to slap my mouth.

A volcano almost erupts off the magnificent piece of art, but it's not lava spewing from the crater. It's a storm of steam dashed through with cracks of lightning. It's a swarm of *beasts* prowling down the craggy slope, their fur gray and pallid, stumpy maws locked in ferocious snarls that bare their ivory sabers.

*Vruk.*

I swallow the swell of bile burning the back of my throat as my gaze rips from the tapestry and drifts to the one just right of it. I dart forward and grab it by the hem, flipping it.

Release a little sob.

I scour the brutal scene of Vruks shredding across the weave—muzzles splashed red, bits of their savage kills scattered about.

Severed hands, arms, heads ...

At the center, a woman with black eyes and hair the color of fire is stretched over a boulder, her fiercely beautiful face caught in a twist of anguish.

I gasp at her extended canines. The tapered tips of her ears.

*Unseelie.*

Her gaze is lifeless, her broken body at the mercy of the haunched beast feasting on her abdomen. Its paw rests on her chest, an extended talon punched through the spot where her heart would lie, blood leaching from the wound.

I'm struck by the mental vision of Rhordyn walking amongst the Irilak, his ears sharpening. Canines *lengthening*. Then his unseeing eyes while I burn beneath the feel of a phantom kiss pressed against my forehead.

*Don't cry ...*

My knees threaten to crumble, an ache surging in my chest that buckles my spine.

With a shuddered breath, I shuffle to the right in uneven

steps, doing what little I can to brace my heart before gently flipping another tapestry.

The shape of Arrin is woven upon an otherwise black background, and within the borders of the lost territory is a mound of bloodied roses. Most are red, but some are the haunting hue of the roses that sprout from my shoulder, threaded with a sparkly string that glimmers in the firelight.

Standing atop the mound is a man dressed in a green cape; *Arrin's* colors.

I can tell he's Unseelie by the points of his pierced ears and the harsh cut of his beautiful face. By the opaline blood dripping from his extended canines.

A broad-shouldered silhouette dwarfs him from behind, his menacing presence making the hairs on my arms lift.

My fingers twitch to reach forward and rub away the blackness so I can see his face.

His eyes.

My gaze drops to the tapered tip of a sable talon protruding from the Unseelie's chest. Blood has seeped through his green cloak, as though the man behind him just stabbed him through the heart.

I dash to the next tapestry, flipping it—like turning the pages of a book I can't gobble down fast enough.

This scene is similar, but the black silhouette is gone, the green-cloaked man atop the mountain of roses now folded in a lifeless lump. The border is no longer black, but a beautiful, ghastly illusion that makes it appear as though numerous bloody swords are threaded through the weft, pointed toward Arrin, each wielded by snarling Unseelie.

*War.*

*Someone murdered the High Master of Arrin, and the entire continent went to war over the unclaimed land ...*

My heart hammers so hard I can hear it rushing in my ears.

I flip the next tapestry.

Silvery dunes are overlooked by a riot of angry, swollen clouds riddled with luminescent forks. Gathered people—no, *Unseelie*—are stalled mid stride, weapons dropping from their hands as they run from bolts of lightning powering down from bulbous, gray clouds.

There's wild fear in their inky eyes that weep bloody tears, mouths agape, jagged lines of silver scribbled across their skin, swallowing some of them whole.

I feel the image take root inside my chest. Weigh me down.

Reaching out, I trace the forks of lightning, some innate part of me *knowing* that these hidden tapestries are ancient threads of history. That I'm peeking through the folds of time at the decimation of the Unseelie.

Given what I know of their history, I should be looking upon these weaves feeling *lightened* ...

Instead, a deep sadness overwhelms me.

Frowning, my gaze drifts to the right, and I find my hands shaking when I reach down and grip the hem of the next tapestry. This one is large, harder to flip, and my shoulder muscles ache as I wrestle it over.

I drop the drape against the wall in a puff of dust that makes me cough. I bat at the swirl of it, squinting through the haze.

My eyes widen, and cold dread seeps through my veins, chilling me to the bone.

A lone hill graces the center of the tapestry, littered with hundreds of wildflowers stitched in the boldest colors.

I've seen a likeness of this image before, back at Castle Noir. Hung before the hidden passageway that led to my secret nook where I'd watch the monthly Tribunal. A tapestry I've looked at many times, heart swelling with a curious sadness I could never understand. A sadness I feel *now* nipping the backs of my eyes as I study the perfect stitches. The way the flowers tilt their faces toward the light. The shape of the petals, like a flurry of tiny flames.

And I just *know* ...

Both tapestries were woven by the same pair of hands.

Night sits upon the shoulders of the palace like a weight, choking the life out of it, giving it a lonely, cold aura despite the muggy air. Even so, I'm not surprised to find Old Hattie in her room off the lobby, sitting on a stool before her loom—her long, silver braid coiled on the floor.

Tucked behind a half-open door, I barely feel the tired ache of my eyes while I watch her weave, huddled within an orb of lantern light. Her fingers move with grace and speed, like the missing two have never been there.

I hunger over every twist and knot, bright threads woven and pulled as taut as her hunched shoulders. She uses the warp stick to tighten the line, and my gaze drifts to the half-finished masterpiece.

A nest of flowers surrounds what appears to be the makings of a pale face, the vibrant pops of color so achingly familiar a lump rises in my throat.

*Wildflowers.*

She makes a small grunting sound that shatters the sleepy silence, and her hand lifts from the threads. She doesn't turn from her task as she crooks her finger—a quiet request for me to approach.

A chill scurries up my spine.

I'm sure most people don't sense me coming and going, dashing through the halls and slipping through rooms. Melding with the shadows.

Not unless I want them to.

Clearing my throat, I tuck my hair behind my ears, checking the dark, empty foyer through the doorway to my right before I ease forward. Old Hattie edges along the wooden stool, setting her lantern on the floor and patting the empty space.

I draw a shuddering breath, then sit.

She collects my blistered, bloody hands and holds them tight, her skin so fine and papery it makes my breath hitch.

They don't even feel *real*.

Frowning, I look into her pale eyes, noting the sheen of tears glazing them as she tightens her grip, cradling my visible hurts. But there's something about her sorrowful gaze that makes me think she sees the pain beneath my skin, too.

"I'm fine," I lie.

Smiling gently, she shakes her head.

I break eye contact and squeeze my lids shut, feeling her fingers coast across the burn mark on the inside of my wrist. She makes a soft humming sound, then eases both my hands toward the tapestry.

Realizing her intentions, I try to pull back. "I don't

know what I'm doing," I say, but her grip only tightens before she twists spools of color around my fingers, guiding me to make the weaves.

I resign to her whim, awkward at first—uncertain— but there's confidence in Hattie's silent instruction. In the way she manipulates my hands so that together, we move almost as fast as she does on her own.

My hammering heart slows, worries melting, mind fixating on the twist of thread as she guides me through her craft.

Many minutes slip by, and I wonder over the spool of time *Hattie's* spent on the weaves she's made. Over the stories she's told in her own abstract way.

Perhaps, like me, she spins circles to escape the noise in her own head.

She uses her warp stick to tighten another line, giving the flowers a little more shape, and I look at her.

Hands stilling, her powdery gaze strikes me.

"I've seen these flowers before," I whisper, and a line forms between her brows. "On the wall at Castle Noir."

Her hand comes up to cover her mouth, and a whimper slips out, features crumbling as tears spill.

*Shit.*

Perhaps I've made a terrible mistake. Poured salt in old wounds that haven't healed.

I reach for her hand—

The clock above the mantle chimes, and Hattie jumps, her wild gaze whipping to the door. Then her hands are moving fast: elbow resting on her flattened palm, the other pointed to the ceiling. She flips the supporting hand and stretches the fingers on that reaching one, making it look like branches waving in the wind. She moves again, making a V shape with her fingers, the tip of her middle finger touching her upper cheek before pointing the same gesture forward, grunting at me.

I shake my head. "I-I don't know, Hattie. I'm so sorry ..."

A groan drones out of her, and she pushes her lantern at my chest, stealing nervous peeks at the clock. Then she's fisting my shirt, lugging me to my feet with a strength that belies her frail stature. She shoves me toward the door so hard I stumble back, catching myself before I fall flat on my ass.

My mind whirs; heart hammers.

"Fwee!"

Her rasped voice shakes me to the bone.

She *can* talk ... she just can't do it properly.

She makes the second hand gesture again, waving her stretched hand. "Fwee!"

"I— I don't ..."

"*Fwee!*"

Fwee ... Fwee ...

*Tree.*

"You ... want me to go to the *tree?*"

She nods so fast I fear her head might topple off her bony shoulders.

The sun's probably about to rise, and I've only ever visited the tree at night ...

My grip tightens on the lantern spilling harrowing shadows across her face now lit with a spark of *hope*.

Beautiful, chest-breaking *hope*.

I offer her a soft smile and nod.

Pushing free of the shadowy jungle, the world opens for me like drapes drawn to the warm kiss of morning.

Loose hair and shirt dancing with the tousling sea breeze, I step closer to the tree clinging to the edge of the cliff like a gnarled hand, the budding sun casting the ocean in bronze ripples, heating my skin and enriching my senses.

Despite the warmth spreading through my veins, blooming beads of luster and making my fingers tingle, a deep melancholy washes over me like the rising tide ...

Last time I was here, *he* found me.

Held me.

Comforted me.

Then I screamed at him and told him terrible things—cold echoes that chill me to the bone.

Arms wrapped around my middle, I step close enough to the cliff that I can see down to the stony shore below; to the weather-worn dinghy I noticed when Cainon led me to the abandoned Unseelie burrow.

I let my gaze coast across the ocean to the small island sitting in the bay, and my heart skips a beat.

Another.

There, littering the simple mound, is a dappled blaze of color.

Red, orange, pink, purple, yellow—

Wildflowers. *Thousands* of them swaying with the breeze, their vibrant petals bared to the rising sun. Clumped together in places, scattered in others, cushioned by lush green grass so bright and bold it reminds me of the grounds at Castle Noir.

My knees give way, and I crumple, pressing my palms upon my heaving chest as a restless energy squirms to life and pumps through my veins ...

There's something out there; something Hattie wants me to *see*.

# CHAPTER 16

*Baze*

Leaning against a stack of crates, I flip the token between my fingers as I watch the long ferry cut across the river, sail bulging. I screw my nose up at the smell of fish and bodily waste baking in the evening rays.

A desperate chorus of yells rips my attention to three cloaked Shulák standing on the back of a cart, tossing loaves of bread at a hoard of children with sunburnt cheeks, chapped lips, and tattered tops. They dive on the offerings like gulls, then fall into a squealing, scrapping heap.

I shudder, ripping my gaze away.

The ferryman—a large lump of a man who takes up an entire seat built for three—coaxes his vessel against the wooden pier. Leaning forward, he huffs and puffs, tossing a length of rope around a post, his face flushed from exertion.

Two scrawny men pass me by, dark shadows cushioning their hollow eyes, looking like regurgitated death. They stop at the ferry, scratching their skin, nibbling their cuticles, edging from foot to foot. They hand the ferryman plain silver tokens and step down onto the vessel.

I move forward, setting mine into his plump, sweaty hand. He closes one eye and looks through the small glass window punched into the center.

According to Blythe—the unfortunate man whose robe I'm wearing—this particular token is *special*. It says I can be trusted. That I've been vetted, my faith tested, and that I've proven myself worthy of initiation. Of this personal, in-the-flesh meeting with the infamous *Madame Strings*.

The ferryman lifts a brow, eyeing me from beneath the hood of his gray robe. "You Blythe?"

I nod.

He offers me a slimy half smile that makes me want to scrub my skin with a pinecone. "Lucky man."

*He wouldn't be saying that if he saw the state I left Blythe in.*

The ferryman pockets my token and jerks his chin at an empty seat directly in front of him. He unties the boat and maneuvers us away from the pier, the sail filling with a blow of wind that shoves us forward, cutting against the current's flow.

We sail toward the opposite riverbank—the small chunk of Parith on the other side of the Norse still embraced by the wall.

The wind buffers me with the sour stench of the ferryman's body odor while he whistles a droning tune I could certainly do without. We move toward a huge gray temple made up of spire-like shapes—tall as the city wall, its ominous facade as abhorrent to me as the mountainous presence at my back.

I shudder.

We nudge the pier, the rope secured by a gray-robed male who scans us over.

The two haunts at the front continue to fidget.

"Wait here," the ferryman grumbles, then steps onto the pier, making the boat bounce around so much I'm surprised it doesn't flip. Speaking in hushed tones, he converses with the other Shulák, tokens clinking when he hands them over.

He points at me.

Leaning forward, I plant my forearms on my knees and hone my attention on my clasped hands, feigning disinterest, still feeling the residue of last night's bender despite the ripening hour.

Waking to a splat of gull shit on my face, wrapped around a streetlamp, steeped in what I *hope* was my own puddle of vomit was a new low. If Rhordyn had seen me, he'd have been so bitterly disappointed.

But he's not here because the bastard made his own mistakes.

We *all* made mistakes.

I shackle the thought somewhere deep and dark as the other robed male steps forward, sweeping his hands wide. "Welcome. I'm Brother Beryll. Please disembark the vessel and step upon our holy shore, into the arms of our great Gods where you will be nourished by their bountiful bosom."

*What a load of krah shit.*

We're ushered across the courtyard, the stone beneath our feet inscribed with a sea of scripture.

*Maars's prophecies.*

Despite the dense heat, my skin sprouts goosebumps.

Dwarfed by the temple's mountainous size, I keep my gaze ahead as we move up a rise of stairs, through a mammoth set of doors, into a lofty interior lit by beams of daylight shafting down from above. A sight that makes my gut flip. Makes my fingers itch for the flask tucked within the discreet pocket lining my robe.

A couple of stoic-faced Gray Guards boasting their signature chainmail and simple breastplate whisk the other two men through a high archway—more bounce in their step than they had half an hour ago.

I frown. "Where are they going?"

"To be cleansed. This way."

Brother Beryll leads me along a maze of quiet corridors, and I take note of every twist and turn, stashing the information in the back of my mind. A shaft of light illuminates the slow-dancing, powdery particles wafting through the air in a smorgasbord of muted colors.

*Candescence.*

My knees threaten to buckle, gums throbbing as my canines punch down beneath my mask, my instincts flaring to fierce, feral life.

Clenching my teeth so hard I fear they might shatter, I force my feet forward.

Force my features to remain smooth.

Brother Beryll receives a ring of keys from a guard standing beside an open doorway, and I'm led into a tight room crammed full of trestle tables heavy with rocks of sugar, dusted in the fine powder the air is thick with. I cough, fighting the temptation to lift my robe and cover my mouth as we weave between the rows.

Men with shaved heads hunch over pestle and mortars,

casting wary glances my way, grinding down chunks of sugar they chip off the blocks. Though a few aren't grinding sugar at all.

They're grinding *thorns*—mixing it with sugar.

Diluting it down.

Shrill crunching sounds pierce me to the core, dragging nails across my eardrums. Violence swells, punching at my ribs, peddling my blood into a fiery rage.

We head toward a door at the far end of the room, and I watch a man sprinkle more of the delicate, crystalline spikes onto a small set of scales from a packed-full jar ...

*No ears.*

I tame the growl threatening to chew through my tone as I ask, "They come already plucked?"

"Of course," Brother Beryll boasts, slipping a key into the lock and clunking the bolt to the side. "They're taken straight off living male stock."

A shiver streaks through me.

*Living male stock ...*

"If any more females exist, they're *well* hidden," Brother Beryll continues, pushing the door wide. "We've done our part, hunted high and low in the name of the stones. Though we got close to finding Shadow's Hand years ago, we're yet to fulfill our duty to the Gods and their great creation. But we will," he says with such stable determination the insides of my cheeks tingle.

I'm certain everybody in the room can hear the erratic thump of my heart. That they can tell I'm an intruder dressed in the skin of a dead man.

That I want to rip the blade from inside my right boot and tear it through their jugulars.

*But then who would lead me to Madame Strings?*

He gestures for me to move past, and I slip into a darker room lined with rows of wooden shelves. Some are stacked with gray coins, some with gold, some with jars of the Candescence-sugar blend.

My heart grows heavier as I sweep my gaze around the space, hands tightening into fists hidden under my scooped sleeves.

"This is where our stocks are stored." He picks up a jar and tosses it high, snatching it in such a carefree manner that I picture my hand wrapped around his throat.

Picture his skin turning a sickly shade of blue.

"You'll pay for one of these, take it, sell it, and return for the next. The funds are then sent to the Glass Palace."

*Interesting.*

He reaches out his empty hand, and I clear my throat, digging through my pocket and pulling out a gold drab. I make the trade, skin crawling the moment my fingers wrap around the glass so tight I'm surprised it doesn't shatter.

"You have plenty of stock," I state, pocketing the jar.

"We do, but it goes fast, which is why we dilute it. The city is thirstier than it's ever been. This month's shipment came in from the Glass Palace this afternoon." Brother Beryll drops some plain gray tokens into a leather pouch and hands them to me. "Anyone who is hooked and can't afford the cost can be given one of *those*. Payment for their trip across the river, where they'll receive the opportunity to kneel to the stones in exchange for a regular supply."

I nod, remembering the gaunt, jittery males who joined my crossing. Realizing just how smooth and fucked up this operation is.

"And don't forget to limit what you give to the children. We don't want an army of runts. We need them fully mature before they become regular users."

I swallow bile, nodding, picturing my thumbs gored into his skull, bursting his eyes like puffballs.

"Of course."

"In exchange for your hard work, you will be given your own room here in the temple—food, clean water, and the blessing of the Elders. You will also be gifted a daily dose of Candescence."

"Right," I mutter, scanning the room as my rage simmers into something thick. Potent.

*Deadly.*

"So … when do I meet Madame Strings?"

He lifts a brow. "Eager, are we?"

*You have no idea.*

I'm led down a coiled staircase, then a long, stone corridor lit by flaming sconces. Guards open huge stone doors that creak their protest, and the heavy scent of spicy incense swirls around me.

"Enjoy," Brother Beryll says, offering a slimy wink that makes my skin crawl.

Soft moans coax a frown as I ease past drapes of sheer gray material tethered to the ceiling. Nudging into the open, my boots become tethered to the stone.

Ahead is a heaving pit of flesh—people with glazed, faraway gazes, paired off or gathered in writhing groups, naked aside from the women decorated in strings of silver bells that tailor to their voluptuous curves and jingle as they bounce, roll, *thrust.*

Guttural moans, sated groans, and the building cries of passion fill the large room ignited by bowls of flaming oil balanced on pedestals. The ceiling is high, the floor padded with plush gray furnishings: chaises; massive floor pillows; thick, fluffy rugs; and a mammoth four-poster bed sitting in the center of the space.

My gaze coasts across the mounds of flesh and fuckery, seeing small bowls of iridescent powder placed on pillows and stools throughout the open room, glimmering in the firelight.

A low growl boils in the back of my throat, my rage spurred into a hissing, spitting beast.

A curvaceous woman peels from a tangle of limbs and body parts moving about the bed, an elegance to the way she makes each step look featherlight. Streaks of gray swirl across her bronze skin, smudged in places.

Our gazes collide—her eyes so blue and bold, a contrast to the blackness smudged around them, splaying toward her temples. Sharpened bits of bone pierce her lobes, and delicate inked lines trace from her full lower lip down her chin and neck before flaring across her plump breasts that bounce as she sways toward me.

"You must be the new runner," she purrs, her voice laced with a suggestive slur that would usually spur straight to my cock. But I'm too distracted by the strings beaded with tiny bells that are coiled around the dreaded lengths of her long, tawny hair. That and the commanding glint in her eye, as though she's used to being in charge.

My heart is a thundering roar in my ears.

*Madame Strings.*

Pushing back my hood, I run my hands over my scalp, missing the tug of my hair. "Yes."

Her eyes hunger over my face. The expanse of my shoulders.

"I'm here for the induction," I continue, and she steps so close I'm struck by the citrus punch of whatever fragrance she's wearing.

Threading her hand around the back of my neck, she leans near to my ear and draws deep before teasing wisps of breath upon my lobe. "*This* is the induction," she murmurs, and my skin pebbles for all the wrong reasons.

Head cocked to the side, she toys with my robe in a suggestive way.

I swallow thickly, crunching my hands into balls. Fight the urge to shove her off. Wishing I'd had the foresight to get blind drunk before I stepped onto that fucking ferry.

*Get it together, Baze.*

"I thought the Shulák valued chastity before coupling? I see no cupla on your wrist."

Her eyes ignite, the corner of her lips curling as she studies me like she sees my nonchalance and wants to fuck it right out of me. "I'm coupled with my faith," she says, then slides her finger past her lips and *sucks*, hollowing her cheeks.

The faintest stir of excitement strikes the most basic part of me while a flood of disgust almost chokes the rest.

With a knowing glint in her eye, she pulls her finger free with a wet *pop*, then dips it in the bowl of Candescence perched atop a stool beside us. My blood chills when she brings the sparkly substance to my lips, stepping so close her breasts flatten against my chest. "Open for me."

Ghosts gnaw at my brain like flesh-eating worms ...

*Yield for me, my pretty boy.*

*Your Lord takes care of you and gives you what you need.*

My mouth grinds open, like someone just gored a bar between my teeth and wrenched them wide.

Disgust surges through my veins.

She stamps her finger upon my tongue, making it tingle. "Close."

I do—squeezing my eyes shut at the same time, feeling those molecules of luster burst in my mouth.

"Now," she says, her voice a husky rasp. "*Suck.*"

My demons scratch at the underside of my skin as I obey, certain the tight veil covering my true self doesn't exist at all. That I'm naked, on my knees on a cold stone floor, begging for my Lord to bend my head to the side, lengthen my neck just the way I like.

For him to strike me with his drugging bite.

A groan slips free and strips me bare.

"Good boy," she whispers, and a shiver climbs my spine.

Tightens my balls.

*You're my favorite, pretty boy.*

*Your Lord loves you.*

She pulls her finger from my mouth and dips it in the bowl again, sucking the powder off before she sashays around me, peeling off my robe.

It falls to the floor in a heavy heap.

She lifts my shirt up over my head, exposing my torso and low-hanging pants. Her gaze roves while she hums appreciatively, and I've never felt so filthy.

So small and pathetic.

*So fucking sober.*

The musk of her arousal smears the back of my throat.

She pauses before me, pupils blown, eyes glazed with a familiar shimmer that suggests she's beginning to feel the punch of light now coursing through her system.

For most Aeshlians, consuming the hard, sharp, sparkly stuff our body absentmindedly sprouts is a recipe for short-term amnesia. A few, potent minutes of blissful *nothing*. When I was little, it'd hit me so brutally I'd forget who I was. Where I was.

Why the world was so ugly.

Then I got older, bigger. Sexually matured. It started having ... *other* effects that would make my skin crawl when I finally came to.

Not that it stopped me.

After years of chewing my own thorns, the hit lost its luster.

She takes a step back, and her hand skims down her abdomen, past her navel. "You're *perfect.*" She tips her head and looks at me from beneath heavy lids. "Such a pretty pet."

*My pretty boy knows how to please me.*

*Your skin bursts so perfectly.*

Her middle finger sinks into her core as she works herself to the tune of her throaty moans and tweaks her dusky nipple into a hardened peak.

"Can you feel it yet?" Her voice is a thirsty plea, her shoulder moving faster, *faster—*

*Can you feel that, my pretty, pretty boy? That's fucking love, that is.*

"Yes," I say.

*Lie.*

She groans, grabs my hand, and drags me toward the bed.

# CHAPTER

*Orlaith*

## 17

Caped in my heavy cloak and a fresh layer of
determination, I move through the gloomy jungle
alight with chirping crickets, the air so thick and
warm it clings to my skin.

Guided by boastful shards of moonlight, I ease through
the thick foliage, finding the trail Cainon took me down
when he led me to the Unseelie burrow.

Emerging onto the exposed shore, silence greets me, the
ocean a stretch of silver that looks smooth enough to tiptoe
across—all the way to the shadowed island crouching in
the distance.

I sigh.

*If only it were that easy.*

"Please be there," I murmur, plucking my path around
the cove, making out the sharpest peaks by the way
moonlight hits their jagged faces. "*Please* be there …"

Seeing the small boat nestled amongst the rocks, my
shoulders slump with relief.

I make short work of the knot tethering it to a large stone, then dump my cloak in the hull, roll my pants, and drag the boat along the rocks toward the glassy bay, wincing at the shrill, grating sounds that score the silence.

Not exactly the quiet getaway I was hoping for, but there's no turning back now.

Wading thigh-deep into the cool water, I ease the vessel off the shore and glide it across the surface, then half leap, half tumble into the hull, limbs flailing as the boat rocks. Scrambling up, I find my center of balance and settle onto the seat, slide the oars down the rowlocks, then roll them forward and *pull.*

The paddles skim the water, carving across the still.

I don't move an inch.

Frowning, I glance over my shoulder at the island in the distance ...

*This might take a while.*

With a groan, I roll them so far forward I grate my knuckles on the rim, then dig the paddles deep into the water, and *heave.* The boat jerks a few feet, and a gleeful sound bursts out of me, swiftly smothered.

*Suck stones, Cainon. Look who can row her own boat.*

I throw the oars forward and dig them deep again, again, *again*—shoulders burning, arms straining, gaining slow but steady traction toward my destination. I push free of the small bay and into the open ocean, the water a mirror beneath me, throwing back a perfect reflection of the moon and sprinkled stars. It's almost heartbreaking to rip a line straight through the middle.

Cutting a glance across my surroundings, my feet tingle,

the sensation spearing up my legs and into my guts. I pause, suddenly aware of the vastness beneath me ...

I release a snarl and plunge my oars into the water.

*Don't think.*

*Just do.*

Blisters bulge on my palms, agitating my still-raw wound, a lather of sweat slicked down my spine by the time the boat scrapes along some shallow rocks that threaten to tear a hole in its hull. Glancing behind me, I see the shore no more than fifty feet away.

A relieved sigh *whooshes* out of me.

Pulling the oars back through the rowlocks, I lay them in the hull, stretch the ache from my burning muscles, and grip the side before easing off the seat, slow and cautious.

Teeth gritted, I lift a leg—

The boat wobbles uncontrollably.

"Shit!" I squeak as it tips past the point of no return, dunking me into the salty depths, my hair a heavy swirl around my flailing form. Remembering the sharks that chased our dinghy when we disembarked the ship, I shove off the rocks and clamber to my feet, finding myself in waist deep water.

The vessel self-corrects, like it's mocking me.

Keeping a watchful eye on the surrounding water, I toss the oars in the hull, grope around me until my fingers tangle with my cloak, then scoop it up and slop it onto the floorboards. I wrap the rope around my hand and pull the boat to shore where I nudge it between two rocks, then loop a tether around the tallest one.

*Fingers crossed it holds.*

I twist my hair into a dripping knot and secure it above my nape, scoping the steep shoreline, seeking the simplest path onto the grassy mound. Gripping hold of rocks to steady myself, I scale the ridge, out of breath by the time my feet disappear amongst thick, fluffy grass.

Moonlight paints my upturned face as I dig my toes into the soil, inhaling air sweetened by the musk of wildflowers that brush against my calves, painting them in whispers ...

An ache flares within my chest.

I've spent so many years wondering about that tapestry in Castle Noir. Now that I'm here—standing within the woven depths beneath a litter of peeping stars—I feel as though I'm bobbing atop an ocean far different from the one I just traversed.

An ocean of *secrets*.

Hearing the desperate echo of Hattie's rusty voice, I shove forward, paving a path across the mound, scouring the land. Searching for ... something.

*Anything.*

My feet sink into a patch of freshly tilled soil, and I frown, crouching to sift some through my fingers. "Odd," I mutter, and continue on, stubbing my toe against something hard nestled amid the grass.

Biting down on a squawk, I drop to my knees, brushing aside tufts of grass and lofty flower fronds, revealing a man-made chute capped with a metal grate.

My stomach drops.

I whip my head around, scanning the moonlit vista. The dark, distant smudge of the palace.

*It can't be ...*

Tingling with nervous tension, I scramble back to the island's craggy shore and clamber down. I scout the circumference, hunting between glistening rocks, breath catching when I discover a shadowed tunnel like the one Cainon led me down when he took me to the burrow.

The *Unseelie* burrow.

My heart thumps like a wild animal jailed beneath my ribs, and I stumble sideways, gripping hold of a rocky outcrop to steady myself. Feeling the hairs on my arms lift, I glance over my shoulder and look upon the palace. Back down the dusky tunnel.

My instincts fist my spine, attempting to drag me across the bay. *Screaming* at me to clamber into that boat and row for my fucking life.

But my curiosity has her nose in the air, urging me forward so she can scamper into that shadowy hole and uncover its secrets.

*Well, I've come this far …*

Dragging my hand along the lumpy wall, I follow the staircase down into the darkness, the air thickening with each uncertain step. Ripening with an all too familiar, potent scent.

Blood.

But it's muddied by other musks that make me want to breathe through my sodden shirt; sour, rotten smells that remind me of the shantytown beyond the wall. Makes the voice in the back of my mind scream louder.

Louder.

*Run!*

Skin pebbling, I spill into a curved hallway lit by flaming

torches, and my heart sinks at the sight of cells lining both walls.

*Another Unseelie burrow.*

I force myself to look into the first cell on my right, and my stomach knots, hand whipping up to wrangle a wail.

Burnished firelight spills through the bars, igniting a slight, slumbering person tucked in the corner beneath a soiled blanket. Their hair is unevenly cropped, cheeks hollow, mouth lax as they breathe soft and slow.

Too slow.

Festering wounds tarnish their dark skin, like someone ... or some*thing* took bites so deep they almost tore off chunks of flesh.

My vision blurs with unshed tears, my heart a lump of lead.

This burrow ... it's no ancient, ugly scar nobody talks about anymore.

It's a fresh, gaping wound. It's everything Cainon warned me against.

*Run!*

"No," I rasp, and scour the next cell, releasing a soft whimper that cleaves straight from my split chest.

A red-haired woman is hunched on a filthy mattress, barely an inch of her visible, pale skin unscathed by welts, bruises, *bites*.

I can't imagine Rhordyn doing this to anybody.

I just ... *can't.*

That voice continues to scream at me as I force myself further down the twisting hallway, counting each breathing inhabitant within each small, stuffy cell.

Men.

Women.

*Children.*

Nobody stirs as I drift past, their dreams perhaps a better place to be than the horrors of their reality.

Moving through a shaft of moonlight, I see a male huddled in a ball by the bars of his cell. A mop of filthy iridescent curls falls across his brow, concealing all but the peak of his thorned ear.

I stumble to a halt.

*Aeshlian.*

A vision of Baze flashes. Of his scarred skin and pale, lackluster eyes after I ripped that ring from his hand. Of the way he dragged his gaping shirt across his chest like he was desperate to hide his scars.

*I know the hurt is loud—*

His past words—once a balm to my wounds—now anchor my heart somewhere deep and dark where there is no light.

Was *this* his loud hurt that still whispers to him now?

A lump forms in my throat as I glance up through the grated layers. Focus on the spindly silhouettes of a few delicate wildflowers arching over the sky-hole's edge, like they're peeking in.

A painful thought wraps my heart in a thorny vine ...

Hattie knew about this place. She knew and somehow sent a tapestry to Castle Noir perfectly depicting this very island. A pretty picture to adorn the stark, black halls ... or a clue?

A plea?

A woven scream she couldn't voice, shipped off for someone to *see?*

Perhaps she knew something I didn't allow myself to explore—that there's a *goodness* in Rhordyn she trusted. That if he received the message and understood her meaning, he would have helped these broken people.

*He would have helped.*

That wound inside my chest throbs so hard and deep my hand flies up, fingers gouging at my breast as I marinate in the pool of guilt shoving down my throat.

Choking me.

As I battle the urge to use what little luster I have to forge a dome and corral the thorny guilt up against my sides—because I *want* to feel this. *Deserve* to feel this.

My.

Fucking.

Fault.

I look at the broken boy again ...

*My penance.*

Determination uncoils inside me like a serpent, unhinged maw set to strike, fierce fangs leaking beads of opal venom. Swatting a tear from my cheek, I continue down the curling hallway. Continue looking left and right, running out of fingers to count, punishing myself with the ghoulish sight of withering bodies and festering wounds.

I will not leave these people here to rot.

I *will* free them. Get them off this island.

But *how?*

I'll need a boat far bigger than the one I came in. Less shitty.

I need help ... *lots of help.*

The hallway straightens, and filtered light illuminates

a domed cavern ahead, akin to the one in the abandoned burrow but *bigger.*

I gasp at the sight of a monstrous man lumped in the center, wearing only a pair of tattered pants. His high, bladed cheekbones, heavy brows, matted hair, and thick scruff do nothing to distract from the cruel cut of his jaw. Deep, slumbering breaths wrestle out of his parted mouth, exposing the honed tips of his long canines ...

*Unseelie.*

My knees give way, assaulting the cold stone floor.

A beam of moonlight pours upon pockets of bulging muscle, igniting glassy veins that fork across a portion of his brassy back like lightning strikes. Dull metal cuffs bind his wrists, each tethered to chains so thick it's a wonder he can move at all, the flesh around them folded back like sleeves of skin that healed then tore, healed then tore, leaving a bloody mess that tells a tale of his entrapment.

His *pain.*

His massive arm is draped over a slight male with tawny, lackluster hair and wide, unseeing eyes pointed toward that hole in the ceiling. Like the last thing he sought was the faraway sky.

My mind whirs so fast I'm certain the room's tipping ...

*What the hell is this?*

A shuffling sound whispers at me from behind, and I spin.

Small, pale hands cling to the bars of the end cell, and I look past the metal, seeing a nest of rosy curls, a dainty face, and big, auburn eyes staring at me, shaded with too much hurt for one so young.

My stomach churns.

The child blinks, and tears slip down her soiled cheeks as she releases a heaving sob that cracks the silence.

Making calm shushing sounds, I crawl forward. "It's okay," I whisper, softening my features with a smile I pray she can't see through.

I reach between the bars and cup her face.

Her lids flutter, like she'd forgotten what it feels like to be touched with tenderness. It's an arrow through my heart, lit with fire that ignites my veins.

I may not be able to save them all tonight, but I can save her.

I can save *one*.

"I'm going to get you out," I promise, my voice a punch of steely determination.

Relief crumbles her face.

Damp, heavy tangles tumble down my back as I tug my hairpin free and delve it into the lock, then twist, flick, *shove*—tipping my head so I can listen close. My hands tremble, hindering my progress. Urgency swells in my chest like a thundercloud.

A growl threatens to rip free, each turn of my hand one too many.

*Come on.*

*Come on.*

*Come on—*

The hairs on my nape lift.

A scurry of motion draws my gaze to the girl shuffling backward, disappearing into the shadowed corner of her small, foul-smelling cell.

My hands still.

I spin, heart jolting at the sight of Cainon behind me, the flaming sconces casting his face in ghoulish shadows that cut his features into harsh, terrifying segments.

I gasp, shoving to a stand.

He darts forward in a blur of motion, and my lungs flatten, head thwacking against the bars so hard lights flash across my vision, a deep throb bulging my brain. My hairpin clatters to the ground as the hard, unforgiving panes of his body lock me against the metal, caging me in his dominating essence, making it hard to draw a full breath.

He smothers my mouth with his salty hand, and my eyes flare, gaze bouncing back and forth between his own.

His pupils have blown so big there's nothing left of the blue.

"Cai—"

"*Hush,* petal." His grated whisper assaults my prickling skin, slamming my heart into a ferocious rally.

A frown touches his lips, and he tucks a tendril of damp hair off my face, warm fingers brushing my thumping carotid once.

Twice.

He leans forward, lips grazing the length of my neck like a lover's caress, hovering over that frantic, fluttering beat. "We don't want to wake him," he murmurs, his voice deep and dangerous.

A bolt of fear shoots up my spine.

*Him* ...

My gaze nips at the slumbering monster chained to the floor, and I swallow—hard—a sense of dread settling on my shoulders like stacks of bricks.

Cainon nuzzles my neck, his words a pattering attack on my fragile flesh. "This is the only time he's ever truly at *peace.*"

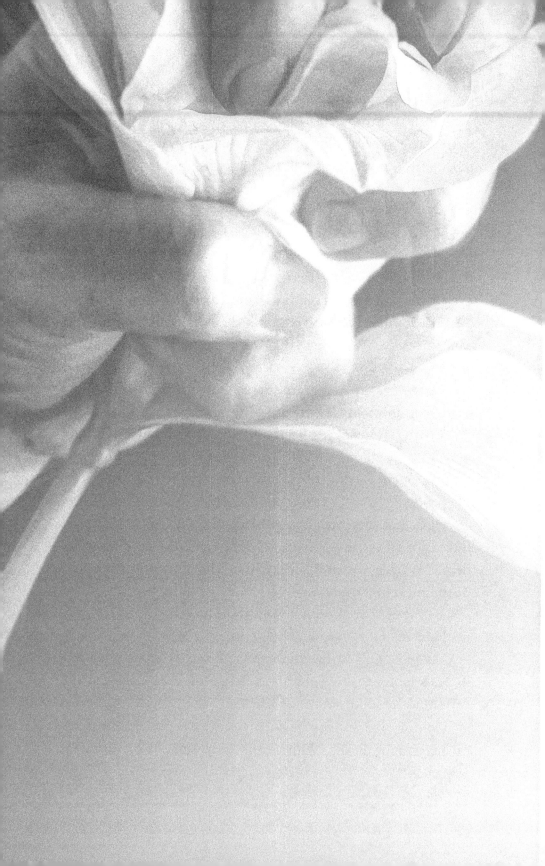

# CHAPTER
*Cainon*
## 18

I arch back, using the pad of my thumb to roll her bottom lip so far I expose her clenched teeth, then thread my fingers through her hair that looks like honey in the blazing light—tangled in a mass of knots I itch to tame.

Her cheeks are flushed, sodden shirt clinging to the outline of her heaving breasts, that bold gaze darting between my eyes. Fearlessly seeking.

Little does she know, that's exactly what I want. What stirs my fucking pulse.

That fearless gleam that makes her eyes sparkle with a luster I yearn to catch. Cradle.

Consume.

That same fearless gleam she had when she pinned me against the wall with her hairpin at my throat. When her thick, golden locks unspooled and tumbled about her face, falling past her waist in a churn of untamed disarray.

My fierce beauty hidden away—cloistered and unsullied— with supple, unspoiled skin begging to be marked.

Claimed.

*Perfect.*

My hands tighten into fists that crush her hair, straining the strands against her scalp. She doesn't flinch, even though I know it must hurt.

I sigh.

"So fucking *perfect.*"

She sucks a breath like she's going to speak, but the words die on her tongue. I yearn to tip forward and taste their strangled remains. Instead, I rest my forehead against hers, pushing until there is no give.

"I really wish you hadn't seen this, petal."

I feel the pulse of her whirring mind ...

Does she realize what she's ruined? What she's smacked out of my outstretched hand by coming here?

A chance at normality.

Silence stews, tension crackling like a dying flame I want to blow life into. But she's seen too much. Now I have to plant my pretty flower in the ground and take Ocruth by force. What a fucking shame.

Behind me, *he* rumbles in his sleep ...

"Who—"

"My father," I admit, and her breath hitches.

"You ... You told me he *passed.*"

I thread my fingers deeper into her messy, messy hair, tugging the wet tangles. "He did."

I study her eyes. The questions swimming within their orchid depths make her look like an addled sprite blinking up at me, choking on her own naïvety. She has no idea how big the world is. How small and delicate *she* is.

How fast I could rip into her.

Drink her dry.

How fast I could have her screaming for me to let her go while her body begs for more.

And if I *truly* unleash? If I listen to the voice that picks, picks, *picks* at me—give in to the savage urge welling in my chest, threatening to rupture, making my fingers curl and my mind whirl with grisly possibilities?

My hand threads around her neck like a collar, gently squeezing, a throb flaring to life in my hardening cock ...

I could control the breath flowing into her heaving lungs. Watch her lips turn blue, panic igniting her eyes. Feel her struggle beneath me, powerless against my crushing might. Cast her into a sleep she'll never wake from, then peel the skin from her flesh to examine her inner workings.

Turn her into a beautiful, bloody mosaic. My own personal masterpiece.

But I would never do that to *her.*

Couldn't.

The moment I looked into those orchid eyes and felt our souls collide, watched her breath hitch like she could feel it too, I knew she was for me.

*Mine.*

Gifted to me by the Gods themselves.

She couldn't walk away fast enough, but she already had me *hooked.* Under her fucking spell.

I hunt that fluttering pulse ...

She just needs time to catch up. To taste me.

For me to taste her.

She'll have plenty of *time* down here while she mulls over her mistakes. A caged eternity to take me into her iron-clad chest and accept the fucking truth standing right before her. Accept *us* and forget the sick bastard who manipulated her into believing she was *his*.

"What happened to him?" she rasps, pulling me from my thoughts.

"The Great Purge almost ripped him apart," I mutter, though the words still come out like they've been sharpened on a whetstone. "Tore him down to his base urges. Turned him into an *animal*."

The last word strikes like a blow, and my delicate flower flinches.

Looking over my shoulder, I study the monster. Remember the strong, cunning man I used to know. He's in there, somewhere. Every time he begs for death, I see a little of my father peeping through his inky eyes. A little more of the man who fed that bestial, broken part of me and called it perfect.

Called *me* perfect.

He never looked at me craven and quaking. Never begged me to change. He gave me *everything*.

Until Rhordyn took him from me.

"That's all that's left of the man who raised me. If I hadn't kept him safe all these years, gone above and beyond to keep him fed and healthy so he doesn't have to leave this place, he would've been hunted. *Slain*."

The refugee kid locked in the cell behind Orlaith lets out a squeal.

I narrow my eyes on her—a small, huddled shadow in the gloom, peering at me through eyes bulging with pure, undiluted fear. His next fucking meal if she doesnt stop looking at me like that.

"You feed him children," Orlaith says, distracting me, her voice barely a whisper.

I sigh.

*Almost* perfect.

"He's picky. Sometimes he refuses to feed unless he's given something ... irresistible. I have to mix it up. Vary his diet. Get him excited."

Her gaze slays, fearlessly picking me apart. A look that spears straight to my fucking loins.

Shrugging, I run the back of my hand up the smooth expanse of her throat. "I have no choice, petal."

"You *always* have a choice," she chides.

My heart stills, a whisper from the past creeping to the surface, wrapping around my neck.

Tightening.

*Ignore the voice in your head, Non. Listen to mine.*

*My voice will never hurt you or tell you to do horrible things.*

*My voice is right—not wrong.*

*My voice is love.*

"Don't talk to me like that," I snap, and realize my hand has clamped down. Orlaith claws at it, mouth gaping, eyes bulging like glass marbles glistening in the firelight. "*Mother* talked to me like that." I tilt my head, lean back, then grip my shirt by the collar and rip, spraying popped buttons.

The yawning front exposes the scar almost directly above my heart. The pale, risen remnants of the moment my own flesh and blood decided the world would be better off without me.

*Another bleeding heart.*

I remember the look in Mother's eyes when I woke to

that talon sliding through my chest, like she was hurting more than *me*.

"She'll never speak again because her aim wasn't as good as yours," I chuff, flashing Orlaith a half smile. "You—on the other hand—put Rhordyn down so beautifully."

Tears shred down her cheeks.

I let her go, hoping she'll fall to her knees. Disappointed when she doesn't.

She folds against the bars, color flooding her face as she coughs and gasps, cradling her flushed throat.

*Always fucking fighting me.*

"*Only because you,*" she heaves through swift, serrated breaths, "*played me ...*"

*I did.*

There was something poetic about manipulating the woman he thought was his into stabbing him through the heart. The woman he *loved*—I could see it in the fucker's eyes.

"I had no choice," I say, serving bite-sized pieces of a truth too big to swallow whole. "He was sniffing too close."

Her bloodshot gaze nips to Father as she gulps air, clinging to the bars at her back like her spine has been ripped free.

Rhordyn may have spared me years ago when he stormed the palace like Kvath come to weigh my hollow heart. When he looked *down* upon a frightened, *powerless* boy with the pathetic blood of my mortal mother flowing through my veins, but failed to notice my *father's* blood warming my soiled heart.

And if he knew I was harboring my bestial, broken father who didn't quite die during The Great Purge?

"You were the only one who could get close enough to eliminate him." I step forward and thread my hand up to cup her cheek. "You saved me. Saved *him*," I say, jerking my chin at the man I'd rip myself to shreds to protect.

"Sacrifices," she sputters.

Again, I drag my hand down her delicate neck, blotched red from my tight grip. "Yes." My fingers rest upon her carotid, ripe and swollen with fluttering need.

A flame sparks inside my chest, her hot pulse flicking at my fingers, churning faster, *faster*. Begging me to split her skin.

Set it free.

My throat works as I brush my thumb across her silky, untarnished canvas. "I can't let you leave, Orlaith."

The child begins to sob, drawing my gaze toward her frail form. Still she's looking at me in that same haunting way.

The same way *she* looks at me.

The child releases another whimper, and a growl brews in my chest, fingers itching to tighten around her tiny throat and stem that *fucking* sound—

"I know," Orlaith whispers, and the air flavors with metallic spice, interrupting my train of thought.

My attention homes on the trickle of blood oozing from Orlaith's nose, descending over her lips, her chin, the background noise paling in significance to the sudden, aching thirst making the nerves beneath my tongue burst with tingles ...

Her lashes sweep shut as I smear it across her lips, painting them red like the night I tasted them for the first time. The night she wore a dress that looked like blood pouring down her curves, puddling around her feet.

My perfect muse, following my lead, dancing just for me. *Mine*.

Her lids flutter, and she opens her mouth, seeming to hesitate. "I have a confession, too."

I tilt my head to the side, twirling a wet length of honey hair around my finger. "About?"

"Rhordyn *did* drink me."

A violent jolt of jealousy almost shreds me in two, and my hand fists her sodden locks, jerking back her head.

Heart thumping, my narrowed gaze scours her untarnished neck for any sign I may have missed that the broody heathen ripped into *my* pretty flower. Scored her delicate skin with his monstrous maw.

All I find is smooth, untarnished perfection begging to be marked.

*Bled.*

She can't be meaning the scar on her wrist. It's too small to be made by a man such as *him*. I always pictured her making that mark herself.

"Are you lying to me, Orlaith?" I swallow thickly, tapping her carotid. "There's nothing more primal than drinking from right here. Nothing more *dominating* than pulling from such a vulnerable source."

"He never drank from my neck," she rasps, and I frown, wrestling with her boggling allegations that just don't stack.

Nothing brings me closer to feeling like a God than when I'm latched onto a warm neck, listening to the slowing *whump* of a dying heart. Deciding between my voracious greed and withering mercy. Rhordyn may be mused by saving small, pathetic lives, but the same voracious hunger that sits inside my chest bestrides him *twofold*.

If he drank from her, there's no way he didn't bite what's mine. *Somewhere.*

*Unless she's playing me a fool …*

"*Where?*" I growl into her ear, feeling her shudder against me.

*If it's her inner thigh—*

Her eyes glisten with unshed tears. Slowly, she lifts her hand, boasting the tips of her fingers.

Tiny, pale dots mar them, barely noticeable even to my eyes.

"Needle pricks," she whispers, and my heart stills. Eyes widen. Hers harden with unfathomable hurt—a look that punches through my chest and rocks my rotten core. "Every night for nineteen years I dripped myself into a crystal goblet and set my offering in a small wicket door, even though I knew not what he was. *Why* he needed it. Every night for nineteen years he climbed that tower and took, and took, and *took.*"

My heart stills.

"*Every* night?" I confirm, frown deepening. "Did *you* ever drink from *him?*"

A laugh bubbles in the back of her throat that's beautifully unhinged. "Rhordyn? Bleed for me? Of course not. Not until I stabbed him through the heart," she bites out, and I swear some of the light slips from her eyes as a shiver rakes through her delicate body.

*Fuck.*

I push closer, mind whirling as she shudders against me. "Petal—"

"I loved it," she admits, and my blood runs hot when I see no lie in her open, aching eyes.

*Luscious, shocking creature likes to bleed …*

"Loved *h-him*."

I want to strangle the fractured whisper from existence the moment it leaves her lips.

I shove my hips forward, crushing her against the bars.

She swallows, her eyes losing more of their luster as the next words croak free through chattering teeth. "And all I w-wanted, all I fucking *needed*, was f-for him to want me just as much as I w-wanted him. To see the *pleasure* in his eyes when he t-took what I was freely giving."

I snag her wrist, gripping tight.

She should have been *mine* from the start. Tucked into *my* palace—*my* bed. Eating *my* food.

Giving *me* her fucking blood.

"Don't you see, Cainon? Rhordyn never l-loved me." Another fat tear rolls down her cheek as she nips the tip of her finger, releasing a bright-red bead of *her*. Spicing the air with more of that rich, potent scent that makes me picture embers crackling against my tongue.

It drips down the length, and I watch; transfixed.

Fucking hypnotized.

She squeezes the tip, releasing another bulb, and my heart leaps when she brings it to my mouth. Her face knots—features drinking the angry firelight like they were made to burn together.

"He just loved my *blood*," she snarls, then shoves it past my lips.

# CHAPTER 19

*Orlaith*

T hat scribbled, scalding mess of black slashes the underside of my skin, my skull, but the intense pain pales in comparison to the flutter of fierce determination swarming through me as liquid warmth oozes from my nose.

Down my chin.

I hold Cainon's inky stare—unblinking—watching him *suck*.

Listening to him *swallow*.

I refuse to let my face crumble. To unveil the cracks weaving across my heart, my soul, and my collection of crystal domes I frantically forged to keep from falling apart as I stripped myself bare. Fed my blood to the wrong man.

*Don't cry …*

A tendril of sadness weaves through a fissure and coils around my heart, constricting, making each thump of the tender organ *sting*. A sob threatens to burst forth, and I snip the rogue weed, then pluck at my thinning luster to patch up the dome it spilled from.

A shiver rakes through me, and I rip my finger free of his mouth.

Cainon gasps, heaving, studying me with boggling complexity—mapping every fleck in my eyes like he's drawing lines between them, trying to sketch a shape.

*The Unseelie fed off the life force of others, Orlaith. Men. Women. Children. It bolstered them. Gave some of them yield over the elements. Filled others with unparalleled strength.*

I watch, remembering Cainon's buckling words, bracing for whatever comes next.

A crackle of power singeing the air? A surge of bone-crumbling strength? Maybe he'll cleave a hole in the stone with a snap of his fingers, or forge flames like the Gypsy from *Gypsy and the Night King.*

Cainon continues to search my eyes with unsettling vigor.

"What is it?"

His head tilts, eyes narrow, and I'm forced to suffer through a pause. "I ... was expecting something," he finally says. "A pull, perhaps."

*A pull?*

Shoving aside my confusion, I snatch the loose thread like it's my salvation, flavoring my gaze with *challenge*—something I learned from a hard man who I'm certain would flay me if he were here.

Alive.

If he knew what I'm doing. What I'm about to say.

But he's not.

I paint a pretty lie in my eyes and gather my soiled words. "Well ... maybe you need a little more?"

The frown slides off Cainon's face, and his features harden.

*Sharpen.*

"Are you *offering* yourself to me, petal?"

I open my mouth, almost spilling a prickly sprout of denial before I hack at its roots. Feel it wither against my tongue. "What if I am?"

He releases a deep, gravelly growl that lifts the hairs on the back of my neck, then threads his fingers through my sodden locks, gripping so hard I choke back a scream. "*Why?*"

That caustic *thing* beneath my skin swells to a splitting degree. Everything feels too tight.

Too small.

My heart thunders, head spinning, words clanking together like boulders, making it hard to pick the right ones.

"I said *why?*"

*Because I need to become indispensable.*

*Because I need your trust if I'm to get out of here and save these people.*

He steps closer, his hard, hot body again crushing me against the bars.

Too close.

*Focus, Orlaith. Focus.*

"Because I know how it feels to hide the monster within," I rasp, pulling a strangled breath. "To wear a brave face while all that ugly stuff inside gorges on everything you love."

The muscle in his jaw bounces, his stare unflinching, penetrating—a tower of menacing brawn poured upon me, oozing arrogance and something ... else.

Something that makes another tendril of sadness twirl up my ribs and peck at my heart.

*There you go again, pushing me away.*

*Would it be so hard? To love me?*

*Her aim wasn't as good as yours.*

His earlier words strike me like a volley of stones, and that beating organ inside my chest spears itself on a rib as I piece together the fragments of his damage ...

His bestial, broken father on the floor.

The way he spoke about his mother.

The scar on his chest.

I look into his hollow eyes, and all I see is a lost, lonely boy desperate to prove his worth. He's reaching for a love that isn't his, and I understand that brutal beast too fucking well.

I hung off Rhordyn's every move since I came of age and noticed him around the castle. *Truly* noticed him as more than just the High Master who offered me refuge and took my daily offering. I noticed his stoic dominance and unflinching manner. His rich, rumbled words that bored beneath my skin and rattled my bones.

My soul.

I noticed the way my heart began to race every time he cast fleeting looks in my direction, like a single word from his mouth could will it to stop.

To start.

I grew in a pot of unreciprocated love, then went into shock when he came to Bahari, crumbled that pot in the might of his crushing fists, and shook all the soil from my roots.

So I pushed him away. Broke him down.

*Hurt him beyond repair.*

Listened to another man speak, then silenced the one I love.

This deep, heavy pain hangs off my ribs, making them bow from the weight ... a pain I refuse to stuff away as I look deep into Cainon's eyes, achingly aware of the cage at my back. The lives tucked behind the bars lining this curling wall.

My resolve hardens.

Cainon preyed on my vulnerabilities when he took me to that burrow and molded me into his personal assassin. Though I hate the thought of wielding those same ugly tools, I'm not above scrapping in the pit of moral mud.

Not here. Not now.

"I know what it's like to feel undeserving of any sort of love but the one that's unreciprocated," I rasp, and his body locks.

Goes eerily still.

I settle my hand upon his scar, spores of self-hatred soiling my insides like an undusted mantle. "We've both been forged by a conditional love that broke us into crumbs people still manage to choke on. Perhaps there's something poetic in that? In *us.*"

The words are vile, rotten things ...

Cainon looks at my hand, studying it like it's some sort of gift he's not sure how to receive.

I'll never forgive myself for preying on his weakness. But with that little girl's sobs still echoing in my ears, I'll do whatever it takes.

I'll be a monster—for her.

For *them.*

186

I tap my cupla with the tip of my bloody finger. "I could love this," I whisper, the sour, lumpy lie slipping off my tongue.

His eyes take on a devastating shade of black that spoils my insides, blazing across my face in a way I imagine the sun scorches the dunes of Rouste.

Perhaps that's exactly what I deserve.

To burn.

I wipe my chin, dragging the silky, wet smear down the side of my neck. He hunts the motion—like he's feeding off the crimson picture I'm painting. "Give me what Rhordyn never did," I say, thoughts of *his* icy lips skimming my yearning pulse almost bringing me to my knees.

A pit-size lump swells in my throat ...

*Don't cry.*

"Give me what I *crave*."

Another low, sawing growl rattles his chest. Runs me through with a strike of fear I'm swift to smother. "It'll hurt, petal. My teeth ... they're not as sharp as a full-blooded Unseelie. There's nothing *gentle* about my bite."

A bold smile curls my lips.

I want him to make such a mess of my neck that I can never look at myself the same again—eternally reminded of this filthy act of survival that makes me want to shred my skin.

"*Good.*"

He grips the side of my face, a harsh assault I lean into as he smears more blood across my lips. "My pretty flower. So full of surprises."

My entire body bristles.

*If he only knew.*

Eyes glazed with lust, he explores my neck in the same manner I do a rock before I swirl paint across the perfect, unspoiled surface. If I live to paint another, it'll be jagged and split, full of holes for heavy truths to burrow from the light. I'll use nothing but the grayslades and their varying shades of silver and ash.

*Don't cry—*

"Where, petal? Where shall I bite this pretty neck of yours?"

*Run!*

Swallowing a whimper, I push my hair back from the right side of my neck and arch for Cainon. A flower that thrives in shadow tipping toward the scorching sun. "Here," I whisper, and tap my thumping carotid, ripping the weeds of self-disgust blooming inside my chest.

Stuffing them beneath a dome.

His eyes ignite, his throat working, and I know I've pleased him with my rotten answer, building another dome for a thorny vine of shame that won't stop pricking all my tender places.

Cainon rumbles low, dragging his thumb back and forth across the sensitive skin, and I close my eyes—hide somewhere happy. Picture a coil of stairs and cold, black stone.

The taste of honey buns.

The rich smells of the kitchen. Frost nipping at fertile soil, and a tapestry of fresh, vibrant shoots that often threaded above the surface a season before they were due. Destined to die.

I think of *him*.

*Rhordyn.*

Think of how his gaze sliced across my skin, making my heart lurch, like it was trying to leap from my chest to his. Think of how it felt to have his mighty weight upon my body, crushing me into the mattress.

Making me feel *safe*.

I can almost feel his icy breath pouring upon me with each rumbling exhale. Can almost hear his voice—a guttural grate that told me not to cry.

*Don't cry ...*

"Fucking perfection," Cainon mutters, warm lips coasting my pebbled flesh, ripping a hole in the illusion like a punch to the face.

Suddenly, all I can smell is salt and citrus, those whispers inside me surging to savage life, a soft wail cleaving through the messy chatter ...

*Run, Serren!*

My knees shake, a sick, squirming sensation wiggling through my chest, up my throat.

A deluge of dense, flourishing *fear*.

*Too much.*

Scrambling through my insides, I scavenge unripe grains of luster, like a litter of sparkly sand I crush, *smooth—*

He strikes, latching onto the taut stretch of muscle and flesh, and I rupture in a blunt blaze of crippling pain that rips through my jaw and spears across my shoulder. I shudder, the half-finished dome falling forgotten as I wrestle the yearn to curl my spine. To tuck into a small, protected ball while I pour free of the raw wound in a hot, bubbling rush.

He claws at my body, my hair, ripping my head so far back my neck feels like it's going to snap, his thick, throaty moans curdling my blood. My mouth falls open, a scream bludgeoning up my throat, but my sound won't come.

The only sound is that of him *swallowing—again.*

*Again.*

*Again.*

Panic flares, kicking, clawing at my ribs. It loses fight like a spent breath.

The world falls away, leaving nothing but paralyzing pain and the unyielding, gluttonous tug at my skin. Itchy bulbs pop across my shoulder, my clavicle, and I picture the fresh flush of blooms unfurling as my lungs fill with a heaviness that feels like liquid ice.

A stark chill seeps through my bones.

My muscles twitch and tighten, lids growing heavy, and I wilt against his arm like a decaying stem. The flaming torch heads blur until they're a pretty smear of white, orange, red.

Black.

I drift.

Floating ...

Floating ...

*Weightless, I tumble toward that seeing end, zipping through the inky forest with a swarm of glowing orbs. Again, we whizz past a decrepit castle that sits on the edge of a sheer cliff, and I'm hailed by the sweetest voice riding the wind's current in lilting notes I want to chase:*

A persistent warmth oozes through me ...
A deeper, more demanding blackness catches me in a
clawed hand and yanks me against the grain. I feel myself
falling in the wrong direction, away from that soft, sad
song I want to hear the rest of.
Wait ...
Wait!

**"No."**

I'm ripped into a watery embrace, tethered to an ancient,
mighty unknown that electrifies me with icy rage and
challenges me to draw breath.
Arctic hands cradle my face, a phantom kiss pressed to
my lips that feels like a whisper given shape. Given life
and love and a fluttering, thumping, hammering heartbeat.
A whisper for my wrongs. Another for my rights.
A whisper for the words that cut, the lies that struck, and
for a love that took more than it had a chance to give.

191

*A whisper for every stone I set amongst that curling wall.*
*Bits of myself I purged to a man who kept everything safe*
*but himself.*

*A whisper for ...*

# HIM.

# CHAPTER 20

*Rhordyn*

## '...RHORDYN.'

*The rough, whispered thought comes to me like a blow of wind rustling the trees. Like a star shooting through my cold oblivion.*
*I strain to catch the next, feeling it burst against me. A punch of warmth.*

'... making my heart lurch, like it was trying to leap from my chest to his ... his mighty weight upon my body ...'

*I crush the thought against me—a quenching pocket of air in this inky void—reaching for another.*

'... feel safe ... his icy breath pouring upon me ...'

'Don't cry.'

*The last words don't sound right—too deep and harsh.*
*They sound like … like …*

Me.

I slam into something hard and hostile, my essence compacting down, stretching against the limited space. Too tight. Too—

*Real.*

My lids snap open, pupils tighten, and I draw a sludgy breath, squinting through my smeared vision, trying to untangle from the dream's sticky web.

The feel—the *sound* of moving water comes to me, and I blink, clearing away some of the cobwebs clinging to my mind. A curling river reflects the moonlight, weaving between arched trees connected by drapes of messy vines.

*Where the hell am I?*

Wheezing wet breaths into my heavy lungs, I roll my gaze around. Notice I'm lumped against a precarious bundle of logs stacked upon each other by the water's swirling flow. Snapped twigs and branches have impaled my leg and torso, poking out the other side, skewering me in place.

*Fuck.*

My vision sharpens on the talon still lodged in my heart. Despite the prickly ache deep inside my chest, I find myself sadistically proud of her perfect shot.

*Nice try.*

Groaning, I try to move, but it's as if

194

my muscles and bones have seized. Something nudges at my shoulder, followed by a dull pull.

I crank my head to the side in slow, painful increments, sketching out the shape of a massive black krah perched on a wet log behind me, lit by slabs of moonlight shafting through the canopy, a sliver of gray, rotten flesh caught in its clawed hands.

Is that—

*I think it fucking is.*

His tufted tail peeks over his shoulder like a charmed snake, swaying from side to side, both sets of leathery wings curled around his crouched body as he blinks those large gloomy eyes. Head cocked to the side, he puts the piece of flesh in his mouth and gobbles it down.

*Did he just ... eat me?*

He releases a shriek, exposing a savage maw of razor-sharp teeth, and hops onto my arm, claws piercing my flesh. I lift my other to swat him away, then roar in agony as searing pain rents through my hand. Like it was hammered through with a nail.

The krah flaps off, and my eyes narrow on the festering wound in my palm. I turn my hand over, inspecting the black scrawls of rotten veins just beneath the surface of my pasty, waterlogged skin.

*How long has the talon been in me?*

My gaze rolls up, past the small flock of krah being led in circles by the one that was feasting on my flesh, seeking the bloated moon that sits low in the sky. Mocking me with its near fullness.

Panic rips me in two.

I draw another rattled breath, checking that tiny

lustrous seed—like a star tore from the sky and settled amongst my ribs. A bright, twinkling beacon, contrasting my fucking dim.

The only star I'll ever kneel to.

Rich, wriggling, *foreign* fear squirms through me like an earthworm, and my skewered heart stills, skin prickling all over. That *thing* inside me bristles, arching up, head to the side.

*What the fuck is going on*—

A scent seeps from the seed—salty.

Citrus.

*His.*

A blunt bite of crippling pain latches onto the side of my neck, the septic ache in my heart *nothing* compared to the ravaging hurt that tears across my shoulder, up into my jaw ...

Not *my* pain.

*Hers.*

The cold, carnal violence inside me *roars*, and my fangs slide down, murderous rage crackling through my veins ...

*He.*

*Fucking.*

Bit *her.*

Thunder rattles the sky, electrifying the air, and the ancient, otherworldly runes carved across my flesh dig their teeth deep enough to draw blood. More of her agony shafts through me, bold and screaming and so fucking clear I ache in places I never knew existed.

*Cainon's a dead man.*

I suddenly feel as if my neck's about to snap, my throat aching with the urge to scream—

'*My sound won't come.*'

Her thoughts strike like that fucking talon, and my muscles bulge with the urge to *shred*. I chain that thrashing darkness inside me, snarling through gritted teeth as I try to sit up.

Try to *move*.

Thick, putrid muck erupts up my throat with a spluttering hack, pouring down my chin. A slicing pain lances through my chest every time my heart trips over a punctured beat—paling in comparison to the phantom tug at my skin. Like he's draining her in greedy draws ... biting deeper ...

*Deeper.*

Another *boom* of thunder, and the malice inside me gnashes at his chains.

My lungs fill with liquid ice I can't seem to shift, a sensation that chills me to the core. Because they're not *my* lungs ...

They're hers.

I scramble for that seed, reaching for it—

Its twinkle sputters out.

Another violent roar rattles my ribs, and my gut flips. Head tipped to the side, more thick goo pours out of me in strangled heaves.

*Orlaith ...*

I sift every ounce of warmth from my blood and feed it to the roots tethering the precious seed to my wretched soul—willing it to ignite.

To thrive.

*Beat!*

My internal scream goes unanswered. Not even the

fleeting whisper of a thought to tame the shadow slashing at my insides, tearing me to ribbons.

I hunt for more scraps of heat in all my dark and dusty corners, a stark, condemning cold threading through my veins.

*Fucking beat!*

Those roots begin to singe, curling up, tearing from my insides in slow, agonizing pulls. The seed begins to implode, like it's falling into itself, creating a hole I'm certain all of existence could sink into.

Every cell in my body stills, a deadly calm washing over me as I watch her try to leave.

*Doesn't she know I'd follow her to the fucking end?*

I punch my internal hand between my ribs and sink my claws into the seed, feeling them pierce through that hard outer shell that wrestles me. Trying to rip from my grip like she *wants* to go.

To *die*.

'*Wait*—'

Her taut, frantic voice comes to me.

'*Wait!*'

I'm *done* waiting, Orlaith.

## 'No.'

The faintest flicker ignites, and I retract my claws, catching it like a firefly. I crouch forward and blow more warmth onto the frail, throbbing ember, giving it everything I have.

*Breathe,* I growl, nuzzling it. I brush my lips against it and order it to fucking *live*.

Another luminous pulse ...

*Another.*

Relief douses me from head to toe, but I shut that feeling down.

*She needs me.*

*Now.*

Still cradling that seed—my *salvation*—I lift my leg and slide my thigh free of the wooden saber, releasing a spurt of inky blood that reeks of impending death. A howl gurgles up my throat, almost splitting me down the middle.

I cough, sputter, heave, vision smearing, the wooden mound beneath me creaking as I look at the remaining stick jutting from my gut.

*Fuck me.*

Face twisting, I arch up, the stick sliding free of my innards, each knobbled bend grating against my bones.

I snarl through gritted teeth, heaving choked breaths, more rotten, foul-smelling blood piping from the gaping wound, dribbling into the water in an inky swirl.

Chin pressed to my chest, I look down at the talon again ...

I thought if she lashed her damage at me hard enough, dealt me the pain I deserve, it would make me feel better about ... everything. Instead, that prickly ache won't ease, and the more I look at the fucking talon protruding from my chest, the worse this feeling gets.

Growling, I reach for the hilt—

The rickety mass beneath me shifts, and I still, poised. I feel the next creak in my fucking marrow.

Everything gives way with a turbulent *splash* that swallows me whole.

I'm churned up, tossed about, pinned beneath the might of rolling tree trunks. More liquid pours into me, and my barely beating heart slows, lungs convulsing as my body jerks and spasms.

*I don't hate you at all ...*

The whispered echo of her words are the breath of air I can't pull. They're sun on my face, and the smell of spring crushed against me. They're a warm, comforting hand escorting me into the eternal shadow of a bitterly cold oblivion I've grown too familiar with.

Something hard collides with my head, and the pain slips away.

Darkness consumes me.

# CHAPTER 21

*Orlaith*

at drops of icy rain splat upon my cheek, my nose, my lips, and I emerge from a sludgy sleep I want to fall back into. Everything rocks beneath me with a violent sway that tips my hollow guts, the deep, painful throb boring through the side of my neck so raw, tender, and exposed. A hurt that feels filthy and wrong.

*So wrong.*

A hurt I want to slap my hand over and hide.

Another raindrop splatters against my forehead, obliterating some of the thorny vines bound around my mind, muddying my thoughts. I tune into the banging, sloshing beat as my world glides forward in slow, steady increments, the smell of a summer storm heavy on the air.

I open my eyes.

A churn of bulbous clouds clot the slate sky—

Shock blazes through my chest, making my breath hitch.

*Cainon let me out.*

*It worked.*

Relief surges up my throat, then chokes me when a vision flashes: short swirls of rosy hair; wide, terrified eyes and frightened sounds; cells and cells of battered lives, now entirely dependent on *me*.

My new reality kneels on my chest like a mountain.

*Me*.

Crushed beneath the mighty weight, my lids yield to the downward tug, and I close my eyes.

Another raindrop strikes my lips with a splash of cold that shivers through me.

*The sky is crying.*

I want to scream. Tell it to stop.

To not waste its tears on me. Tell it I *deserve* this burden.

The backs of my lids flash with a burst of white that electrifies the air, and a deafening crackle follows, so violent I flinch.

Another forward shove sends water sloshing up the side of the boat as a fervid gaze rakes across my skin and leaves a prickly trail. "You're *mine*."

The familiar voice cuts through me, curdling my blood, spilling my will to think and feel.

I fall eagerly into the dark.

# CHAPTER
### Cainon
## 22

I tap my thigh with the vial, watching *her* from where I'm reclined against the wall. Her spine is hunched, shoulders tucked forward, that long, silver hair unbound and puddled behind her stool as she works the bright strands wrapped around her trembling fingers. Threads them into place.

Drawing deep, I screw my nose at the heady scent of desperation seeping from her pores.

I'm late, but really, she's only got herself to blame. After all, I was cleaning up the fucking mess *she* made.

My gaze lifts, narrowing on the half-finished tapestry she's working on. You can see the rapt attention she's poured into the design—the colors, the tension of each bulging thread. It all fits together in perfect, blissful harmony, and I'm certain that's all she's ever wanted. All she cares about.

Perfection.

Her love for the craft ... it's *endless,* poured all over the walls downstairs; a constant mutating thing that grows and fucking *grows.* I have nightmares of those tapestries spawning mouths and taking big, bloody bites of me, masticating my face until I barely recognize myself.

I should burn them all, but I'm too good to her to even consider it.

Too lenient.

She uses her weft stick to tighten the layer, the instrument jiggling with the uncontrollable shake of her hands. She releases a frustrated grunt, pushing some rogue tendrils behind her ear with a dash of her hand. Again, I tap the vial against my thigh.

"Are you enjoying that?"

Her flinch is a whip snapping at my heart, making that voice inside me pick.

Pick.

*Pick.*

She always does it—*every time.*

There's a pause before she nods but doesn't look back. Doesn't seek me out with the tender stare I crave. She used to try, but her eyes didn't lie, and I could see the roiling fear below the surface.

Again, I look at the tapestry, tilting my head to the side as I study the half-finished piece of a face shrouded in a nest of flowers. I note the shape of the woman's eyes and the half-moon irises, the burst of orchid threads a stark contrast to the rest of the piece.

In it, I see Orlaith.

"You like her," I murmur, and the air between us tightens.

Her head bobs. Slow.

Cautious.

"I like her, too." I saunter forward, heavy boots

hammering the stone. "The talon Orlaith came here with is gone."

Her hands still. Even the tremble abates for a beat before reigniting tenfold.

Disappointment clogs my throat.

I had my suspicions, but seeing it confirmed is a different beast entirely.

"She used it on Rhordyn," I admit, forcing back a breath burdened by her undiluted fear. Guess I should be used to it by now, but she shouldn't have the *right* to be scared of me.

I'm her fucking child.

"A little bird once told me you sent a tapestry to Rhordyn's territory. Call me sentimental, but I tried to find it. You know—wanting to keep the entire set intact because I'm such a good son." I study the flowers she's pieced together thread by tedious thread. "I failed, of course. Though, for you, I guess that's hardly a surprise. But after finding Orlaith on the island tonight, I wonder ... were you trying to send *clues?*"

Her shoulders stiffen in the silence.

*Blessed fucking silence.*

I cross my arms and study the back of her head. "Is that true, Mother? Did you hope Orlaith would see me through *your* eyes and do what you failed to do?" I grip her stool and whip it around, wooden legs screaming against the stone. "But where would you be without me, hmm?"

She flinches again as I crouch, bringing us face to face. She doesn't even bother to hide the fear in her wide, pasty eyes.

"Dead," I pronounce. "You'd be *dead*. Need I remind

you, the only reason you're still *breathing* is because I need your filthy blood to keep Father from slipping away entirely."

She makes some sounds I pretend not to hear, molding her hands into shapes I never bothered to learn the meaning of.

I drop my head, massaging the bridge between my eyes. If I wanted to listen to her speak, I would never have cut out her tongue.

"I heard you talking with Father, you know. When I was small. *Pleading* with him." She becomes still, and I can feel the warm tickle of her undivided attention blazing across my face.

There she goes again, trying to manipulate the situation by feeding me drips of hope that she *cares*.

I lift my head, looking up at her from beneath my brows. "I heard you say that what I lack in power I also lack in empathy."

Her mouth falls open.

"That you're *frightened* of my capabilities. Ironic, since you mated a monster. I'm not sure what you were expecting to end up with."

All the color slips from her face that used to be beautiful once upon a time. Before I started starving her of the thing maintaining her youth. A little petty, but I do hold a good grudge.

"Any weakness I have is because of you," I scoff. "My pathetic, *mortal* mother who can't even look at her own son without shuddering. You're the reason I'm not stronger. The reason I'm pure bloodlust and no fucking *power.*"

I reach up, and she flinches as I snag some silver strands

and squeeze them between my thumb and finger, desperate to tame them.

Later. After I've dealt with my pretty flower.

*She's* my priority now.

"By the time I've done what Father never could and claimed Ocruth as my own, perhaps I'll finally be worthy of your love," I say, tucking her hair behind her ear.

Her face scrunches, garbled words dropping from her mouth like pebbles. Tears gather in her eyes, and all I see is a paltry, desperate, dramatic ploy to gain the upper hand.

Not today.

I grip both sides of her face, stilling her jaw and those mutated noises. "You almost ruined everything," I seethe, upper lip peeling back, my gums aching with the promise of elongated canines that never emerge. "*You almost ruined everything!*"

The words blast out of me with a violence that ricochets off the walls.

I press my forehead against hers, rolling my head one way, the other. "But she loves me," I whisper, a slow, rumbling laugh building in the back of my throat. "She loves me in a way you *never* did."

Mother trembles in my grip, tears slipping down her cheeks, her knobbly, frail hand settling upon my heart. Making my flesh burst with goosebumps—a sensation that scurries up my spine. "I ooh ove ewe, Gnong. I *ooh* ove ewe!"

*I do love you, Non.*

Perhaps I need to sew her fucking lips shut, too.

"No, you don't." I rip her hand off my chest, then shove

back and push to a stand, looking down on her. Feeling sick to my stomach. "I have the scar to prove it."

Another whimper, and my mouth twists in distaste.

I jerk my chin at the empty spot on the stool beside her. "Hand. Now."

Her breath stills, face crumbling with a guttural sob. She shakes her head, mumbling words that find no berth.

"*Now!*"

Another flinch. Pathetic sounds whittle free as she lifts her hand, feebly tugging at her clothes with clawed fingers.

As if that will help.

She gasps as I seize her wrist, a mere stick in my firm grip. I place her hand on the stool, palm up so I can see the calluses that have built up over the years from the constant twist and tug of the threads she dearly loves.

The middle one has the most.

I eye it like the enemy it is, knowing it speaks the language of the only love she really knows—her *craft*. I whip my blade from my boot and slam it through the base of her finger, severing it just below the knuckle.

Blood splatters my face, and she releases a loud, curdling shriek that ripples through the palace.

I think I made a similar sound when she tried to put me down.

"Be grateful," I mutter, sheathing my dagger. "I should be taking *two*."

She tucks her bleeding hand up close to her chest and cradles it, big, heaving sobs racking her frail form as she looks at me through eyes glazed with immeasurable hurt. Like she didn't bring this on herself.

A trail of blood dribbles off the stool, pooling on the ground.

I unstopper the empty vial and snatch Mother's hand, collecting the ruddy liquid from the severed stump while her chest heaves with silent sobs. Punching the cork back into place, I use her water pitcher to rinse my hands. I dry them with a cloth I throw on the ground, pulling the other vial from my pocket to wave in her direction, Father's blood sloshing about.

A desperate sound bludgeons past her chattering teeth as she stumbles off the stool and falls to her knees, looking up at me like a begging dog.

"Not today," I say, a smirk grazing my lips. I tuck the jar in my pocket before I give her my back.

Today, she can *suffer*.

# CHAPTER 23

*Baze*

Madame Strings's heady musk clings to me, making my skin itch more than it usually does. Making me want to scrub it with a dry loofah until I scrape away the sensation, though I doubt it would help.

This sensation—this filthy *itch*—goes all the way to my fucking marrow.

Now that I'm here, choking on her scent, I realize I've spent so long living in my own filth I'd forgotten how it feels to breathe fresh air … but it's hard to justify a different existence when every beat of my fucked-up heart feels stolen.

Undeserved.

Swallowing the nausea clawing up my throat, I look down at Madame Strings's hand resting upon my naked thigh. Her head is on my chest, lashes spread across the apples of her cheeks, lips slightly parted as she breathes soft and slow. The gray paint on her creamy skin is smeared all over her plump curves. The same gray paint that's now on my hands. My body.

Tainting my fucking soul.

Saliva gathers beneath my tongue, and I battle the urge to vomit.

She groans in her sleep, rolling, long ropes of golden hair fanned to one side as she settles on her front, nuzzling into the gray sheets. She splits her legs, back arched, like even in her sleep the Candescence is still wisping through her system, telling her greedy body she wants more.

I wonder how old she really is. How long she's been bolstering her eternal youth and beauty with thorns plucked from *my* people.

Probably a while, based on the way she fucks.

She mumbles as if she's going to wake, then settles into a steady rhythm of deep, even breaths. I would be relieved if I could feel anything at all, but my mind's a graveyard littered with the bones of too many people I knew and loved.

Lost.

If a krah swooped down and shat on me now, I'd probably fucking welcome it.

I sit up, drag my hand down my face, then look past the floaty curtains shrouding the bed and the swirls of incense smogging the air, scanning the room that's lost its beat. Men and women are passed out in tangled piles or draped across the rugs, the furniture. Wherever their most recent surge of candy-induced pleasure landed them.

Easing off the bed, I locate my pants and pull them up, not bothering to find my top or the robe I came here in. Stepping over a man who fell asleep with his cock in his hand, I swipe a bottle of spirits off a low stone table, tipping it over the fluffy rug as I make for the fireplace.

I grab a metal poker, another gush of nausea rearing up my throat. I splash more spirits about the room, over chaises, floor pillows, and up the side of the bed, take a single saluting sip, then drop the empty bottle and kick over a bowl of blazing oil, its contents sloshing across the floor.

Leaching toward the plush rug.

Not bothering to glance over my shoulder, I grab another bottle of spirits and make for the door, a violent roar blasting to life as catastrophic heat singes my shoulders and the back of my bare head.

I barely feel the burn.

I pull the doors shut behind me, threading the metal poker through the handles and sealing the reek of frying flesh inside. Closing myself off to the fisted bangs on the stone. The cries for help.

The blood-curdling wails.

Thick, white smoke billows from beneath like an upside-down waterfall, freckled with little sparks of iridescent shine that sow a seed of determination deep inside my gut.

The doors begin to shake ...

"*Gleish nam vel arft tha ke, astan da. Gleish nam vel arft tha ke,*" I murmur, then give the smoke and the screams my back. "*Gleish tes ta* vaka *nam vel arft tha ke.*"

There's an eerie silence about the temple as I move through cold, lofty corridors like a ghost chasing its next haunt, following the path I gouged in my mind when Brother Beryll brought me this way earlier. The path I pictured myself walking over and over again while I was deep in that woman and my own self-hatred, feeling nothing but what my body was telling me to feel.

What *she* was telling me to feel.

Fine evanescent dust shimmers in the shafts of moonlight spearing through holes in the ceiling, making my gums ache as I catch sight of a lone guard pacing back and forth before the door to the production room.

I set my bottle on the ground, step up behind the large man, grip his head, and rip it sideways, a guttural *crack* echoing through the silence.

His body thumps to the floor at my feet.

Seeing my reflection in his sightless stare, I snarl, unbuckle his sheath, and drape it across my chest. I pull out the short, gold-tipped spear that feels foreign in my fist, frowning, weighing it.

*Guess it's not the time to be picky.*

I stash the man behind a column, retrieve my bottle, and ease into the silent room packed with long trestle tables, heavy dust settled upon the tops like a sprinkling of sparkly snow. Frowning, I notice footprints in the powder coating the floor.

I set the bottle on a table and, softening my footfalls, follow the shuffled tracks to the back storage room, peeking past the door that's cracked a smidge.

Brother Beryll is hunched over near the shelves of thorns, the firelight from a flaming torch casting his gray robe in shades of orange and black. My brow lifts as he uncorks a jar, pockets two thorns from the small stash, then plucks up another and repeats the process. Like a greedy, foul-smelling rat.

Now I don't like him even more.

"Yoo-hoo," I say, shoving the door wide.

He leaps so far into the air, he smacks the back of his head against the shelf, rubbing the hurt while he straightens, looking at me. His eyes bulge, mouth falling open, stare slashing from my bare chest to the spear in my fist.

"*Y-you ...*"

"Yes," I mutter, twisting the ring from my finger and pocketing it. My fake skin loosens its tight grip, like cool water spilled across my flesh—not that it makes me feel any less filthy. "*Me.*"

All the color leaches from Brother Beryll's face, and he stumbles back, flattening against the shelves.

I advance.

His panicked gaze scrawls across my disgusting scars, and I wonder if he feels sorry for me. If he's scared, or remorseful, or if he just sees me as a fucking animal that slipped out of its cage.

"I— I didn't ..."

"Don't bother," I bite out, upper lip peeling back. I slam my stolen spear through his chest, cleaving it between his ribs, shredding his heart. Blood bubbles from his gaping mouth, and he crumples to the floor. "It won't save you."

My pulse roars in my ears while I watch the light leave his eyes, hoping it will make me feel better.

Disappointed when it doesn't.

Clearing my throat, I stuff the spear in its sheath and snatch a large-handled basket off the floor. I drag my arm along the shelves, sweeping the jars of thorns and ground Candescence into the basket's hollow. Taking every last ounce into the production room, along with Brother Beryll's torch, I uncork each jar and sprinkle the contents upon the wooden trestle tables—a pretty, morbid offering to the only God I worship. The only *God* who has the power to bring justice to this fucked-up, unbalanced world.

*Death.*

I crack the bottle of spirits, splash it upon the tables, then use the flaming torch to ignite all three. Color and light explodes, violent heat scalding my knuckles as I back toward the door slower than I should.

"*Gleish nam vel arft tha ke, astan da. Gleish nam vel arft tha ke,*" I rasp, then clamp my teeth down on the promise.

*I will find you, brothers.*

*I will find you.*

# CHAPTER

*Kai*

## 24

Seated against a crystal boulder, I dangle my hand in the blood-red stream that cuts through the grassy plateau in gurgling twists and turns. Around me, iridescent spires reach for pink, wispy clouds, their tips bearing little windows large enough to poke a head out.

Just.

Some spill tumbling vines with purple blooms tipped toward beams of morning light shafting between the gaps.

It's a sight to behold—otherworldly—but Lychnis has never felt ... *normal.*

It's believed the Goddess of Light couldn't stand to watch the decimation of her beautiful creations. That she tore from the sky on a crescent moon and fell like stardust, swallowed by the sea. That the ocean birthed her in the form of this island; the geyser her blood, forever flowing.

All I know is that it didn't always exist. That the ocean hailed us—a call to arms that whispered through the waves.

*'Get apple! Get apple!'*

'I don't want a fucking apple,' I growl at Zykanth, scouring the tree his attention is narrowed on—ten times larger than it was last time I saw it.

Many moons ago.

Its branches bow under the weight of plump, green fruit being gathered and placed in baskets by a pair of Aeshlians shrouded in brown cloaks.

The woman tucks a drape of hair behind her thorny ear, her attention coming to rest on me.

I quickly look away.

Seeing them the other day rocked me to the core. I'd stumbled back to our nest in disbelief, suddenly exhausted, certain I was going to wake and realize it was all a dream. That I wouldn't be forced to look into the eyes of the ones I'd failed and pretend that nothing happened.

So I did just that—for days.

*Avoided.*

This morning, Vicious took me by the hand and dragged me out the door, leading me down the too-familiar path to the oasis—extorting her unique power over my impulses. Perhaps knowing I'd fucking follow her anywhere.

*'Get apple!'*

Clearing my throat, I stuff a loose shard of crystal in the pocket of my holey shorts that Vicious pulled from her ramshackle pile. 'There. Treasure in my pocket. Now shut up about the apples,' I grind out, gaze drifting to Vicious.

*'Precious little savage one. Mine.'*

She's cross-legged in a patch of tilled soil, dressed in her too-big shirt, her slender, sun-kissed legs covered in dirt. Her hair is a shock of white scribble, eyes like the burning horizon.

My insides ignite.

'Yes.' I swallow thickly. 'Yours ...'

Two children totter about, cast beneath her watchful eye. The smallest plays in the dirt, lustrous curls bouncing about her heart-shaped face while she piles soil into heaps she pats into different shapes. The other can't be older than six, her hair longer, one side woven into braids adorned with crystal beads. She rips vegetables from the soil, inspecting each with a serious look as she dusts them off, piling them in a basket she could curl up inside.

She offers a carrot to Vicious, who frowns for a long moment before taking it.

Biting it.

Her face screws up, and she spits orange chunks into the soil, then wipes her tongue with the sleeve of her shirt to the bursting tune of the child's laughter.

The faintest smile tilts my lips, disappearing when I feel the woman Aeshlian watching me again, filling my chest with a tidal wave of guilt.

*Does she recognize me?*

*Hold me accountable?*

I wouldn't blame her if she did. If she shoved me against a spire and swore in my face, tears streaking down her cheeks.

This oasis ... It used to be home for *scores* of Aeshlians going about their daily tasks: hacking tools from chunks of crystal, tending crops, preparing vegetables to be baked in ovens dug into the soil. Children frolicking in the stream, picking wildflowers in the sun. Happy and carefree.

A pure existence now tainted.

A slashing memory strikes—of petrified screams

bouncing between the spires. Of the sea air soured with the potent tang of blood that splashed the soil near the base of that supersized apple tree. A tree that appears to have gobbled up the offer like it was freely given, expanding from the unnatural punch of light it took from the Aeshlian blood.

My chin falls to my chest.

*'Get the apple!'*

I groan.

Sensing movement to my left, my heart lurches, eyes widening when Anver sits beside me—arms draped across his bent knees, hands clasped together. A fur pelt accentuates his broad shoulders, his hair shorn on both sides, framing thorned ears, the rest twisted in a rope of beaded braids that fall down his spine.

He turns his head, exposing a scar slashed through his brow and eye that wasn't there last time I saw him, his strong jawline and chiseled cheekbones softened by the fine elegance of his ethereal breed. "It's been a long time, old friend."

His gruff voice rolls like barreling waves thumping against my chest.

"I ... thought they got you all."

I swear the light in his eyes dims, and he cuts a look at the children as a heaviness settles between us. "Almost." He clears his throat. "Some of us survived in the island's deep hollows, hidden behind one of my shields. We only came out once we were emaciated from hunger, and by then the island was abandoned."

Failure claws up my ribs and sits upon my shoulders like some flesh-eating beast.

There were *years* of peace before the island was discovered by outsiders, by which time our guards had dropped. Many *bruák* came all at once, flying across the ocean on vessels with iron spears bolted to their decks. With empty hulls ready to pack full with warm bodies.

Blasts of power ripped the air and scorched the sea, and we couldn't stop them all.

The ocean ran sparkly and red as the sound of death filled the air, accentuated by agonized screams as babes were torn from mothers' breasts.

*Our treasure was taken.*

The sky shook, and darkness stretched above. The sea rippled, then went deathly still, becoming a ravenous, meat-eating trap for those of us who survived. Our penance, perhaps. One many of us swam into the jaws of.

Plagued by unimaginable guilt, some originals braved the mainland to hunt for our treasured friends, then failed to bring forth their tails when they came back to the ocean—having spent too long on legs. Some cast the search too wide and ended up in the wrong ocean at the wrong time, struck by the bolt of power summoned from the sky that brought an end to most of the Unseelie.

But the *Aeshlians* ...

First, they were feasted on, then hunted to the brink of extinction right beneath our noses.

"We failed you," I choke out, dropping my stare to the grass.

"No, you didn't."

I look sidelong at Anver, frowning.

"We may be immortal, but it is as unnatural to be without an end as it is to be without a shadow. Even Gods and Goddesses chose to rip from their oblivion because they know the *truth*."

"Which is?"

He drops his voice to a low murmur. "Without an end, loss stacks upon your chest like stones. The loss of your home, your loved ones, your *mind*. I have watched both the making and breaking of my kind, and through it all, I have come to realize that mortality is a gift. Those with endless life end up destroying themselves," he says, face etched with sorrow. "Or others."

His words gore at my chest while he evokes a false smile and looks forward again, welcoming the man and woman carrying the basket of apples toward us. I clear my throat as both Aeshlians dip their heads, the female extending an apple in my direction.

My eyes widen.

A *gift*.

Zykanth erupts into a giddy swirl as shock electrifies me from within, and I reach out to accept it. "Thank you ..."

She bobs her head, offering me a shy smile before drifting off with the male. They ease beneath string laden with fish flesh drying in the sun, disappearing through an entryway in one of the crystal spires.

I look at the apple, conscious of its weight; of the bright, healthy tone of its lime-green skin. I can almost taste its sharp sweetness, the underside of my tongue tingling in anticipation of the crisp meal I can't bring myself to sink my teeth into.

To enjoy.

Not after seeing all the blood that spilled across that soil.

With thoughts swimming much faster than the sickening

churn of my guts, I look down a path. The swiftest route to the ocean from here.

"You have claimed her?" Anver grunts out, the question striking me unawares.

My attention drifts to my bite mark on Vicious's nape, half concealed by a gush of wild hair as she digs small holes with her bare hands, making way for the pouch of seeds the eldest child is dispersing throughout the patch.

*'Back off, little sparkly legs. My savage little chosen mate.'*

A rumbling sound boils in the back of my throat. "I am hers, and she is mine."

"Then why the bleak eyes?"

I sigh, running both hands through my hair, fisting the strands. "Because I know of another Aeshlian," I admit, voice low, afraid the wind will carry my words somewhere dangerous. "A *female*."

He loosens a breath, and I feel his gaze bore into the side of my face. "She evaded the huntings?"

A chill nuzzles between my ribs, burrowing deep, and I catch his bulging stare. Take in his whitewash complexion.

"She spent most of her adolescence on the coast of Ocruth. She's since traveled south aboard the ship that shot my drake."

Zykanth flinches, coiling into a knot, and I give him a tender stroke.

"Bahari ..."

I nod, and a grim mask of foreboding settles upon Anver's face.

"Her true self is hidden by a force not of this world, but I've seen too much not to worry." To picture her being strung from a tree. Hacked to pieces.

Burned at the stake.

I clear my throat and avert my stare, shivering.

"My drake is healed now. At some stage, perhaps soon, I may have to risk the waters. I can't take Vicious with me. If the beast that guards these islands were to hurt her ..." I shake my head, teeth gritted as Zykanth unravels, thrashing against my ribs, again, and again, and *again*.

Can't risk it.

Won't.

"May I ask ... how long has she been here?"

I notice Anver watching me closely, the faintest line drawn between his brows. "A while," he finally says, as though picking the words with caution. "She came to us savage. Didn't seem to understand right from wrong, or how to communicate. She was just—"

"Vicious," I finish, and he nods, turning his gaze on the vegetable patch.

"Ailith and Siah are the first young born on this island since The Great Hunt, and your Vicious has grown a special bond with them. But it's taken *years* of gentle coaxing and cautious gifts to pull her this far into our fold."

*Years ...*

The word plops into my guts like a rock, confirming my suspicions.

*Years ... without her tail.*

Meaning my beautiful, wild Vicious has a tombstone in her chest in place of the churning, beating life force I couldn't imagine living without.

Inside me, Zykanth releases a deep lament that rattles

my bones and the strings of my heart, and I try to swallow the ball of emotion rising up my throat.

"Perhaps losing her drake hit so hard she let go of her humanity ..."

Silence stretches for so long it becomes uncomfortable, and I catch Anver's gaze. He's watching me with precision, something roiling behind his crystalline eyes.

He lifts a brow. "You have been ashore too long, old friend."

The words are heavy, like he's passing me something sacred.

"What—"

A blur of motion has my attention snapping to the youngest child bounding toward us—giggle chiming, smile beaming, curls bouncing.

"Geil de neh veshta, nav Ashta!" she gushes, clapping her dirty hands, smelling like damp soil and flowers.

Reminding me of Orlaith.

"Geil de ne veshta, nav Ashta! Hath te nei—"

Anver wraps his big hands around her shoulders, stilling her steady bounce. "Use the common tongue, Ailith. Remember your lessons."

With the most dramatic sigh I've ever seen, she screws up her face, as though thinking hard. "Favor, please." She taps her lips, gaze rolling toward the sky, back again. "Gift ... for Ashta?"

I can't help but smile.

Anver laughs low before cupping his hands together. "Close enough," he says, crisp light shafting between the gaps in his fingers—a gift born straight from the bowl that did not pass down the generations, making Anver the last with the ability to solidify his light. A few moments later, he lifts his hand, revealing a dainty bloom of luminescent crystal.

*'Treasure!'* Zykanth trills as the little girl claps and bounces, squealing with delight. *'Treasure, treasure, treasure!'*

"Thanking you favor." She dips her head, takes the bloom, then dashes toward a path between the spires, cloak fluttering in her wake.

"I better follow," Anver grinds out, pushing to a stand, casting me in his broad shadow. "Make sure she doesn't fall down the hole."

*'I like holes. Holes hide sparkly things.'*

"Where's she going?" I ask over the inner ruckus of Zykanth's ramblings.

There's a beat of silence, and a reverence ignites Anver's eyes. "The *well*."

Zykanth almost cracks free of his cage as his excitement bubbles over, and scales erupt across my chest, making me itch. *'Go. Move little legs. Follow little shiny one and big shiny one. Get pretty treasure for little savage one.'*

Vicious watches me stand and pocket the apple, and a warmth swells inside me beneath her curious gaze. I follow Anver along the lofty path sandwiched between sheer crystal blocks, slowing when it chops into a staircase that tunnels down. Light filters through the crystal, casting prisms of color across our skin as we edge into the bowels of the island.

The air is crisp and fresh, but hauntingly still, making me cautious of every shallow breath, lest I stir something I shouldn't.

The stairwell opens into a small cave, its walls and

ceiling adorned with clusters of long, blunt crystals. Ailith stills a few steps from a jagged split in the ground, lowers onto her belly, and wiggles toward the sharp edge, dangling her arm over the side, holding the rose aloft.

She drops it.

Hearing a distant plop, Zykanth surges against my ribs, trying to propel me over the edge.

*'Move, little man. Get beneath big ribs. Zykanth get treasure for soft little mate.'*

'You won't fit, you silly sea snake!' I growl internally, scratching at the scales erupting across my cheek as I creep forward.

"Why drop it down there?" I rasp, my voice echoing back at me.

Anver smiles.

"It's a gift," he rumbles, and I cast my gaze into the chasm bathed in a mottling of light filtering from above.

Something glimmers below, making my pulse race, igniting Zykanth into a boiling swirl.

*'Treasure,'* he bleats. *'Dive, little man!'*

I wrestle him down and lock him away, but still my heart powers along at a ferocious pace ...

It's a *trove*.

# CHAPTER 25

*Orlaith*

I reach my arms above my head, my stretching groan morphing into a hissing wince as a blaze of pain shoots through the side of my neck.

My eyes pop open, my vision a haze of gold and blue, hands padding at a bandage wrapped around my throat like a noose.

I sit up, heaving air, certain I'm starved of it.

That I'm choking.

Heart pounding, I unravel the bandage in frantic, trembling motions and toss it aside, fingers coasting over the tender patch of ravaged skin throbbing with a deep ache.

I swallow a whimper, forcing myself to breathe slower. *Slower.*

A room comes into view—all ornate gold furnishings and lapis lazuli walls. A dressing room packed full of gaudy dresses that aren't made of much. A soaring, spectacular view of a glittering city that hides so many ugly secrets.

My room.

I look down at the pure white sheets pooled around me, tongue tingling as a wave of nausea swells.

*Definitely* my room ...

*It's okay,* I remind myself, breathing in through my nose, out through my mouth—chapped lips thick with thirst. *You're out.*

*You're useful.*

I think of the little girl with red hair. Imagine finding a way to pull her free of that cage, wrap her in a hug, and tell her it's going to be all right.

Clinging to that thought, I reach for a glass on my bedside table, almost knocking it over in my haste. I cradle it with both hands and tip it to my lips, guzzling so much water I feel it sloshing around inside my belly.

*It's going to be all right.*

Shuffling sideways, I ease my legs over the edge of the bed and set my feet on the cold stone floor, a blue sleeping gown tumbling about my legs ...

I swallow thickly, choosing not to think about how I was changed into this silky, strappy garment. About my long, near-perfect plait tied off with a blue bow to match, a few sprigs of hair loose from my sleep.

Sweat slicks between my breasts, down my spine as I settle the empty glass back on the table, clinging to it with a clawed hand. I hang my head forward and breathe.

*Breathe.*

*It's going to be okay. I'm going to get them out.*

*Somehow.*

I cut a glance around the room, gaze narrowing on a glass jug full of water sitting atop my vanity. This deep, unquenched *need* flares within me. Like I've been stumbling through a dusty desert for days on end and have finally found a well.

I snatch the empty glass and rock to my feet, my body too heavy—such a contrast to my too-light head as I shuffle toward my vanity. Gripping the chair to steady myself, I pour my glass full, then drain the contents in gluttonous gulps, spilling some in my eagerness.

Slamming it down, my chest heaves as I wipe my mouth, braving a look in the new mirror that replaced my shattered one.

A tight breath cuts through my parted lips.

*He took too much ...*

Dark circles cushion my flat, lack-luster eyes, lips hued blue, skin a sickly shade of gray—so thin in places you can see the map of my veins sketched below the surface.

I look like I just clawed back from the brink of a death that's still clinging to my edges. How can I save a burrow of people—save a *territory*—if I can barely save myself?

*Your kind needs sunlight to survive. It's why Rhordyn had you housed in the northern tower all these years. It got the most of it.*

Zali's words strike me like a slap, and my gaze shifts to the open balcony doors. To the slabs of buttery light pouring past the billowing drapes, bringing with it the smell of freshly fallen rain. My feet move of their own accord, and I drift toward the doors like I'm attached to a tugging string. The drapes part as I step onto the balcony, and warm sunshine embraces me.

I shudder from my fluttering lids all the way to the tips of my toes.

Moving past the bench, I lean against the wall for

support, then lower to the ground and stretch my legs—bunching my dress up to expose more of my flesh to the sizzling rays. Flicking the straps off my shoulders, I rest my head against the stone, close my eyes, and turn my attention inward.

Transfixed, I watch beads of light bloom amidst my gloomy insides. One by one they swell, like winking stars sprinkled across a dusky sky.

*Small seeds grow into big, strong things ...*

The backs of my eyes prickle with the promise of tears as I marvel at the fierce, ethereal beauty. At countless seeds of the strength I need to brace my spine and save those innocent lives.

Plucking some with slow, gentle grace, I cup them close, worshiping each one like I do a perfect stone scooped from the shore of Bitten Bay. I squish them, smooth them, take my time molding them into small but mighty domes I stack inside my chest. All the while, that raw, shameful pain in my neck throbs with each hammering thump of my heart.

I can't afford another mistake. Another weakness.

There's too much on the line.

Every clipped step down the stairs echoes the tap of my heels, my chin high and spine as strong as my freshly soldered determination.

A reticule hangs off my wrist, Cainon's cupla bound around the other, feeling heavier than it ever has. My hair is a crimped gush over my shoulder, my dress an intertwining maze of gold and blue strips that show too much of my sun-kissed shoulders, my legs ... *every other part of me.*

But it was the one laid out.

Izel found me asleep on the balcony and told me I'd been instructed to get ready. That Cainon has something to show me in the city.

A gift I will receive before the people of Parith.

All I really heard was *city* and *people of Parith* and a plan took shape inside me like a web of tripping wires—risky. Dangerous.

*All I have.*

I refused her help getting dressed so I would have time to make the appropriate preparations.

Walking past a tall hallway mirror, I catch a glimpse of myself and pause, struck by my eyes—bright with the sun's luster, yet hard as flints. Like my soul has been snatched and stuffed beneath one of the many crystal domes nailed against my insides. A pretty graveyard for everything that makes me vulnerable.

I lift my hair, checking the bite mark; raised, raw, and angry-looking, throbbing with its own beat.

Reminding me of its shameful existence.

The bandage pulled too much attention—made me look *weak*—but my hair is the perfect camouflage.

Draping my heavy locks upon the hurt again, I continue down, nearing the foyer, Cainon coming into view with his back to the stairwell.

He's clad in a finely threaded tunic trimmed in gold, his arms crossed, hair brushing his broad shoulders in loose, salty waves that make him look a little different than normal, though it doesn't trick my thundering heart. Doesn't stem my urge to backtrack.

To *run*.

He's still the same predator whose eyes lost all their hue before he tore into my neck and almost drained me dry. Still an ancient animal forged from a time when power ruled the world.

I swallow thickly, lifting my chin as I round the stairs, like I'm stepping into a gilded Unseelie burrow. Reminding myself that I have a plan—I just have to grit my teeth and hold on until tomorrow night.

I just have to play the fucking part.

Cainon's speaking with a woman dressed in a flowy gray robe. Her hair is woven into a crown of silky, golden locks, fine lines bordering dark-purple eyes, blue bursting from their pupils.

The same pretty shade as my friend Gael's.

*Her mother.*

A few of my domes rattle, vicious, thorny emotions threatening to spear up as I remember the story Gael told me.

Remember the scars on her back.

As I look at the upside-down v carved between her eyes and battle to keep my knees from crumbling.

I hold the woman's gaze all the way to the bottom of the staircase, and her brow buckles.

Cainon turns.

"Orlaith. I was just coming to get you," he rasps, his hot, hungry stare raking across my skin. "But I got caught speaking with the High Septum ..."

I paint a soft smile on my face, looking into his ravenous eyes. "I'm sorry I beat you to it."

His throat works.

The High Septum reaches out and takes his hand, tugging him toward her. Frowning, he breaks my gaze and leans her way.

She whispers something in his ear.

Flicking me a sideways glance, Cainon gives me his back. The High Septum looks at me again, eyes narrowed, her hand slipping from his arm before she limps across the foyer and disappears through a side door—snapping the tension I hadn't realized was crushing my lungs and making it hard to breathe.

Cainon clears his throat, turns, and extends his hand toward me. "Such exquisite beauty should hang off my arm. *Always.*"

*Play the part.*

Reinforcing my domes, I dish him a shy smile and thread my hand around his arm, every cell on edge as he tucks me too close to his side and leads me in the direction of the main exit.

I steal a glance at the side door. "Is the High Septum the Shulák's ... leader?"

"Yes," he says with a laugh. "She'll be overseeing your trial and officiating our coupling tomorrow."

That's unfortunate—I'm pretty sure she hates me already. Or at least doesn't *trust* me.

Probably justified, since the feeling's mutual on both accounts.

"You look astonishing," he continues. "Positively *edible.*"

I flick him another forged smile despite my bristling skin. "Thank you."

He spins, charging me back behind the large, golden door, snatching my breath. He cages me against the wall with such dominating force, my fingers twitch for the blade I'd usually have strapped to my waist or thigh. Thankful I don't as I find a little vine of rage coiled between my vertebrae. Untangle it.

Stuff it under a dome.

"I like that you removed the bandage," he purrs. "That you're wearing my bite proudly beneath this pretty, pretty hair."

His words crawl across my skin like the prickly caterpillars that nibble on my rose bushes. The ones that would leave a rash on my hands when I'd pluck them off.

"I'm so glad you approve," I lie with a sultry slur that tastes like spoiled fruit, slamming another layer atop my creaking domes as I think of a warm kiss upon my head and a deep, bone-rattling voice seeping through the layers of my skin.

A voice I'd give my *life* to hear again ...

*Don't cry.*

Cainon sweeps my hair off the side of my neck, his fingers brushing the bite mark, and my skin flushes with goosebumps for all the wrong reasons. But they add to the ruse. Make it look like I'm *enjoying* his rapt attention.

Like my body's responding to the low rumble boiling in his chest as he pushes so close there's hardly room for me to breathe.

"It's still so raw." He swallows, the sound rattling the

235

chains of the painful memory of him latched onto my flesh, drawing greedy gulps.

Itchy pops flare across my shoulder.

"It still smells like your blood *tastes*." He drags his nose up the side of my neck, releasing a pained groan. "And if I don't stop doing this, I'm going to rip into this pretty neck and ruin your lovely gown."

I repress a shudder as he tilts back and grabs my hand, kissing my knuckles while looking at me through blown pupils. Drinking me in a gentler way than the one I'm certain he's imagining.

Pining for.

"Later," he promises, flashing me a serpentine smile that's all teeth before he drapes my hair back over his mark and tugs me toward the exit.

*Later.*

I frantically reinforce my domes again …

*Play the fucking part.*

Swallowing waves of nausea, I'm led through the courtyard and out the palace gates, the sun blazing upon my face and all my bare patches of skin. We near a clopping swell of saddled horses and armed guards, each adorned with golden helmets winged at the sides. The horses' eyes are half concealed with blinders, their manes hidden by flat, interweaving peels of gold that mold to their shape.

We move through the throng, approaching a huge white horse held in place by a stoic-faced Kolden. Cainon grips me around the waist, lifts me, and sets me upon the thick saddle blanket, the animal shifting in a tight, agitated prance.

I grab a leather strap as a blow of wind tousles the

strips of my dress, exposing the swell of my breast and the curve of my inner thigh.

Blushing, I smooth the material as best I can with one hand, gripping the horse with the other. But a quick glance at the guards assures me they either didn't notice or they know better than to steal a peek of what's deemed their High Master's property.

A *boom* rips through the silence, and I jolt. Some of the horses buck and squeal, the one beneath me tossing his head about and making my heart bolt. A litter of blue light rains from the sky, burning out before it hits the bay.

Cainon snatches the reins off Kolden and leaps up behind me, pulling me tight against his chest. I'm sealed between his legs, my heart hacking at my ribs as I catch Kolden's fleeting stare—his jaw set, eyes hard.

He turns toward his own horse, and my gaze spears across the bridge, dread sitting heavy in my gut. "Do we have to go far before we reach this ... gift?"

"Not far," Cainon whispers in my ear, his excitement evident in his hitched voice.

More bristled bumps explode across my shoulder. Up the side of my neck.

Cainon digs his heels in, and we jerk forward. The beast leaps into a rocky trot, then a smoother canter that has my entire body rising and falling between Cainon's thighs.

"Relax, petal. I only bite behind closed doors."

I slam another ready-made shell atop the dome containing my self-disgust, then force myself to lean back, molding to him, feeling my blood curdle as a rumble of appreciation rattles from his chest through my back. It's so close, so intimate, that I feel a chunk of my heart cleave off and crumble away like sunburnt soil.

*Breathe.*

*Just play the fucking part.*

We race over the bridge beneath the sun's severe glare, trailed by an orchestra of hooves clopping against the cobbles. I keep my hair plastered around the side of my neck as we break onto the esplanade and slow, moving through the city streets, a sea of men, women, and children emerging from doors and stores and tight side alleys to follow our path. Some of the smaller children tug at the adults' shirts or hands, frowning, questions pouring from their mouths in a jumble of garbled words.

*"Whada we doin', Maamy?"*

*"Ah we goewing to see mowah da pwetty sky spahkles?"*

The adults remain tight lipped, quelling the children's questions while nipping glances at the guards who escort us through the streets.

A heavy sense of dread settles upon my shoulders, even as I harbor a seed of hope tucked in my reticule—searching the crowd for a familiar face.

*I just need one.*

More and more people swarm, packing in around us, until we come to the end of the street, spilling into a massive cobbled square. The buildings surrounding it are tall and chunky, each boasting tiers of balconies stuffed full of people—their attention nipping at a large object draped in blue fabric.

A cold sweat breaks across the back of my neck.

Down my spine.

The guards behind us fan out around the perimeter,

halting their horses in a steady, unified formation as hundreds of men, women, and children spill in after us.

*So many people ...*

So many pairs of *eyes* that it's hard to convince myself they can't all see through my cracks. Can't see the lie in the way I'm leaning into Cainon's chest, or in the soft smile I pass him when he plants a too-hot kiss upon my ear.

I almost expect somebody to stand up and scream it. To call me out.

To sow seeds of doubt in Cainon's mind that prevent me from saving those poor, innocent people trapped in his father's burrow.

Cainon pulls our horse to a stop beside a stone podium draped in billowing blue curtains trimmed with gold thread. He leaps off, then reaches up and helps me down.

I barely feel him grip my waist, or my shoes setting upon the stone. Barely feel his hand press against my back, ushering me up the stairs, into the podium's sheltered cove high above the ground.

We move to the balustrade where we look out across the crowd still compacting into the square, parallel lines of armed, stony-faced guards keeping them from filling a path of empty space between us and the obscured structure.

The crowd erupts—booing, yelling, screaming obscenities at a person being dragged by two burly soldiers.

My heart dives.

*What is this?*

The prisoner's head is concealed with a sack loosely tied around their neck, making them blind to the fruits and vegetables being hurled their way. They ricochet off the guards' armor, but the prisoner flinches every time one finds its mark.

My stomach threatens to turn itself inside out as threads of understanding begin to weave together.

*This is not a regular gift.*

I maintain my passive act, gripping hold of the balustrade to prevent my knees from crumbling as Cainon steps up behind me, then sets his hands on either side of my own—ensnaring me. I suck a tight breath, my heart thundering so hard I fear he might hear it.

"This is all for you, petal."

I tilt my head to look at him. "Me?"

His eyes are wide, his smile bright and expectant as he nods.

My stare slides to a stack of arrows with blue fletching, their heads cushioned by bounds of white material—perhaps to protect the arrowheads from hurting anyone by accident.

They remind me of the chrysalides I used to find on the milkweed back at Castle Noir. I'd snap them at the stem, tote armfuls up my tower, and set them in a vase to keep them fresh so I could watch the butterflies hatch. I found such joy in seeing them fly for the first time, then flutter out one of my open windows.

I cling to the happy memory with trembling fists as the drape is torn off in a ripple of blue, revealing a pyre standing proud in the center of the square, constructed from hay, branches, and a tall log.

Muscles tensing, I fight to control the tremor threatening to cleave me down the middle as the prisoner is bound to the wooden pole.

A hush falls over the crowd.

The bone-chilling silence haunts me, muscles tensing, Rhordyn's words booming in my ears like a thunderstorm:

*Things are done differently here. That boundary is only ever cut into when they're preparing to burn someone at the stake.*

The memory of potent, charred flesh blasts the back of my throat as the sack is yanked off, revealing a man with golden skin, sandy hair, and azure eyes that find me instantly—sharpened with pain and fear, darkening with ire.

My blood runs cold.

*Vanth.*

# CHAPTER 26

*Orlaith*

I step back from the balustrade, trembling hands outstretched, like they will somehow shield me from the scene.

Cainon takes my wrist, turns me to face him, and I gasp when he places a longbow in my hand, staring at the lofty arc of polished wood.

A terrible awareness blooms beneath my ribs ...

"Do you know how to shoot one?"

The harsh cut of his voice spurs the storm in my stomach, and I look up into his uncomfortably earnest eyes. My gaze flicks to a big metal bowl set on a stone pedestal beside me, brimming with flaming oil, then to the arrows and their fluffy, flammable tips.

The heavy weight of dread fills me, shoving the air from my lungs and leaving little room for me to breathe.

"I—"

*Fuck.*

I give him a tight nod, and a pleased smile grazes his

lips. He checks the ties at each end of the bow caught in my white-knuckled fist.

Barely seeing them, I scan the crush of people pouring into the square while the tempest churning inside me devastates my nerves and threatens to power up my throat. Fissures weave across my crystal domes, releasing wispy tendrils of tangled emotion that crawl up the sides of my chest.

"I can't—"

"Don't worry," Cainon coos. "Nobody will dare snicker if you miss."

"No, I mean I *can't* do this, Cainon." I shove the bow at him, letting go. It wobbles for a bit before he snatches it, slashing a glance across the crowd. "I can't—*won't* light that pyre."

He pours over me like a menacing statue, making the space feel too small.

Too cramped.

My heart labors as he leans in, the tips of his fingers brushing my cheek with his too-hot touch, his anger a violent swell lashing me in waves. "I *smelled* you on him, you know." The words blow up my heart rate, scaling my skin like thistles. "Smelled the remnants of Vanth's ... *desire* locked within the fibers of his clothing after he was detained for almost murdering you."

"I don't understand what you're saying ..."

Silence stretches, his brows knitting together as he looks down at me with a crushing sort of finality. "They need to see that you're *mine*. They don't *touch* what's mine, Orlaith. Not unless they want to die." Again, his fingers skim my cheek, traverse my lips. "And if you don't take the first shot, you'll be seen as *welcoming* his crude attention. And perhaps you were. How do I know you weren't *begging* him to fuck you?"

My breath flees. "I— I *wasn't*—"

His eyes harden like flints, a darkness toiling within their depths. "*Prove* it," he bites out, wrapping my fingers around the bow, those two words stoning me over and over ... shackling me to this nightmare.

This hell.

I swallow a surge of violent words, and my heart bolts as he cups my cheek, tips my head, and shifts my hair, gaze darting to that ravaged spot on my neck. Cainon rumbles, pummeling me with brutal, bloody promises.

*Prove it ...*

I want to stretch out those words and twist them into a twine to tighten around his throat. Watch his eyes bulge as he begs me for mercy—

A bell tolls, ringing out across the crowd, snapping me from my violent reverie. Cainon drops his hand but remains close, his body a scouring heat against mine as we turn our attention to the pyre.

A squire climbs onto its base, dressed in a blue tunic, stockings, and a leather belt. He has a feather in his hat that flits in the hot, humid breeze.

He unrolls a white scroll, then begins to read aloud, his baritone easily carried across the hushed crowd. "*Vanth Augustine, Second of His Name, has been convicted of grievous crimes against the High Master's promised.*"

"Remember, you're only sparking the match," Cainon murmurs into my ear, and it's a battle not to squirm away from his barbed breath. "It will mean so much to me."

My legs threaten to buckle, and I'm forced to lean against the balustrade.

"*For his misdeeds,*" the squire continues, "*he has been sentenced to death by fire! Shunned in life, so too shall he be shunned in death.*"

"*Shunned in death!*" The crowd roars the words to the haunting beat of drums. "*Shunned in death!*"

I don't want to be here, drawing on the smell of sweat and fear, watching a crowd jeer for blood. I want to be in my rose garden, dragging my fingers across flushes of bold blooms, admiring their depth of color.

"*Shunned in death!*"

I want to be sodden and salty, stretched out on the black-stone beach, the sun on my face as Kai churns through the waves—always watching.

Always close.

"*Shunned in death!*"

I want to be in Rhordyn's Den, curled beneath the covers and surrounded by walls of black, sleeping away the day.

Hiding from the world.

Cainon steps behind me, and I can feel the frantic pace of his pounding heart, his hard, throbbing manhood pressed against me.

He's ... *enjoying* this.

"He needs to *suffer,*" Cainon grates out, his voice carved with a menacing lilt.

"*Shunned in death!*"

I can't think, can't speak, can hardly breathe as I scan the wild crowd, some with an upside-down v carved into their foreheads.

Their fists punch the sky every time they bellow the vile words.

I catch sight of a tall man with salt-and-pepper hair and bold blue eyes that spear right through me, and my cheeks heat with a flare of shame. I break Gun's stare, looking down at Zane tucked close to his side, draped in the cloak I bought him. Watching me with wide eyes, like he doesn't recognize me.

Neither of them are chanting.

My throat swells, and I rip my gaze away, blinking back tears. The bell tolls again, and the crowd becomes silent, though the drums continue to beat.

Cainon places his hands over mine, urging me to lift the bow. Forcing me to look down the line of the unarmed weapon to where Vanth is trussed up a hundred feet away, his eyes now bulging with unmistakable fear.

Cainon points toward a lump of hay. "Shoot right there. It'll ignite the pyre's base, and he'll burn nice and slow."

His words are the smell of scorched flesh torn from the past, presented to me like a gift. They're more death pinned against my already haunted conscience.

A terrible tremble rattles me from the inside out ...

"You've done *much* worse," he purrs, creating more fissures in my domes.

Spawning more sprouts of crippling emotion.

"This will be a breeze compared to stabbing someone through the heart at close range."

I swear the ground softens beneath my feet, my hands now coated in *his* blood as I watch him slip away.

Fall backward into a frothy waterfall.

It's an effort not to sob. To split apart and *scream*.

I step from tragedy to tragedy, toting death like tombstones collecting beneath my ribs. And I realize with heartbreaking finality that I got the wrong monster in that jungle.

*I got the wrong one.*

"Don't be nervous." Planting a kiss on my cheek, Cainon shifts toward the stack of arrows, plucks one up, then swipes the bandaged tip through the fire. A churn of flames swallows the bind of white material, and a collective gasp echoes from the crowd.

A sea of eyes turn to me as Cainon helps me notch the arrow, and a woman somewhere howls—a coarse, throaty sound that curdles my blood.

I don't look in that direction. Don't want to see who that haunting eddy belongs to. Vanth may have done a terrible thing, but he's still a son. A brother.

Perhaps a promised.

My chest becomes so crowded with wild weeds of emotion that each breath feels choked, and I struggle to remember the reasons why I'm biting down on words like crunching glass. Why I'm wrestling my morals into a wrangled knot while I wear the stoic face of a woman I'm beginning to hate.

*The little red-haired girl still caged in that burrow— the way she flinched when I reached between the bars and cupped her cheeks.*

*The male lying dead on the ground, his flat stare seeking the shaft of moonlight spearing down from above.*

A terrible realization settles upon my shoulders ...

I have no choice. I have to sow more death into my already sullied conscience.

I have to play the *fucking* part.

I drop inside myself, gather a wobbling stack of crystal shells, then begin untangling the mangled mess of my emotions trailing through the patchy carcasses of my untended domes. I corral them back where they belong, slam new domes into place, then pull a deep, shuddering inhale.

*Breathe, Orlaith. Find a quiet place inside and chase the silence.*

Baze's words come to me from the past, and I steady my grip on the weapon, lifting it, looking down the line of the arrow and past the blazing tip. My gaze doesn't land on Vanth but on a broad-shouldered male in the crowd behind him swathed in a royal-blue cloak, arms crossed and face hidden within the shadow of his hood.

My heart leaps, then stumbles over a foray of frantic beats.

I don't have to see his features to know who it is. To remember the torment roiling within his eyes before I turned my back and left him lying on the sand, broken and beaten with his scars on display, desperately trying to cover himself.

*Baze …*

Part of me wants to run to him. To beg him to drag me away from this hell, kicking and clawing at his skin while I struggle to scream—because he knows better.

*He always does.*

The rest of me wants to tuck into a ball and hide from the man who taught me how to use a bow, now watching me point one at a person trussed against a log with a wet patch blooming at his crotch.

"Your hands are shaking ..."

Cainon's voice pierces my thoughts, and I'm reminded that there's a predator standing behind me. A predator *Baze* has a prickly history with.

*I should have your head for that, boy.*

My insides flinch at the chilling echo of Cainon's words—almost a promise.

One wrong move could spur Baze to do something stupid that draws attention to himself. Gets him hurt.

Killed.

That sizzling darkness slithers free of the chasm inside my chest, and I feel it worming beneath my skin like fiery eels. A deadly promise of its own.

Swallowing, I straighten my shoulders and lift my chin, shifting my gaze back to the pyre. If I pretend he's not here, not watching, then I won't draw any attention to him. I won't have to look myself in the eye and see how much I've changed.

See the monster I've become.

"Orlaith?"

"I'm fine," I say—a pretty lie for my poisonous, shameful truth.

Cainon steps to the side, and I pull my arm farther back, the fletching brushing my ear. The flaming tip dances in the wind, my hair doing the same as I catch Vanth's wide, aching stare.

His lips move, muttering something overshadowed by the woman's howling screams.

I fail to force my heart to slow, remembering the broken look in Vanth's eyes after he shot his brother through the heart. The way he drank from that bottle of liquor as though he truly believed it was going to burn the blood off his hands.

I remember the way he growled at me to *scream*—like my own pain was the only remedy for his own.

*He's suffered enough.*

I lift my aim a smidge, threading a breath between my parted lips. I close my eyes, find a small sliver of silence tucked beneath my ribs, and release the string.

The arrow loosens, and I hear the distant thud, followed by a hush that blankets the crowd.

The howling stops, the only sound now the roar of my own blood gushing through my ears as I slam more shells atop my crumbling crystal domes.

"You missed."

I open my eyes.

Vanth's head is slumped forward, a blossom of blood swelling from where my arrow protrudes from his heart.

*No, I didn't ...*

There is no dousing surge of relief for the fire in my veins. No breath of fresh air that can clear the rotten filth from my lungs.

Tears well in my eyes, but I refuse to let them spill, slamming another shell atop the dome containing my flourishing self-disgust.

I look up at Cainon who's clutching the rail, chewing his lip. "I'm sorry."

"It's fine," he mutters, taking the bow. In a few swift motions he's snatched another arrow, set it alight, notched it, and then it's whizzing through the air so fast it's impossible to trace. It lands amongst the straw, and a violent burst of flames lick up the side of the pyre. Up Vanth's legs.

His body.

The smell of burning flesh hits, and it's an effort not to fold forward and vomit as I force myself to watch his skin bubble and blister, blacken and melt, until all that's left are his charred remains and a swirl of ash on the wind.

Cainon speaks with one of the guards below the podium while I stand beside the balustrade, fingers wrapped around the railing, bits of ash littering my dress and hair.

Drifting through my torpid insides.

I watch the thinning crowd, hunting a dark-blue cloak and a rebellious dash of sandy hair. Perhaps Zane feels my gaze on him because he finally turns, glancing up at me when his uncle stops to have a word with someone.

My heart leaps into my throat.

I unlatch the reticule from around my wrist and tuck it between two railing rungs, desperation widening my eyes.

He frowns but gives me a terse nod.

Pure, unguarded relief floods my veins, and I well up from the force of it, clearing my throat as I offer him a tight smile.

If anyone else were to notice the bag and pluck it from its hiding spot, they'd find it empty.

But *Zane* ...

He'll scope the lining, find the small slit in the side, then worm his fingers down and feel the folded notes I tucked within. One a placation, the other a plea—a note I pray makes it into his uncle's hands *soon* because I'm running out of time.

Cainon assists me down the stairs, and I'm boosted back onto the horse. A blow of wind wails through the lofty buildings, playing with the tendrils of my dress, lifting my hair off my neck just as Cainon climbs up behind me and settles me between his thighs.

But my attention isn't on the man at my back, wrapped around me like the bars of a prison cell. It's on *Baze* standing amongst the crowd.

Though his face is cast in shadow, I can feel the hot rake of his stare upon the bite mark as I hurriedly pull my hair back down to hide it. I feel that same stare scrape across my wrist, my cupla, like he sees it for the shackle it is.

He begins weaving through the crowd, shoving people aside in his haste.

Charging toward me.

My heart thrashes so hard and fast I'm certain I'm going to be sick, eyes widening with a silent plea.

I shake my head ever so slightly.

*No, Baze.*

*No—*

He doesn't still, doesn't even slow, drawing almost close enough for me to leap through the air and land in his arms. He's about to push free of the crowd when Cainon kicks the horse forward, catapulting us down the path so hard and fast I'm shoved against his chest.

He weaves his arm around my waist, tucking me close, and I want to feel repulsed. Want to sit in that feeling until it seeps through my skin and rots me to the core. But I can't feel anything beyond this wild fear wrestling inside my chest ...

*Baze saw.*

# CHAPTER

*Rhordyn*

## 27

Lungs convulsing for breath I cannot pull, I grope at the water, the river dumping me against rocks that pummel and pierce.

I dredge through the surface of the raging current with a coughing, retching heave. A torrent of thick, putrid liquid pours up my throat, lost to the violent churn of frothy rapids dragging me *away*—my surroundings a blur of blue and white.

I fist the talon and try to heave it out, screaming as I'm jerked against a rock so hard it shifts the weapon sideways, digging deeper into my rotten flesh.

*Get out of the river.*

*Just get out of the fucking river.*

I'm tossed around like driftwood, water punching up my nose and sloshing over my head. The current lugs me around a sharp bend toward a burbling abyss, and I choke down a breath before being sucked down the steep deluge, spat out into a steady stream of calmer water that allows me a moment to breathe.

Look around.

I catch sight of a low-hanging branch a second too late, trying to thrash against the current, fingers brushing it before my body loses strength. I'm ripped beneath the water, tumbling, mining the strength to move.

To try again.

*Seeing her face on the backs of my lids.*

Roaring, my muscles power into action, and I punch above the surface again, heaving my leaden arm up to snag a vine draped from another low-hanging branch. I lash against a boulder with bone-buckling force, my chest absorbing the brunt. A blade of pain impales me, forcing more liquid from my lungs with a bubbling choke.

Black dots blot my vision, multiplying, and my next heartbeat is slower than the last …

*No*—

With a growl, I plow through the blur and whip my other arm around the large, slippery boulder, my entire body clinging to its weight. Sharp ridges slice into my waterlogged hands as the current yanks at my legs and threatens to snatch me under.

I heft myself farther up the rock, one painful drag at a time, until I reach a plateau where I can roll onto my back. Groaning, I grit my teeth, looking down at the talon's hilt protruding from my chest, haunted by visions of her hand wrapped around it.

Fuck.

I grip it and *pull*.

It tears through the ladder of ribs with a bolt of searing

pain and a gush of rank-smelling blood. I throw my head back and *roar.*

The sky shakes, krah swarming as I put pressure on my ruptured chest. I look up, forcing my focus to narrow on my surroundings, wheezing through shredded echoes of the paralyzing pain.

I'm at the base of a ravine, sandwiched between sheer walls of dark-blue stone, scarce light shooting through the jungle's thick canopy.

*Still in Bahari.*

Through the gaps, ribbons of color dash across the ripening sky.

Evening.

*No.*

*How long have I been out for? A day? Two?*

*More?*

I hunt the few patches of sky, desperate for a glimpse of the moon so I can map its phase.

A frantic surge swells inside me when I fail to find it.

I exhale a rattling breath and roll sideways, coughing foul-tasting bile across the rocks while I cup that tiny seed notched in my chest, alight with a twinkling shine, its delicate roots woven deep where they belong.

Relief loosens some of the muscles in my chest and throat, making my next breath easier.

Smoother.

"Keep beating." The order is growled as I push onto all fours, looking up at the sheer cliff from between the gaps in my sodden hair.

My heart plummets.

It can't be higher than fifteen feet, but right now—with

a half-healed hole in my guts and leg and a split in my heart—it looks like a fucking mountain.

*Just keep fucking beating.*

With the talon still clutched in my fist, I crawl, stumble, and slide across algae-slicked rocks, black blood leaking from the rotten wound in my chest. I reach the vertical cliff, mapping its clefts and bumps, ignoring the black blots gathering in my vision like a swarm of flies.

I push to a swaying stand and slam my fist forward, impaling the talon deep into the rock face a foot above my head. Tightening my grip on the hilt, I hang my weight and lift myself with a chest-cleaving howl, certain my entrails are spilling from the puncture in my gut.

That the muscles in my thigh are fraying.

I dig my fingers into a cleft in the stone, scuff my sodden boot against another, then rip the talon free and swing myself higher. Stab the talon deep again.

*Again.*

More black blots muddy my vision, my body growing cold and heavy, forcing me to pause. I glance down at the sharp and slippery rocks below ...

*Not now.*

*I'll fucking die again.*

I tighten my grip on the talon as the world begins to blur, Orlaith's past words grating across my heart.

My soul.

*I just love you so much it hurts.*

I roar to the sky and the stone and this hole in my fucking chest stealing all my strength, wondering if she can hear me shredding the air as I rip the talon free and stab it into the rock. More blood oozes from my split chest, pushing between clenched teeth, bubbling past my tight lips.

She has no idea what's coming for her.

I pull and stab, pull and stab, finally hauling myself over the ledge. I flop down upon steady ground, wrestling wisps of breath.

*You're the happily ever after I don't deserve.*

A deep, gravelly laugh scrapes up my throat, wet and sticky, reeking of the rot leaching through my veins.

*You can't escape me, Milaje. You'll have to trap me in an iron coffin and drop me in the middle of the fucking ocean, and even then, I'll haunt your dreams.*

*Your nightmares.*

*I'll haunt you even when you try to die.*

My tattoos chew as I swipe at my chest, snagging the length of leather hanging around my neck.

The muscles beneath my tongue tingle ...

*No.*

Snarling, I shove to a stand, more warmth oozing down my torso. I wobble, slamming against a mossy tree, finding the other side bare.

*South.*

I lift a heavy boot. Thud it down.

Another step.

*Another.*

I keep moving, shoving past waxy shrubs, shouldering trees, hand clawing at my chest like it wants to gouge between my ribs and cradle that twinkling seed.

Just get to her ...

*I just have to get to her.*

My stuttering heart slows, breaths staggering. My head

goes light and airy, shadows dancing at the edge of my vision.

"*Stay awake!*" I wheeze past the rotten muck gathering in my lungs. Drowning me a little more with each wet heave.

My limbs grow heavier, and I swear the soil begins to ripple beneath me, making each step less steady than the last. My knees give way, and I hit the ground like a boulder.

A familiar deadly chill slips through my veins, and my head rolls to the side, like the world's tipping …

"Fuck," I gurgle as the blackness chomps down.

# CHAPTER 28

*Orlaith*

"You sure you're okay, petal?"

I nod, offering Cainon a soft smile even as the world tips, using the handle to the door of my suite to stop myself from falling.

*Plummeting.*

"Of course," I say, the blazing candelabras swaying. I blink away the haze, trying not to slur. "Go to your meeting. I need time to prepare for the trial tomorrow, anyway."

"Yes, you do." He steps close, rumbling in the back of his throat. It's a teeth-gritted battle not to flinch. Not to *recoil* as he presses a too-hot kiss upon my head that cleaves off another chunk of my heart.

Crumbles it to the nether.

He smells like fried flesh …

We *both* do.

"Get some sleep," he instructs as he moves toward the foyer door and swings it wide enough that I see Kolden standing sentry in the hall beyond, his stare firmly set *away.* "Tomorrow's a big day."

Passing me a hungry smile over his shoulder, he leaves, shutting the door behind himself.

I picture the lid of a coffin settling into place.

Releasing a shuddered exhale, I close my eyes, waiting until his steps fade down the hall before I crumple against the door, folding forward, hand slapped upon the wound on my throat. Cainon's bite mark—freshly torn.

Freshly *feasted* on.

I open my eyes. See the room's spinning.

Repress a whimper.

*Get inside—just get inside.*

I twist the door handle, stumbling as I push it wide. My legs buckle, and I watch the stone floor rush toward my face—

I'm jerked upright, bolstered by a hard body.

"Fuck," a deep, familiar voice hisses.

*Kolden.*

He sweeps me into his arms and shuts the door, then carries me farther into my suite and sets me on the bed. Shafts of silver moonlight pour through the open balcony doors, making my broken heart ache.

Mind drifting amidst the muddy haze of my heavy thoughts, I reach for the light, wanting to tangle my fingers through it ...

Kolden takes my outstretched hand and wraps it around a glass, nudging it toward my mouth. "Drink," he orders, tipping it to my lips.

I force the water down my throat until there's no more, and he lowers the glass, crouching before me.

An aching quiet settles between us as I gently untwist a vine from around my ribs and spine, gathering it like a spool before pulling its roots from the tender organ in my chest. A vine that sprouted from the splits in my heart, blooming a burst of dull, silvery flowers while Cainon clawed at me—his teeth so deep in my flesh I could feel them grating against my tendons. Like it was trying to tell me this is wrong.

*It's all wrong.*

I pinch the petals closed on the big, ashy blooms nipped with streaks of silver, tuck them amongst the vine's coiled mass, then reach for one of my ready-made domes and ease it into the hollow, cradling its wilting corpse until I can no longer watch it slip away. Until I can no longer feel its dying breath kissed upon my brow.

*Don't cry.*

I pin it against my insides with all the rest of the domes that are starting to look like gravestones.

"You need to go," I whisper, blinking, a tear rolling down my cheek. If Cainon catches Kolden in my room, there will be another burning.

I'd rather die than go through that again. Than watch those flames gobble him up.

"No," he growls, the impasse boiling. "With all due respect, my loyalties now lie with you."

"Why?"

He sighs, holding my stare as he says, "They just do."

My face crumbles, and I look away, desperate to avoid his eyes while this sudden surge of emotion strangles me.

The air between us tightens, and I feel his gaze scrape

across my throat. Across that raw ache thudding in my neck, making my stomach pitch with the need to vomit.

My cheeks burn as I reach for my freshly bound braid and drape it over my shoulder. "I'm fine, Kolden. I asked for it."

His stare hardens. "Asking out of want and asking out of *need* are two entirely different things."

*What I want, what I need, and what is right are three entirely different things.*

The backs of my eyes burn, Rhordyn's words landing a different blow than they did when I was bound in a red dress and my own cloistered naïvety.

I told him I wasn't as innocent as he thought. He told me I'd look back on the moment and realize I was wrong.

It hurts how right he was.

Nipping a glance at the door we came through, Kolden clears his throat. "What do you need me to do, Orlaith?"

Heart hammering with a feeble, hopeful beat, I tilt my head to the side. "Do?"

He leans forward, an intensity burning in his stare. "How can I *help?*"

A surge of relief impales me, a sudden alertness clearing some of the fog from my brain.

He wants to *help me.*

I dash a tear off my cheek, sniffling. "Do you ... Do you happen to know where the High Master's fleet is stationed?"

Kolden frowns, then gives me a tight nod that would bring me to my knees if I weren't already sitting.

My throat works, prickles bursting against the backs of my eyes as I release a shuddered breath, feeling the tides swirl around me, turning ...

Finally fucking *turning.*

"The—ah—urn over there," I say, raising a trembling hand to point at it. "There's some bits of parchment and a stick of sharpened coal stashed inside."

He stands and walks to the urn, lifting the lid and reaching in. I close my eyes and breathe, trying to stop the room from swaying.

*It's going to be okay.*

Kolden passes me a piece of parchment, and I flatten it against my thigh, then scratch a jittery note upon the surface—difficult with a shaking hand.

Signing the paper, I hand it to him. "Please take this to the mail tree and ask that it be sent to Cindra at Graves Inn. If you'd scribble your own instructions on how to find the fleet, that would be greatly appreciated."

I pause when I see the tiny crystal bloom sitting in his palm. The imperfect one with a few jagged petals from where I cracked them off.

Heart tumbling, my hand becomes still as I lift my eyes, looking at him. "I found it at the markets," I whisper.

The hard glint in his stare tells me he doesn't believe me before he even speaks. "If one of the Elders were to come across that—"

"I'll get rid of it." The words come out harsher than I intend them to, sown with a frantic seed.

His jaw hardens, and he regards me with intense focus. With another curt nod, he sets it in my palm, curls my fingers around it, then takes the parchment and makes for the door, easing it shut behind him with quiet finality.

My pulse roars in my ears, my tremble returning twofold—so rampant that when I push to my feet I almost crumple to the floor again. I make for the wall and lean against it, choking back the smell of smoke, citrus, and salt dousing my hair. My skin.

*This fucking dress.*

Groaning, I rip at the strips of material barely holding me together, feeling them tear beneath my jittery fingers as I stumble toward my washroom. I don't bother to turn the dial on the mounted lantern, opting instead for the comfort of the silver light spilling through the frosted windows.

I place my bloom on the ground and crank the faucet, then step beneath the spill of water that pours from the cleft in the wall, gasping at the rushing torrent of chill that drenches me from head to toe. Cupping my hands before my mouth, I draw deep, gulping drags that surge straight down my arid throat—shoving back images of Cainon's mouth on me. Of his teeth tearing at my already shredded flesh, making the same thick sound every time he swallowed.

*You bleed so beautifully for me …*

My body surrenders to the weight on my shoulders, and I crumble to the floor, hand slamming down to absorb the force. I screw up my face and release a silent scream that morphs into chest-wrenching sobs.

There's still so much that needs to fall into place, and with this fresh throb in my neck, with the smell of scorched flesh sitting in the back of my nose like a thick smog, I feel hopeless.

Drained.

*I can't afford to feel either of those things.*

I blindly slap at the wall and turn the faucet to warm, snatch a bar of pumice-infused soap, and scrub myself—

the warm water unlocking the complexities of the citrus-scented bar and making me want to gag.

Time slips by as I scrub harder than I ever have, the bar turning paper thin, disintegrating against my chafed skin.

I rest my head upon the wall, water puddling in my lap, and stare blankly ahead, my vision of the washroom distorted by the flowing wall that makes me think of Kai. How everything felt lighter with him around. How he would flash me one of his mischievous grins I couldn't help but mimic and my worries would sift away.

Just thinking about him almost makes me smile.

Lifting his conch to my lips, I tilt it, then pour three small words into the hollow scoop that gobbles them up ...

"*I miss you.*"

I instantly hate myself when the words come out raw and choked, weighing down the shell. Because I know he'll worry, and that's the last thing I want.

Swallowing thickly, I tuck the conch close to my heart. Something little shifts beyond the spilling water—darting through the door, then settling on the ground. My curiosity scrapes together my remaining dregs of energy, and I ease onto my knees, pushing my upper body past the gushing sheet.

Wiping my eyes, I look at the familiar sprite lost amid the steam, though I can still make out the tiny black piercing in the tip of her tapered ear, poking free from cloudy curls sticking out in all directions.

"Hi, Spider Bite."

She blinks at me.

My gaze drops to the package she's hugging against

her chest, as though it's the most precious thing she's ever been given.

"Is that for me?" I ask, composing my voice.

My face.

She nods, hopping forward, her fluffy brows bunched, worry staining her big, inky eyes.

"I'm fine," I rasp, flopping my hand onto the stone between us—palm up. "I just ... haven't eaten enough spiders today."

Her frown deepens, and I internally curse myself. I'll probably end up with a stack of them stuffed beneath my pillow later.

Another hop forward, the fierce flutter of her lacy wings softening her landing as she settles beside my hand and sets her package in my palm.

I curl my fingers around it.

"Thank you," I whisper, retrieving the bloom and placing it close, nudging it toward her. "For your troubles. You've been doing a lot of fluttering about for me lately. I'm sure it's very tiring ..."

She crouches, picks it up, and tucks it against her chest, looking down at the bloom, back at me, head tilted and eyes wide. With a slow nod that gains strength and speed, she leaps off the ground in a dusty blur, then darts through the doorway, disappearing from my line of sight.

I open my hand, looking at the parcel. Wondering.

*Hoping.*

I pick at the delicate knot of string binding it all together, unraveling the layer of silk to reveal a round, white seed no larger than the tip of my pinky finger.

For a moment, all I can do is stare, a lump swelling in my throat that's hard to swallow.

*He did it.*

Zane got my message. Made sure it got to his uncle. Meaning Zali got hers, as well.

*You're amazing, kid ...*

I clutch the seed within my fist and cradle it close to my heart, then ease onto my back, eyes closed, battling the wave of emotion threatening to wear me down.

Such a tiny, seemingly insignificant seed, but to me ... it's *everything*.

It's *hope*.

Not only do I have the antidote I desperately need for my plan to work, but this seed is a sign that Gunthar's on board with everything I need from him.

The rest is up to me.

My eyes pop open as I snarl, rolling onto my front, pushing onto my hands and knees. I crawl toward the doorframe and haul myself up, securing a towel around my trembling body.

I clamber toward my vanity, kiss the tiny senka seed, and poke it into the soil amongst my flush of wildflowers that will hopefully conceal its eventual bloom.

There's a knock on my door, and I groan, my finger still stuffed deep in the dirt. "Yes?"

It creaks open, Kolden's voice booming through the thin gap. "Izel is here with your evening tea and cake. Are you happy to accept her?"

I almost decline, but then I think of my growing collection of bane bush berries—the ones I've been plucking from most meals delivered to my room.

*It wouldn't hurt to have a few more.*

I wipe my dirty finger on my towel, then begin loosening my braid. "Thank you. Send her in."

Izel breezes through the doorway, balancing a teacup and a plate with a large slice of ... something I've never seen before—layers of custard and pastry all perched atop each other in a pretty stack. I eye it curiously, still unraveling my plait as she sets the refreshments before me with a little golden fork.

"I thought you might like some chamomile tea to help you sleep," she says, offering me a soft smile that lights up her blue eyes—usually hard like flints.

It almost knocks me off my stool.

The candlelight illuminates her tidy bun and burnished skin as she draws a shuddered breath. "It's been a ... rough day for us all," she croaks, and I feel those words cleave between my ribs, wanting to coil around the ache.

"It has." I return her smile. "Thank you, Izel. I really appreciate the thought."

With a dip of her head, she leaves, shutting the door behind herself.

My smile morphs into a frown.

She seemed ... *sincere.*

*Maybe our relationship is finally turning a corner?*

I toss my hair over my shoulders, then lift the top layer of pastry, find three teensy berries smudged amongst the custard, and sigh.

*Maybe not.*

I clean them on my towel, then push both plates aside, yanking the drawer open. I retrieve the tiny vial I've been filling with the bane bush berries, corking the top before

I pull out my dagger and wave the already charred length through the flame of a stubby wall sconce.

A deep sense of nostalgia blankets me like a frosty breath blown across my neck ...

I whip the blade through the air, waiting until it's cooled before I press the honed tip into the pad of my thumb, hissing as a bite of sting punches through my flesh. A bead of blood swells, rich and red and thicker than usual.

I let one, two, *three* drips splash directly upon the seed, then cover it with soil and ring out my braid, showering the mound with a healthy dribble of water. "Please bloom," I whisper.

*Please.*

"You can do it. I *know* you can."

Giving the small pot an encouraging pat, I suck the hurt on my thumb and turn my attention to the bed, edging toward it on frail legs that seem to be finding their strength. I thread my hand beneath the mattress, fingers grazing the leather sheath *he* gave me.

I tug it out, brushing my thumb across the straps, the buckles, pulling it close and drawing deep through my nose, catching the faintest wisp of crisp, robust *him.*

My domes rattle, the seed of a whimper slipping through my tightening throat ...

I tuck the sheath away again with a tenderness I wish he saw, then screw my eyes shut and shake my head. Once.

Twice.

I grasp my chisel and whip it out, a fire igniting in my chest.

*I have a hole to finish.*

# CHAPTER
*Kai*
## 29

She's bound against my rib cage, tucked beneath my arm, beautifully naked—her cheeks flushed with a glorious glow that makes my heart thump with satisfaction. That makes a different part of me thump with the swelling warmth of deep, ravenous *want*.

I groan as my cock tents the furs. I'm just reaching over to brush the back of my hand across her cheek when Zykanth slams his tail against my ribs—like a chastisement.

My hand whips back, and I bare my teeth at him, releasing an internal growl that rattles his cage. 'What in all five seas was *that* for?'

'*Little man let soft little mate sleep big sleep. Soft little mate tired.*'

Frowning, I reach back, slipping my hand under my head instead of traversing it over her curves, looking up at the crystal ceiling that's ablaze in a riot of color from the moonlight shafting in through the window. Wondering when *Zykanth* became the voice of reason.

Not sure how I feel about that.

He's right, though. She's probably exhausted. But just the thought that she's exhausted from *me* gets me fucking harder, and that's not going to fix anything.

I should get up, get some air. Maybe … *go for a walk.*

Zykanth rumbles his approval. '*Yes, walk little legs. Down track, over grass, down track, down stairs. Down, down, down …*'

'I know what you're up to,' I mutter, easing off the snowy furs. Rolling another, I fold it around her like a nest before I press a kiss against her temple. I pull on the patchy shorts—far too short and tight—and, with a groan, tuck my throbbing cock into the constricting material. Threading the buttons into their holes, I steal another glance at Vicious …

*Maybe just a quick—*

Zykanth snaps his maw around my rib, and I wince, deciding it's best to take this tussle outside.

I head out the door, snipping it shut behind me.

"You're acting weird," I growl, the crisp night air a refreshing nip to my skin. Working wonders on my hot, hard want as I weave down crystal trails, escorted by ribbons of color hanging low in the sky.

'*Soft little mate need rest. Little man blind.*'

'And you're a pain in my balls.'

I tell myself I'm just going to check on the vegetable patch the young ones planted earlier today—at least until I *pass* the vegetable patch and can no longer continue lying.

I had no idea there was a trove beneath this island. Some lucky drake must have camouflaged the entrance *very* well all those years ago. It's impossible to fathom what unlikely treasures such a cunning beast would have hoarded ... until they no doubt became a feast for the beast that now roams these waters.

An uncracked trove over a thousand years old ...

Salivating, I swallow.

'Just one look,' I warn Zykanth, who's practically dragging me forward by his bitten grip on my spleen. 'No touching.'

'*Little touch?*'

'You never just *touch.*'

'*Steal instead?*'

Exactly.

I jog down the quiet tunnel bathed in filtered moonlight mottled with every color of the rainbow, spilling into the cavern, coming to a stop a few steps away from the well I watched the young one drop that sparkly rose into.

'*Why stop?*'

'I don't know,' I murmur, a shiver running the length of my spine as I look at the skewed rift, something tapping at me that I can't quite put my finger on. 'Something feels ... wrong.'

'*Little man turned soft man.*' Zykanth thrashes against my rib cage so hard I grunt, but he doesn't stop. He keeps going, going, going, making it hard to draw breath—like I'm taking fisted blows to the chest. '*Forget how to drake.*'

'How about— I shove a— clam in your— mouth?' I grit out between violent blows.

'*Big talk for little man with tiny legs.*'

Sighing, I ease forward, looking down the sheer drop to the glimmering water below, feeling my eyes glaze.

Zyke stills, charmed by the sight, sending a *tap-tap-tap*

down into the abyss as I swallow thickly, the urge to have and hold and cradle and *steal* boiling in my chest …

*'Yes! Yes! Yes! Steal treasures. Build big trove for little chosen one. Much work. Zykanth only one who thinks important things. Little man think with wrong head.'*

Actually, he has a point. We absolutely need a bigger trove. More treasure to impress her.

*'More seaweed for soft bed.'*

'Okay, you've convinced me,' I concede, praying there's an exit that doesn't spit me out in the ocean. Or that I can find a way to climb up through the hole again afterward. 'It would be nice to get my tail out …'

Anver's right—it's been too long.

*'Yes. too long. Exercise tail in trove. Swirl, swirl, swirl!'*

'If we find anything good, I guess we can just take it back to the hut and store it amongst Vicious's pile of knickknacks.'

*'Yes! Impress little savage one,'* Zykanth trills, churning round so fast he's a scaled blur. *'Steal, little hands! Go now.'*

Heart thumping hard, I take off the shorts, happy to toss them aside as I move to the pinched end of the hole. Shifting to the edge, I plant one hand on either side of the jagged cleft and ease forward, drop all my weight into my shoulders, then lower my feet toward the depths.

A tingling sensation kindles at the tips of my toes, rippling up my legs. My skin tears, scales peeling to the surface, bones extending—blunt tips tapering off. My feet elongate, stretching out like curling waves that swish and sway to the flexing dance of my mighty muscles.

A smile spreads across my lips as the point of our frilly

tail brushes the surface of the water far below, euphoria flooding my veins—

'I miss you.'

The words whisper up from the water's depths, sharpening, spearing through my heart and making my stomach convulse. Making Zykanth still so fast my arms buckle.

*'Treasured one ...'*

My smile drops as I cling to the edge of the well, her voice raw and halting. Churned out on a sob. Her words not an admission, but a *plea*.

I swallow the bile rising in my throat, releasing a pained groan ...

*Orlaith needs me.*

Her words haunt me, her chilling whisper pulsing up and down my spine as I look at Vicious sound asleep coiled within the nest I bound her in.

I study her beautiful lines, aching at the thought of leaving her.

Knowing I have no choice.

It's too dangerous for her out there in the big wide ocean. I may not make it across the abyss myself, so I can't risk taking her in Zykanth's mouth.

Won't.

She stirs, blinking up at me, her eyes like sleepy suns that glow in the dark amongst her whitewash of hair.

"Mine," she says, reaching for me with one arm.

I give her a melancholy smile. "Yours, Vicious. Always yours."

She frowns as I push my pants off and tuck into the furs beside her, lengthening her body so the plump curve of her ass is pressed against my thighs. She stretches around, twisting at the waist to set her hand upon my cheek, then searches my eyes in slow sweeps, like she's trying to delve beneath the waters.

"Mine," she repeats, lifting my hand off her hip and coaxing it down the slope of her belly.

*Farther.*

Easing me toward her wet, swollen entrance.

I groan, running my fingers through her, swirling around that nub that makes her jolt against me.

Her lids flutter closed as she squirms, arching her neck, baring a stretch of beautiful sun-kissed skin to my hungry mouth. I lave at her, feeling her skin burst with goosebumps beneath my lips, grazing my teeth along her delicate flesh.

"Mine," she cries, tilting her hips so she's splayed against my hardening cock, rocking, lifting her leg and draping it over my thigh—telling me exactly what she wants.

I raise my left leg and split hers apart. "Yours, Vicious," I whisper upon her throat as I open her with my fingers, coaxing the head of my thick, aching cock against her entrance. "*Yours,*" I growl, and drive up into her clamping depths with a spear of my hips—wishing this could fix everything. Wishing this could shift the heavy guilt from my shoulders.

Devastated by thoughts that she won't understand.

275

# CHAPTER
## *Orlaith*
## 30

I slip down the stairwell, checking over my shoulder as I spill into the lobby on silent steps, my chisel tucked in the back pocket of my leather pants. Dashing toward Old Hattie's room, I frown when I poke my head in and find her stool empty, her weft stick still lodged at an odd angle in her half-finished tapestry.

An uneasy sense of dread roosts upon my chest.

I force myself to continue, dodging from shadow to shadow in case anybody else is roaming the palace at this late hour. But it's quiet.

Empty.

It's not until I'm charging down the stairway that leads to the hall of tapestries that I hear the first sounds of life: a faint *ping-ping-ping* coming from the direction of my hole.

My pulse scatters.

Slipping my hand in my pocket to grip hold of my chisel, I peek over my shoulder, then ensure my wet hair is plastered against my wound as I tiptoe along the dark hall, edging toward frail slivers of fiery light spilling from behind the tapestry that hides my hole-in-progress.

It bumps and swells like somebody's bunched behind it, that muffled *ping-ping—ping* chipping apart the silence with relentless force.

Approaching with slow, cautious ease, I keep my steps soft until I hear a muted whimper. Goosebumps burst across my skin.

*I know that sound ...*

I lift the tapestry and release a flood of lantern light, seeing Old Hattie tucked in my hole in her soiled nightgown, her knobbled limbs all torn and grazed.

I gasp.

Startling, she spins. Cheeks tracked with tears, her wide, bloodshot eyes almost spear straight through me. The potent punch of her fear clogs the back of my throat and nearly brings me to my knees, but then her face crumbles with what looks like relief.

Her entire body jerks with deep, silent sobs—her sound somehow managing to stay locked in her chest, more fresh tears rolling down her cheeks. Her beautiful, talented hands are lumped in her lap, gnarled and blistered, one still clutching the hilt of a worn kitchen knife and a scrunched rag she must have been using to muffle the sound.

A bloody bandage covers her right hand, though the shape is ... different. Like her middle finger's—

My other hand slams against the wall to steady myself.

*Her finger's gone.*

She continues to convulse, soundless sobs racking her frail form.

I find it hard to believe Cainon would let something like this happen to his governess. Not under his roof.

*Unless ...*

A hideous thought worms to the forefront of my mind, gnashing flesh and bone to get there. "Did *Cainon* do this to you, Hattie?"

The crush of her face, the silent heave of her chest ... It's all the answer I need.

I remember the pretty story he told me about this poor broken woman, painting himself out to be her hero. Such ugly, rotten lies.

I lift the rattling shell containing my anger, letting it squirm a slashed path up my throat. My jaw hardens, teeth chattering with the power of my untethered rage, this deep ache pushing down into my canines, like they're trying to pop out of my gums.

Crouching, I remove the knife from her grip, gently catch her trembling hands, and press my forehead against hers—waiting for the tide of her emotions to drop. When the convulsions finally break, I pull back and capture her weary gaze. "I've got this," I whisper, forcing a soft smile when all my edges feel sharp.

*Piercing.*

"I'm going to make it better, Hattie. I promise."

A strangled sound whittles out of her, and she cups my cheek, nodding. I help her from the hole, her knobbly limbs unraveling with a gush of stone shards that have me blinking at the mess, wondering if I forgot to dispose of the last lot.

Must have. There's ... *too much.*

Hattie hands me the lantern and shuffles down the

hallway without looking back—her feet bare, hair a loose, wild trail of silver dragging along the floor in her wake.

She disappears into the darkness.

The tapestry bulges the slightest amount, and I ease it back, frowning as I brush more shards into the hallway. Tucking into the hollow, I set the lantern down and run my hand across the deep dents of Hattie's progress, finding a hole I can almost fit my fist through.

For a moment, all I can do is stare, coasting my fingers around the honed edges, drawing on the musty scent pouring in from behind, tinted with the distant, familiar smell of death.

Of *blood*.

I shake my head in disbelief …

*She broke through to the other side.*

# CHAPTER 31

*Zali*

The streets are bathed in gray, the air still thick with smoke from the burning that wafts through the alleys, blotting the rays of the rising sun.

Robed worshipers shift through the streets in silent flocks. Even the Gray Guards are still out in tromping droves, dressed in their signature chain mail and iron breastplates stamped with an upside-down v, longbows in hand, quivers sheathed down their spines.

I duck into a side alley to dodge another barreling charge, two of the guards speaking of a fire at the temple yesterday morning. About their *stores* being lost in the blaze.

I can only guess what that means.

A smirk stretches across my face ...

*Karma, you fierce thing.*

Their footfalls fade, and I push on, my hood pulled far enough forward to hide my face from anyone who might be peeking through windows to see what all the commotion is about. Not everyone would be able to recognize me without my sword strapped to my back or my sigil pinned to my cloak, but I can't be too careful.

The Inn's sign creaks in the breeze, stirring up wisps of smoke that had settled over the cobbles as I pull the heavy door open. The bell tolls my early-morning welcome, and I ease my hood back onto my shoulders, surprised to find Graves already up, looking at me from behind the bar.

Quill poised over a piece of parchment, he raises a brow.

I give him a firm nod.

*All set. Now, it's just a waiting game.*

Graves gives me a tired smile, then waves me on before disappearing through the back door, fanning the scent of freshly baked bread into the room. I weave between tables topped with upturned chairs and make for the stairs, climbing to the second floor.

Standing before my room, I'm just about to dig my key into the lock when I realize the door is already cracked open. The rich, woodsy scent of nightshade catches me off guard, slamming into the back of my throat, almost knocking me off my feet.

*Baze.*

I swallow the cloying lump in my throat, battling the tremble of my upper lip threatening to curl back.

*He should know better ...*

Shoving the door open, I step into the dim room and close it behind me.

Hand pressed against the wall, Baze is standing before the window, looking out upon the waking world.

I still, frowning at the fine stubble on his head. My gaze carves the expanse of his broad shoulders, and my heart drops at the peeled and blistered skin spread across the taut blades.

"Baze ..." I rush forward, fingers poised above a patch of bubbled wounds.

*Burns.*

Clearing my throat, I move to the bathroom, dampen a washcloth, and race back, about to drape it across his sores—

He turns so fast he's a blur of motion, catching my wrist in his fist. "Don't," he says, the word a quiet wound, his eyes shaded with a daunting shadow that makes my skin prickle.

I breathe in his scent, woodsy and floral spiced, and the heady musk of ... *sex.*

He's been *fucking* somebody.

My upper lip threatens to peel back before I catch notes of something else mingling with the potent smell ...

The acrid tang of *smoke*. Of fried flesh—*not his.*

Either he was at the burning, or—

Remembering the Gray Guards charging through the streets, my stomach pitches.

Not charging.

*Hunting.*

"The temple," I whisper, sliding back a step, raking my gaze across him like I'm seeing him for the first time.

He drops my wrist, keeping his lips tight, watching me retreat another step.

Another.

"You're the reason the guards have been out in droves," I snarl, feeling all the blood drop from my face, replaced with a punch of *rage*. "I told you to keep away!"

His chest shakes with a silent laugh, a twisted smile breaking across his face as he runs his hand over his bald head. "What's the point?"

"Don't say that," I growl through a snap of teeth.

His face smooths in the blink of an eye, and he leans against the windowsill, stretching his legs before him and crossing them at the ankles. "I need to ask you something."

The words are clipped, and even though his eyes are shaded by the lack of light in this room, I can feel the accusing slice of his stare.

Some of his anger ... it's directed at me.

"Well, ask me."

His gaze drops to the floor at my feet, and he seems to hold his breath, like he's reconsidering.

My patience frays. "Don't fucking cower from the question, Baze. *Ask!*"

He sighs, condemning me with an unblinking stare. "I saw her today. At the burning. She was trying to hide a *bite mark* on her neck."

My lungs turn to sandstone, hand flying to my mouth.

*Cainon fed on her ...*

Something darkens in Baze's eyes, making me recoil as I realize—

"You thought I knew."

His silence is answer enough.

I storm toward the bed and crouch, reaching beneath it to retrieve a small wooden box, tipping the lid as I stand. "There is *nothing* in here that suggests she's been in danger," I say, showing him the note some kid left at the bar for me after the burning, as well as the one Cindra received from

Kolden and Orlaith. Shoving the box against his chest, I look up into his eyes. "*Nothing.*"

"But she is," he growls, pummeling me with his breath—untainted by spirits. In fact, he looks utterly sober, eyes clearer than I've seen them in years, which only makes his actions and the erratic energy rippling off him *more* chilling. "She's in danger. And there's something in her eyes that tells me she doesn't even give a fuck."

*Shit.*

This is not a conversation that's mine to have. It's hers. Unfortunately, I'm incapable of lying to him.

I just can't bring myself to do it.

"I know," I admit, drawing a slow breath as I drop my gaze to his chest. "I've also seen that look in her eyes."

Tension cuts the air.

There's a palpable pause before he threads his finger beneath my chin and tilts my head, forcing me to regain his eye contact. "I'm going to need you to be a bit more specific."

The softest push of his finger, and something inside me melts.

"I ... found her in his bed, overdosed on caspun. I don't think it was her intention, but—" I swallow, watching the color drain from his face. "I could tell she wanted to follow him ... if you know what I mean."

His eyes glaze, stare drifting behind me for a long beat. Then he shoves past, storming for the door.

I whirl.

"Where are you going?"

"To fucking *get* her," he barks, and my pulse pitches.

I sprint forward.

He opens the door, but I punch it closed. He turns, staring ahead, becoming still.

Thoughts churning, I press the box against his chest again, nudging it gently. Urging him to look.

To *read.*

"There's a plan, Baze. We're so close to securing what we need to break into Vadon's territory and stem these Vruk attacks at the source, but everything hinges on the first part of the ceremony taking place. It's the only way we can get the ships without inciting war."

"You're telling me to put the ships above her," he states, voice flat.

*Dangerous.*

"It's what she would want."

He whirls so fast I'm suddenly pressed to the door, his hands slamming either side of my head, an untethered look in his eyes. "Because she has *survivor's guilt!*"

My upper lip peels back, my energy swelling against his until we're an angry clash of tension. "We're in too deep. If we pull the plug now, we lose *everything.*"

I let my eyes say what my words do not. That I'll lose this one chance to get what I need to protect my people.

The only family I have.

"Tell me," he snarls, dropping his head lower so we're eye to eye, dousing each other in violent exhales. "Would *Rhordyn* sit idly in the background if he were here? If he'd seen what I saw in that city square today?"

I grit my teeth so hard they ache.

He's right, of course. But I have a duty. If I led with my heart, I would never have survived The Vein.

The dunes.

I would not have become High Mistress.

Out there, everything's a weapon if you're desperate enough. I wonder if Orlaith is beginning to realize that, too. I can't wrap my head around a reality where she'd let Cainon bite her unless she had a very good reason.

But I can't dwell on that right now.

"I have to make the right decision for my people," I say, my voice a knuckle-bearing blow.

Baze clicks his tongue, then pushes off the door and leans back, crossing his arms over his chest as he dips his head to the side.

The look he gives me is a shiv through the ribs.

"Perhaps that's what you've been doing all along. Perhaps *that's* the real reason you didn't tell me she was listening outside the office that day when Cainon proposed their coupling."

The words land like a blow to the jaw, and I suddenly wish he was drunk.

"You don't mean that ..."

He sniffs, turns, and picks his sword up off the end of my bed. "I'll do as you've *ordered*," he says, voice spiked with enough venom to stop a heart. "But if anything happens to her, I'll never forgive you. Or myself."

He shoves the box against my chest, pulls the door open, then leaves me choking on the smell of smoke, sex, and rage.

# CHAPTER
*Kai*

## 32

Steps heavy, I weave up the jagged stairway carved into the lofty tower of crystal, cresting a rise that releases me onto a small plateau—like someone scooped out some stone and made a sheltered inlet.

A diving platform.

I look out upon the ocean that's a stretch of glass bathed in the same soft peach as the sky. It would almost be impossible to pinpoint the horizon if it weren't for the icebergs scattered across the still.

I look down the cliff to the ocean far below—a jump I've made many times.

*Before.*

Now the prospect feels a bit like leaping into a gaping, monstrous maw ready to crunch down on me, slurp the meat off my bones, then spit them out on the shore. The beast that roams these waters does not discriminate between what she does and does not eat.

Destroy.

Is she down there now? Looking up at me? Waiting for me to jump so she can *pounce?*

Crouching, I run my hands through my hair, tugging at the roots as Orlaith's admission *tap-tap-taps* at me.

*I miss you.*

*I miss you.*

*I miss you.*

The sawtooth edges of those three words shred my heart straight down the middle.

*If something happens to her, I'll never forgive myself.*

*She needs to be here—with her people.*

*She needs to come home.*

'What do we do?'

Zyke has been so silent inside me, coiled in a knot of scales and frills, watching through big, green eyes. The erratic beat of his indecision pulsing through my blood and bones.

'*Soft little mate safe in sparkly rut hut.* Not *safe in too still sea. Zykanth swim real fast with big strong tail. Check on treasured one. Find soft little mate sparkly rock for big sorry. Little man poke soft little mate with tiny love stick. Soft little mate make big forgive.*'

Fuck.

I need to speak with her. At least *try* to make her understand.

I push up, spinning. Heart stilling at the sight of Vicious cresting the rise of steps.

Her hair is a wild dash of disarray, eyes like rising suns—still heavy from sleep as her snowy brows pull together. Confusion stains her stare, and she looks to the drop behind me, back again.

My skin pebbles, responding to her nearness like the sea tides to the moon.

She shakes her head, and the two halves of my heart fall away from each other.

*She knows I'm leaving.*

"I have to, Vicious ..." I steal a step forward, crushing the space between us while she looks at me through wide eyes. "I must help a treasured one. You stay. I go. *Dangerous.*"

*Too* dangerous for her.

"Mine," she growls, shaking her head, tears slipping down her flushed cheeks as she steps forward and tips onto her toes, then takes my face in her hands. "*Mine!*"

The hurt in her eyes plows through my layers like a fucking gaff.

"Yes," I rasp. "*Yours.* I'll return *soon.*" My determination to outrun the hungry waters will also get me back. To her. "You stay. *Safe.* Nothing can get you here so long as you stay out of the water."

Confusion swims in her glistening eyes, then her expression hardens, upper lip peeling back as a snarl builds in the back of her throat. "*Come.*"

My lungs compact.

*Come ...*

The second word she's ever spoken and it's another spear through my fucking chest. Because I want her to come more than anything. Want to take her to my trove and show her my treasures.

She's my chosen. I want to go everywhere with her—always.

*Forever.*

But there's a hungry beast lurking in the water. I'd never forgive myself if something happened to her because I lured her away from her safety net.

"*Come!*" she screams, the words clawing at me as she paws at my face, my arms. As she nuzzles into my chest.

'*Little chosen one thinks big strong. One chomp, gone.*'

A pained sound rips up my throat.

I walk her back against the crystal until we're a clash of hard and soft, and take her face in my hands, looking down into her wide eyes. "You can't, Vicious. You *can't.*"

Her features scrunch up, and I feel my heart do the same.

I dip my face into her neck and press a kiss to her flesh—

She shoves at my chest so hard I stumble back toward the edge, heaving breath, looking into wild eyes.

'*Hmm. Little chosen one bit strong ...*'

Her lips are peeled back from her teeth, forehead a crush of fine, snowy brows as she heaves serrated breaths, eyes blazing with a heartbreaking mix of pain and rage.

*She doesn't understand ...*

I close my eyes, choking beneath the oppressive weight of this harsh reality.

'*Go little man. Make big jump. Zykanth find big treasures. Make little savage one not mad.*'

He's right. Prolonging this hurt isn't going to make it any better. I just need to go.

*The quicker I go, the quicker I'll return.*

"I'll be back," I rasp, sliding back a step.

Another.

My feet tingle with the promise of frills and scales.

"*Coming back*," I growl, and a snarl saws up her throat.

When I can no longer take the pain in her eyes, I spin.

Run.

*Leap.*

The fall is too swift, the plunge too slow—the water a crispy gulp to my sea-starved heart.

I pull a breath through my gills, feeling the power of the ocean pour into my bloodstream as my bones stretch and swell, jaw popping.

Skin ripping.

Shorts *shredding*.

A slew of piercing teeth spears down from my expanding gums with clamping might, scales peeling upward and smothering my soft skin. Water wings sprout from between my ribs, fanning, and my legs bind into a massive, mighty tail.

With a powerful churn of our body, Zykanth spears through the crystal clear like a silver speck in a sky full of black—a desperate, heart-pounding dash. The ocean rumbles against our skin, and an angry current begins to shove and pull.

Twist and heave.

To gush against our scales and make our frills flutter.

*Shit.*

'Faster, Zyke! We're too out in the open!'

'*Quiet. Zykanth not focus when little man whine.*'

We spear toward the shifting icebergs, their glistening roots reaching into the dark depths. We worm between their shifting might, slurped down tightening gaps, chased by booming blows as we narrowly avoid being crushed—once.

Twice.

We come to a vast, empty space—the next iceberg a distant beacon in the gloom.

*'Little man hold big rib.'*

I do as he says as we surge into the emptiness, the dappled, flickering light coming from above barely a match for the darkness surrounding us, almost at the berg when a coiling whirlpool appears below.

A hungry current that *snatches* us.

We're pulled into its murky depths, rolling and thrashing, powerless against the spiraling fury. There's the flash of a buttery tail within the raging swirl, a stream of bubbles that blow against our face, before we're spat out amidst the calm like a chewed bite.

Free.

Fucking *free.*

'Go, Zyke. Go!'

We power through the ocean, punching free of the abyss, heart hammering, tail churning. Pushing us farther and farther away from our Vicious.

Zykanth releases a chilling squeal into the churning sea, my heart still perched on a cliff at our backs.

Knowing I've done the right thing. Hating myself anyway.

*Forgive me, Vicious ...*

# CHAPTER
*Cainon*
## 33

I scan the crowd, relishing their palpable excitement.
*Feeding* off it.

Every inch of the tiered seating is crammed with wide-eyed men, women, and children jostling, laughing, the smell of their eagerness and greed a potent reminder that there hasn't been a public trial for *years*. Not since my Low Masters and Mistresses became hooked on Candescence.

People stopped dying; stopped bringing new flesh into my well-stacked monarchy.

I like it this way. When your lifespan is never-ending, you swiftly learn the great quality of surrounding yourself with people you trust.

Or *control*.

I lean back in my chair, arms folded, knee bouncing in anticipation. Feeling like one of the kids who keep jiggling in their seat, asking when it's going to start. My personal viewing platform is tucked within the rows of seating high above The Bowl, offering a clear view of the entire amphitheater.

The *best* view.

A subtle knock on my door has my head snapping to the side. "Yes?"

It creaks open, and my guard speaks through the gap. "The High Septum, Master."

"Let her in," I say, shoving to my feet.

The door swings wide, and Heira limps through, dressed in her ornamental robe—similar to her usual but with a shimmery overlay—the door shutting behind her.

"Finally." I take her hand and tuck it in the crook of my arm, escorting her to her solid gold cathedra right beside mine. "I was beginning to think I would have to make the announcement without you."

She smiles up at me, but it lacks its familiar twinkle. "I wouldn't miss it for the world. The tempest is quiet today, is she not?" Heira muses through a wince as she lowers to her seat, and I think of the surging pound that usually drums against the bluff this cavern is dug beneath. "Seems the Gods are listening."

"Hopefully that's a good sign," I murmur, pulling back her hood to reveal a long, perfectly woven plait.

Disappointment drops into my gut like a rock.

Frowning, I ease it back over the seat and let it flop. "You already braided it ..."

"I knew we were going to be short on time," she says, reaching over her shoulder to give my hand a placating pat. "But I'd *love* some refreshments."

"Of course," I say, clearing my throat. "I have all your favorites."

Nipping a glance at the big stone doors Orlaith will soon emerge through, I move to the table at Heira's back stacked with food and begin setting some strawberries in a bowl, then some grapes and cubes of cheese. "Is everything okay?" I ask. "You seem ... *tense.*"

"I am particularly troubled, I admit. Yesterday morning there was a situation at the temple. It's what I wanted to speak with you about before your *promised* came down the stairs and stole your attention."

*Fuck.*

I pause, looking at her over my shoulder. "Apologies, Heira. I intended on coming across the river last night, but I had a meeting with a Regional Master that ran late."

I don't tell her the reason it ran late was because it *started* late. Because I got distracted feasting on my pretty flower. I get the sense that it won't go down well, given their frosty encounter yesterday.

"That's why there's been more Gray Guards on this side of the river?" I query.

"Correct."

"Nothing too serious, I hope?"

"Unfortunately, yes. Very."

I frown.

Setting the bowl on the small table beside her, I notice the tightness around her eyes as I drape myself in my cathedra and gesture for her to continue.

She picks a strawberry off the pile and rips off the greenery. "An ungodly *rat* infiltrated our ranks and set fire to a month's supply of Candescence," she seethes, and my eyes widen.

"How did *that* happen?"

"I'm uncertain, but we're hunting the culprit." She bites into the strawberry with a brutal sort of savagery I can appreciate, swallowing her mouthful. "They also set fire to a room full of worshipers. Only one survived. She's badly injured, suffering from burns and smoke inhalation, but I trust we will receive a full description of the vile, scuttling rat once she's able to do so."

*No wonder Heira looks so fucking riled.*

"I'm sorry. I know how much this will impact your duties to the Gods." I reach for her hand. "Is there anything I can do?"

"Pray the Gods have a plan that will work in our favor," she says, giving me a tight smile that doesn't reach her eyes. "This is a painful setback, not only for us but for *everyone.*" She scans the crowd like she's scouring each face. "I refuse to let *anything* get in my way of finding Shadow's Hand— least of all this strike of ungodly malice."

I nod my agreement as she rips the green off another strawberry and bites into its flushed flesh.

The drums begin to pound—deep, thudding *booms* that make the air feel like it's beating against my skin. My heart flips, attention whipping to the doors at the top of the stairs, watching them creak open.

A silence blankets the crowd.

A string of robed worshipers file down the steps, hoods pulled low over their faces. They pour around The Bowl, forming a complete circle, hands clasped together so the draped scoops of their sleeves connect.

The drums take on a different, more frantic tempo that stirs the rate of my heart, and two Elders step onto the stairway in synchronized harmony, garbed in their ceremonial robes akin to the High Septum's.

Orlaith emerges behind them dressed in a spill of plain gray fabric, stealing my breath. Her hood is draped around her shoulders, hair braided to look like a golden crown sitting upon her head. The crowd erupts with a deafening roar of elation that spurs all the way to my hardening cock.

Clearing my throat, I shift in my seat, watching her descend the stairs in that liquid way she moves—like her feet barely touch the ground. Reaching the bottom, she's led between two of the tall, glass aquariums dotted around The Bowl, coming to a halt.

Her flat eyes are cast ahead as the Elders ease the cloak off her shoulders.

*Fuck.*

A gray bodysuit clings to every dip and curve of her lithe, ethereal body like a second skin, covering her arms, her legs, her *neck*—concealing the pretty flesh I love so much. Bringing my greedy nature a spike of satisfaction.

Her cupla is on bold display, so bright against the gray. *Mine.*

*All mine.*

"She is a very beautiful woman, Cainon."

I glance sidelong at Heira, who's watching Orlaith with a baited sort of intrigue. "She is, yes."

"For someone who spent most of her life too afraid to leave the grounds of Castle Noir, I did not expect to encounter such a fiery presence." She peels her gaze away and looks at me from beneath her hood. "I thought the girl to be a mute, skittish thing."

My mind tumbles back to last night. To the way Orlaith's

body opened for me like a blooming flower when I latched onto the side of her neck and drank her silky warmth. To the deep, guttural moan she released that almost had me ripping into her in other ways.

I twirl my cupla around my wrist. "Anything but," I rumble, eating up Orlaith's curves with my ravenous stare.

*Anything but.*

"She is not going to steal you from me, is she?"

Heira's strained voice knocks me off guard, snatching my stare. I lift her hand and brush my lips across her knuckles. "*Never,*" I growl, a promise and a plea. An answer I thought she surely knew.

Relief floods her eyes, and she gives me that soft, nourishing smile I love so much, then turns her attention forward again. Together, we watch other Shulák splash Orlaith with sacred water scooped from the bowl of Mount Ether, preparing her for the trial while they chant to the rhythm of the thudding drums.

Orlaith doesn't blink, doesn't flinch, and for the first time, I notice the dark circles beneath her eyes. Her pasty complexion.

I frown.

Her body is obviously struggling to keep up with my ... *rabid* demands. I must try to stop sooner next time, but it's just so fucking hard to control myself with her when she gives herself to me so beautifully.

So *willingly.*

"Arrangements have been made," Heira says, interrupting my inner musings.

"For?"

"Should Orlaith fail the trial today, there will be no

burning, but a whipping instead. In the city square. Thirty lashes. Enough that she will look as though she's beyond repair, though I'm certain you will still find use for her."

Relief floods my veins as I squeeze Heira's hand. "I appreciate your discretion."

"But *should* she fail, I have contingents of Gray Guards camped out near the western border between Bahari and Ocruth, and I've ordered the bulk of our militia farther inland—closer to the Norse. We're more than prepared to help you take the Ocruth seat of power by *force*."

Jaw hardening, I give her a tense nod, watching one of the Elders draw the gray silt from the shores of Mount Ether down Orlaith's forehead, nose, lips, and chin. The drums quicken their thudding, pounding like the beat of a panicked heart. "I'm certain that won't be necessary. I have full faith that Orlaith will climb out of The Bowl and this transition will be smooth."

"Let us see. As always, I put my trust in the Gods."

There's a pitch to Heira's tone that makes me frown, and then she's standing, reaching for the amplifier on the table beside her. She brings it to her lips, and her stern voice rips across the quieting crowd like an avalanche.

"Men, women, children of this *magnanimous* territory, we have gathered here this morning before the full moon's rise to witness our first Ether Trial in over a hundred years!"

Heira raises both arms skyward.

Everybody cheers—the energy infectious.

"Today, the Gods will judge this woman standing before you all in the color of Ether. They will deem her worthiness to sit beside this *great* man," she looks down at me with that wholesome smile, sparking a fire in my swelling chest that burns like a thousand embers, "to cradle his offspring in her womb, and to support him in his selfless endeavors to protect our territory against that which could strike us down!"

There's another eruption of applause, like fists bashing my ribs, and a lopsided smile breaks across my face.

"The tempest is silent ..." Her words—softer now—carry like a verbal shiver I can feel all the way to my bones. "The Gods are *listening*, weighing this woman's thoughts and fears. Her *faults*. Today, before every person in this amphitheater, they will pass their judgment."

The crowd chants in unison, stomping their feet at a ferocious pace, filling the space with the sound of thunder.

*"Judgment!"*

*"Judgment!"*

*"Judgment!"*

"During our preparations," Heira says, sedating the crowd, "Orlaith was asked which creature she was drawn to. As is tradition, that very creature will now be released into The Bowl."

*Finally.*

Father used to say this important decision told truths about someone's character.

Anticipation makes my heart race as the drums begin to pound—hard and fast—and my gaze bounces around the tanks while I wait to see which one will drain.

Which creature was she drawn to? I want to know everything about my petal—her strengths, her weaknesses. What makes that tangled mind *tick*.

The tank containing the electric eels begins to bubble, and dread drops into my stomach like a bag of ice as the creatures disappear through the plinth, then squirm up from the depths of The Bowl.

*Fuck.*

My gaze slashes to Orlaith's widening eyes, then to Heira lifting the amplifier to her mouth again. "Let the trial begin!"

The crowd erupts, chanting, punching their fists toward that hole in the ceiling.

I feel myself fall off that excited cliff, plummeting fast. "She chose the *eels?*" I whisper-hiss, sweaty and fractious, my control fraying by the millisecond.

"I, too, found it interesting. They're such slippery, silent killers," Heira says, setting the amplifier back upon the table, hissing a pained sound as she settles beside me. "Did you know, contrary to their name, they are not closely related to other eels but a form of carp? And they actually breathe *air*. Their very visage is a lie." She plucks another strawberry, not even bothering to rip off the green before she bites into the ruddy flesh.

*This is a fucking disaster.*

"No one has ever chosen the eels or the piranha," I grind out between clenched teeth, trying to keep my lips from moving too much. "Why the fuck *would* they?"

Heira shrugs, swallowing her mouthful. "Perhaps she feels like she has something to prove?"

I frown, looking at Orlaith—wide-eyed at the edge of The Bowl. All the color has returned to her cheeks, making her look flushed.

"Or perhaps she wasn't aware the *choice* had such an important role to play?"

Heira cuts me a harsh glare. "Failing to prepare is

preparing to fail. A Bahari High Mistress should have foresight in *spades*." She takes my hand in hers, and I bite into venomous words as her thumb circles around my knuckle.

I look down at our intertwined fingers, back up into her softening eyes.

"She is in the Gods' hands now, my boy. If it's meant to be, she will climb out of that bowl, gain respect from your people, and rule by your side with great honor. Trust the process."

Her words hammer me into place, making me look at the situation from a different angle. One not governed by my fucking heart.

She's right ...

*She always is.*

I swallow, giving her a tight nod before lifting her hand and planting a kiss upon her knuckles, then returning my focus to The Bowl.

The Elders edge back.

Orlaith takes two stiff steps toward The Bowl, nostrils flared, chest pumping swift breaths, a glint of fire and fortitude in those orchid eyes.

The crowd murmurs, a restless energy swirling, and I release Heira's hand,planting my elbows on my knees so I can give my pretty flower my undivided attention.

Orlaith's stare drops to the stone plinth the empty eel tank is seated on, then moves clockwise. She traces the metal arch spanning The Bowl, her gaze fixing on the rope tied to the highest point—perfectly central—suspending the golden bell atop the body of water.

She looks back at the empty tank before a steely smile touches her lips.

I frown, fisting my hands together, gaze cutting to Heira. Her expression is pensive as she watches the scene with rapt regard.

Orlaith stomps around The Bowl—more endearing than it should be—then stops beside the empty tank, looking past it to cut Heira a glare that sends shivers up my spine.

*What is she doing?*

My frown deepens, and time seems to stretch.

Orlaith flicks a fleeting glance at me, then whips her body around, propels her foot forward, and slams her heel into the tank.

A collective gasp animates the crowd as it topples ...

Then shatters all over the floor.

# CHAPTER 34

*Orlaith*

Cainon watches me as glass skids across the stone, his brow furrowed, wide eyes conflicted—like he has no idea what's going on.

Or that he's sitting next to a snake.

It's almost enough to make me feel sorry for the guy, but then I remember he's up there while I'm down here, battling against the odds to rescue people he's deemed disposable, and that feeling chokes itself to death.

Breath powers into my heaving lungs as I look at the High Septum, a simmer of fire in her eyes. My mind flashes to an earlier time when a similar stare crowned with a similar mark ripped across someone I loved before an axe was swung.

Before my brother's blood puddled on the floor.

I repress a flinch, tension crackling between us. She pushes to a wobbly stand and leans against the balustrade, like she's about to scold me from her lofty, ornate perch.

The faintest hint of satisfaction flares beneath my ribs.

*Go ahead, bitch.*

I scan the bind of brethren looped around The Bowl, murmuring between each other. I'm not surprised to find Elder Creed staring right at me, his eyes a disapproving glint within the shroud of his hood. Perhaps he's annoyed that I made such a mess of his pristine amphitheater?

I'd feel bad if he wasn't such a dick.

*Electric eels my ass. Where's my fucking rockfish?*

Again, I look at The Bowl. At the eels bellying through its illuminated depths. I've tried to climb out of that thing so many times, and spinning circles has gotten me nowhere.

Elder Creed's instructions from the first day ring in my ears ...

*Only once you manage to climb back out on your own have the Gods found you worthy of this coupling.*

He said *nothing* about not making use of my surroundings. He also failed to mention the trial would be rigged with two electric eels ready to shock me to death before I've had a chance to set things right.

I figure the gloves are off.

I flash the Elder a lupine smile, pretending I'm enjoying this charade much more than I really am, then bend over and snatch a piece of glass off the ground.

Dodging the treacherous litter of shards glimmering in the sunlight, I tiptoe around the edge of The Bowl, coming to the thick metal pole arching over the body of water, supporting the rope that hangs from its highest point. The *rescue* rope with a bell on the end I slapped every time I almost choked to death during my failed attempts to climb free of this stupid thing.

If it chimes, I forfeit.

Fail.

*Not this time.*

Biting down on the shard of glass, I shake out my legs, wipe my sweaty hands on my thighs, then press my weight upon the pole that's almost vertical this far down. I reach high, grip tight, and pull myself up, shoulders burning, suddenly thankful for this silky bodysuit that allows me to glide with relative ease. I curl my legs and, bracing my feet against the pole, reach up with my other hand and haul myself skyward in one sliding motion.

Repeat.

The higher I climb, the more my feet tingle from the rapidly soaring height, a sensation I try to ignore as the pole begins to curve, forcing me to heap my focus and dwindling energy on maintaining my center of gravity.

I feel the High Septum's stare like a brand upon me, making my teeth grit. If this place has taught me anything, it's that everyone has their own motives. Most people are more than happy to tread on a corpse if it gives them an extra foot of height above their enemy.

I'm tempted to wave my middle finger at the woman, purely to satisfy my flourishing hate.

Don't want to lose my balance, though.

Another pull reopens the cut in my palm, and I look down the line of the rope to The Bowl far below as blood drips.

Drips.

My heart leaps into my throat. From all the way up here, I can see the long, dark shapes skulking through the water, disturbing the still, my skin nettling with the thought of them brushing against me.

*Shouldn't have looked down.*

I slowly lift my hand to pluck the shard of glass from between my teeth, aware of the crowd's murmuring as I carefully begin to sever the rope in steady cuts. Every slice frays more of the tawny fibers, and the shard bites into my already ravaged palm.

I wince, more blood dribbling from my bunched fist

*Drip.*

*Drip.*

Far below, the water ripples with each fat bead that leaks from my deepening wound.

Once only a few frail strands remain, I center myself so my chest is on the bar for stability, gripping hold of the rope with my spare hand as I cut the final tether. The weight of it falls into my tight grasp. A smile grazes my lips before gasps echo around me, and I realize I'm tipping sideways.

"Crap ..."

Scrambling to snatch the bar, I'm forced to drop the glass *and* the rope, left hanging upside down with my hands and legs bound around the pole—not quite ready to face the inevitable. There's a splash beneath me, and all the blood rushes to my head as I let it fall back, seeing the rope now slinking below the surface, its frayed end chased by a slithering eel that bumps at it with rapt curiosity.

I groan.

Just my luck to get *curious* eels.

My skin tingles under the scrutiny of a thousand pairs of eyes watching my every breath, every blink, every bead of blood dripping into that pool. I alter my hold again so both hands are facing the same direction, then draw a deep breath and uncross my legs at the ankle, letting them drop.

My bloody hand begins to lose grip, pinkie slipping free, tension building in my chest like something stretchy bound around my hammering heart.

I stare at the perilous plummet below, at the eel flicking its tail at the surface like a silent threat.

"*Please* don't electrocute me," I plead, drawing my lungs full as I loosen my grip on the bar.

Gravity yanks me down.

# CHAPTER 35

*Orlaith*

**W**arm water swallows me in a splashing gulp.

I plunge deep and fast, colliding with the stone bottom, pressure bulging my eardrums. A burst of bubbles punch from my lungs, skin tingling with the instant sense that I'm not the only living thing in the dark bowels of this bowl right now.

I fumble around for the rope, stretched arms sweeping until my fingers connect with the coiled lump. I snatch it up and shove off the bottom, more bubbles escaping as I kick skyward, reaching toward the sunlight painting my upturned face.

Breaking free of my inky prison, I draw greedy breaths, treading water, head swiveling, gaze darting for any sign of my slippery friends. An eel pokes its snout above the surface and gulps a mouthful of air less than ten feet away, and a shiver scuttles up my spine.

*Make it quick.*

I sift the rope through my fumbling fingers, trying to haul the heavy bell toward the surface.

Something bumps against my arm.

My breath flees, like I've just leapt into an icy lake that's seized my chest.

My hands still, gaze rolling down, becoming transfixed on the eel nudging me. My attention whips to a ripple of disturbed water—the other eel rapidly approaching from another direction. The gasps and screams of the crowd fade into oblivion as every cell in my body stands at attention.

*Please don't shock me.*

It slows, then disappears below the surface, and I feel it slither against my leg, curl around my foot. It drops away, but the other bumps into my shoulder this time, and the hairs on my nape lift.

*Please, please don't shock me ...*

It seems to squirm its entire body along the expanse of my back, and my skin bursts with goosebumps that make me want to shudder all over. It moves away, and cheers ring out across the roiling crowd as a quenching breath powers into my lungs. I spin to double-check they're gone, then let the welling shiver rake from the base of my neck to the tips of my toes.

Peeking at the High Septum's blazing eyes, I keep lifting the rope until I can finally grab the bell, then try to worm my trembling fingers into the knot and loosen it. A growl boils in the back of my throat, frustration welling. I try my teeth, but all that does is almost rip them out of my gums.

Cursing, I look down past my churning legs ...

*I need to find the glass.*

Drawing my lungs full, I dunk, flip my body upside

down, and *kick*—pulling at the water with my free hand, propelling myself toward the bottom one lopsided pull at a time. All the noises from above muffle into oblivion as I reach the dusky depths, equalizing the ache from my ears before brushing my hand across the stone floor. Hunting for the lowest dip where I hope the glass has settled.

The breath in my lungs begins to burn, making my chest jerk with the suffocating urge to inflate. I'm just about to push to the surface when I hear the scrape of glass on stone.

My heart lurches.

I retrace the same sweep, slower this time, the shard's sharp edge slicing into my finger. My hand tightens around it as an eel slithers down the length of my arm, making me want to shed my skin.

My throat spasms, a gurgle escaping my lips, and I shove skyward, frantically kicking, my legs tangling with the rope. I *feel* the eel chasing me, shivers raking over me as I scramble up, breaking through the surface.

Gulping breath, I slice at the rope in short, frantic swipes, flushing the water with the constant ooze of blood seeping from the stinging slash in my palm.

The curious murmurs of the crowd are a distant drone. Flicking disturbances and sporadic ripples haunt my peripheral, stirring my pulse and this anxious ball squiggling through my chest.

I rip the bell loose, holding Elder Creed's shadowy stare as I stem the urge to toss it at his head. Limbs heavy with exhaustion, I release it and the shard of glass, then bind one end of the rope into a large loop. I spin, legs screaming their objections, gaze landing on that stubby stone plinth the eels were housed upon.

Lifting the rope above my head—and to the collective gasp of the crowd—I whip it around, then *throw,* maintaining my hold on the tail end as the loop flies through the air ... and slaps against the side of The Bowl.

A surge of disappointment slams into me.

*This was much easier in my imagination.*

I drag the loop close, pull a ragged breath, and toss it again. The sound of wet rope slapping against stone impales me with the lance of failure, and I curse.

*Much, much easier in my imagination.*

I dare not look at Cainon's platform, not wanting to see the satisfaction on the High Septum's face.

Again and again, I reel the rope in and toss it. Again and again, the crowd distracts me with their antsy murmurs as I fail.

Fail.

*Fail.*

"*Come on,*" I growl, sitting deeper in the water as my legs begin to tire, shoulders growing heavy, strained. I battle to draw air into my aching lungs, water sloshing into my gaping mouth, making me choke and sputter.

I drag the sodden length to the surface and grip the loop, skin flushed from this tepid water slowly boiling me alive. Using every last bit of strength I have, I throw the rope, already preparing to wind it back when the loop slots perfectly over the plinth.

My stomach lurches, and I blink back tears of relief. Gasps and cheers blast the amphitheater full of riotous excitement I can feel in my bones.

I pull the rope taut and test the catch it has on the stone, a smile splitting my face when it holds true. Pride pumps through my veins in a hard, hot rush, and I almost laugh, reeling myself toward the side. I place my feet on the edge and secure my grip, preparing to haul myself up—

Something flicks against my waist before a bolt of paralyzing pain snaps through me, ripping up my arm to where my cupla rests against my wrist. Every muscle in my body bunches before a cool numbness replaces my bones.

A surge of screams is the last thing I hear before a shrill ringing fills my head.

I drop through the tiers of a deep, watery grave, unable to draw breath. Shock and fear are replaced by a light, airy feeling ... like I shucked the layers of a heavy existence I can't grasp the meaning of.

Who am I? Why am I here, slipping toward a silky darkness?

My back thumps against something hard, and I'm no longer sinking, but looking up at a round window of light that's too small and far away. Like I'll never be able to catch it, even if I try.

*Try ...*

The word picks at me, making me feel something.

*Uncomfortable.*

A dark, fluttering shadow circles high above, like it's churning within that beam of sunshine that almost looks like a moon—stirring it up. I want to grasp at it, a fading urge that slips out of reach.

I'm caged in this watery end.

Within this body that doesn't work.

*Caged ...*

A thought niggles at me, prods, then *bites*—visions flashing.

*Metal bars.*

*Big eyes.*

*Curly red hair.*

A *promise*—its steely echo blooming inside me like a flourishing wildflower.

*I'm going to get you out.*

A gurgle wrenches up my throat as fiery determination flames within my heart, turning my blood into a sizzling rush. I force my seized muscles to work. To *move*. To scoop at the water in powerless pulls that don't shift me fast enough toward that distant surface, but they move me.

*They move me.*

With each sludgy kick, with each desperate wade, my body becomes more engaged.

I punch through the surface to the frantic gasps of the crowd, treading water while I choke on sips of breath. Willing more strength into my muscles that still feel bunched and broken. I ease toward the side, flapping around until my hand collides with the rope, retching more water free of my laden lungs.

My savage snarl cuts the air, and my upper gums ache as I lift my legs, set my feet upon the stone, then tighten my hands and *pull*—hauling my spent body from the tepid water, pouring everything I have, everything I am, into the slow but steady ascent.

*I'm going to get you out.*

I repeat the promise to myself until I'm busting over The Bowl's lip.

The crowd erupts—hoots and cheers and squeals of delight as my head swirls, heavy lids threatening to tug down.

I look at Cainon, seeing him standing—applauding. Boasting a proud smile that curdles my guts.

Beside him, Heira's also clapping despite her thin lips and scathing stare that fills my hollow belly with a gluttonous feast of satisfaction.

I crawl across a litter of sharp shards, pushing up, kneeling before Elder Creed, broken glass slicing into my kneecaps as I look into his wide eyes and flash him a smile that's all teeth. "Nice try," I slur, wobbling. "I hope they shock you while you're trying to sift them out."

*Darkness.*

*Past*
*Before the Great Purge*

# CHAPTER
## *Rhordyn*
# 36

My stomach is as hollow as the thin air heaving into my lungs, thighs burning with each frantic step I scale up the crumbling path of Mount Ether's summit, tracking the scent of vanilla beans and damp soil all the way to this dead and dusty end.

Clinging to sweat-slicked skin, my shirt reeks of my dashed journey, mind racing even faster than my feet. The cold air tangles with hot steam rising from clefts between the stones, another scent riding the tails of the rich, sulfuric taint this place breathes into the atmosphere ...

*Fuck.*

I haven't stopped since I realized Rai was gone. Haven't tired. I tire *now*—sipping the smell of her blood.

A savage sound saws up my throat, and I quicken my pace, moving so fast the craggy, gray stone around me blurs. There's only more heartbreak to be found here, in this place. More twists of the talon already hilt-deep in a rotting wound.

The sloped path chops into stairs so steep one misplaced step would send me plummeting, but I take them two at a time, powering myself up and up and up—

I spill upon the volcano's crown, a flat band of rubbled terrain that wraps around the caldera, supporting a clutch of stone monoliths—their piercing tips lost through the swirl of clouds. Stairs curl around the massive shards of gray rock, creating perilous paths that scale the individual spires, giving access to inky words chipped into the surface.

The *tap-tap-tap* of Maars's chisel echoes down from above, chipping at my bones as I search my surroundings in desperate sweeps.

*Can't see her.*

That wildness inside me *roars.*

Charging right, I sprint past stone after stone until I come to the one foretelling the elements of Rai's unraveling—right at the base. One of the first ribbons of script to be plucked from the bowl and carved upon this stone.

I have to crouch to run my hand along the words that are chiseled just as deep through the folds of my brain:

*Fate will flare for storm and stone,*
*Hearts broken by the scratch of death.*
*Rot will sow. Hate will grow, Hover upo*
*—an end that will fail to land its blow.*
*Seven times, her death will rise. Eight,*
*the strike will land. Wrath spills from*
*a bloody hand. Her wrath will*
*spill from a bloody hand.*

A fresh smear of crimson is swiped across the stone, and I rub it between my fingers, smelling it.

"Fuck."

The ground shakes, like some beast beneath my feet just took a breath and grumbled.

Like something disturbed its *sleep*.

I charge toward the edge of the bowl. Sliding to a stop, I look down the slope that plummets to the large crater lake, still ruffled by the echo of Mount Ether's moan. Ribbons of black scripture frolic beneath the dull-gray surface, flicking at it, as though begging to be snapped up and inspected.

Chipped into the stones by Maars's gnarly hands.

My gaze snags on the tapered outcrop jutting toward the center. On the woman standing near the end, her black dress blowing about her small, frail form, the torn strips dragged by the handsy wind.

Long, silver tresses swirl around her in tangled scribbles, her right hand smothered in blood that drips from the tip of the talon clenched in her white-knuckled fist.

My heart dives.

*Her wrath will spill from a bloody hand.*

I leap and slide down the craggy slope with a volley of loose rocks and shards of stone that tumble into the water, disturbing the steam wafting off the surface. Another restless rumble rattles the ground, the entire world seeming to shake. I stagger, taking tentative steps toward the frail outcrop.

"*Rai!*" I boom, and she spins, striking me with her bold black eyes set within the canvas of her fierce, regal beauty.

Her features are sharp, her cheekbones matching the bladed angles of her shoulders, arms, and legs; her pale complexion a stark contrast to her lips—the deep red of spilled blood.

Even gaunt and half starved, she's unparalleled.

Everything that's *good* in this world, steeped in the sourness of loss.

I step onto the ledge, swirling, sulfuric steam dampening my skin. She throws her hand toward me, and the clouds ignite with a fork of lightning that carves down from the sky.

"*Stop.*" Her ripped voice hacks through the empty space between us.

I hold her gaze and take another slow, steady step.

"Don't you *dare.*"

She speaks softly now, her tone gentle like the bedtime songs Mother used to sing to us when we were small. My responding snarl is as hard and coarse as Father's stony regard.

I hunt the unhinged glint in her ebony eyes—the darkness bleeding into the surrounding skin like dusky veins pushed to the surface. I hunt that severed talon hanging from her hand like the lingering threat it is, chewing on my compulsion to lurch forward and rip it from her bony grasp.

Another step. Another.

She shuffles back in silent retreat, and my heart vaults.

I still, hands crunching into fists so tight my knuckles pop.

Silence settles between us, a great beast crouched on its haunches, plotting which of us it's going to pounce upon.

"You *knew*," she scolds, the words the crack of a whip. Knew the prophecy. Knew that she would find him.

*Lose* him.

"Yes."

I knew and never told her. Never warned her of the pain her path was paved in.

Another layer of hurt hatches in her eyes. "Why didn't you tell me?" she cries. "I expected that from Mother and Father, but *you*—" Her voice breaks, and something in my chest feels like it's twisting, gouging at my insides. "I thought you *cared*."

*Caring* was watching her find a love that made her glow. It was hearing her speak about dreams of her own family—a family I knew she'd never have.

*Caring* was hunting for ways to manipulate the fates while she lived in peaceful oblivion, not knowing that the happiest days of her life were about to come to an abrupt and heart-wrenching end. That she would be forced to watch her mate decompose from the inside out, helpless to fix him.

*Save* him.

She pushes her shoulders back and lifts her chin, swatting a tear from her cheek. "Mother and Father—"

"Are coming." My voice is cut with the promise of something fierce threatening to split through my skin. "I was faster."

I'd powered across the plains once I'd realized she escaped the castle. The sun tore across the sky five times while I tracked her scent, driven by the knowledge that she was out here—alone—being feasted on by her broken heart.

I look at her bloodied arm as the wind pulls her scent

to me, punched with the metallic tang of not just *her* blood, but also that of a goat.

*Fuck.*

"You asked Maars a question ..."

Her gaze calcifies into a cold, bitter mask. "Yes."

"And?"

"He told me why I don't die no matter how many times I *stab*."

I flinch from the blow she landed with such precision, visions of her flashing into the forefront of my memory: her lifeless body cast across her blood-soaked bed; the room smelling like the death she craved—the death that didn't stick the first time ... or any of the times that followed.

A loosely tied ribbon falls from her hair, the strip of white swirling through the air before landing atop the lake in a splash of sizzle and steam, the material swiftly disintegrating.

I chance another stolen step forward, hand raised as if to tame the wild, broken beast before me. "What did he say?" I ask, picturing my hand delving between her ribs, gripping hold of her hurt.

Crushing it.

"Our father." Her head rolls back, and a laugh spills from her, manic and twisted. "Our *father!*" She screams and waves the talon through the air, wobbling.

Stumbling.

Her foot scores the edge, and a wildness swipes at my insides, every muscle in my body poised to leap as a piece of stone breaks off and plops into the water, scattering the scriptures.

I blow out an exhale as she finds her balance and

straightens, then half turns to watch the ripples cast across the pallid water. Slowly, her gaze drops to the talon, its severe length curved at the tip, dripping blood. "The only way for me to join him is to impale myself through the heart with this. Covered in *his* blood."

*His—*

*Her mate's.*

"And where the fuck am I going to get that? He's *dead.*" The words pop out of her with a bubble of soiled laughter. "He's ash on the wind because the stars refused to answer my plea. Not even a *whisper.*" I track the tear caressing her cheek. "Because they don't *care*, Rhor. Because we're nothing but a colorful splash of entertainment upon the tapestry of their immortal oblivion."

Another rumble throws more ripples across the water while I try to remember the girl Rai was before she was cast in this shadow of loss …

All I can see is the ache in her eyes when Heath heaved his last breath, her beautiful face twisting into something I could *feel* in my chest.

All I can hear are the sharp shrieks that ripped up her throat. Pleas for me to let her go when I caught her trying to leap off the cliff at home—determined to break herself apart on the jagged rocks below.

She drugged herself with sips of a half-death she believed would bring her closer to *him*.

Seven times I watched her eyes go flat and empty, then sat beside her bed and waited for them to open again—hoping that maybe she'd come back better. That things would go back to the way they were before.

That the words on the stones would be *wrong*.

"But I think I've found a way to get their attention," she whispers, glancing out across the lake, and a shiver climbs my spine. Rakes across my skin. "After all, that *stupid* book I found said all of creation poured from ... here."

Realization almost clefts me down the middle, my gaze darting to her bloody hand.

The talon clenched in her fist.

*Her wrath will spill from a bloody hand. Her wrath will spill from a bloody hand. Her wrath will spill from a bloody hand—*

*She's going to toss the talon in the water ...*

"Rai, no—"

"*Why not?*" she screams, face contorted with a mix of heartache and rage. "They watched *him* rot from the inside out." With a shrug, she takes a step toward the perilous drop so that her toes are nudging the edge. "Their precious world can do the same."

"You're not thinking straight," I growl. "You throw that talon into the pool and you yield to the words. You fucking *yield.*"

She tips her head and laughs, the sound poison to my ears.

For a moment, I'm happy Mother and Father were slower than me. That they're not here to witness this.

It would kill them.

"*Anything* could spill out," I continue. "And it won't be the Gods that suffer. Not truly."

It will be the people.

The *innocents.*

"Can you wear the weight of that?" Her laughter tapers as I take another step forward and hold her narrowing stare. "Because the Rai I knew cried when I had to put a foal out of his misery after he got crushed against that tree and snapped his spine."

"Your Rai is *gone*," she snarls, upper lip peeled back to reveal her piercing canines. She lifts her chin and looks down her nose at me, like she despises me—*truly* despises me. "But I don't expect you to understand, Rhordyn. You've lost *nothing*."

"I'm losing *you*," I rasp, and her eyes flare, shoulders bowing as if an arrow just struck her chest.

I hold her gaze, unblinking, a swirl of ashy wind whipping her silver mane into a deeper state of disarray.

She drops her head, breaking my stare, her shoulders folding further.

"Rai—"

"You can't fix me, big brother. You can't erase my hurt."

Another step, and I could almost reach out and touch her. Grab her. Rip her from the edge and pull her to my chest. Instead, I bend my knee and *kneel,* dropping into her line of sight.

Her breath catches as she's forced to look straight into me. To see the raw desperation in my eyes as I say, "Not if you don't let me *try*."

Her lids sweep shut, chin wobbling, and for a moment, I think she's going to step over the edge.

To jump.

Instead, the talon clatters to the stone, and relief punches me in the gut as she crumples into a pile of sharp limbs and filthy flesh.

I resist the urge to reach for her, knowing the moment is fragile.

"It's tiring, you know," she opens her eyes and looks at me with a deflated expression, "having you as a brother."

I lift a brow.

"I'm kidding." Her lips slant into a tired smile. "I love you, even though I'm so mad I could shred holes in the world."

I grunt, letting my shoulders buckle as I rub my eyes. *Maars and his fucking chisel.*

"Do you remember that old fort you dug for me in the sprite warren after I begged for a castle of my own?"

I glance up at her.

"It took me three moon cycles," I mumble, tipping back onto my ass and scrubbing at my scratchy face. "A swarm of sprites would nip me all over every time I brought out a bucket of soil."

Her smile grows, her features beginning to soften, the darkness sinking from the skin around her eyes, pupils tightening until the gray has returned for the first time in weeks.

Months.

Relief slathers my insides.

"That's how I learned my first curse word, you know." I frown as she continues. "I saw you emerge from behind the mail tree swatting at them like bees, and you had this look on your face like you wanted to stomp them but wouldn't."

I thought she was oblivious—that her dug-out castle was a complete surprise.

"You ... knew I was making it?"

She nods sheepishly, tucking a lock of knotted hair back off her face. "You looked ridiculous dragging that trolley packed full of my dolls and teddy bears and lacy pillows across the grass. I was so excited because I knew that meant it was almost done. That I was about to *see*." She pauses, swallowing, looking down at her hands. "Then you showed me ..."

I remember that day clearly. Remember the way her eyes lit up as she dashed from room to room, squealing, almost tripping over her feet with excitement. I remember the silence that swept through the warren when Father crunched himself down and prowled through to her fort every night for a full moon cycle—Rai insisting she had to sleep in there, determined a princess should never leave her castle unattended.

Of course that meant us, too.

Our parents fawned over Rai like she was their entire world, and I never begrudged them for it. Not when they knew her time was limited.

Besides, she's my favorite person, too.

"It was the happiest day of my life," she whispers, and this weird feeling claws at the back of my throat, making it feel tight and choked.

Clearing it, I rest my arms on my knees and stare at the stone beneath us, wishing I could speak the words inside my head. Knowing they would come out wrong.

Jumbled and too sharp. Or too blunt.

How do I articulate how much she means to me? Perhaps I should just tell her that I love her, too.

I open my mouth—

The volcano rumbles with a burst of fury that makes the ground jolt in tandem with my heart, and a strident *crack* splits the silence as a fracture weaves through the stone between us.

My head whips up.

The ground gives way.

She plummets.

A burst of undiluted fear widens Rai's eyes and electrifies me from within. I lurch forward, arm whipping out, snatching thin air.

Time seems to slow, her hair a storm around her face, bloody hand reaching for me—a desperate, hopeless plea. Her terrified gaze never leaves mine as her mouth opens in a tortured scream.

Her body folds, arms outstretched.

There's a splash, and for a split second, her tragic stare spears through me, resigned to her fate ...

Then she's gone.

# PRESENT

I open my eyes to find myself reaching through the grass, muscles bunched like I'm preparing to jump through the ages and fail all over again, that mournful ache in my gut just as gnashing as it's ever been.

Groaning, I roll, squinting at the shafts of light piercing the dense canopy, the air warmer.

Thicker.

*How long has it been this time?*

I paw at my chest, feeling around the edges of the sore, sticky wound that's not healing fast enough, then snatch the soft bladder hanging from the string around my neck. Easing onto my knees, I lean back as I pop the cork and tip my head like I'm exposing my throat to the very contents of this fucking thing. I suspend the nozzle over my mouth and wait for her to drip.

*I killed my mother ...*

Orlaith's words attack me as she hits my tongue in a cold splat, and I let her confession spoil every other inch of my body that's not weeping rot.

She passed me those words like they were a bloody weapon she'd first used to stab herself. If she'd given me time to speak, I would have told her the truth. Would have given her another reason to plunge that talon through my chest, confessing it was *me* who stilled her mother's heart.

*Me.*

I close my mouth around the crackling ember of *her*—unable to stop myself from drawing a breath through my nose and savoring her taste ...

She's a swirling prism of color and light tingling my taste buds. She's amber warmed by a beam of sun, leaking down the side of a pine tree and heaping in the soil, begging me to extinguish her with a heady gulp.

She's a flower, so fresh and full of life—crushed between my teeth as I swallow. She's a sun in my throat, sinking low, igniting me from the inside out.

She's everything I love.

*Everything I hate.*

The hairs on my arms and legs stand on end as she calms every bristled cell; the sharp edges threatening to gouge through my flesh. She soothes the gnashing teeth and the serrated edges that never dull.

That restless beast beneath my skin rumbles—a deep, satiated sound as my blood begins to boil, making me want to rip out my veins. That same heat pools in the tips of my fingers, electricity crackling through my muscles, making them twitch and tighten.

Making my binds *chew.*

I tip my head and laugh at the sky.

"You fucked up," I mutter as my senses hone, and I become terribly aware of every root beneath the soil, the pulse of energy slugging through them. Of the air rushing past me like a blown breath I could choke or feed. Of the water barreling through the chasm below, alive with heaving might I can feel thrashing through my arteries.

And below the earth, beneath the roots and the rocks, beneath the layers of death and decay and bones and long-forgotten secrets ...

*Obsidian.*

"I'll *never* let her go," I growl, then fall forward, digging my hands into the dirt, pouring every single fucking drop of that heat into the ground. Giving *her* to the soil and the trees and the seeds and the stone, when all I really want is to keep her tucked beneath my ribs.

*Safe.*

A mighty rumble breaks apart the silence, and a flock of krah scatter as the ground begins to shake. As trees snap and fall, crumbling a hole in the canopy.

The ground splits, the same sensation spurring through the tips of my fingers as a ring of massive obsidian sabers erupts in a burst of soil and stone, spearing upward. The grass takes on a richer shade of green. Silver vines crawl up the black stones, budding, flushing with argent blooms that slant their faces toward the sky.

There is nothing silent about the way I curse the Gods, planting this refuge in the soil. A permanent safety ring for anyone who might be stumbling through the shadows, hunted and hungry.

I will not fall silently into their fate.

*Neither will she.*

My spine arches, skin itching, fingers threading so deep I lose sight of them entirely. I pour until not a *drop* of her lustrous warmth is trapped inside my chest. Nothing but the seed—silently pulsing.

And for a single precious moment, I can almost will myself to believe she's free of me.

Of this.

Just ... *free*.

# CHAPTER 37

*Cainon*

M en, women, and children scuttle into the corners, looking at me through wide, bulging eyes as I stride past cell after cell. Like they believe they're seeing Kvath in the flesh, hunting the next soul he wishes to snatch.

Despite the way those stares grate at me, this powerful sensation surges through my veins, making me feel bigger.

*Stronger.*

Down here, *I* pull the strings. Weave whatever the fuck I want.

*I'm* in control.

I'll be feeding into this desire soon—so close to taking the seat of power in Ocruth. Taking *his* family home. Flattening it to the ground.

A big, final *fuck you.*

It'll be even sweeter with Orlaith at my side. I'll wait until she's in heat, then fuck her in the rubble. Fill her womb. Make her mine in every way.

After tonight, I'll be surprised if she ever thinks of him again. I plan on keeping her locked away in the coupling chamber until she's so *spent*—so smothered in my cum and scent—that the only word she remembers how to say is *my name*.

*Mine.*

I exit the hall to find Father coiled on the ground at the edge of his feeding arena, his chains pushed to their limits, stressing the twisted, crumpled skin at his wrists. His head is tucked beneath his arms, hands threaded together and resting over the back of it like a shield.

He's trembling, crouched in his own puddle of piss, blood dribbling down his back—a sure sign he's been moving around, stretching his limbs, the glass bolts' tapered tips shredding through his muscle and flesh.

I look at the woman slung across the ground with her throat torn open, her hair a spill of strawberry wine. Her wide, unseeing eyes glisten like amber gemstones in the beam of evening light spearing from above.

I pinch the bridge of my nose. "Dammit," I mutter with a shake of my head, screwing my eyes shut.

The last thing I feel like doing before my coupling is digging a fucking hole, but I can't leave the body here. If I don't remove them fast enough, he becomes possessive, clinging to them like some sort of pet—hauling them about, chatting to them.

Telling them he loves them.

I think of the time he clung to one so long it began falling apart, forcing me to remove it in bits.

"I went too far."

My eyes snap open at Father's gnarled, rusty voice, gaze

narrowing on him. His head is lifted, inky pools cast on me, but there's ... *something* about them that makes him look more animated than he usually is.

"Father?"

They flatten again, punching my gut full of disappointment.

"I went too far," he repeats, and I sigh, dragging a hand down my face.

"It's okay." I step over the line, making for the dead woman. "You did nothing wrong. You sent her to a better place."

I remove the key from my pocket and crouch next to the body, unlatching the shackle around her wrist, her hand still warm and floppy. Tossing the iron cuff upon the stone, I pause to massage my temples.

*Fucking hell.*

Perhaps I'll just move her back to her cell? He won't be able to see her from there. I can leave her until tomorrow night and just pray she doesn't stink up the place.

"*I went too far. I went too far. I went too far—*"

"Fucking hell," I mutter, wiggling the key into the second lock.

The sound of chains whipping across stone wrenches my stare sideways, a gasp powering into me at the sight of him, *right there*—an inch from my face—his eyes an inky blaze of horror.

I fall back, landing hard on my elbows.

He crawls atop me and fists my shirt, his putrid breath blasting my face as he drops so close our noses crush together. "*I went too far!*"

A bolt of fear snaps through me, making my lungs seize.

I swallow, forcing myself to breathe. Think.

*Speak.*

"It's okay, Father. It's okay. I'll take care of it ... I always do. Always will."

His eyes soften.

"It's okay," I repeat, my words slow and soft. "You're okay ..."

He blinks, frowns, then folds back and scurries across the floor. He snatches an old shirt of Mother's from his twisted nest of rags, crushing it close to his chest before he bunches up at the edge of the circle and tries to make his body small. Once he's nothing but a trembling knot of muscle and sinew, he begins to rock back and forth with a tortured swing, the glassy cracks in his skin shining silver in the moonlight, threads of crimson dripping down his back.

*"Bring her to me. Bring her to me. Bring her to me—"*

Letting my head fall back against the stone, I sigh and wipe his spit from my face. "You know I can't do that. What if you break her? You'll never forgive yourself."

*And I'd lose you entirely.*

"Besides," I grind out, rolling sideways, pushing up. "You don't need her. You have *me.*"

His constant chant is a fucking axe to my brain as I release the remaining cuff, grab the dead woman by her ankles, and drag her toward the hallway—her long, strawberry hair a wispy trail in our wake.

Everyone watches us pass, their stares burning holes in me from all angles.

Lumping the woman in the corner of her cell, I snatch the catchpole I left leaning beside her door. I don't bother to lock her in, moving down the hall, dragging my hand along the bars as I scour each quivering inhabitant, pausing by the child with curly red hair.

I frown.

She's in the middle of her cell, bound on her side with her eyes open but sightless. I hardly believe she's breathing until her chest expands with a jagged inhale.

Guess she didn't take well to watching her mother get mauled to death. I probably should have considered that before I put her in the cell right beside the feeding arena. A look like that ... she's practically *begging* for death. I doubt she'd even run if I put her in the chains.

I'd have as much luck snapping him out of his spiral if I threw her mother's corpse back in the arena.

"Fuck," I murmur, backtracking.

I pause before the cell containing a male Aeshlian with coils of iridescent hair. Big, crystalline eyes blink up at me—a little dull on shine.

He needs sunlight. A perfect excuse to give him time in the chains.

"You're up," I say, leaning the catchpole against the wall.

All the color drains from his cheeks.

I dig my key into the lock, and he shuffles to the back wall. The fresh reek of piss fills my nose. "*No! No, please! I-I can't go out there again—*"

"He needs a pick-me-up," I declare, grabbing the catchpole.

I stalk into the cell as the boy pulls into a tight, trembling ball. It's really fucking hard to get the prongs around their necks when they act this way.

I kick him in the ribs, and his head whips back, a scream spilling as I clamp his throat and drag him toward the door. He continues to kick and thrash and squeal, his desperate sounds morphing into big, wrought sobs that draw every other inhabitant to the forefront of their cells.

"Shh-shh-shh," I coo, snapping a shackle around the young man's wrist, tethering him to a long length of chain that's bolted to a pole in the circle's center. A chain longer than Father's, giving his prey the false sense of security in this small outer band.

Giving them *hope*.

Pathetic fucking hope. The main ingredient of disappointment.

Shuddering, Father tries to scuttle farther away, more blood leaching from his torn-up wrists. "No," he cries. "*No-no-no-no—*"

"I know what you need, Father." I snap the second cuff into place. "It's okay."

I loosen the catchpole, toss it aside, then stalk toward the man I'd give my life for. I crouch before him, grab a fistful of his own chains, and give them a playful tug, flashing him a reassuring smile. "Come on. You used to say their blood made you feel good. And there's nothing wrong with feeling good."

He snaps his head around, looking straight at me with wide, aching eyes. "I want it to end, my son. *Please!*"

My heart stops.

"Wh-*what* did you say?"

His chest swells. "My *son!*" he roars with the ferocity of a thousand war drums.

He slams his hands into my chest, all the breath punching

from my lungs as I'm thrown backward. My head smashes against the stone, lights forking across my splitting vision as I look up at him—standing at his full height, like the mighty, powerful warrior he once was. Teeth bared, his canines glisten in the firelight, his inky eyes on harrowing display.

"*Father ...*"

The word comes out choked.

His face contorts, and he crumbles down, like someone just ripped several disks from his spine. He snatches Mother's top off the ground and scurries toward the far edge of the arena where he resumes his silent rocking.

*My son ...*

He hasn't called me that in ... *centuries*.

Throat thickening, I breathe the echo of his words like the nourishment they are, watching him shudder in the corner ...

My face hardens, a fierce ball of determination welling in my chest.

He wants me to let him go—to end his suffering. I can't. Won't.

Ever.

*My son ...*

Those two words could fuel me for an *eternity*.

I push up and wobble to my feet, rubbing the back of my head, and make for the boy in three long strides. Gripping his torn and soiled tunic, I drag him along the floor toward the ray of light shafting down from above.

He kicks and screams, clawing at my arm. I discard him on the ground, watching his eyes ignite as he scuffles onto his ass, gaze whipping between me and Father muttering incoherently, rocking to his own twisted beat.

I step back, hold the boy's wide, frightened stare sparkling in the light, and whisper, "*Good luck.*"

He clambers to his feet and scurries toward that chalky line he thinks will save him from the unhinged predator at his back.

Father's head snaps up, features sharpening. His shoulders swell as he snarls.

Salivates.

The boy doesn't make it far before Father barrels him over with bone-crunching force, pinning him to the ground, stretching his neck to the side. He latches onto the opaline flesh, and iridescent blood explodes across his rabid face.

It hurts seeing him like this—a twisted shadow of the man he used to be. The man who *loved* me despite …

*Everything.*

But it's better than not having him at all.

# CHAPTER

*Orlaith*

## 38

I bathe in milk, honey, and fragrant oils for exactly one hour. I know because I watch every minute, every *second,* tick by on a clock above the mantle as a team of quiet servants scrub me, pluck me, shave me in places that make me want to scrunch into a ball and hide. Instead, I stuff every wisp of emotionally driven weakness beneath my field of tiny domes, then plaster another bigger, *stronger* dome atop the lot—a double layer of protection that instantly loosens my bones, my muscles, leaving me with nothing but stony determination that will hopefully carry me through the next few hours.

Nobody seems to blink an eye at the wound on my neck as I'm dried with a thick, warm towel. My hair is combed into a cascade of tumbling curls, my skin slathered in a lotion that smells like orchids—sweet and musky.

I'm swathed in a blue silk dressing gown and escorted from the bathing chamber. Six women bunch around me, and we move through the lofty corridors like a single unit;

past guards who nod curtly and servants who bow or curtsey, as though my steps are now paved by the Gods.

It couldn't be further from the truth.

Kolden opens the door to my suite, and we gush past, the door shutting behind us. Izel and another handmaiden are standing by my dresser that's littered with stubby bottles, bowls of gray slop, and tins of cosmetics.

I glance out the open window, the gluttonous moon rising above the cityscape that glitters in the distance— bloated with heavy promises that don't pack the same punch when I'm feeling …

*Nothing.*

Sounds of merriment spill across the bay: the thunder of drums, a chorus of voices, and more of those loud *pops* as seeds of light shoot up into the sky and explode into a myriad of falling stars.

Izel gestures for me to sit before my vanity, and a few fine braids are bound around the crown of my head, pinned in place and adorned with tiny blue flowers. My nails are painted with something that makes the tips look like they've been dipped in gold, the dark circles under my eyes dusted with a powder that matches my skin tone. My lashes are swept into dramatic curls with a liquid that tints their length, the ends embellished with golden dewdrops. Finally, my lips are stained blood red, each sweep of the brush making them tickle.

I'm escorted to where a heavy shard of silver light pours in through the open balcony doors, my robe slipped off my shoulders, baring my naked body that feels like it no longer belongs to me—a thought that skims the surface of my hardened mind rather than gnawing through its spongy flesh.

Someone lifts my hair and picks at the latch on my necklace. I whip around and snatch her wrist.

A hush falls upon the room as I shake my head. "This stays on."

"But, Mistress," the unfamiliar handmaiden sputters, big blue eyes nipping at Izel, "we *must* remove all jewelry except your cupla. It is tradition."

"Then I will do it myself when I'm ready."

There's a moment of hesitancy before she dips her head in quiet submission, and I drop my hold on her.

I turn my attention back to the moon, sighing internally.

The servants each hold bowls of that gray slop that smells like sulfur, wielding delicate brushes. They get to work painting my body—adorning me in cold, tickling lines, swirls, and flicks that make me shiver all over.

I glance down, and my eyes widen when I realize what they're doing. Painting me in scriptures I've seen before— scrawled across Rhordyn's skin—tailoring to every dip, curve, and hardened peak of my body.

*Enhancing* me.

That big, internal dome rattles, like the ones beneath it popped off or shattered. I slather more light upon it and force myself to stare at the moon. Watch it rise in daunting increments. Focus on everything I must do and the steps I must take.

Simple. Empty.

Superficial.

A wild gust of wind whips past the curtains and glazes my skin, lifting the hairs on my arms like an electrical charge that seems to swathe me. As if leaning into it, my entire body sways—

A servant takes my arm, urging me to step into a garment puddled at my feet. The dress is lifted—a sheer, shimmery sheath that looks less hardy than tissue parchment ... though I guess that's the point.

Easy to shred.

*Who needs proper clothes when all this night is really about is what's between my legs?*

Another thought that glides across the surface before I blow it away like the seeds of a dandelion.

They ease the gown over my painted breasts and settle it into place, its neckline cutting a straight line from one shoulder to the other. The back is low and draping, long sleeves the shape of bells. It's opaque from the knees down, but through the rest I glimpse the scrawls of scripture tangled across my sun-kissed skin. The more intimate parts of my body are cleverly hidden beneath swirling trails of shimmering gauze.

Something I'm thankful for.

The servants who scrubbed me in the bathing chamber back away, heads bowed, their murmured words crawling across my skin like ants: "*We serve as one. We serve as one. We serve as one—*"

They exit through the door with the unfamiliar handmaiden, leaving only Izel, who caps the cosmetics on my vanity. Her motions are loud and disruptive now that the others have gone, snapping lids down and clanking things into place. "I'll leave you to your pre-ceremonial prayers," she says, glancing at me through the mirror, her expression guarded. Perhaps she's pissed that I didn't drink her poison tea or eat her poison cake. "I'll be back with the fertility tonic."

Her words hit like a punch to my dome as she turns on her heel and leaves.

All I can do is stare at the closed door, struggling to remember what it is I have to do. The next step I have to take.

*Nobody said anything about a* fertility *tonic ...*

I shake off a full-body shudder, slather another layer of light upon my trembling dome, and snap into action—unlatching my necklace. My fake skin barely gets the chance to peel down before I loop the chain around my ankle twice and resecure the clasp, thankful the opaque hem of my gown conceals the contraband.

I uncap the lip lacquer, then open my vanity drawer, pull out my cloak, and retrieve the small vial I stashed behind it. My heart drops when I see the cork—no longer a tawny tone but stained black, soaked with the liquid it was meant to stopper.

*Shit.*

I cut a glance at the door behind me, then dig my hand into the drawer and grab the vial of leftover bane bush berries from Izel's suspected assassination attempts. I tip them across the bench and pick the ripest ones, retrieve my pestle and mortar from the other drawer, sprinkle the tiny berries into the hollow with a few drops of water, and grind them into a slurry.

The liquid is thick and gray at first, before finally turning loose and dark as ink.

I lift the mortar and tip the liquid bane toward the pottle of red lip stain.

*One drip.*

*Two—*

Enough to kill a dinner party worth of people if it were dispersed within a jug of water.

I frown.

Maybe I'll try to squeeze out a little more? Cainon's half Unseelie, and I need to knock him out for a good long while. At the very least, I need him asleep until the High Septum cracks open our coupling chamber at sunrise, hunting for evidence of my freshly stripped virtue—or so I've been told.

Another drip.

*Another—*

The door clicks shut.

My attention snaps to the mirror before me. In it, I see Izel near the entrance, paused, a small bottle of grass-colored liquid in her hand. Her shrewd gaze shifts over the mortar. The berries sprinkled on the table. The pottle of red lip lacquer.

Finally, she looks at *me*.

In her big, blue eyes is the deep seed of knowing. Vile, poignant, accusatory *knowing*—which only confirms my suspicions.

*She spiked my meals with the berries to begin with.*

Tension cuts the air, and I settle the mortar on the table, swallowing, brutally aware of just how fragile this situation has become. *Burn-me-at-the-stake-rather-than-couple-with-me* fragile.

"Izel, please don—"

She spins toward the door, the fertility tonic thudding against the rug.

My vision smears as I move too fast and all at once, chewing the space between us in a few strides, making me feel as if I left my skin over by the vanity. Swallowing a violent, rocking surge of displacement, I bind her with my arm and smack my hand upon her mouth.

She bucks and twists and tries to wrestle free, but my bones are hardened by the alloy of my desperation.

"Stop, Izel. Please. You *have* to listen."

She continues to twist and grunt, teeth grazing my palm, trying to sink into my flesh.

I press my lips close to her ear, my whisper sharp and urgent. "He's a very bad, very *twisted* man. Just stop trying to bite my hand and give me a second to explain."

She goes completely slack and still, and I breathe a sigh of relief, closing my eyes.

"He's Unseelie," I whisper, tainting the air with the haunting admission. "He's got men, women ... *children* entombed in a feeding burrow beneath an island in the bay."

I wait for any reaction at all.

*Nothing.*

Just the sound of her breathing hard and fast through her nose.

"I— I have a plan to rescue them. Their lives depend on it."

I give that information time to settle, feeling each second tick by faster than the last while I stare at the door. Expecting someone to burst in at any moment to hail me for the ceremony.

*We can't stand here all night ...*

I draw a tight breath. "I'm going to let you speak now. Please don't do anything stupid."

The second I lift my palm, she screams.

I slam the heel of my hand into the side of her head, and she crumples. Fists assault the door as Izel's limp body thuds to the floor at my feet.

"Orlaith?"

*Fuck.*

I leap over Izel and dash to the door, pulling it open just enough for me to peek through the gap up into Kolden's daunted expression. "Can you keep everyone out for a moment?"

He looks past me, eyes widening. "*Is she—*"

"Going to have a very bad headache when she wakes up?" I mutter, and a sharp curse batters me.

"*How?*"

"She saw me mixing liquid bane with my lip lacquer."

All the color drops from his face, and he tries to shove the door.

I frown, pushing my weight against it. "What are you doing? Stop that."

"Step aside," he growls. "I'll make it quick. She won't feel a thing."

*Holy petunia*—he means to kill her.

"That is *not* happening!" I whisper-hiss. "She doesn't need to *die*. Just ... watch the door so I can stuff her somewhere."

The muscle in his jaw pops, but the sound of booted steps has him glancing over his shoulder. "The guards are coming to collect you. I can buy you another two minutes—tops."

The door snips shut.

I draw a deep, shuddered breath, surveying the room, trying to work out where to stash my unconscious handmaiden so I won't be worried about her waking midceremony and busting ... *everything.*

I can't tie her up and gag her. What if nobody finds her and she perishes? That doesn't sit well, even with my emotions lumped beneath a stab-proof barrier.

My gaze hones on my dressing room, an idea flaring to life like a lantern's flame ...

*I'll smuggle her down the stairwell and lean a chair against the door. When she wakes, she can leave through the hidden exit that will spit her out amid the jungle—far enough away that I'll hopefully be long gone by the time she tattles.*

*Good plan.*

I boot the fertility tonic away, wrap my hands around her wrists, and drag her backward, huffing and puffing, straining against her weight. "This is all ... for nothing," I mutter, as if she can hear me. "I'm about ... ninety-four percent certain it can't even kill him. He'll just have a ... nice, big, hopefully really long nap. Not that you can talk. Your ... moral compass doesn't exactly point ... true north. What were you even going to say? *'I found the High Master's ... promised using the berries I tried to ... poison her with?'* Come now. You're smarter ... than that, Izel."

I lug the secret door open, heave her partway down the stairs, set a lantern beside her so she has protection against the Irilak should she venture into the night, then lean back with my hands on my hips while I catch my breath. "Try not to roll down the stairs in your sleep," I say on a sigh, then move into the dressing room, close the secret door-mirror behind me, and shove one of the heavy, ornate dressing chairs in front of it.

*There.*

I dash into my suite, catching sight of a dark shadow perched atop my dining table. My heart leaps up my throat, and I still, the sound of my rushing pulse a roar in my ears.

A massive black krah cocks its head to the side, watching me through inky eyes that seem to reel me in.

*Perhaps it's come to shit on me and stake my death in the soil?*

"Not now," I hiss, striding forward with a flick of my hands. "I've got too much to do. *Shoo!*"

It flaps into the air, swooping leathery-winged circles about the ceiling, then lands atop the pole connecting two of my bedposts, scampering into a sitting position. Staring down on me from its lofty perch with a strange imperial bearing that would put me on edge if I wasn't so busy staying *off* the edge.

It turns, curls its lanky tail around the bar, then plummets backward—hanging upside down as it shuffles its wings until they're tucked around its body like a sooty cocoon. I think it's settling in for a nap, except it doesn't close its eyes.

Just continues to watch me.

I sigh, sit on my stool, and use the long brush to blend the liquid bane through the red lip lacquer. "Don't judge me," I mutter, glancing at the krah in the mirror before painting my lips with careful strokes that smother the bloody tone, replacing it with a rich, deadly color.

A loud knock almost has me jumping out of my

skin, and I fumble with the lacquer, tucking it in my drawer. "Coming!"

I delve my hands into the cramped flush of wildflowers, like splitting a book down the center, revealing the big, white bud sitting an inch above the soil atop a thick stem, all bound up with its secrets tucked away.

I blow on it.

Five petals uncurl, cupping a clutch of milky filaments capped with tiny beads of light, each petal the size and shape of the pad of my thumb.

A smile fills my cheeks, and I draw on the rich, spicy fragrance that makes the back of my nose itch.

"Aren't you clever," I whisper, then pluck two petals and tuck them beneath the crown of braids wrapped around my head.

I peek up at the krah again, setting my finger against my poisonous lips as it blinks at me.

"Shh ..."

# CHAPTER 39

*Orlaith*

I'm escorted down a vast hallway of roughly hewn stone, gray like the robes from my nightmares.

Every step is coddled by a clanking cage of synchronized guards, each adorned in a glinting shell of golden armor. I doubt there's much that could penetrate the wall of metal and brawn surrounding me from all angles. Seems a bit of an overkill since the hall is empty aside from us—the majority of the palace's servants celebrating in the streets with the people of Parith, shooting their pretty light show from the esplanade, getting drunk and high and singing their merry tunes.

The muffled sound of a thudding drum continues to call us forward, strengthening with every step I take, beating in rhythm with my languid heart. I know I should be nervous. That somewhere deep below the layers of shiny defense I've stacked inside myself, I'm just a small, frightened girl who wants to curl up beneath the bed and hide.

But fear is a luxury I can no longer afford—not for myself.

I slather more layers upon the crystal dome that's keeping me tame. Keeping me from thinking too much.

Feeling too much.

We reach the end of the hall, and the front guards peel away, revealing a pair of large granite doors flanked by two robed Shulák who dip their heads and bow.

I cringe inwardly. There's not one single part of me that wants their respect, and if I wasn't so busy stuffing everything down, I'd probably say as much.

I smooth another layer of light upon my rumbling dome.

The doors are pulled wide, releasing a roll of thick, white smoke that spills across the floor, cloying around my ankles like insipid vines riddled with iridescent sparkles. I frown, crouching. Wafting some up against my face to smell it.

"*Orlaith*," Kolden hisses, reaching out as if to grab my wrist and drag me away, before his gaze darts to the other guards. He clears his throat, resuming his position while the breath tingles down my throat, all the way to the bottom of my lungs.

This warm, gooey feeling unfurls within me.

*Strange.*

I look at the smoke again, so caught up in the glimmery, seductive swirl that the next volley of drumbeats has my stare snapping up.

I suck a sharp breath.

The massive square chamber ahead ... It's *odd*.

Flaming wall sconces are bolted to the lofty walls containing an ocean of heavy smoke stretched before us, freckled with specks of color that catch on the orange firelight spilling across the expanse. Every now and then there's a riot of undulating motion that makes the smoke tide, revealing a flash of flesh or a whip of honey-colored hair.

The thick musk of sweat, spice, and sex shoves me full of seedy promises with every hoarse inhale. And the *sounds*—the deep, desperate grunts and high-pitched cries of passion ... They settle inside me like a flush of tepid blooms unfurling from their coiled constraints.

It reminds me of a forest nymph's lair, except all the action is caught beneath that sea of smoke. I doubt they can even see what they're doing. Who they're touching.

Round, flat rocks sit just above the surface of the heavy smog like stepping stones, dotting a path through the middle to a pair of stone doors bracketed by two more Shulák.

My curiosity peaks as the spilling atmosphere tangles with my hair and licks shivers across my skin. Kisses a line down the ladder of my spine. It tweaks my nipples and makes my body feel warm. Tingly.

A little more ... *free.*

"What is this place?" My voice sounds funny. Sultry, even.

I'm not sure why.

One of the Shulák lifts a cloth to his mouth, then follows a swooping trail of steps down into the smoke and disappears from sight, the other turning his attention to me. "The Pit of Impurity. The Impurists are doing the act for which they were branded. Ten have been chosen at random to redeem their soiled souls by becoming a Vessel of the Gods. The utmost privilege."

"Oh."

*That makes no sense.*

Kolden nudges my foot with his boot, and I look at him—a pillar of fortitude staked at my side.

*Don't breathe more,* he mouths.

I frown.

*That's hardly good advice.*

I'm about to tell him exactly that when the Shulák scales the staircase, rising free of the vapor that wafts off him. He leads a naked woman by the hand until she's standing beside me—blue eyes glazed, nipples peaked, cheeks as flushed as her lips that are smudged in sparkly stuff. Her hair is a tumble of creamy curls that fall well below her pert bum.

She reminds me of ... someone. But I think that *someone* had different colored eyes. A friend, I think? Her name's on the tip of my tongue, but I can't quite pin it down.

It keeps wriggling further away.

"This is where your escorts leave you," one of the Shulák announces, taking my hand and easing me forward. "You—a Paragon of Purity advocated by the Gods—will now cross the Path of Athandon, walking above the Impurists who have failed to gain passage into Mala this eve."

Failed to gain—

*Huh?*

I look over my shoulder, catching a final glimpse of Kolden's furrowed brow before the doors snip shut with a thud of finality that feels significant.

I think.

Maybe it's not significant at all?

I nuzzle into that heat still nesting in my lungs and decide on the latter.

Our hosts gesture us forward with sweeps of their robed arms, and I realize they mean for us to jump from one stone to the next until we reach the doors on the other side. Unsure how the woman next to me is going to manage *that* in her current state, I hitch the hem of my decorative sheath, take her by the hand, and lead her across the treacherous terrain.

We kick up swirls of smoke with every leap, something heavy thumping against my ankle with each frolicking bound, the girl's giggles a tinkling echo that patters upon my skin—like this is a merry game of hopscotch.

*Perhaps it is?*

"Wait!"

The girl pulls her hand from mine, and I peek over my shoulder to see her crouching, eyes sparkling with mischief. Her hair hangs forward, revealing long marks on her back that are raised and red and look like they hurt.

This big, shiny thing deep inside me rattles.

*Strange.*

She scoops up some of the smoke and blows it toward me like she's trying to spur a fog-fight. It wafts against my face like a pleasant splash of frothy water.

I smile, her infectious joy warming my blood into a bubbling rush.

We leap from stone to stone, pausing here and there to splash each other with smoke. I realize I'm laughing, too.

*This is fun. I like this place.*

*Why did I not want to come here?*

*And what is this floaty white stuff? It smells like sexy things. Makes me want to feel the way this woman looks.*

*Captivating and free.*

She wafts more smoke at me, and it slips down my throat like a cool, crisp drink, then settles in my lungs with a comforting heaviness that pops and crackles.

I giggle again, certain I'm floating on winged feet.

We leap onto a podium, and two robed people pull some stone doors open. A warm breeze nips at my skin as we jog up a flight of stairs that seems to cut through the sky before wrapping around the outside of a stone tower.

We sing to the stars and the wind and the sound of heaving waves below as we frolic up the stairs that curl round and round.

I like these stairs. I think they will lead me somewhere safe and sunny, but I'm not sure why.

Stopping, I look down, back the way we came ...

The girl tugs my hand. "Come on!"

"I want to count them."

"Next time." She giggles, giving me another tug. "We're almost at the top! I want to fly to the stars with you!"

*That sounds nice.*

I smile and chase her round and round some more. We spill onto a big circular stage that's supporting a ring of high towers, each carved with strange words. I look up, seeking their tapered tips, my mouth popping open in wonderment when I see how close we are to the moon—huge and silver and *beautiful*, painting my upturned face in a pour of fresh light that ignites every cell in my body.

I want to dance naked for it. To drag my fingers through my hair and cup my heavy breasts. I want to climb onto all fours and bay to it like an animal full of nothing but rich, primal, *wanting* sounds squirming up my throat.

"This is a *wonderland!*"

My words echo …

echo …

echo …

The woman giggles and tugs me into a spin, and we twirl for the moon, her creamy hair like liquid silver beneath those rays of light.

I'm not sure why that makes my chest hurt.

I stare at that silver moon again as somebody tugs me sideways—

I land on my knees on a large, soft pillow, and my stare levels with a pair of blue eyes.

The man before me has hair the color of a tumbleweed, the tousled tips brushing broad, bare, muscular shoulders. Pretty gray words are painted down the sides of his neck, over his chest and chiseled stomach where they disappear beneath the waistband of his pants.

I savor the words. Part of me even wants to *touch* them. But there's something wrong with them. As though they're in the wrong place …

Or *something.*

He's a beautiful man, but my body doesn't respond to him like it did the moans and the smells and the deep, throaty grunts.

Like it does the silver moon.

*Why am I here with this man I don't know in this place that is so very strange?*

My mind squeezes, like a muscle trying to contract. I'm

certain if I squeeze it hard enough this will all make sense again.

"Petal," the man says on a throaty laugh. "It's hit you hard, hasn't it? I can barely see the purple in your eyes. We'll have to build up your immunity."

I don't know what he's talking about. Who is this *petal?* I don't think that's me.

Hearing it doesn't make me feel good.

Somebody begins speaking strange words that make no sense, and I look up at a robed woman with long hair bound in a very tidy braid, her eyes such a pretty blend of purple and blue—though I don't like the way they're looking at me.

*I don't think that woman likes me very much.*

Kneeling before her is the naked woman I danced beneath the moon with, her kind eyes staring right at me.

She giggles.

*Such an infectious sound.*

A glint of something long and sharp catches my attention, and a splash of warmth hits my face. Dark liquid pours from a line drawn across her throat, down her breasts.

Frowning, I look at her eyes, but they don't see me anymore.

She's no longer giggling. Instead, her mouth is *gaping.*

Some of that dark liquid is collected in a bowl, and more robed people close in to carry the girl away, leaving a trail of wet splats that make me frown. I try to squeeze my mind again, but I just can't squeeze it hard enough.

I try it from a different angle. Nothing.

I thought this was a wonderland ... Now I'm not so sure.

*Think.*

*Think …*

I look at the man before me.

He tilts his head to the side, the blue in his eyes giving way to more and more black. "Is this the first time you've seen a sacrifice?"

*I don't know what that is.*

"Maybe not?"

That seems like a good answer—halfway between a yes and a no.

Just as confused as I am.

He makes a low humming sound. "They're done to appease the Gods. Mainly Kvath, Jakar, and Bjorn—who created the universe with the convergence of their mighty powers. Death, blood, and a balanced number of sacrifices for a fruitful coupling."

I frown, not certain I want any of this fruit he speaks of. His words don't chime like the girl's giggles.

They don't make me feel happy inside.

I crane my neck, trying to see where she went as the woman in the robe says more words that mean less and less.

The man before me dips his fingers into the bowl of dark liquid, painting the slippery substance upon the stone bangle around my wrist as he looks into my eyes— something possessive in his stare that makes me feel strange.

"Tonight, the Gods will pierce the veil between our realms to witness me pierce the veil between our bodies. Tonight, I claim you before them—as mine. Forever."

I frown, not so certain I want this veil to be *pierced*. It sounds painful.

Unpleasant.

He takes my hand and dips my fingers into the wet stuff, too. Like a puppet on a string, he coaxes me to paint *his* stone bangle while I'm told to repeat things:

*"Tonight, we will open the veil to the Gods while I open my body to this man, surrendering my blood and binding us for eternity."*

I don't like the way the words taste. How they feel in my mouth. I want to take them back.

My wrist is grabbed real tight, forcing my hand to flatten. Something sharp is dragged along it, drawing a line of sting that makes something big and sparkly and smooth inside me shake.

Shake.

*Shake.*

The man clasps my hand in his, and his own is wet and warm.

I squeeze my mind so hard I'm certain I'm making a mess of it, turning it into a mangled lump while I try to force its juices free.

*Think!*

My hurt is bound in a strip of material, and the man helps me to my feet. I'm led between two of the towers and over a line of those pretty scripted words painted with something red and wet I'm told not to smudge.

I'm not sure I wanted to touch it, anyway.

We step into a large, shallow dip the same shape as the moon above us. It's smothered in white pillows that look soft as clouds. There's white blankets and white rugs and more white pillows I keep tripping over because I can't stop staring *up*.

The moon is so big and bright and silver. It sits perfectly against the bold sky.

I love it.

I want to touch it, catch it, pull it close to my chest.

*Why am I here? I should be up there …*

I trip on another pillow, but the man has me by the arm. Laughing, he lowers me to my knees, then leans close to my ear. "They're going to summon the Gods now to witness our coupling."

*Coupling.*

*Coupling.*

*Coupling …*

I don't know what that is, but I don't think it's something I want to do. I just want to sit here and stare at the moon. Picture what it would feel like if I could drag my finger across it. Would clumps of silver come away under my fingernails? Or perhaps it would shave off in curls? Maybe it wouldn't be hard at all but a wet paint I could smear all over myself?

I think I would like that.

More weird chanting of words I don't understand, and I look around, seeing many robed people standing between the towers.

"*Vliagh, ashten de na, malika nei. Vliagh, ashten de na, malika nei. Vliagh, ashten de na, malika nei—*"

I frown, feeling each strange sound pat my skin, becoming more insistent with each repetition … as though they're trying to tell me something.

"*Vliagh, ashten de na, malika nei. Vliagh, ashten de na, malika nei. Vliagh, ashten de na, malika nei—*"

The man on his knees before me is looking at me funny,

holding my hands real tight. "Are you okay, petal? You've gone very pale."

His words are so soft and squishy compared to the ones being chanted. Perhaps it's the repetition that's making me look at them harder. Making me examine them from their infinite angles.

No ...

It's something I can taste on the air. Something that reaches beyond the bounds of my mind, like they're ancient. Otherworldly.

Like they were hewn from a faraway star.

The words grow heavier the more they're stacked upon each other, building a static tower that feels as though it's reaching for the moon.

*Beyond.*

"*Vliagh, ashten de na, malika nei. Vliagh, ashten de na, malika nei. Vliagh, ashten de na, malika nei—*"

A warm, prickly current wiggles beneath my skin and makes me shudder, seeming to wrap around ... my shoulder? My neck?

*Deeper?*

It tugs, tugs, *tugs*—like trying to yank a worm from the soil.

A sharp whistle flares to life, drilling into my ears. I want to clap my hands over them and block out the sound, but I can't because the man's got them caught. Just like this *thing* caught on my collarbone, like I'm on the end of a line.

"What's that ringing sound?"

The man frowns, looking at me even funnier than he was before. "There is no ringing sound, Orlaith."

*I don't think that's my name ...*

"*Vliagh, ashten de na, malika nei. Vliagh, ashten de na, malika nei—*"

The sound raises a pitch—or ten—and my vision goes wobbly, like something inside me is trying to shake loose. The pain in my ears grows until my right one feels hot, my eardrum swelling with a pulsing pressure that's *buckling.* Like my entire skeleton is trying to shuck its skin and worm through my right ear.

I rip my hand free and use it to cup the hurt, blocking the teeny, tiny exit, features twisting as the hazy fog draped across my brain seems to suction out of the hole like sand flowing through an hourglass. My ear *pops,* like when I dive too deep without equalizing, and whatever was trying to worm out snaps back into place so hard and fast only the man holding onto my hand keeps me from whipping sideways.

"*Vliagh, ashten de na, malika nei. Vliagh, ashten de na, malika nei—*"

Things bead back to me like fat raindrops wetting the sun-scorched soil ...

*Coupling ceremony.*

*Promises.*

"*Vliagh, ashten de na, malika nei. Vliagh, ashten de na, malika nei—*"

My mental focus sharpens the image of the man holding me steady, frowning. "Are you okay?"

*Cainon.*

*Poisonous lips.*

"*Vliagh, ashten de na, malika nei. Vliagh, ashten de na, malika nei—*"

*Him ... gone.*

The last one is not a drop at all, but a drenching.

A *drowning.*

My squishy mind hardens to full, devastating focus, like I've just been picked up out of one place and dropped into another. I have no idea which way is north. How long it's been since those doors closed on Kolden.

I have no idea where the girl went—the one I danced beneath the moon with.

But Cainon and I, we're kneeling on a massive bed of white pillows and throws, and that can only mean one thing ...

Panic riots through me as I check my dome, finding it strong and secure, relief almost crumbling me, though I paint another layer atop it just to be certain. "I'm fine," I lie, giving him a sweet, poisonous smile.

The chanting stops.

An eerie silence befalls us. So quiet, I can hear the constant workings of my body: the snap of a blink; the *whoosh* of my heart squeezing; the way my lungs squish with every breath I pull.

Something cool I cannot see or smell brushes against my face, leaving a prickly trail that makes my heart skip a beat I'm certain everybody can hear.

I look up into Cainon's eyes, a rumbling sound boiling in his chest like a greedy promise.

*Poisonous lips.*

My gaze is drawn sideways, to where the High Septum and each of the robed Shulák are filing out between two of the towers, disappearing through the curtain.

"Where are they going?" My voice is too loud, *screaming* even though the words were whispered.

"The palace sky roof. They'll bow before the moon until it sinks," Cainon says, taking on that deeper tone he gets when he's hungry.

For me.

*Poisonous lips.*

"They've left us alone to consummate before the Gods."

Frowning, I follow the direction he's pointing.

All the breath leaves my lungs, the sight making me feel like something just shoved its arm down my throat, gripped my guts, and tore them free.

*Oh my ...*

*No.*

*No-no-no ...*

The beautiful, happy woman I led across the stepping stones is nailed to one of the spires, blood spilling down her naked body, her chest cleaved with special instruments that bare her vacant cavity.

She's still, like a broken doll pinned against the wall, and ...

She's *watching* me.

But her eyes don't appear like they did before. The now-golden orbs dazzle in the moonlight like blazing suns. Just looking at them makes me want to scrunch my lids and hide from the radiant glare.

I wrestle the urge to vomit and rip my stare from the sight. Look to the next.

Regret it instantly.

Another woman—this one with shorter hair and more voluptuous curves—is presented in the same macabre way.

Her wide, *seeing* eyes are like fog caught in a ball, swirling so fast they make my head spin.

My blood curdles, heart pounding hard to slush it through my veins as I close my eyes and breathe ...

*Breathe ...*

*What the fuck is this?*

*What.*

*The.*

*Fuck.*

My morbid curiosity gnaws through its chains and takes another bite of the scene.

Blood-red irises and black, slitted pupils stare out at me from the next unlucky victim of this mass slaying—a thin man with long hair and spindly hands hammered to the stone. But those eyes are anything but dead, and they're looking at me like I'm *prey;* a piercing stare that makes it feel as though there's something wrapped around my throat.

*Tightening.*

That voice inside screams for me to *run.*

Another icy trail breezes across my lips. A phantom touch—so safe and familiar I want to lean into it. To tuck beneath it and hide from this living nightmare.

I look over Cainon's shoulder to a broad man tacked to the stone, his head pinned upright by nails hammered beside his ears. His ribs are splayed, baring another chest cavity. No heart, lungs, intestines.

Empty.

But his *eyes*—they're a swirl of quicksilver sprinkled with stars that would bring me to my knees if I weren't already here.

They're the opposite to the hollow insides, churning with so much violence the waves ripple through the space between us, splashing against my chest to the beat of my thundering heart.

And they're looking right at me.

# CHAPTER

*Orlaith*

## 40

reathless, I'm held captive by that bruising stare, like the man himself has my lungs in his ghostly fists—tightening his grip.

*Tighter.*

That sparkly fog I was inhaling must have built illusions in my mind. That's the only way I can reason with ... this.

*Him.*

*Maybe I'm going mad?*

Even so, I want to drop Cainon's hand and run over there. Fall to my knees before that poor, wasted life hanging from the stone and beg for Rhordyn's forgiveness. Tell him how stupid I was. How *naïve.*

Tell him I'm doing everything I can to atone.

Those beautiful eyes move, casting an icy trail over my lips ... my chin ...

Cainon threads his fingers through my hair and pins it back with a firm grip on the side of my head, baring my torn-up throat, showing more flesh to that charging gaze that slides across my neck like an avalanche.

A bolt of lightning snaps through the sky above, and I flinch.

"Don't be afraid," Cainon murmurs—a comforting coo I barely hear over the ringing in my throbbing ear. He points toward the swelling storm. "Jakar is showing his *approval*."

My heart jumps into my throat as he tips forward, rumbling low, his lips almost brushing mine. Like he's about to steal a spiked kiss.

*Yes.*

I arch forward, urging him on.

*Do it.*

Another head-splitting *boom*, the sky rattling its chains so hard the stone beneath us shakes.

Cainon's breath skims my lips as he makes a chuffing sound, then pulls back, eyes glinting with a blaze of lust. "Patience, petal," he says on a gravelly laugh, regarding me with such intense focus I feel pinned in place in more ways than one. "I want to *savor* your body before I taste those pretty lips."

I don't want that. Not one bit.

I want him to taste my poisonous lips, then fall in a heap so I never have to feel his breath on me again. Or his teeth in my flesh.

*So I never have to know what it feels like to have him move inside me.*

He shifts so fast the world blurs, and then I'm spread out on my back, all the breath knocked from my lungs as he brackets me in with his flexing might—stretched atop me in a way that makes me wither inside.

Makes that dome rattle and rumble, a scratch, scratch, *scratch* grinding beneath it.

He sinks his face into the crook of my neck. "You're *mine*," he growls, his words stained with his twisted, tainted affection. His too-hot touch skims down my leg, fingers tangling with the hem of my gown. He slides it up, and my entire body locks.

Another bolt of lightning scribbles across the sky, and desperation shakes me loose from the inside out.

If it rains, the poison will be washed from my lips. This will all be for *nothing*.

And I'll have to ... with ...

*No.*

Cainon nibbles my jaw. Runs his tongue along the skin. I harden my spine—my heart—and grip both sides of his face, forcing him to meet my steely gaze. "Kiss me," I command, my voice a husky groan.

Another violent *boom* rattles the walls as his eyes ignite, like I just sparked them with a match.

"*Now.*"

With a bone-rattling growl, he crushes our lips together.

I let my hands drop and open myself, a willing victim to his lashing tongue while he pours thick, throaty sounds past my poisonous lips.

But I don't just need him to kiss me ...

I need him to *swallow.*

He tips back for breath, his hands a cradling prison for my face, and I pull my lip between my teeth and bite so hard warmth dribbles all the way to my chin.

371

Releasing a sawing sound, he lunges forward again, digging his tongue so far into my mouth I can barely breathe. His hands maul my hair, like he's purposely screwing it up so he can spend hours untangling it later.

Breaking the kiss, he leans back on his heels. "You're a *delicious* creature," he grinds out. His throat works, and I picture a mix of noxious blood slipping down into his belly as his eyes turn inky. "*Mine.*"

I battle the urge to flinch.

The word wounds—every time. Because I'm not his. Not anyone's.

*Not anymore.*

I belong to the silver-licked shadows of my own mistakes.

He moves to grab my right ankle, but I shove the left one at his chest instead, stuffing the other beneath a pillow.

A hungry smile stretches across his face as his hand tightens around it, fingertips grazing up my calf. "Pushy tonight, aren't we?"

I nod.

He releases a dark chuckle that rattles my bones, then plants a kiss on the arch of my foot. I want nothing more than to rip away from his touch as he pecks another upon the inside of my ankle …

Just above it …

My heart sits in my throat like a rock.

I hold the saliva pooling in my mouth, knowing where those kisses are heading. Knowing I'd rather swallow this poison than feel his lips *there.*

Watching me, he peppers a haunting trail all the way to my knee, my heartstrings fraying a little more with each too-hot peck upon my crawling skin.

I want him off me.

*Want him off, want him off—*

His next kiss wavers, and my stomach flips as his pupils swell. A black, bubbly froth leaks from the corner of his mouth, and the backs of my eyes sting, my face threatening to crumble. My knees wobble with the urge to squeeze together, like they've been released from a catatonic spell.

He drops my leg. Claws at his throat.

My entire body begins to tremble.

Blood rushes to his head, the veins in his temple and forehead swelling to the surface as his chest heaves deep, gurgling breaths—reminding me of the people he's condemned to rot on the outskirts of his city.

A drop of satisfaction drips upon my chest.

A bubbling, choking cough, and something flashes in his widening eyes as he shreds at the skin around his neck—a mix of emotions too complex for me to trace. *"You—poisoned me—"*

*Checkmate, asshole.*

Lids drifting shut, his limp body sways forward, making my heart vault. I try to scramble backward—

*Not fast enough.*

His body lands upon me with such hefty force all the breath is punched from my lungs, my mouth gaping. A trickle of saliva slides across the back of my throat, making the muscles clamp down like a knee-jerk reaction.

*Fuck.*

I whimper, shoving at his body, trying to kick him off with my free leg. More saliva pools in the back of my throat. Lightning threatens to crack the sky into shards, and I hear the patter of raindrops before they batter my skin.

My movements become frantic, this trapped feeling inside me swelling.

*Swelling.*

*Get him off—*

Cainon's ripped backward, plonked to the side in a heavy lump, revealing Kolden standing over me with a scarf wrapped around the lower half of his face. He yanks it down so it's hanging around his neck, kneels, and pulls me into a seated position.

I dig my fingers down my throat. My stomach clenches, and a flaming surge of bile pours up and out of me in a gushing torrent. I spit, splutter, heave all over a pillow, feeling numerous celestial stares rake across my skin—like they're watching this show unfold with rapt attention.

Gasping, I tip back, tears streaming down my cheeks, mixing with the rain now pounding upon the pure white pillows, drenching my hair and skin. I cut a glance at the red, slitted eyes as I wipe my lips with the back of my arm, painting it with a poisonous smear.

Call it intuition, but something about them makes me think that particular God *wants* me to choke.

"Where did you put it?" Kolden barks, and I rip at the tiny braids around the crown of my head, hands trembling, hunting for the petals I stuffed beneath them. When I come up empty-handed, I get onto all fours and begin flipping pillows and throws while Kolden does the same.

A dark realization dawns.

*They must have fallen out … Maybe blown away …*

I look at Kolden sideways. "They're not here."

His eyes widen. "Did you swallow some?"

*Maybe I got it out in time …*

I nod.

"*Fuck,*" Kolden growls, pulling his scarf up. He whips another out from beneath his chest plate, wraps it around my face, then sweeps me into his arms.

He spins, and I catch sight of those chilling silver eyes boring through me like a savage pledge. A gaze that follows us until we slip out of sight.

"I think I'm okay," I say, yanking the scarf off my face. I'm certain it's making it harder for me to breathe. "You can put me dow—"

"No," Kolden grinds out between muffled breaths as he powers through eerily quiet hallways with me tucked against his armor. "You'll speed up your heart rate and pump the bane through your system faster."

I go to argue, but a cough comes out instead, barking up my throat.

"Fuck," Kolden hisses, then tucks into a cupboard, slapping a hand over my mouth.

I wrestle the urge to cough again, chest jerking as booted footsteps come, then go. Perhaps a guard making rounds.

Kolden pushes his head out and looks both ways before ripping down his scarf and charging on. I let the cough free—this one wetter than the last.

We make it all the way to the main lobby before my vision starts to split. By the time he's sprinting toward the door where he usually stands guard, my breaths are gurgling, throat tightening with each restless draw.

I whimper, my stomach turning cold, then numb—the same numbness creeping up my throat much faster than I'd like it to.

Thoughts roll through my head like boulders ...

What if I die? I didn't tell Kolden I have people to save or my plan to free them. And now my breaths are so wet I doubt I'll be able to get the words out before my last heave.

*Shit.*

"You're okay," he grinds out, shoving into the lobby as that numbness reaches the back of my tongue, making it feel floppy. I lose the ability to keep my head upright. "You're going to be okay. Just hold on."

He powers past the door into my moonlit suite, and I watch the world slip by upside down. He settles me on the ground, my limbs like felled branches.

Kolden stomps away with hurried steps, then tromps back again.

"Which one, Orlaith? *Point.*"

Wheezing, I look through slitted eyes at the four different-colored petals he's waving at me, then let out a mangled groan when I fail to move my arm. I focus on the white one and try to jerk my chin at it. Guess I get the point across because he cranks my mouth open and lays it on my tongue.

"*Chew!*" he bellows, stamping my mouth closed, like he thinks I'll spit it out and get straight back to dying.

*I can't die yet. I've got promises to keep.*

That foreboding chill seeps further up my tongue, the deadly numb trailing just behind, and I grind my teeth against each other one slow, chattering chew at a time. The spicy petal mashes with the frothy stuff that was forming, setting fire to my taste buds and making the back of my nose burn.

"Swallow," he orders, and I oblige, feeling it sear a path

down my throat and pool in my belly, chasing away that numbing sensation with everything it touches.

*Torches.*

Relief weaves its roots through my chest.

Kolden opens my mouth and places another petal on my tongue. "Again."

I want to tell him it's unnecessary, that this stuff is so potent it could reignite a graveyard of poisoned folk, but it takes less energy to chew.

That burning sensation spreads, paving a fiery path through my veins, making my hands and feet tingle with the rush of warmth. I flap my floppy arm about until my hand connects with the golden urn, remove the lid, then wrap around. My entire body convulses with the force of a violent, lung-scraping cough.

Wet stuff loosens from my chest and splats out of me, dribbling down my chin.

*Again.*

Teeth chattering, I peek up from the urn, clinging to it like a lichen tethered to a rock. Kolden's standing over me with his arms half crossed, right hand massaging his jaw as he watches me with stern eyes.

"Ships?" I ask.

"I haven't heard yet, but no news is good news."

I nod, then bark out another round of splattering coughs that echo through the urn, spitting more thick stuff free of my heavy chest.

*That's good.*

I peer up again, feeling goo stringing from my chin like a sticky spider web, seeing the smear of blood on Kolden's chestplate.

I frown, catching his stare.

He glances down, sees what I was looking at, and begins ripping at one of the leather straps on his shoulder that tethers the chestplate to his body. "One of the Elders stayed back and was lagging by the door, getting off on the sounds. You'd been in there too long. I got concerned," he grinds out, his motions growing sharp and desperate, until the buckle finally pops loose. "I did what I had to do, then stuffed him in an urn before I charged in."

My stomach roils.

Cainon could have still been awake. Somebody in the smoke pit could have clambered out and seen him—though I doubt it. They were pretty well occupied.

Even so ...

"You"—I clear the tickle from my throat—"saved me."

*More than just me.*

He tears at the strap on his other shoulder, jaw set as he unbuckles the sides and lifts the piece, then lumps it on the bed. He drags a hand down his face.

"Thank you, Kolden."

He grabs a piece of tissue parchment from my vanity and hands it to me. "You can repay me by getting out of this city. Now."

*Oh dear.*

"Slight problem ..."

A frown shadows his eyes as I swallow thickly, cutting him a cursory glance before I take the parchment and use it to wipe my chin. I toss the scrunched-up ball in the urn, then clonk the lid back into place, giving the thing a little pat before I push to a wobbly stand.

Wavering, I wait until I stop seeing doubles before I lift my chin. "There's something I have to do first, and I'm not leaving until it's done."

# CHAPTER

*Zali*

## 41

A storm churns at our backs, roughing up the waves and giving us a forward shove that has sped up our journey at a gut-spilling rate.

I like rolling waves of sand. Wet ones ... not so much.

I only hope it's not too rough for Gunthar and his small crew to make it out of the bay once Orlaith is free of the ceremony. And I hope like hell nobody raises the sea gate before they leave.

My thoughts turn to Baze and the cutting words he slashed at me before he left my room ...

*If anything happens to her, I'll never forgive you. Or myself.*

My stomach does another sickening churn.

He never met us at the docks, despite me sending him a sprite to inform him of our plans. Like he severed himself from the pack.

From *me*.

In the end, it was probably a good thing, since every

man was checked for burns by a flock of Gray Guards before being allowed to board the ships loaded with enough reserves to last a few months at sea. Not that we'll need it all.

Precautions.

The crewmen also stacked the hulls with 'empty' barrels containing the loved ones of every sailor who boarded one of the seven whaling ships now trailing us through the howling, moon-soaked night, the lids cracked off the moment we set sail.

Every Ocruth warrior Rhordyn and Cindra smuggled into the city over the past number of weeks is dressed in blue, weapons concealed, demeanor calm as they work the deck to the booming tune of the distant storm, casting glances ahead. A sea of stony faces betraying none of the nerves I'm certain they're all feeling.

Kolden's note spoke of a guarded outpost that usually boasts up to ten soldiers overseeing the building of the ships, but I'll believe that when I see it.

The only definites in this world are the ones you forge for yourself.

Cutting through dense, bucking waves, we veer around the edge of a mounded island clothed in thick brush and numerous palm trees, visible beneath the bold moonlight.

I frown, wiping a splash of seawater off my face. "This can't be right," I mutter, Cindra stepping up beside me. "I was expecting crops of cedar." I scuff my boot against the floorboards. "That's what his ships are built from ..."

"Hmm." She holds onto the mast as we tip down the face of a smaller wave, the waters finally calming now that we're sailing around the island's protected side. "Perhaps they're outsourcing the timber for the ships?"

"Good point ... unless they have their own plantations farther around. Either way, I'd like to know we're on the right track. Perhaps check with Rowell?"

*If we've been given the wrong coordinates, we're screwed.*

Cindra nods, disappearing toward the back of the ship.

With the fierce wind easing, the boat has slowed, and the men hurry to tighten the sails as we navigate the dark coastline at a smooth pace. We coast around a rocky outcrop, relief surging through me when the island practically yawns—boasting its gaping maw. The sheltered bay is larger than Parith, cut with a steep stone backdrop.

Ship hulls line the shore in various stages of construction, suspended in massive wooden cradles.

I scan the wide waterfront lit by flaming torches placed in intervals around the bay. About thirty-five blue-sailed ships pock the water.

Not nearly as many as I was thinking.

Shit ...

We'll be down on numbers, and I won't get the privilege of sinking any remaining ships as a silent *screw you* to Cainon.

I look behind, making sure Cindra's waving the flag for the others to hold back while we cut through the water toward a thick, stubby pier jutting from just beyond the point, the end illuminated by twin torches.

Seven armed men stalk toward us.

"This is going to be interesting," Cindra murmurs at my side as Rowell drifts the ship against the dock, somebody else throwing down a rope to one of the waiting guards—each of them looking up at us with pinched brows, glazed eyes, and flushed cheeks.

One of them hiccups.

"I think they're *drunk*."

"Any excuse for a bender," Cindra muses, and I hum in acknowledgement, tucking a string of oily black hair behind my ear—my fiery locks slathered in a mix of coal dust and lard that makes me smell like the rotten mop below deck. Messy, but necessary.

*Drunken guards mean they're less likely to see through my disguise.*

The crewmen lower the gangplank, and I'm the first across it.

One of the soldiers squints at me a little too hard, like he's picking apart my sooty disguise. I smell the alcohol on his breath before he says, "Who the hell are"—*hiccup*—"*you?*"

Relief fills me.

The man at the front with a barreling chest and heavy lines at the corners of his flint-blue eyes lifts his hand without looking back at the man, a quiet command for him to shut it. "What's the meaning of this?" he barks, nose scrunching as he leers up and down my body, then does the same to Cindra.

My skin crawls.

I pull a squashed scroll from the beeswaxed pocket of my cloak, thankful to see no water has seeped through from our sodden journey.

I hand it over, and he unravels the parchment, frowning

as he reads it. "The High Mistress's dowry, aye? No cunt is worth that many ships."

I bite my tongue so hard it bleeds, hand twitching to reach for my blade …

"First I've heard of this load of krah shit," he grumbles, then hoicks a wad of spit at the pier.

*Unsurprising.*

"Be that as it may, it was prearranged. We've been instructed to escort as many ships as we can up the coast."

Tension cuts the air as he looks up from the scroll, folding it; pocketing it. "You'll have to wait until the morning. Once I can confirm with the *High Master,*" he says with a condescending lilt. "I'm sure you understand."

*I'm sure I don't.*

"Sir, these are direct orders from your new *High Mistress.*"

He spits a bubble of laughter. "She could be a cow's udder for all I care. I answer to no female. Never have— never will. So you can either sleep on your ship and wait till morning; fuck right off back the way you came in that shit heap you sailed here in; or go inside that building down there"—he jerks his thumb over his shoulder—"get on your back, spread your thighs, and make yourself useful, you over-assuming cun—"

A whistling sound pierces the air and a warm splash kisses my cheek before the guard's head slides clean off his shoulders, thudding to the ground by the tip of my boot.

His body quickly follows.

"I really *fucking* hate that word," Cindra bites out, kicking his head over the edge of the pier. "Men like him are the sole reason I swore them off for good."

384

The other men draw their swords, bellowing in confusion.

Rhordyn's soldiers pack in behind us, the sound of their loosening weapons music to my ears.

"I'm just impressed you beat me to it," I say, shoving my cloak off my shoulders and pulling my own sword free, whipping it through the air as another guard dives forward.

Cutting through his belly like butter.

Seems the disguise was unnecessary after all.

Dressed in blood and seawater, I watch wooden dinghies ferry crewmen, women, and children from the whaling ships we came here on, dispersing them evenly across our newly acquired fleet.

Cindra steps onto the pier and makes for where I'm standing amongst the blood of the men we slew. Having ditched her blue garb, she boasts her Ocruth gear that tailors to her fierce curves—her pale hair splashed as red as the bloodlust in her gray eyes.

"There's a barge stacked full of glass blocks farther around the harbor," she says, pointing across the busy bay. "As well as another boasting a *curious* red sail that's stacked full of cedar."

*Interesting.*

"I guess he's trading glass for the logs he's used to build his ships," I muse, and she nods.

I knew Parith was receiving an abundance of glass-laden barges down the Norse, but I assumed it was being used in the thriving city—not traded off continent.

"I'm going to have a look around," I murmur, stalking down the blood-soaked pier.

I pass a large wooden building at the end, built against the cliff. A dwelling we plowed through once we finished off the guards. It was mostly empty, apart from sleeping quarters, a shit ton of rum, and two young, black-haired, sparsely dressed females who appeared to be high on Candescence. *Too* high to do anything other than allow Cindra to lead them back to the ship where they could sober up.

Both of them bore bruises.

It didn't sit well. Still doesn't. There's a rage toiling beneath my skin, and I'm not sure how to douse it.

The pier spills out onto a scooped shore that cushions the base of the cliff, taking me past piles of timber, wooden piers that jut out into the bay, and more looming ship hulls under construction.

*Where are the builders?*

I come to a jagged cleft in the cliff face, and realize I'm at the entrance to a cave, nose scrunching as I draw on a fetid blend of excrement and body odor.

Frowning, I pull a blazing torch from one of the holsters nailed to the wall and step into the shadowed interior, past wooden boxes overflowing with tools. The only sound is that of my footsteps as I ease deeper into the cave system, the rank smells thickening, until the stone wall gives way to metal bars.

*Cells.*

I look into their gloomy interiors, and my heart dives.

Droves of men, women, and even a few children are bundled together—filthy. Black and tawny garbs frayed at the hems, bearing holes the size of fists that betray the frail bodies beneath.

The *refugees*—the people who have been fleeing to Bahari with hope in their hearts that they were stepping into a safer existence …

He's been using them as *slaves*.

"Fucking *dog*," Cindra growls from behind me, and I almost leap out of my skin. I was so deep inside my head and aching heart I didn't hear her approach.

"We need to find the keys," I rasp, swallowing. Struggling to keep my upper lip from peeling back from my aching teeth. "Some might not want to come, since they came here to escape the Vruks, but we have to offer."

I clear my throat, hating the emotion prickling the backs of my eyes. Hating that I failed so many of these people.

Some of *my* people.

They came to Cainon for refuge, and he put them in cages.

*I'm going to kill him.*

# CHAPTER 42

*Orlaith*

"You actually dug this with a ..." Kolden pokes my blunt chisel out past the tapestry he's stuffed behind, giving me privacy while I change my top. "With *this?*"

"It wasn't always that stumpy," I murmur, threading my arms through the holes of Rhordyn's shirt—his leather satchel on the ground at my feet, pulled from the urn on our dash down into the palace's bowels. I pull the shirt over my head, unable to stop from shoving my nose into the fibers and drawing deep.

Sating my lungs full of *him*.

That dome inside me rumbles so much a little bit of crystal flakes off the otherwise perfect surface.

*Shit.*

The shirt tumbles halfway to my knees, my legs clad in comfortable leather pants, feet bare, hair loose and heavy since I lost my hairpin in the burrow. The sheath Rhordyn gave me is bound around my thigh, my dagger snug inside.

I buckle Rhordyn's sword across my chest, tuck his leather satchel into my knapsack, then slip the handle over my shoulder and bunch my hands into fists, feeling more myself than I have in …

*Too long.*

I pluck my wooden sword off the ground, picturing Rhordyn's wisteria vine tangling through my fingers, up my wrist and arm, infusing me with mighty strength.

"I'm good," I rasp, tightening my hand around the hilt. "Let's go."

Kolden edges back and looks me over, gives me a firm nod, then wrangles his square body into the very small, very round hole again and wiggles through. Once his boots aren't tenting the tapestry, I pull it back and clamber in after him, crawling over blue dust and a few remaining shards of stone.

Poking my head out the other side, I scan left and right down the tunnel dimly lit by our torch lying on the ground, the acrid smell of death and decay coming to me on a soft breeze that whistles around corners.

Kolden stands about four feet below, reaching up with empty hands. He shed all his golden armor back in my suite, left only with what he was wearing beneath—simple brown pants and a blue tunic—his gold-tipped spear strapped to his back, tawny hair half down and draped around his shoulders.

"You've explored this tunnel?" he queries. "There's a hive of passageways beneath the palace—remnants of the old structure that was torn down years ago. Are you certain this one goes to the right place?"

"I'm certain." I hand him my sword, which he places

on the ground, then maneuver my body until my legs are hanging over the edge, waiting for him to grip my waist before I drop.

He settles me on the ground amongst a litter of stone shards, and I wipe my hands on my pants. "I ran it this morning to check if it goes to the right place," I say, picking up my sword. "Barely made it back in time for the trial preparations. This way."

I take off to the left.

Kolden's on my heels, accompanied by the *whoosh* of our flaming torch as we power through the tunnel that dips and rolls, like it rides the waves of the ocean's currents—the ocean I can almost feel pushing down on us from above with its mighty force.

The tunnel becomes short and wide, then so tall and narrow we have to turn sideways to edge through. Some segments of the walls are smooth, others sharp enough to slice a hide.

This tunnel ... it wears so many emotions that when I ran down here this morning, without my *own* stuffed deep, some areas made me want to curl up and cry.

We continue chasing the stench of death until we're spat out through a small entryway on the other side of the burrow's domed feeding arena lit by blazing torches. Cainon's father is tucked on his side, eyes closed, bunched near the center where a torrent of rainwater gushes down from the sky-hole and pours through a grate in the ground.

Fierce bursts of light spill down from the angry sky, igniting the glassy veins carved into his flesh. The dried, jagged threads of blood that have leaked from it—stitched across his skin.

He's rumbling in his sleep, every deep, even breath a rockslide, making the hairs on the backs of my arms stand on end.

"He's chained," I whisper over my shoulder, settling my wooden sword and knapsack on the floor. "Earlier, he was sleeping at the edge of that white line, and his chains were pulled taut. He can't reach us."

The storm continues to bang its drum as Kolden follows me around the arena's edge, sticking to the outer side of the white line that maps the entire circumference. Despite knowing we're safe, I keep a watchful eye on the slumbering form, though it's not until we near the mouth of the prison-cell tunnel that I notice something in a sporadic burst of light flashing down from the leaky sky-hole.

A flop of iridescent curls ...

A pointed ear with crystal thorns lining the shell ...

*Somebody's tucked beneath the monster's arm.*

My feet stop, that dome inside me creaking as I take in the deep bite mark on the Aeshlian's neck, his closed eyes, lips slightly parted. I look at his chest, willing it to inflate.

Willing him to *breathe*.

The faintest flutter of his eyelashes, and I feel the motion in my chest like a butterfly sprung to life.

*He's alive.*

"Orlaith," Kolden whispers in my ear, and I almost jump right out of my skin. "We must prioritize the people in the cells."

He's right. I'll have to leave this boy till last.

With a heavy heart, I drag my gaze away from the haunting scene and dash around the corner, then fall to my knees before the child with curly red hair. She's tipped on her side in the middle of her cell, bunched like a ball, blank gaze cast ahead. *Through* me ... like she's not even seeing me.

A porcelain doll broken on the floor.

I frown, dread settling on my shoulders like some clawed beast just perched upon me, waiting to snatch up the whittling life.

"Hey, sweetie," I whisper.

She doesn't even blink.

My heart skips a beat.

Finding my hairpin in the middle of the hallway, I set my sword on the stone—

*We must prioritize the people in the cells.*

Kolden's words register like a blow to my chest.

How did he know there *were* cells? All I told him was that there were people to rescue, hidden beneath an island in the bay. That I knew of a secret entry that could get us in and out with relative ease.

A metallic jingle cuts through my thoughts, and my hand snaps down to my dagger, fingers tightening around the hilt.

The girl's pupils narrow, registering something beyond me with a flash of familiarity.

Registering *him.*

I swallow, feeling the air shift as Kolden steps up behind me. My heart drops as he digs a key into the lock.

Twists it.

Clicks it open.

*Why does he have a key?*

A prickly thought snares me like barbed wire ...

"She knows you," I whisper, my voice hoarse; fragile.

"Yes."

I harden my resolve and reinforce my trembling dome, hand twitching to reach for the dagger tucked against my thigh.

I refuse to accept a reality where I fail to save this little girl's life.

I. Refuse.

If I have to go head to head with Kolden right here in front of her, I will.

He reaches past me with his other hand, and I release a raw, primal noise from somewhere deep inside my gut. He pauses for a second, then pushes the door open.

I expect him to pick me up and try to shove me in— poised for the fight that will surely ensue. Tension crackles between us, my gums igniting with an intense ache to gnash my teeth against something hard and unforgiving.

With a deep sigh, Kolden pulls the key out of the lock, and I feel him shift closer, like he's crouching. Voice hot on my ear, he says, "I was ordered to look after Calah while the High Master was away."

My thoughts scatter, turning my insides into a battleground.

He had the chance to save these people, and he didn't.

He. Fucking. Didn't.

That crystal dome rumbles so violently my entire body trembles.

What will be left of me if the dome erupts? What will be left of him? So much has happened since I built it. I have no idea what's grown beneath. What I'm going to be forced to face once I finally lift the lid.

I look over my shoulder, right into broody blue eyes,

and Kolden winces, as though I just struck him with something sharp.

Funny, since that's exactly what I'm considering.

Hunched behind me, he hangs his head, keys dangling in his limp hands. "I—" He sighs, keeping his attention cast to the ground. "Very few of them will come to me, but I can help by opening the doors."

He pushes to a stand and, without even a glance my way, walks to the next cell to the internal tune of my creaking dome while soiled words gather on my tongue.

*Not now, Orlaith. He's not the priority now.*

*These people are.*

I slather another layer of light on my dome and focus my attention forward.

Gaze fixed on where Kolden was crouched, the girl is unmoving, the color drained from her skin, hair a blaze against her sickly pallor.

The shadows beneath her eyes are so dark and daunting.

She's got a look to her I've *felt* before, in my chest. Like some parasitic leech that takes greedy gulps of your will to climb out of bed in the morning. To think.

To *breathe*.

It's the look of someone who feels trapped inside their body.

"I'm just going to clear the other cells," I whisper, giving her a soft smile even though she's still looking straight through me. "I'll be right back, okay?"

No answer.

Another creak of my dome as I pin my hair into a bun, then dart to the next opened door, smiling at a man with a shock of brown hair. He's bound in a filthy blanket in the corner of his cell, looking up at me with big eyes that split my chest despite the fact that everything's tucked so deep.

"It's okay," I whisper. "We've come to get you out."

His brow buckles. "You can't be real. You were dead."

His words steal my breath.

I shake my head. "Not dead. I'm very, very real—I promise. And we don't have much time, so—"

"I've seen what dead looks like," he says, chilling me to the bone. He untangles, bracing himself upon the stone and pushing to his full height, though his body stays stooped from spending too long crouched in the corner. "You were dead." His harrowing gaze slides to the mangled cluster of people shuffling past. Placing a trembling hand on the door, he staggers out of his cage.

*Strange.*

Brushing his words aside, I focus my attention on coaxing more people out of their cells, their dazed and confused expressions turning to sheer terror as we ease around the edge of the feeding arena, past the sleeping monster.

I leave the bedraggled group in the tunnel with instructions to wait, then go to help the remaining captives.

Thirty-three bony, trembling, wide-eyed men, women, and children later, I pause by a cell containing a red-haired lady who's tucked on her mattress with her back to me. I try to pull the door open, but it won't budge.

I turn to Kolden who's ushering a man and woman past, both bound in rags they hold tight against their emaciated frames. The final two prisoners—aside from this woman, the little girl, and the boy in the feeding arena.

Some of them have been going to Kolden, following

him out. Freedom still tastes sweet, even when it's served by the man who led other captives to their demise.

I reach out my hand. "Can you please pass me the key?"

He pauses, looks at me with a guarded expression, then urges the others to continue—one of them leaning so much on the other it's surprising they don't topple over.

Kolden cuts a glance behind me, stepping forward.

I step back.

He sighs, stare drifting to the prisoners still hobbling down the hall, then back to the woman behind me. "Not that one," he says, dipping his voice lower than usual. "I locked it for a reason."

What the ... *fuck?*

"I'm not leaving *any*," I growl, and his eyes soften.

"She's already gone, Orlaith."

My heart drops, his words crippling my ability to stand.

I snap my hand out and hang my weight on a bar as he runs to catch up with the others, taking the arm of the woman dragging her foot and wrapping it around his neck, supporting most of her weight.

My head turns, gaze delving between the bars. The woman's red hair spills across the stone, and realization chokes my next breath, that dome inside me shaking, *shaking* ... like something's rustling around beneath it.

*Is she the little girl's sister? Mother?*

*Did the child watch her die?*

I move down the hallway, each step feeling more weighted than the last. Like there's something inside me that's growing bigger by the second. I near the little girl's space.

She hasn't moved.

Entering her cell, I crouch low and soften my steps so as not to startle her. I swipe her hair back from her cheek, her flesh warm despite her vacant eyes. "Your story doesn't end here, sweetie ..."

She doesn't answer. Doesn't blink. Doesn't flinch.

My lungs compact.

"Small seeds grow into big, strong things," I rasp, easing my hands beneath her bent body. I lift her, tucking her close to my chest so she can feel the beat of my heart. "But they need sunlight and warmth to set their roots in the soil."

Her body stays limp against mine ... There's *nothing*. No sign that she's alive other than the soft *whump* of her heart.

Too slow.

Too steady.

I want to scream at her. Beg her to show me something. *Anything.*

Instead, I whisper upon her brow, carrying her free of the cage, a lump forming in my throat. "You can't get either of those things in here."

A frail breath shudders through her, and it's the most beautiful gift I've ever received. A tear rolls down my cheek as I tighten my grip.

*Something.*

# CHAPTER
## *Orlaith*
# 43

I ease the child into the arms of one of the more healthy-looking females who appears to be able to bear her own weight. Brushing a curl back from the child's face, I give the woman a tight smile. "Hold her close, please."

She nods, dropping her tender gaze.

Turning, I stride to Kolden, who's easing a man to his feet, preparing for our trip back through the tunnel. "Do you have the key to the shackles?" I ask, indicating the boy tucked beneath Calah's arm.

Kolden gives me a wary look. "I do. But—"

"Get this lot moving through the tunnel—weakest in the middle, strongest at the front and back. Then meet me in the arena."

"*Orlaith*—"

"I'm not going without him," I say, charging on, the only weapon on my body the dagger sheathed at my thigh. The rest are useless where I'm going, anyway.

I burst into the arena, making my way around the edge

until I'm standing within eyesight of the Aeshlian caught beneath the Unseelie's arm. There's a shackle around his right wrist, probably his left, too, considering the squiggled lengths of chain lying on the filthy ground.

His wide, iridescent gaze is pinned on me.

Again, I look at the big, bulky arm draped over the boy's midsection, a heavy understanding rooting in my chest like a mountain.

The moment he tries to wriggle loose, the beast will wake.

Which leaves me with one option.

A single glistening tear slips from the corner of the boy's eye, like he can see the train of my thoughts. The intention in my stare.

*Go*, he mouths, and I feel that word poke between my ribs and charge into something squidgy.

I shake my head, sensing Kolden's presence like an approaching landslide. "We can't draw close enough to release the shackles without waking him," he grinds into my ear. "The only way to get them out when they're under his arm like that is to creep in and grab the chain, then drag them past the line, but you don't want to do that unless they're dead. Calah gets excited if you try to rip his toy free. Most of the time he tears the bodies to bits on their way out. Being drunk to a slow, sleepy death would be a much kinder way to die."

I shudder from the base of my skull all the way to the tips of my toes. I'd already thought that option through and came to a similar conclusion, but hearing him spell it out like that is sure to haunt me for the rest of my life.

"The boy's stuck there," Kolden tacks on, slamming the

words down like the swing of an axe. "He knows it. It's why he just told you to leave. We've got a tunnel full of people we have to get out of Parith before the High Master wakes and hunts you down. We need to *go*."

His logic is clear. But like my cloistered emotions, his words don't land their blow—pitiful against the might of my crystal dome and the stony grit of my determination.

I refuse to let that boy watch us leave him here to die. I'd rather rot in here myself.

Studying the chains lumped upon the ground, snaked about in swirls, I map their trajectory if either man or monster were to move this way or that.

A flash of light rips through the sky-hole, igniting Kolden's wide eyes as I backstep over the line to the tune of booming thunder. All the color saps from his cheeks as I take slow, backward steps deeper into the dead zone.

Toward the monster.

I spin.

"Orlaith, *no*—"

"I'll distract Calah," I tell Kolden over my shoulder, "but I need you to act the moment he moves. Get the boy free. If Calah catches me, *leave*. Run and don't look back. Take everyone straight to Cainon's personal ship. Captain Gunthar is there with a crew ready to sail to Ocruth."

A tear shreds down my cheek as the last word falls from my lips, and I realize it's from a tender vine of relief curling around all the broken bits of my heart ... an emotion I didn't think to stuff away.

Why would I?

I've been pretending my soul didn't tumble over the

400

edge of a cliff with the man I murdered, kept busy by all these circles I still had left to spin …

*Secure the ships.*

*Complete The Bowl.*

*Rescue these lives.*

Now with my circles connecting, the silt settling, I'm staring down the throat of a life without *him,* and there's this emptiness below my ribs that makes me feel like it would be easier to just … fade away.

It makes me more disposable than the boy.

Another bolt of lightning ignites the space and lifts the hairs on the back of my neck. I draw my blade, wrap my bound hand around the sharp end, and *slice*—ripping open the same wound I used to lure Rhordyn to his death.

The monster whips up his head, nostrils flaring as he draws long whiffs of the air like a dog sniffing at the wind. A low growl permeates from somewhere deep inside his chest, and he rolls forward into a predatory crouch, tangles of filthy, matted hair falling across his screwed-up brow.

His stare flays my skin. Cracks into my bones. Slurps at my marrow—like he's tasting all the bits that were used to put me together.

There's a glimmer of something else in his inky eyes …

Relief?

It ignites and dies so quickly I question it was there at all.

My vision narrows, senses heightening. I keep moving, every preplanned step chased by the sound of my blood drip, drip, dripping in my wake as I coax his attention farther around the arena. He finally shifts, dragging his leg along the Aeshlian's torso, moving off him entirely—not once breaking my stare. He doesn't even blink.

Kolden creeps toward the boy, face etched with fierce determination. I'm thankful for another bolt of lightning as the Aeshlian gathers his chains close to his withered body. The constant pour of water absorbs the sound of him shuffling across the floor in slow, staggered movements, trying to pinch the gap, his wide, terrified gaze firmly cast on the back of Calah's head.

All the while, Calah prowls closer to me, a deep, abrasive snarl ripping past his bared teeth, his hunched body all bulging might.

That voice inside screams for me to *run.*

I sidestep.

He mimics, the glint in his eye howling his excitement.

I sidestep again.

He snarls, smashing his fists against the stone like he's preparing to charge.

I'm vaguely aware of Kolden reaching the boy. Easing the key into the first shackle—slow and silent as a mouse creeping around a sleeping cat.

I sidestep again just as the first shackle is set down on the ground with delicate precision, and they get to work on the second.

Kolden fumbles with the key, my heart lurching as it clatters against the stone so loud I feel it in my bones.

Calah's entire body locks up, his head whipping around.

*No.*

I flick my hand, splashing my blood across the side of his face.

His head banks in my direction, slower than a rising moon. When I finally see his eyes, a gasp cuts into me.

Every last droplet of humanity has drained away, his features sharper, canines *longer*. Like his entire being has honed into the perfect apex predator—all dark, ancient savagery.

I hear the second cuff clatter to the ground, notice Kolden lifting the boy and running as Calah charges, his roar vibrating through me.

I spin, sprinting—

He hits like a boulder, punching the breath from my lungs. I'm spun by a ruthless grip on my hair, head ripped back, throat bared. He strikes, snatching the scream slicing up from my lungs, releasing my blood in a hot gush.

A surge of pain crunches down on my throat, fills my skull, lashes the underside of my skin. It tears at my muscles and sinew and bones with deep, powerful, gluttonous drags, wilting me from the inside out.

*Get away,* I internally scream as I'm clawed at.

Bent like I'm made of clay.

Warm, wet pressure erupts from my nose and ears, bleeding more of me.

"*Get th*— ... *away* ... " I reach for my ankle, tangling my fingers with my necklace. "*Plea*—"

Calah releases a bubbling breath against my flesh, and the draining tug on my skin abates. His lips unlatch as I slip from his loosening grip, falling back upon the stone in a listless heap—gasping. Weakly clawing at the slippery stuff spilling from my neck.

He wavers from side to side in a sinking sway, blood

dribbling down his chin as all the darkness leaks from his eyes, leaving them the brightest blue I've *ever* seen.

He looks straight at me, snatching my breath, the most pure, untainted smile grazing his bloody lips.

"Finally," he rasps, eyes softening with unmistakable relief, before they go flat and lifeless—all the light draining away.

He crumples with a heavy thump that rattles his chains, staring sightlessly ahead; chest unmoving.

Eyes unblinking.

*Dead.*

I sob, my gaze traveling up the folds of a familiar black cloak, delving into the iridescent eyes of a man I've only seen once before. On the beach at Castle Noir.

My next breath is choked.

The scars on his neck are raised and gnarly beneath the spill of firelight, his chest heaving with a frantic, battering beat that has no rhythm. Like he's clambering through each one, wrestling them into submission.

Baze's eyes are pinned on Calah, and I look to where he's staring—to the curved tip of a Vruk talon protruding from his heart.

The vision does something to me. Makes that dome inside me release a big, creaking groan as something scrape, scrape, *scrapes* at it from beneath.

*Don't cry—*

I break my stare and stagger to a stand. "Baze?"

No answer—not even a blink.

I take a wobbly step around Calah, reaching, pausing when I see shadows battling within the tumultuous depths of his eyes.

A flash of *conflict*.

I look down at Calah, back at Baze, then lift a trembling hand and cup his cheek. He flinches, pupils tightening as they land on me.

The faintest spark of ... something, and a line forms between his brows, his gaze shifting down to my neck, up to my eyes again. He makes this deep throaty sound, before threading his hand through my hair and crushing me against his chest.

I buckle.

*Break.*

Every wisp of emotion that was nesting in dark spots and hiding between my ribs congeals into a sawing vine that shreds me open, baring my messy insides to the man who's always seen my bruised and battered heart.

He tightens his arms and digs his face into my hair. "Don't cry, Laith ..."

Clinging to him, I sob harder.

"You should hate me," I finally manage to choke out. "I— I ..."

*I've done so many terrible things.*

He plants a kiss on my forehead, leaning back to wipe the tears from my cheeks with the edge of his hand. "Part of me does," he admits, and I revel in the way that blow lands.

I deserve it.

*I deserve so much more.*

Looking again at the wound on my neck, his jaw hardens. He reaches beneath his cloak and rips a strip of material off the hem of his shirt, brow pinched with concentration as he gently binds me. "I'm certain the feeling's going to be mutual once we have a moment to clear the air, but we'll work through it," he says, tying off the wrap. He licks his thumb and uses it to rub off some of the paint on my shoulder. "That's what family does, Laith. We untangle our shit, no matter how messy the knot is."

*Family.*

I didn't know how much I needed to hear that word until now. I tuck it deep inside, like he just gifted me a root-bound tree and told me to plant it somewhere that brings me joy.

"We don't fucking run from each other. We *fight* for each other. Period. And if you ever leave me stranded on a beach like that again, I'll kick your ass from here to the fucking stars and back. Do you understand?"

Another tear tracks down my cheek, a smile almost slipping free as I nod, running my hand up over his bare head.

Family.

*I have something to fight for after all.*

"Hate to interrupt," Kolden grinds out, "but we're tight on time."

My eyes widen as twin canines push so far down from Baze's upper jaw they're dimpling his bottom lip. He whips around in a blur of motion, charging forward until he and Kolden are chest to chest. "Who's this dickhead?"

Kolden's expression doesn't waver as he looks up at the menacing tower of muscle and fierce, primal fortitude poured over him.

"My guard. He, ahh—" I stumble over to them, sniffing, trying to push between them but failing to find the strength. "He saved my life."

"Not from where I was standing," Baze bites out, like

he just slaughtered the words, then spat them in Kolden's face. "He wasn't the one being used as *live bait*."

Gods.

"My idea. And not now, earlier in the night. When I almost choked to death on liquid bane."

Baze goes eerily still, dissecting me with a split-second sweep of his eyes. "Well, good for him. So did I. More than once if you count that time you fell down a sinkhole in the garden when you were six."

*I'd forgotten about that.*

"Very impressive," I say, successfully wedging myself between them. I place a hand on both their chests and give them a firm shove that's probably not as firm as I think because my body is still a bit floppy feeling. They both take a step back anyway, which I appreciate. "But we really do have to go. The others will be halfway down the tunnel by now."

Baze's eyes cut to me, then to the Aeshlian tucked against the wall beside the exit, watching through the gaps in his bunched limbs. Looking at Kolden again, Baze sucks air through his teeth, pulls his ring from his pocket, and stuffs it on his finger, tinting his skin and brows and smoothing the sharp edges of his ears—holding Kolden's eye contact the entire time.

"Tell anyone and you're dead." He turns in a churn of black fabric, ripping the talon from Calah's back with a wet *crunch* that makes me flinch.

Kolden clears his throat.

"I'll do a sweep of the place," Baze mutters, storming toward the hall of cells with a sword strapped to his back. "You go ahead."

He moves out of sight, and I breathe a sigh of relief, letting my hand drop from Kolden's chest. He clears his throat and takes off down the tunnel.

I look at Calah. At his swelling pool of blood and big, bright-blue eyes that stare blankly ahead.

I think about that haunting smile. About the way he looked at me when he smelled my blood, like he could see beneath my many layers to the darkness tucked beneath my skin.

Like he could see my ability to end him and *wanted* it.

# CHAPTER 44

*Orlaith*

It's a slow, tedious trip through the tunnel with only a few torches to light our way, Baze and I offering support to those in need of someone to lean on. A blow of wind whistles around the corners and lifts the hairs on the back of my neck, making the dark feel so dominating I'm certain it could crush us in a blink.

I steal a glance over my shoulder, into the prowling gloom that creeps after us, always remaining three steps behind.

I'm not sure how much time has passed since the ceremony, but it feels like too much. It feels like *time* is what's whistling around the corners, urging me on like some whispered warning.

Murmurs come to me down the line, and I look ahead, seeing the crowd drift to one side like tipping water. My breath catches as Old Hattie hobbles into view, dressed in the same haggard clothes I saw her wearing last, her bandage still stained with blood and the filth it collected while she was hacking at the wall with a kitchen knife.

Her steps are unsteady, body crimped forward, insipid eyes cast ahead, like she's seeing something we are not. Like she's hooked on a line, being dragged forward one shuffled step at a time.

Her face is a twist of mournful agony that triggers something inside me. Makes that big dome rumble so loud I'm certain everybody can hear it …

She carries a dagger in one hand, the other shredding at her chest, fingers clawed and tendons taut; as though she's trying to plow through and rip out her own heart.

"Hattie." I reach out as she passes. "Hattie … We got them all."

She doesn't acknowledge me, her tragic gaze fixed ahead.

I take a step forward, fingers skimming across her hand. She pauses, looking down at the point of contact, then up into my eyes, hers igniting with a spark of recognition. A whimper slips out, and she cradles my cheek with her free hand, resting her forehead against mine.

"Come with us," I whisper, and she pulls away, the tenderness in her gaze catching my breath.

She shakes her head, drifts back, and staggers on, the tangled trail of her silver hair the last I see of her before she disappears into the gloom like a dissolving apparition.

A mournful weight settles upon my chest, making the backs of my eyes sting. Because I just know—like some silent whisper nuzzling beneath my skin, nesting beneath

my ribs with the other ghosts I've tucked away—that I'll never see her again.

There's a stillness about the palace as we file through the ornate hallways, past gilt wall sconces balancing candles almost burned down to the nub, taking a quiet route I preplanned because it's devoid of servants at this hour.

Nobody makes a sound. Not even the younger ones huddled in the arms of others or trailing along with their fingers twisted into the hem of someone else's clothes.

We reach a corridor on the main floor, one side lined with windows that take the rain's lashing, the little *pings* creating a haunting melody to our quiet charge.

Bolts of light preface a clap of thunder somewhere in the distance. Baze snatches my shirt and shoves against my back as something shifts from the shadow behind a large urn.

My heart leaps into my throat, another flash revealing a small person stepping forward and pushing back his hood, a roguish smile splitting his face.

*Zane.*

"How did you get in here? And what the hell are you even *doing* here?" I hiss, wiggling free of Baze's hold and wrapping my arms around Zane, stuffing my face into his hair. "It's dangerous ..."

He pulls back. "I got worried. Uncle said you were running late. And there was nothing in your note about ..." he flashes a look at the others still moving down the hall, "*them.*"

I wince.

I couldn't be too specific, just in case the note made it into the wrong pair of hands. I asked for the senka seed, set up the thieving of Cainon's ship, and requested Gun pass a second note to Zali explaining the plan to get me out—that's all I could risk.

"Found them on the way out," I tell him, offering a soft smile before I nudge him forward. "Now let's get you out of here."

Poor Gunthar. He may not have noticed Zane's missing, but if he has, he's not going to be happy.

We reach the others at the door to the courtyard, bunched and shivering and glancing around nervously. I weave through the crowd, finding Kolden with his hand on the doorknob and a grim look on his face. "What's wrong?"

"There's a large contingent of Gray Guards. The High Septum must still be this side of the bridge."

"How many?" Baze asks from right behind me, gripping my upper arm like he thinks I'm about to burst through that door and do something stupid.

Seems his trust has flown out the window.

"*Too* many," Kolden grinds out, flicking Baze a shaded look. "If somebody draws them away, I can get the gate open. Two palace guards will be on the other side of it— Jahk and Tier. Both good men with good morals, and one of them has a kid on the way. I'd like them to live."

"Is there no other route to the pier?" Baze asks, and Kolden and I shake our heads, seconds ticking by like my racing heartbeats.

*Shit.*

"We could all climb down from Orlaith's balcony?

That's how I got in." Baze, Kolden, and I glare at Zane. "S'not *that* hard," he boasts, pulling a plum from one of his many pockets, shining it on his cloak, and handing it to a kid beside him without even passing him a sideways glance. "Orlaith does it all the time. I've seen her from where I fish for squid off the rocks."

I open my mouth, close it, Baze and Kolden now glaring at *me*. "Not *all* the time ..."

"Most nights," Zane clarifies, and I nudge him in the ribs. *Little snitch.*

Kolden clears his throat. "The moment swords clash, more of the palace guards will storm in from all four corners. It'll be a shit show. They'll lock down the palace, lift the sea gate, and we'll be sitting ducks."

Silence stews, thick and cloying, and I can feel the heavy thump of Baze's thoughts well before he utters them. "I'll do it. Those Gray Guards have been pretty hungry for my blood since I set fire to their temple. I'd just have to wander in front of them, flash the burns on my back, and they'd chase me to the Shoaling Seas."

My blood chills, guts cramp, eyes so wide I'm certain they're going to pop out of my head as Kolden and Zane whisper-blurt, "That was *you?*"

Baze winks at Zane, who's looking up at him with reverence—like he wants to be him when he grows up. Which is disturbing. He's not an example of moral aptitude one should strive toward.

"You're not doing it," I bite out, punching Baze in the shoulder.

"Ow," he says with a half laugh, rubbing the point of contact. "That actually hurt."

*Good. Who sets fire to a fucking* temple *in a city full of Shulák?*

"Family *sticks together*," I croak, regurgitating his words. I don't want to leave him behind. Especially with the knowledge that he's made so many powerful enemies in the short time he's been here.

He sighs, dashing his hand up to run through hair that's no longer there. It's not the only thing that's changed.

He's still my Baze, but also … not.

I see it in the way he moves—not as fluid as he used to be. Like he's less at peace with the skin keeping him contained. I see it in the tightness around his eyes and mouth, and the way his eyes go blank when he thinks nobody's watching.

"I thought we would have more time," I choke out.

"You're acting like I'm about to walk to my doom here," he scoffs. "That's offensive. I know you kicked my ass on the beach but let's keep things in perspective." He swipes a tear from my cheek, cracking a smile that's far too light for this moment. "I'll do a little dance for them, make them sweat a bit, before I find somewhere to either kill them quietly or hide—preferably the former—then I'll meet you at home. I have a few things I need to tick off my list first anyway. This is actually a convenience."

I'm not sure why he's painting me such a pretty picture. In my experience, some of the prettiest pictures tell the deadliest secrets.

I hate this. I don't want this. But I can see it's what *he* wants in the way the vein in his temple has pushed to the surface—the same way it usually does when he and I are about to spar and he gets that bounce in his step.

That gleam in his eye.

"You promise?"

"I fucking *promise*." The words come out with such conviction they're clipped with a growl.

I draw a shuddered breath, blow it out real slow. "I'll ... see you at home, then?"

*Home.*

I feel the word all the way to my bones. The pull to be back.

Baze whips me close for a hug that's over too fast, then nudges past, ruffles Zane's wet hair, and shoulder-shoves Kolden out of the way, the latter releasing a guttural grunt. He cracks the door and peeks through while my heart rages against its confines ...

I feel like he's just a dream I'm about to wake from. And I don't want to.

*Not yet.*

"Baze?" I whisper-yell.

He looks at me over his shoulder, brow raised, the blazing light of a wall sconce glinting off his eyes.

"I love you."

His features soften so much I see the dimple pucker his cheek.

For a moment he's the Baze that lured me out from under the bed and told me not to cry. The one who made my first paintbrush, taught me how to write my name, and how to crochet my knapsack.

"I love you too, Laithy."

Then he's gone.

Kolden holds the door ajar until we hear the heavy pound of boots, the sound dispersing into a scuffing echo while my heart labors. While that dome inside me creaks and groans, like something's trying to wrestle free.

He gives me a terse nod and pushes the door open.

I tuck Baze's parting words inside my chest as we spill out into the quiet courtyard and creep around the inside edge, past blue-stone columns and golden urns. Kolden slips down the short archway that leads to the palace gate, and I hear the heavy grind of it lifting, then scuffing sounds. A baritone grunt.

Another.

A few moments later, he pops his head around the corner and ushers us forward.

I herd everybody down the tunnel, past two unconscious guards lumped against the wall. One by one, men, women, and children step through to the puddled grounds beyond, the shielded bowls of flaming oil giving off just enough light to guide our way.

A child has stopped, hands in the air as he reaches for raindrops tangling with his fingers, making my throat cramp with a swelling ache …

It's the look of *freedom*—so pure and rich it could bring me to my knees.

Kolden leads us over the grass and around a hedge, then along a shadowed path that melds into stone steps that snake around the island. A sheer wall of choppy rocks lines our left, and a steep fall to our right meets the heaving sea below. The final sweeping stretch until we reach the ship visible in the distance every time another bolt of lightning cracks across the sky, a single blazing lantern hanging from its mast.

The sign that we're safe to board.

*It's almost over ...*

Something warm swells within me as Zane and I take the rear, the rest of the party keeping a brisk pace. Like they can taste the sweetness of their impending freedom on the rising winds.

Another crackle of lightning scribbles across the sky, uncomfortably close, almost like it's reaching for us. Some of the children scream, a blast of wind battering us so hard it hits with a burst of seaspray ripped off the roiling ocean, salting my lips.

"It's going to be a rough trip out of the bay!" Zane yells, his cape billowing in his wake. "Good thing Uncle knows the waters so well or we'll all be shark chow!"

By the light of another lightning strike, I watch his cloak break free from around his neck, then flutter over my head. He slams to a stop and spins, dashing after it.

My heart lurches, as if trying to punch free of my ribs and chase him.

"Zane!"

*Fuck.*

I hand my wooden sword and knapsack to one of the men ahead of us, then sprint after Zane, the clip in my hair falling victim to another violent gust of wind. "*Leave it,*" I yell over the howling gale, watching the cloak tumble through the air until it tangles with the corpse of a small, gnarled tree partway up the bank, hanging off its spindly branches. "I'll get you another. *Come on!*"

He stops at the base of the bank, looking between me and the cloak before he clambers onto the rain-slicked rocks and begins to climb.

"Shit," I mutter, glancing back at our group now

stretching down the pier's length, some scaling across the unsteady gangplank.

I come to a stop beneath the tree, the sodden cloak flapping in the wind. "Zane, please. We don't have time."

"I've almost got it!" he belts out, gripping hold of the tree, leaning forward, trying to bend the branch enough so he can flick his cloak free. He finally manages to snatch it—

The branch snaps.

Zane plummets, screaming.

I lunge to buffer his fall, and we thud to the ground in a tangle, my head thwacking against the stone, skull-splitting pain throbbing to agonizing life.

"*Are you ... okay?*" I grind out.

He groans, climbing off me. "Yeah. Got my cloak, I'm good. What about yo—"

A blaring horn sounds above the howling wind, followed by a *boom* that rattles my bones. A single bright seed shoots up into the bulbous clouds, turning them blood red when it bursts with such violence the entire sky seems to shake.

Dread drops into my stomach like a boulder, some innate intuition flaring to life.

*Cainon's awake.*

That voice inside screams louder than it ever has before ...

"Run." I roll to my side and nudge Zane to his feet, scrambling after him. "*Run!*"

We explode into action, feet slapping against the wet stone. We hurry down the steep stairs, then launch onto the pier, and another bolt of lightning ignites the churning waves splashing up the sides, dousing the planks in a foamy residue.

The pier is empty aside from us, the ship churning with the ocean's heavy rise and fall. Kolden is standing on deck, next to the gangplank, yelling words I can't make out over the roaring wind. But when the deep vibrato of clanking chains rattles across the bay, even the wind seems to pause.

To *listen*.

*They're lifting the sea gate.*

*Fuck.*

"*Push off!*" I scream through the icy torrent of rain battering my face, waving. "*We'll jump!*"

Kolden seems to hesitate, and I think I hear a woman shriek before the gangplank is raised.

A streak of lightning rips across the sky as the ship begins to crack away. "*Faster, Zane!*"

For a battering moment, the rain becomes a sheet of white, drumming upon the pier, smearing my sight of *everything*. But I sense we're getting close.

*Almost there.*

"We're going to have to jump, okay?" I reach for him. "Take my hand, we'll do it together!"

No answer.

I look to my side—

There's nothing but the rain and the wooden poles and the churning sea clawing at the pier.

I spin, pulse scattering at the sight of Zane pinned to the ground beneath the boot of an armored guard, cheek flat against the wood, eyes wide and wild.

*Scared.*

# CHAPTER
### Orlaith
# 45

My dome creaks and groans as more Gold Guards swarm around Zane like a clanking river of crushing might.

Five—eight—*ten* of them.

All the fight bleeds from me.

I fall to my knees, gasping breath, holding Zane's stare through the shifting obstacle of golden shin guards. This hopeless feeling grips hold of my shoulders and shoves me down so hard I'm certain the pier's going to splinter beneath me.

There's the *swish* of loosening weapons, gold-tipped spears glinting in sporadic bursts of light ripping across the sky. Again, that woman screams in the distance, farther away than before—similar to the sound my mother made when that axe swung.

Struck.

Zane's face crumbles, and I *feel* that look fissure through me like hairline splits in my chest, my ribs, my lungs.

*Deeper.*

Time grinds to a halt as a crack weaves across my crystal dome, the sound so sharp and cataclysmic that I'm certain the world is fracturing.

An inky claw nudges through the gap, slathered in a stretch of goo that drapes between the honed tips of rose-thorn nails, gripping hold of the split's whetted edge. A second claw follows, clamping down on the other side.

More of the splitting sound that threatens to pop my skull, and the gap widens.

*Widens.*

Something flaps beneath the surface, scratching, making me want to bunch down into a ball and scream.

*Scrape.*

*Scrape.*

*Scrape.*

More scuffling sounds as a web of fractures weaves across the crystal—

The dome *explodes* with a shattering blast, bits of it embedding in my organs, my bones, my muscle and my flesh. Leaving my insides in bloody tatters. Lumped amidst the macabre gloom, surrounded by shards of bone and crystal and shredded flesh, is a bony animal cloaked in more of that stretchy, gooey substance it shakes off—splattering the mess against my sides, unveiling more of the creature's ghastly form:

It reminds me of a krah, except it has branches for wings, dead leaves for plumage, and black, fathomless eyes I'm certain I've seen the likes of before. Bits of it have rotted out, a third of its face surrendered to the vile decay, revealing rows of bramble teeth and pockets of gnarled carcass draped with withered vines of black.

Its slender tail curls up, the tip a tuft of singed leaves swaying from side to side as the creature tips its head and *squeals*—a shrill sound that makes my bones ache, threatening to crumble from the pitch of it. Thick tears puddle in my eyes, and when they leak down my cheeks, I smell blood.

The creature flaps inside me, toiling a churn of crystal shards that shred my heart and my spongy lungs, stripping flesh from my bones. It flits high into my chest, nests in my throat, and screams to the sky as blind, icy rage paints my vision red.

Zane squirms and screams, the spear settling against his cheek drawing the faintest line of pink that jolts me from the inside out—like I just got touched by the spindly tip of lightning clawing across the sky.

I push to a stand and rip the sword from the sheath at my back. A thud hammers into my palm, ratchets up my arm, then ripples through my blood like the beat of a song so complex, I feel like it's rewriting the fabric of my being.

A scream punches up my throat that tastes like blood, and I charge; teeth bared, that creature flapping inside me, screeching to the thunderstorm as I whip a man around and slash my blade through his carotid. His warm blood splashes my hand, and the beat drums louder.

*Louder.*

I toss him aside, snarling to the wind and the rain and the frantic churn of gold armor, like wasps buzzing around, threatening to sting what's *mine* to protect.

*Mine.*

My surroundings smudge, and I hack, dodge, *stab*—
fueling that terminal song until it's a thrum in my ears.
Red plumes spray across the pier. Across my face and arms,
drenching my hair.

I'm deaf to the rain. Deaf to anything bar the sword's
pounding song spurring me into a deadly dance of mass
destruction. Gorging on every slashed artery. Every severed
limb and head.

Every dying scream.

I'm a feasting beast, and no matter how many times I
stab, hack, *kill,* I'm still *ravenous.*

I sever the taut ligaments across the back of somebody's
legs.

He staggers forward.

Descending upon him, I fist his hair, ripping his head
back so far I bare his throat to the honed edge of Rhordyn's
sword. I begin to slash it sideways when a desperate sob
comes to me through the murk of my rabid rage.

I look up past a litter of butchered bodies, most of
which I don't recall hacking apart. Stabbing through.

*Gutting ...*

My gaze homes on Zane—no longer pressed against the
wood but on his knees with his cloak clutched close to his
chest. Cainon's standing behind him, eyes wide, inky balls
of blazing accusation. He's fisting Zane's hair, baring his
too-tender throat to a golden blade.

That macabre creature stills, then scurries down into
the chasm in my chest so fast it kicks up crystal shards in
its haste.

All the fight melts from my bones.

"*No-no-no,*" I plead. Dropping the sword, I clamber off

the guard and toss my hands up either side of my head in surrender, the blood coating them oozing down in rivulets.

Cainon looks down his nose at me, the rain dripping off his brutal features while Zane squirms in his hold.

I drop to my knees, shuffle forward, a flush of desperation softening my ravaged insides. "Cainon, please. Take my life instead. *Please.*"

Another crack of lightning, closer now, reflects in Cainon's eyes like the silver fissures of a broken plate.

He pushes the blade deeper into Zane's flesh.

I stop moving. Stop breathing.

Too scared to even blink.

Cainon takes in the scene around us, his only surviving guard now bound in a groaning heap, reaching for Rhordyn's sword. Cainon looks behind me to where I don't doubt the ship is plowing through the savage waves, hopefully past the rising chain. His upper lip peels back, features honing into something truly horrific.

There's not a drop of mercy in his callous stare when it locks on me again.

Trembling, Zane wiggles his fingers into one of the many pockets tucked amongst the folds of his cloak. I see a flash of gold as he pulls out the Bahari token he stole off one of the sailors.

"I have a t-token," he pleads, waving it high enough for Cainon to see, and my heart impales itself on the tip of a shattered rib.

*He's trying to buy his life ...*

Cainon's gaze drops. He plucks the token from Zane's grip, weighing it in his hand. Hope bursts in Zane's eyes— infectious, fragile hope.

Cainon looks at me, and in those inky eyes, I see too much.

Too little.

I see the way this story unfolds—how hopeless it is for me to try to rewrite the ending already scored in stone. To change the fate of this boy who's going to die simply because I love him. Because I'm a black hole that gobbles up everything bright and good and alive.

Because I *exist*.

I break Cainon's stare and look at Zane. Force a smile for him to cling to; a pretty lie to soften the sharp truth notched against his throat.

*It's okay,* I mouth, even though it's not. I mouth it over and over again as his eyes fill with tears.

*It's okay. It's okay—*

"You did this," Cainon says, his voice a chilling monotone full of heinous promises.

I crumple inside because I know he's right.

*It's okay. It's okay. It's okay—*

The blade lowers ...

Zane's eyes widen, and he slumps forward as I look up at Cainon, a seedling of hope blossoming in my heart.

*Is he ... reconsidering?*

The gold token lands with a *thunk* in a puddle of red by my knee.

My heart stops.

Zane's blood-curdling scream flays me down the middle as Cainon lifts him off the ground by his hair and dangles him over the edge of the pier. "Think I'll let the *sharks* do it."

"No," I sob, crawling forward, reaching. "*No!*"

"*You. Did. This.*"

He lets go.

Zane falls too fast yet agonizingly slow, cramming me full of every horrifying detail:

Crumpled features ...

One hand reaching, the other clutching onto his cloak like it'll grow wings and save him ...

The pure, undiluted fear in his eyes ...

I scramble toward the edge, but Cainon lands a boot to my ribs, and I collide with the pier in a dash of blood and water. The sound of Zane splashing into the hungry ocean drives a stake into my gut, and I unspool around it. Not slow and steady, but so fast my entire *being* ends up in a tangled, messy heap.

Lashing lengths of caustic blackness slither up from that chasm deep within my chest, honing their tapered tips, slitting my skin from the inside out. Hissing for me to *kill*.

*Kill.*

*KILL!*

I can no longer hear the wind, the thunder, or the sound of my own heartbeat. I can no longer hear the raging ocean as it heaves and churns—riddled with beasts that won't think before they *chew*.

All I am is brain-bursting pressure and hissing vengeance.

My fingers twist with the chain around my ankle, brutally aware that the jetty is made of wood. That cutting my ugly loose will kill me, too.

I've lost the will to care.

*I.*

*Did.*

*This.*

Blood weeps from my eyes as I hold Cainon's stare and rip my necklace free.

*KILL!*

The pressure doesn't immediately abate. Blackness doesn't burst through my skin and shred everything around me.

I spur the darkness on, screaming for it to *kill*.

*Kill.*

*Kill ...*

Pressure swells until I can hardly see through the blood in my eyes, and I'm certain my skull has just as many fractures as my heart.

*Something's ... wrong ...*

Blood gushes from my nose, forging a warm path down my chin.

My scream fades to silence as my lungs deflate, spine arching back. My chest tips to the sky, and I'm certain my eyes are about to pop from the pressure.

Cainon fists my sodden hair, wrenching me forward while I split apart from the inside out, my arms and hands scribbled in lines so hot my bones are surely melting.

He pinches my chin, and itchy pops flare across my shoulder as I'm forced to look up. The sky cracks apart again with another fluorescent flash, igniting Cainon's wide eyes. Igniting my bright reflection blasting off the mirror of his sable stare.

"*You— You're a—*"

Snarling, I cast my hands into claws and try to shred his chest. He looks down and gasps. Drops my hair.

Stumbles back.

I blink, trying to clear more blood from my eyes, seeing

the grizzly slits in my outstretched hands, up my arms, tapering toward my elbows. Seeing the slither of sizzling darkness just below the surface—a silent promise for a death that won't come.

*It won't come.*

All the color has gone from Cainon's face as that pressure continues to build, shoving at my weak spots. I look to where Zane was tossed over the edge of the pier …

*My fault.*

There's the sound of a blade loosening, and I see the long, golden sword Cainon just pilfered from a corpse while he stashes his dagger in his boot, looking at me like he finally sees the monster I really am.

All I can see is Zane holding up that golden token— begging for his life.

All I can feel is Rhordyn's warm kiss upon my forehead.

I smile at Cainon as he whips back the sword. Laughing, I tip my head and bare my bound throat—hoping for a clean slice.

Because I'm done.

I've got nothing left to give.

*I don't want to be here anymore.*

The air becomes so charged I feel it thumping against my skin, like it holds a pulse of its own. The atmosphere splits as a fork of black-veined lightning cleaves down from above and kisses the tip of Cainon's sword, blazing off in jagged blades. A shrill, strident sound mulches my brain, followed by a *boom* so loud another scream rips from my throat.

The ground falls away beneath me with a sound akin to shattering glass, and I plummet into an icy sea of churning, tumbling water that claws at my body and *roars* at me.

My head collides with something hard.

*darkness.*

# CHAPTER 46

*Baze*

Having spent so many years living in a cell, being stuffed back into one doesn't jar as it should. I'm not hit with a burst of panic. I don't claw at the bars with hope in my heart and a wild urge for freedom wrestling beneath my ribs.

There's no point.

All it does is expel energy I need to breathe, blink, and perform my regular bodily functions that keep me existing. It's the only reason I survived so long all those years ago when my cell became my cold, stony hug. My shoulder to cry on, break against, lean upon.

My fucking *universe*.

I gave up hope and forged myself into the sort of creature that thrives in chains. *Feeds* on them. I traded in so much of the important stuff that I was left with this mangled version of myself by the time Rhordyn liberated me.

Not quite sad to be free. Not quite happy about it either.

That's kind of how I feel right now—not quite happy to

be stuffed in this tiny cell that smells like despair and youth with a perfect, disturbing view of the feeding arena.

Not quite sad about it either.

Because if I weren't here, *he* would be alone. Or in the guts of an ocean beast.

I let my gaze drift through the bars to the cell on the opposite side of the hall. To the small person in the corner, huddled beneath a blue velvet cloak.

Sleeping.

A boy I dove into shark-infested waters to recover because—fuck it—I like the kid. Orlaith likes the kid.

We all like the kid.

I have no hope for me, but for *him* ...

I'd punch a fucking ocean of sharks to make sure he doesn't end up as mutilated inside and out as I am.

I rip my gaze away, spearing it to the powdery sunbeam of morning light spilling from the sky-hole—the storm having passed a couple hours ago. A storm which swelled into a heaving, restless beast that slashed at the sky, shredding the atmosphere into static ribbons.

It settled the internal wound I've been harboring since Zali and I received Orlaith's sprite, even before I saw the bolt rip down from the sky—a scribble of blinding white light threaded with a black vein that side splashed off the tip of a risen sword and struck the pier into glassy smithereens. So bright, I can still see the residue of it on the backs of my lids when I squeeze them shut.

So that sunbeam pouring into the burrow ... it's a sure sign that Orlaith made it free of the angry ocean. Because if she hadn't? The fucking sky would have fallen. And that man right there—crouched over Calah's lifeless body in the middle of the feeding arena—would be dead.

*We'd probably all be dead.*

Cainon reaches forward, sweeping the long, silver hair back from the face of an elderly woman curled up in Calah's limp embrace, her scored wrists crossed before her withered form.

*Self-inflicted?*

I don't look too hard. Don't think too hard about it either. It's just the sort of black hole I could tumble down if I stared long enough.

My gaze drifts to Calah's wide, unseeing eyes, and I half expect him to blink. For them to flick in my direction. For him to stand and stalk toward me reeking of disappointment.

*You were my favorite, pretty boy.*

*How could you hurt me like that?*

*I thought you loved me, too.*

Something tight wraps around my chest, making it hard to breathe, and I cut a gaze at the ceiling.

"They loved each other despite their differences," Cainon grates out, his voice thick with emotion, making me want to bash my head against the wall. "He dragged her down into his burrow, thought she smelled good, then tasted her and realized she was so much *more* than just a pet ..."

Just a pet.

Just an animal in a cage.

"He was the shackle she learned to cradle against her chest despite his ... *flaws*. Then *I* came along," Cainon says, his words echoing through the somewhat hollow burrow. "I was the flaw she couldn't see past."

"I don't want your life story, dickhead. I couldn't care

less if you were shat out of a donkey's ass. It's been a long day, and I'm pretty keen to find the most comfortable position in this shithole and tuck down for some shut-eye." I shuffle, repositioning myself against the wall, wincing when the motion slides the top layer of flesh off the burns on my shoulder blades. "So, if you would kindly fuck off," I hiss through clenched teeth, "you will have my not-so-eternal gratitude."

The thump of his boots echoes down the hall while I hone my attention on a crack in the ceiling.

"You're awfully cocky—"

"That's what the ladies tell me."

"—for somebody in a cage."

*I never left the first one.*

He crouches beside my cell, the smell of blood mixed with his acidic scent wafting into my personal space— something I don't appreciate.

I don't have much of it.

"You know, I still wonder why Jakar chose *Rhordyn* to be the bearer of his runes. Of the great *gift* of his divine power. I'm sure he regretted it when that savage immediately wiped out almost the entire race of Unseelie, then hunted what was left like dogs."

I laugh to myself, loud and twisted. He has no idea how wrong he is …

No. Fucking. Idea.

Jakar didn't gift Rhordyn shit except barbed chains.

"That some people have been led to believe Jakar slaughtered his *own* creations just shows what an undeserving coward Rhordyn was. *God Blessed,*" Cainon muses, the words a snarl of disgust. "*That* animal? Really?

The only time I've ever seen him support the Shulák was when he invited two to the ball, though I'm certain he had blasphemous reasons behind it."

I laugh some more.

Boy's got it in for having a limp power-dick courtesy of his half-mortal heritage. There could be worse things— like watching every female in your race get hunted and slain while the males are farmed like animals.

"Real blessed, that one," I mutter, trying to itch a spot beneath my right wrist shackle, not quite able to reach. *That's gonna be a pain.* "He used to wake up every morning and thank the Gods for their great contribution to his cheerful existence."

The silence stretches so long I could strangle myself with the length of it, and I get the sense Cainon's not impressed with my tone. I probably shouldn't goad him, but this dick just gives me the urge to sling shit from my cage. I figure words are the lesser evil.

Rhordyn should have put him down years ago.

I bet he's a feral knot right about now. Poor Laith. She might've survived Cainon, but Rhordyn's a different story. You don't simply *survive* that man after you nudge against his grain. You weather him like a storm. You batten down the hatches and pray he doesn't rip off your roof and tear you to shreds. And when you step outside again, the world will not be as it was before because he's not a storm that treads lightly.

He reshapes the fucking terrain.

And she didn't just nudge him, she stabbed him through the heart.

He'll eat her for breakfast if she's not careful.

Cainon pushes to his feet, clonks a key into the lock, and whips the door wide. I would get a little excited if I wasn't shackled to the floor by a length of chain that barely allows me to scratch my ass without pulling a muscle.

The hairs on my arms lift as he crouches before me, and I tangle my fingers between each other.

"You know, I always thought you were Rhordyn's pet," Cainon says, and *that* gets my fucking attention. Not enough to look at him, but enough that I shut my mind down and listen. "That he's been feeding you his blood and gifting you long life because he liked your taste."

I swallow thickly, waiting ... Knowing there's a reason for this particular line of babble that makes my skin burn like I've just been rolled in stinging nettles.

He taps my ring with the tip of his finger, freezing the fucking blood in my veins. "That right there—Orlaith wears a necklace with a similar jewel."

My heart drops, and I look at him for the first time since I clawed my way back to consciousness, eyes widening.

*Fuck me.*

His right eye is an inky orb, a burst of black capillaries webbed across the skin surrounding it.

And his *left* one ... It's glass—just like the scribble of thin, glassy fractures that weave across his cheek and temple and stretch into his hairline.

He's a monstrous mix of flesh and translucent splits, some areas leaking threads of blood that drip to the floor.

*Guess the side splash got him in the face. Poetic, all things considered.*

I take note of the smudged remains of gray scripture painted across his naked torso—much like Rhordyn's. Like he's been playing dress up.

A smile weasels past my lips. "You look like shit."

He rips off my ring.

My breath comes hard and furiously fast as my skin peels down, inch by fucking inch, until every visible bit of fragile, pearly flesh is exposed.

Every bite of shame.

Cainon doesn't look surprised, just satisfied he was right. This sick feeling swirls in my gut with all the salt water still sloshing around.

"This makes so much more sense," he says, cutting his stare across my scars, hovering over one high up on my throat. His gaze turns pensive—I think. Hard to tell anymore. "Rhordyn's always had a soft spot for the lesser beings of our world."

My heart smashes against my spine as he runs the tip of his finger over a bite mark on my neck—so small it's always served me an extra scoop of disturbed with my daily ration.

I don't remember getting it, or any of the other small ones.

I don't *want* to either.

He studies me like a three-course meal with a goblet of sparkly blood to wash it down. "I remember you," he purrs, the words silk, binding me up into a sticky cocoon that makes it hard to breathe.

This sinking feeling spears me through the guts.

He cocks his head to the side. "Father used to let me

feed on you when you were doped. He said your blood was his *favorite.*"

Bile rushes up and chokes me. Forces me to swallow.

*Nobody bleeds for me like you do.*

Old wounds bite deeper, a low growl bubbling in the back of my throat ...

*My pretty boy. My favorite.*

I drop my chin, looking at Cainon from beneath my brows.

He frowns, and another thread of blood weaves between his eyes, down his nose where it drips onto my bent knee. "I believe he secretly thought it might awaken some sentient part of me, though he never voiced it."

His words are a buzz in my ears, barely breaking through the deep drone of centuries of pent-up *rage* desperate for release.

I crunch my hands into balls. Picture them tightening around his neck.

"I thought the Gods gave me Orlaith ... That she would be everything Mother was for Father." He shrugs. "Now I realize they've just given me a chance to prove how worthy I am of their special treatment. Jakar tried to strike her today and *missed.*" He waves a hand at his fucked-up face. "I won't."

My fangs slide down so fast I barely feel the sting.

"Rhordyn will fuck you up," I say, deadly calm. "He will push a talon through your chest real slow, right there." I point to the scar sitting just above his heart—*just.* "But a little farther down."

"Impossible. Orlaith made sure of that. Like a fucking

*puppet,* she put the beast down for good." He chuffs out a mangled sound that curdles my blood. "Didn't you know?"

*Orlaith told him she killed Rhordyn ...*

"I played her, Baze. And she danced for me. Oh, how she danced for me. You should have seen the way she arched that pretty neck—a fucking *whore* for my bite."

Even my bones vibrate with rage, and I rip my stare away, looking through the bars to the boy huddled in the corner of the opposite cell, my heart slamming to a stop when I realize he's *watching.* Peeking over the top of his cloak, his eyes visible between tangles of floppy hair.

Taking it all in.

*Fuck.*

I wish he'd plug his ears. Close his eyes.

I wish he'd have made it to that fucking ship.

"Shadow's Hand, right beneath my nose," Cainon muses, shaking his head, laughing.

My heart stops.

Did he see her true self?

Her fucking *mark?*

"You've both been hiding her this entire time."

The words butcher me down the middle. They scoop out my insides, then slop them on the ground, heaped in a steaming pile.

I squeeze my eyes shut. Jerk against my chains so hard I feel them peel some skin from my wrists, immediately quenching that itch.

*He knows ...*

And I'm stuck down here in a fucking cell.

"I'm looking forward to killing her. I'll hang her from a

pike so everyone can see Shadow's Hand in the flesh before I set her alight while you and the boy watch."

My eyes snap open, a snarl slicing between my bared teeth.

*Don't listen, kid.*

I rip at my chains again, again, *again.*

Cainon gives me a serpentine smile and shoves to a stand, towering over me. Looking down on me like the God he thinks he is. "Until then, you're going to the Glass Palace," he says, cutting a glance at Zane, and my snarl morphs into a deep, chesty growl that rattles my fucking teeth.

Cainon dishes me a smirk. "*Both* of you."

# CHAPTER

*Orlaith*

## 47

I wake like a punch to the heart.

My eyes pop open, and I gasp a breath, gaze scouring a net of palm fronds to the powder-blue sky beyond. I rip at my chest with clawed fingers, brutally aware of the shards of crystal dome still wedged in my lungs and withered heart. Poking out of my smashed and splintered bones.

There's a gnarled, overgrown forest of thorny emotion stuffed inside me, filling every dark, shadowy corner. Raw, painful emotion I'm too scared to touch. To handle.

Like I've forgotten *how*.

Silver vines have twisted around my bones and organs, sprouting a nest of pretty slate-colored grayslades bearing charcoal filaments—so fucking beautiful I ache in places I never knew existed.

I don't deserve those flowers.

*Don't deserve them—*

Whimpering, I roll to the side, looking toward the sloshing sounds of the ocean.

A stretch of turquoise water glimmers in the sunlight. Small, frothy waves lap at a thin stretch of dark-blue sand that clings to my skin. My stomach clenches, and I gag, coughing up a vile mix of salt water and bile.

*The storm must have dumped me onto the beach ...*

Rhordyn's shirt hangs off my shoulder, torn in places but bone dry. Like I've been here a while. I pat my thigh, finding my sheath empty, though there's a familiar weight around my neck ...

I finger my necklace, confused.

*How did I secure it after I ripped it off?*

After—

*You did this.*

Cainon's hissed accusation attacks me like a barbed whip slashed at my heart, and I see the look in Zane's eyes as he fell. See him reaching for me—clutching that cloak with his other hand.

A guttural moan morphs into a sob as I crawl toward the water.

*You did this.*

I shove to my feet, stumbling over my steps before I run—colliding with the splashing waves, falling to my knees. The water swirls around my waist while I claw at my chest and tight throat. While I reach behind my arm and *pinch* harder than I ever have.

*You did this—*

I suck a shuddered breath, release an agonized scream.

That jungle of emotion shifts and squirms, thorny vines battling each other for freedom, making them impossible to dislodge. My scream turns into deep, chest-cleaving sobs that threaten to split me.

*Don't cry.*

His words come to me like a blow of icy wind, making my skin pebble.

I look out across the azure water, reminded of the cloak I bought Zane; wrapped for him; poured all my love into.

The cloak that got him killed. Just like I got my *brother* killed.

My *mother* ...

Rhordyn ...

*So many others.*

I think of the jellyfish I once watched from the edge of a cliff. How jealous I was of their freedom to simply ... *drift.* My whole body yields to the idea, aching with the sudden urge to swim out into the depths.

*Just drift.*

I push to a stand, wading through the water, charging forward—

"*Stop.*"

My heart leaps into my throat, the commanding baritone a blow from behind, like a rope snagging around my knees, almost pulling my legs out from under me.

Slowly, I turn.

My heart stops.

I see his eyes first—silver swirls that pierce through the tousled mess of his sea-stained curls, whipping me up inside. His all-consuming stare makes a sob burst up my throat.

Stubble paints his chiseled features, his face a beautifully barbaric masterpiece. He's shirtless, standing amidst the jungle's dense shadows, arms crossed, wearing a pair of tattered black pants that cling to his legs like savage strips of art. His silver-scrawled tattoos wink and flicker, hugging his powerful physique, yielding to every bulging brick of muscle—so much bigger than they were before ...

*Before.*

Even my imagination is forgetting what Rhordyn really looked like. Is painting him bigger, sharper.

More fiercely captivating.

Just more fuel to the blaze of pain I've been cradling since I took his life. Or perhaps I'm wrong? Perhaps I didn't get washed up on this shore at all? Perhaps we *both* somehow made it into Mala and this is really happening; he's really here.

*Perhaps I'm dead, too.*

This rich sense of peace cups my heart with warm hands as I run to him, deep, heaving sobs clawing up my throat as I kick up sand in my haste. I draw close enough to smell his frosty musk on a whip of wind before he drops his arms, drawing my attention to the tattered state of the left side of his chest ...

It looks as though his tattoos have been cut from his skin, one by one. Torn off in messy strips around the red, risen scar directly above his heart. Right where I ...

Where I ...

My feet still.

I look up into his eyes and see they're hard like flints. Register the energy rolling off him, smashing against my chest, making it hard to breathe.

*"You. Bared. Your. Throat."*

He charges—pinching the space between us in a few explosive strides.

A bolt of fear slashes through me.

I turn and run, staggering blindly through the sand, colliding with a palm tree. He slams into me, crushing me against the trunk, leaving barely enough space for me to inflate my lungs.

His fist strikes the tree, the creak of splitting wood tightening every muscle in my body. He shoves his head into the side of my neck and huffs sawing breaths upon the bandage Baze bound me in. "You ... bared ... your ... throat ..."

His tone is hauntingly calm.

Somehow, that's much worse.

"I ..."

I don't understand what's happening. I thought Mala was supposed to be a rich, happy place. All colorful and bright and—

"You looked death in the eye and crooked your finger," he growls, nudging my head to the side. His lips skim my ear, sending a zap straight down my spine as his hand threads around my chest and presses upon my heart. Like he's checking for its beat.

A tender shield despite the catastrophic energy lashing against my skin, gusting down my lungs.

His lips graze farther down, over the bind around my throat, the next words spoken through a crackle in his voice as that hand applies more pressure. "You fucking *yielded,* Orlaith."

"You're dead," I say, my voice a strangled sob. "I—"

*Did terrible, unforgivable things.*

He pushes closer, and I feel the deep, catastrophic beat of his life force thumping against my back like the blow of a beautiful, mighty hammer. "Obviously not."

My soul lurches, my entire being clutching to a single wild thought ...

A thread of *hope*.

He's alive. He's standing right behind me.

The world rips out from beneath my feet so fast my head spins, a relieved sound whittling up my throat that feels stolen.

*Not mine.*

I don't understand this reality. Don't know how to handle it, or why it's been gifted to me.

*I don't understand.*

*Alive ...*

But—

"I got you in the heart ..."

"You missed."

"Impossible." I know where to strike. Baze taught me well. "I felt it push through!"

"Sorry to disappoint," he says, the words bitten with such malice I hear the ones he *doesn't* say. Feel them slice into my chest and slip amidst that messy, mangled forest—a willing victim to those piercing thorns.

For the first time ever, I fucking *hear*.

"I ..."

*Regretted it the moment I did it.*

*Almost followed you over that waterfall—more than once.*

"Yes, Milaje?"

The words won't come out. They're lodged so deep in

my throat I'm certain the only way to force them free will be to vomit them up.

*He's here.*

*He's not dead.*

A vine of relief sprouts from the fleshy mess of my mashed-up heart, its tip perfectly honed, like the needle I used every night to prick the tip of my finger. It dips and weaves about the staggering organ, threading through all the broken bits, tugging the torn edges toward each other like it's trying to stitch me whole again.

Tears stream down my cheeks as I weave my hand out from the crush of us and trace the flexing might of his strong arm, all the way to his hand still pressed upon my heart—

He shoves away so fast I crumble, spinning. My legs fail me, and I career sideways, then lose my balance and fall back into the sand, landing hard on my ass.

Rhordyn stands over me like a storm wrestled straight from the sky, molded into a man.

A monster.

His eyes are black, ears sharp, features so cut and refined I'm convinced he was sculpted by the Gods themselves. That they hewed him from the deepest, darkest corners of the universe.

Looking at him makes me want to fall to my knees and weep.

*He's here. He's really here.*

He reaches behind himself and rips the talon from where it must have been stuffed down the back of his pants. My heart slams against my ribs as he sends it thudding into the sand beside me, that curved length glinting in the sunlight.

He watches me with the focus of a hunter fixated on his prey. "Pick it up."

My breaths become staggered, fumbled things …

There's no feeling in his tone—a cold-blooded challenge that ices me to the core.

"N-no," I sputter, feeling what's left of my heart mulch through his clenched fist.

"*PICK. IT. UP!*" he roars, and I sob, scrambling back. Managing to clamber to my feet while still maintaining his eye contact.

He retrieves the talon and stalks every step I scurry backward through the sand, his stare a savage blend of unflinching determination and frosty condemnation.

I realize, like a stone clipping me in the skull, that he's been masking so much of himself since the start. I'm but a mouse dangling by my tail before his fathomless might. Waiting for him to pounce and gobble me down.

My wild emotions shift amidst my cramped insides, abrading my most tender parts.

Battling for space.

For air.

"It was a mistake," I blurt, scurrying over fallen fronds and shards of coconut husk. "I— I thought you were a—"

"Monster? I am."

"—*murderer.*"

"Also correct," he bites out, like he tore the words from a carcass and spat them at me.

"I thought you fed on *people!*"

There's the faintest softening of his eyes. "Only one. Now and forever."

I stumble over a log that almost cuts my feet out from

under me, his admission turning my insides all warm and swirly.

*Good things I don't deserve to feel.*

"Though she's a literal pain in my chest," he tacks on, and my gaze drops to the red, risen scar on his pectoral.

The scar *I* made.

Another cluster of vines pack amidst my insides, cramming me so full I can hardly breathe for fear of thorns piercing my skin.

Poking through from the inside out.

I almost trip again—something I can't afford right now. I'm certain that if I crumble all the way to the ground, he'll crush me like a stampeding herd.

"Cainon said—"

"I don't give a *fuck* what Cainon said, Orlaith. You listened. You *believed*," he grinds out, his words stone barbs lobbed straight at my gut. "You disappointed me."

My heart dives into an acidic pit of guilt, and I waver, forced to slam my hand against a trunk to steady myself. He doesn't slow his prowling advance, like a shadow chasing its captor.

I clamber into action again, whimpering, my pulse whooshing in my ears. "He showed me an abandoned burrow—"

"His *father's* burrow. The one I extracted Baze from years ago."

I stumble on nothing but my own naïvety, remembering Baze's scars.

*Calah made them...*

Recalling the conflict in Baze's eyes after he stabbed

Calah through the chest, it all slots into place like razor blades.

I blink, tears shredding down my cheeks, face twisting, eyes narrowed on the mighty shadow stalking my every step. "This is what happens when you keep so many *secrets*, Rhordyn! People get stabbed!"

His upper lip peels back, a darkness falling upon us, like all the light just got sucked out of the atmosphere. Big, heavy raindrops begin to fall through the canopy and patter upon the underbush.

"Don't lecture me on *secrets*," he says past lengthening canines. "You're riddled with them. I can smell them on that bandage." He points at my throat, making my cheeks burn, and I slap a hand up to smother the shame. "That *hand*. Even your fucking *tears* reek of them. But don't worry." He waves the talon at me. "I'm not about to stick *this* through your chest because of it."

Another slash to the heart, struck with such precision while I scramble along physically.

Mentally.

*Emotionally.*

"You told me you were going to show me your worst and—"

"You stabbed me in the heart."

"You said I missed!"

"You did," he snips as I clamber backward over a fallen tree. He steps over it like it's a twig he could crush with his bare fist.

"What is it, then?" my curiosity plies, the rainfall growing heavier, plastering my hair to my cheeks. "Your worst?"

"You can't handle my worst. You stabbed me in the heart. By *mistake*. Because Cainon told you to."

"I thought you had your own burrow beneath Castle Noir! I thought you put my people in chains and cages!"

He shakes his head; a single slice to the side. "Never once. Though I might re-evaluate my morals if you keep trying to die."

I flinch all the way to the marrow—stripped bare.

*Too* seen.

"Stop."

"*Never.*"

I moan, almost tripping again. "I ... I thought you were ..."

"Dead?" he bites out, the word a stabbed conviction that slides between my ribs and pokes into something squishy. "I was."

My face crumbles, more tears leaking down my cheeks, melding with the rain. If anything, it only makes him look at me harder.

*Fiercer.*

His head banks to the side as he stalks me deeper into the jungle, forcing me to nip glances over my shoulder, dodging more debris with each fumbled step. "Did it make you feel better, *Serren*? Watching me bleed for you?"

Another flinch.

Another wave of thorny, chest-buckling pain I don't know how to handle.

My back collides with something hard and cold—a large slab of blue stone that's nowhere near as brutal as Rhordyn's body when he powers into me, punching breath from my lungs again. With a mighty strike of his hand, he stabs the talon into the stone right beside my head.

I gasp, every cell in my body shaking with adrenaline.

*He remembers my name ...*

My silent sobs turn into deep, guttural sounds that are ugly and messy and bubble up my throat and nose as he tips my head with a pinch of my chin, forcing me to look into his ebony eyes. Forcing me to face my messy expression ricocheting back. "Did. It. Make. You. Feel. Fucking. Better?"

My mouth opens; closes.

I want to speak. To tell him I didn't want to live in a world without him.

That I still don't.

I want to tell him that I don't just love him. That a single four-letter word could never define the way I feel, nor could it explain the way my soul bled with his absence, driving me to do things that will always stick to my skin like a layer of filth.

I want to tell him I was blind.

Hurting.

That my self-hatred bled off the page and tainted him because I was sick. Traumatized. That I had no idea how to ask for help, or tell him I wasn't okay.

*That I'm still not.*

That my chest is so full of thorny things I'm too afraid to touch. To handle.

But I can't tell him any of that because the people I love get struck down with an axe or my own caustic power. They get fed to the sharks.

The people I love die.

"Answer me, Milaje."

The words are a blunt force that rattles me all the way to the core. They punch down my throat, rip truths from my heart, and pull them out—their dangled roots dripping blood all over the both of us. "No. I've never felt such unbearable pain ..."

Something softens in his gaze as I suck a gasp, my throat raw, like I just breathed fire through it. I heave breath, but he doesn't move. Doesn't stop pinching my chin or forcing me to look in his eyes.

"Then I guess it's good your aim was off." His next exhale is an icy blast battering my lips. "Now, I need you to listen because I'm only going to say this once."

He drops my chin and pushes so close I can feel all the bulging slabs of his rock-hard body. Can feel the solid evidence of his want for me.

A whimper worms up my throat. A desperate, selfish, *needy* sound I chomp down on.

*Not for you.*

*You threw him away.*

He tucks my hair behind my ear and cradles the side of my face; a tender motion I yearn to lean into.

*Fall* into.

A polar contrast to the hard words thrown from his mouth.

"Consider this your first and final warning," he says, leaning so close his lips skim mine—like dragging an iceberg across my cupid's bow. "You bare your throat like that again and the entire world will suffer." My heart skips a beat as he leans back an inch, looking at me with a hardness that dwarfs every other look he's ever given me.

"I can't be held accountable for what rips out of me if I'm forced to watch you die."

*How do I tell him I wasn't baring my throat to Cainon's sword but to the weight of my lethal existence?*

My face crumbles.

His stare flays.

"Are we clear?"

I swallow a sob and nod.

A deeper shade of black sweeps over his eyes, making me feel like I'm in the midst of something ... *else*. Like I'm being watched by not just him.

By something *cataclysmic*.

"Say the words," he rumbles past his canines I'm certain have grown thicker, longer; his chest swelling against me with crushing promises. "I need to hear you tell me that you're clear as fucking crystal."

"I got it, Rhordyn."

He releases a bestial sound that makes me shudder from the tips of my toes all the way to my pebbling nipples, then steps back. I plunge to the sand in a heaving, coughing, throbbing heap, my entire body flushed with a heat that threatens to unravel me.

He rips the talon from the stone and stalks off.

Catching my breath, I watch him through wet, stringy strands of hair as he moves between trees, splashed in rain as he picks up his sword, strapping the sheath across his torso—a rippling tower of menacing might. He snatches something else off the ground, then charges toward me, staring me down like a natural disaster I want to fall into.

"Something you want?"

He's paused a few feet before me, his sword back where it belongs, his eyes still black like the dark between stars.

He's breathing … heart beating …

*Here.*

Alive.

*So beautifully alive.*

Perhaps this is some sort of dream, but it's a perfect one. He's angry, fierce, frightening … but he's here.

*Is there something I want?*

*Yes.*

"No."

This rumbling sound boils in the back of his throat, and he hoists me up. "I told you not to lie to me if you can't do it convincingly." He grips me around the ribs and tugs me forward, my breasts brushing his torso as he slams something into my sheath.

I look down and frown at the hilt of my dagger now poking out the top, then slowly lift my gaze to his eyes.

*He had my blade this entire time?*

*But why?*

Something slashes within the depths of his eyes like a whip of blades. "Because I didn't trust you to wake up with it, Milaje. For good reason."

My heart stills.

*He thought I'd—*

I drop my stare, recalling the moment his voice struck and stilled my feet.

Stopped me from going …

"The boy's fine, Orlaith."

Frowning, I look up into his obsidian stare. "What?"

"I saw Baze pull him from the water," he says, tone softer than it was before. "He's fine."

Realization strikes, widening my eyes.

My mouth falls open as Rhordyn spins, prowling through the jungle while my pulse roars in my ears. While the trees seem to sway with my tipping perception.

*Zane's okay ...*

*Della didn't lose another child.*

My knees buckle, hand slapping out to brace myself against a tree as I cup the words he just gifted me and pull them close to my chest. Smooth them into a shell I use to cradle my broken heart.

*Baze saved Zane.*

I shake my head, whimpering.

Rhordyn's alive. The people who were caged in the burrow are free and hopefully partway to Ocruth by now. The rest of the ships are hopefully *also* sailing to Ocruth ...

*It feels too good to be true.*

Another whimper, and I clap my hand over my mouth to catch the whittled sound of relief, because it *is* too good to be true.

If I let myself fall into this feeling, my walls will crumble. My guard will drop.

I still have *death* coiled within the chasm inside my chest, hunting every step I take.

Hunting the ones I love.

I may have missed Rhordyn's heart, but that sizzling darkness ... It took my own flesh and blood.

*No.*

I pinch the vine of relief threatening to stitch me whole again, and pick it free of my heart one plucked loop at a time—the messy lumps of flesh falling away from each other in devastating increments. I rip it out at the roots, wincing from the sharp pain that almost makes me gag, then tuck it in a bundle at the base of my chest.

I forge a dome—just one—setting it atop the bloody corpse before turning my attention toward the forest of emotions crammed within my chest. So much wild collateral I have no idea where to begin untangling it all without making a bigger mess. Without potentially disturbing that strange, macabre creature I hatched back on the pier—the one I can sense hiding down there somewhere amidst the painful clutter.

Perhaps if I just … *back away? Ignore it all?*

Avoid the haze of the past few days. The bandages. The wounds tucked beneath my skin. Avoid the icky memories that try to tame me into a fucked-up plait.

*Yes.*

Don't touch it. Don't look at it. Don't think about it.

*Avoid.*

I tiptoe out, blink back to the now, and release a shuddered breath.

"Keep up," Rhordyn bellows from ahead. "We have a lot of ground to cover if we ever want to get home."

I scrub at my face, allowing the faintest smile to slip free, along with my gathered tears.

*Home.*

With *him.*

# CHAPTER
*Orlaith*
## 48

Rhordyn sets a rigorous pace over toppled trunks and big shards of blue stone, sometimes slashing through drapes of vines with his sword, the terrain a constant rise and fall. At times we're forced to climb near-vertical cliffs, others we're traveling down the spine of rocky gullies, ankle-deep in rushing water, pausing periodically to fill our bellies from the crispy streams.

Silence mulls between us like the hot, sticky air that clogs my lungs and clings to my skin as we weave deeper into the jungle, brushing past thick, waxy leaves, the canopy so dense barely any moisture seems to escape this humid hell.

I keep resisting the urge to close the distance between us and touch him. To make sure he's really here, and that my mind's not playing tricks on me, dragging me through the jungle by my withered heartstrings.

He doesn't look like he wants to be touched right now—shoulders tight, movements stiff. Every now and then he clenches his hands into fists so tight I picture him strangling something.

Or someone.

I forge along behind him, gulping breath, my calves and thighs more wobbly by the second. My head feels light and airy—perhaps from the higher altitude. I rack my brain, trying to remember the last time I ate ...

But I can't. Since I woke on that beach this morning, I've been walking through a dream—the past few days a big, messy, hurting blur I don't want to think about. Or talk about.

Ever.

Zane and Baze are okay. Rhordyn's alive—brooding, but alive.

He's here. With me.

I'll never take that for granted again.

Keeping my stare firmly pinned to the back of Rhordyn's head, I tug on my cupla, trying to drag it over my squished-up hand for the umpteenth time today. Unsuccessfully.

I want it off so I don't have to look at it. Wearing a constant reminder of everything I gave since I stepped onto Bahari soil is not helping me *avoid* the messy forest of thorny emotion smushed inside my chest.

It's doing the opposite.

After another painful tug, I sigh. If I keep it up, I'll make myself bleed, and then Rhordyn will be all up in my face, inspecting the hurt. Then he'll ask why I don't just unclip the thing.

*Avoid.*

My full bladder makes each hurried step more uncomfortable than the last. Groaning, I slow to a fidgety stop, threading my fingers through my sweat-slicked hair and shoving it back off my face.

Rhordyn pauses, looking at me over his shoulder.

He's not even breathing hard. If it weren't for the shreds in his pants or the sweat beading off his sculpted panes, he'd almost look like he was taking a midmorning stroll.

He raises a brow.

"I need to ... *go.*"

Frowning, his gaze drops to my shuffling feet before slashing a glance around. He points at a fallen log a few feet away. "There's a perfectly good spot. I'll give you my back so you have some privacy."

I blink at it, back at him. That *log* has got all the privacy of the bucket the sailors used on the ship.

"I'd rather perish."

He cuts me a look so damaging I feel it slice into my bones.

I wince.

Wrong choice of words after our earlier conversation.

Sighing, I massage my rumbling gut, though that only makes me want to pee more. "I'll be right back. Just ... wait here," I say, threading between thick shrubs, feeling his icy perusal track me until I shift from his line of sight.

I blow a shuddered breath and edge down a slight hill, finding a sheltered spot tucked behind a rock where I can squat without the threat of losing my balance and tumbling to my doom. I'm just resecuring my sheath to my thigh, about to head back up again, when a soft voice comes to me:

The words feel like vines wiggling on the wind, hooking on my ribs and twisting around my spine. They give me little tugs.

Caught in the clutches of some kind of trance, my feet move of their own accord, easing me farther down the steep slope—running in places, dropping to my ass and sliding in others, a litter of dirt and debris chasing my swift descent through the humid murk.

I've heard bits of this song before ... *somewhere*. Like drips of a dream that keeps slipping through the gaps in a clenched fist.

I want more—the *rest* of it. I want to collect every twirling lyric and pull them close to my chest. Let them whisper their secrets upon my skin.

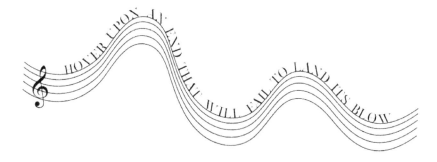

The tune tapers, and I become suddenly aware of a familiar rattling symphony, like a sea of singing cicadas. I push free of the jungle near the base of a frail gorge pinched to the right, as if some mighty hands plunged down from the heavens, gripped the mountain, and began splitting it apart—then paused. Nuzzled within that split is a cavernous slash that's tapered at the top, spewing a radiant gray light.

No sunshine filters through the connecting canopy above, as if the trees on either side are clasping hands. A huge pack of Irilak are huddled in the dense shadow at the cavern's mouth, just shy of the spewing light, like slender slants of vapor caught in some sort of waving trance.

They're watching that hole the same way Shay used to watch my mice treats before I'd toss them over my Safety Line …

A deep rumble belches from the cave, and my heart flops. The Irilak shift in unison, like they're preparing to pounce, and I glimpse a taloned claw swiping at the prowling shadows like a threatened cat.

Realization slams into me.

*Vruk*.

More of that singing voice:

SARAH A. PARKER

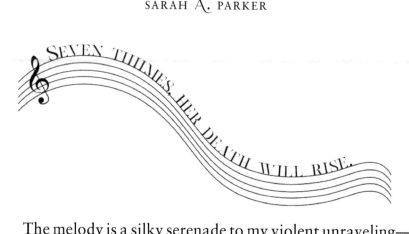

The melody is a silky serenade to my violent unraveling—
my throat tightening, breath failing to wisp through and fill
my aching lungs. I scramble back a step, another, noticing
the strange terrain the Irilak are nesting on: dehydrated
lumps of fur, claws, wide-open maws, and slack, fluffy tails.

*A graveyard.*

*It's a fucking graveyard.*

That cornered beast snarls again, the sound a slash to
my chest.

I spin, colliding with something hard and cold.

Rhordyn's arms band around me, and my entire body
trembles against the might of his embrace, a breath pooling
into my lungs that's all leathery, earthen *him*. His hand
weaves into my hair and cups the back of my head, and I
nuzzle against his chest—no longer ice cold, but *warm*.

*Why is he warm?*

*Here.*

*He's here.*

He tightens his grip.

"It's okay." His voice is a throaty rumble, so much
thicker than it usually is. Something settles inside me, like
a freshly planted rosebush weaving its roots into uncharted
territory.

He tucks me behind a tree, pressing his forehead against

mine. "I'll be right back." Whipping around, he sprints over the morbid terrain of gray pelts before I have a chance to register what he just said.

The Irilak sweep aside like splitting water as he bounds from firm, fluffy mound to firm, fluffy mound, toward his one fucking *weakness*.

"*Rhordyn!*"

"*Stay there!*"

My heart does a nosedive.

If a talon strikes him through the heart this time, he'll—

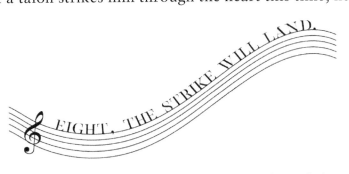

EIGHT, THE STRIKE WILL LAND.

Visions flash of him standing on the edge of that cliff, blood bubbling from his lips, a talon punched through his chest.

Of him tumbling, his eyes flat, lifeless.

A lethal combination of fear and rage saws up my throat, making it hard to fill my lungs.

I look down at my hands, certain they're covered in blood. That it's drying, cracking. Those same cracks weaving through my chest.

*Don't cry.*

That creature scurries out of my dusky chasm, plowing through my internal forest, not even flinching as it swipes its tail like a scythe, slashing my thorny vines and ripping them free with its rose-thorn claws.

Making space.

It uncurls twiggy wings, stretches them, then flaps, flaps, *flaps*—toiling up crystal debris and bits of wild emotion. It tips its head, cranks its maw, and *shrieks*.

The sound splits me down the middle.

Every vine of fear withers, turning crispy and black, freeing more room for my creature's flapping wingspan. I rip my dagger free from my sheath and charge, barely feeling the lumpy terrain beneath my bare and nimble feet, pouncing from one macabre mound to the next.

I plow down the path Rhordyn already paved through the pack of Irilak who seem to turn in unison, their oily perusals scribbling across my skin.

I'm careful to avoid the tapered talons poking up from shriveled carcasses as the cavern belts out another rumbling belch, the smell of sulfur thick on the air. The Vruk is no longer at the mouth of it, swiping for release. It's lumped on the ground with its throat slashed, the grizzly wound leaking a plume of black blood.

*Rhordyn is nowhere to be seen.*

My gums ache so much I grind my teeth together, reaching the rubbled slit, stepping around the beast and charging inside.

WRATH SPILLS FROM A BLOODY HAND.

My creature calls to the haunting serenade—flap, flap, *flapping*. Whisking my insides into a churning mess.

The thick, rancid air vibrates against my skin with each roaring rumble that spews from the bowels of the cavern as

I stalk over sharp shards of stone, barely feeling them bite into my feet, fist tightened around my tiny, charred dagger.

*Don't cry.*

Rhordyn powers around a jagged corner, his arms and chest and face splashed in icky black stuff, eyes like ebony moons, widening. Narrowing on me—the darkness bleeding into the surrounding skin.

He snarls past long, pearly fangs. I return the fucking favor as he closes the space between us in a few powerful strides.

"How dare you stuff me behind a tree, then charge headfirst into possible death!"

"What the fuck are you doing? I told you to stay—"

"Like a dog!"

He slams into me, snipping both our rants as he tosses me over his shoulder, punching all the breath from my lungs. Still, I manage to lift my head.

A stampede of frail Vruk charge down the cavern's luminous throat, galloping in jerky strides. Barging into the walls.

Each other.

Their maws are bared, fangs dripping strings of saliva, ribs and hips so sharp they almost poke through their dull, bedraggled coats. Some bear gory slash wounds, like they've been down there so long, hiding from the Irilak, they've been fighting amongst themselves. Perhaps picking off the weak and wounded in their efforts not to starve.

Rhordyn erupts through the entrance and into the shadowed gorge, one of the Vruk launching after us in a desperate pounce—paws outstretched, talons splayed, tail pointed. It collides with the ground just outside the cave's illuminated embrace.

The Irilak surge like a locust swarm, smothering it, becoming a heaving, suckling mound of black vapor.

I shudder, losing sight of the feeding frenzy as Rhordyn bursts through the trees, charging up the bank so fast my surroundings blur. My creature tucks its wings and scurries through the mess it made, crawling back into my chasm with a swish of its leafy tail—sprigs of emotion shooting from the carnage, packing my insides full again.

We breach the ridge, and Rhordyn flips me off his shoulder. I stumble backward, catching myself against a tree, looking up. His features are a dark twist of wrath and feral condemnation, but it's got nothing on the sawing fear and slashing rage ripping me up inside.

*He could have died.*

*He could have—*

His brows collide, and he peels my layers with a softening gaze.

I spin, giving him my back as I buckle into a knot, digging my hands through my hair, certain a fist is wrapped around my throat—*tightening.*

*He's okay.*

Breathe ...

I scrub my face, trying to loosen the snake bound around my neck, restricting my airflow, making my lungs convulse for breath that won't come.

*Breathe!*

"Orlaith, open your eyes. Look at me." *He's okay, he's okay, he's okay.* "Listen to my voice. I'm here. *Breathe.*"

My head swims, eyes rolling back.

*Weightless.*

I become vaguely aware of my body being tucked against his rumbling chest before I succumb to the clawed clutches of my wild panic.

# CHAPTER 49

*Orlaith*

I wake in a haze, my mind fluffy like the blankets swathed around me and the pillow tucked beneath my head. To the warm brush of evening sunlight pouring through a large window, kissing my cheek, igniting an eddy of dust mites swirling through the air.

*Where ... am I ...*

I reach up to rub my aching throat, wincing when my hand brushes the bandage and disrupts the wounds beneath. Visions flash, hard and brutally fast:

*Vanth's flesh melting off his bones as he burned to a crisp.*

*Sinking to the bottom of The Bowl, trapped in a body that didn't work.*

*Cainon's weight upon me as I scrambled to get free, poison dribbling down the back of my throat.*

*Calah crunching down on my neck.*

*Zane falling.*

*Reaching.*

Each memory strikes like an arrow through my chest—so hard and fast I can't catch a breath before another one hits.

*Rhordyn ... alive. Charging me against a tree. Lashing emotions that stripped me bare.*

*Telling me Baze and Zane are okay.*

The last hits like a hammer to my ribs, crushing them. Too good to be true.

*Was it all a dream? Was it just my imagination playing tricks on me?*

Panic flays me down the middle as I scramble through my muddy mind, struggling to pull air into my lungs. Reaching for the back of my arm, I'm about to pinch when I finally draw a whittled breath through my nose—*him.*

*So much him.*

I sit up, the double bed I'm lying on tucked in the corner of what appears to be a small wooden cabin, Rhordyn's sword leaning against the wall by the only exit. A barrel nests beside the bed, boasting a bowl of plump red berries, a glass of water, and a propped-up fold of parchment.

A note bearing two beautifully scrawled words that loosen the rope bound around my throat:

I grab it, tuck it close to my chest, look at his sword, *breathe*—in through my nose, out through my mouth ...

*Breathe ...*

*He's here.*

*It wasn't a dream.*

Nursing the note like a bandage pressed upon my heart, I continue steadying my breaths with large doses of *him*, gaze skimming my cramped confines.

The large window overlooks the jungle beyond, the trees far enough away that I think this must have been built in a clearing. There's a workbench that runs along that entire wall, a sink in the middle—just beneath the window—the rest of the space cluttered with tools and weapons and crockery, along with chunks of glass, cracked lanterns, and jars of fruit and preserves.

The back wall has a small dining table pushed against it, as well as a freestanding stove with a chimney punched through the roof and a soft seater that's seen better days— the brown fabric patched in places. Strings of drying herbs crisscross the ceiling, spicing the air with botanical smells that remind me of Stony Stem.

My heart pangs at the thought.

Even though the place is packed full of somebody's life, there's an emptiness about it. A hollow aura that makes me think it hasn't been inhabited for a long while.

Rhordyn must have brought me here after I passed out from—

*Avoid.*

I'm okay.

*I'm fine.*

Clearing my throat, I tilt the glass to my lips and drink, the crisp, nectarous water slipping down my throat like a gift straight from the Gods.

*I swear, Rhordyn's got a magic pouring touch.*

A brutal heartbeat of sharp splitting sounds comes to me just as I pick up on the hint of smoke staining the air.

Frowning, I set my empty glass down, as well as the note, and ease off the bed. The wooden floorboards are a strange mix of rough and smooth beneath my feet—like they were harshly milled but have seen the wear of so many steps their sharp bits have been buffered down.

Cradling the bowl of berries close to my chest, I place one in my mouth, moaning at the sweetest, most sensual burst of deliciousness that has ever graced my taste buds as I move through the room. I still before the window, looking past powdery rays of the setting sun and into the clearing beyond, softened by tall tufts of wildgrass and little white flowers that look like sprinkled stars.

There's a small campfire raging within a ring of charred stones, a few stumps of wood scattered about like rustic seats. A metal brace saddles the fire, supporting a black stockpot, whatever's inside spilling a waft of steam.

Two skinned rabbits are laid out on a chopping board, their pelts lumped to the side. Behind it, Rhordyn ...

Shirtless.

Sun-kissed.

Slicked in sweat and soot.

A tower of dark muscle savagely maiming me with each sacrificial sweep of my eyes. I consume him like I did that water, gulping greedily.

*Selfishly.*

He dumps an armful of firewood on a pile, then pauses, looking to the side, as though he's listening to a secret whispered on the wind.

I lean closer to the window, biting down on another soul-melting berry as he dashes sweat from his forehead, then walks to an axe lodged in a stump. He rips it free.

My heart stills.

It glints in the sunlight as he swings it high, his entire body a force of rippling brawn, followed by the splitting sound of the stump breaking apart.

*Avoid.*

I turn from the scene, rubbing the tightness from my chest, bowl of berries forgotten.

Seeking a distraction, I walk to the stack of weapons and run my fingers along the lengths of some short spears, a dagger, and a plain thin sword. The entire thing is shorter than my arm and riddled with nicks and dents, but when I grip the unbound hilt, holding the sword before me, it feels balanced in my hand.

"Not bad," I murmur.

I move farther along the workbench, stealing another glance at Rhordyn through the window, enjoying the way his powerful body moves as he picks up a piece of half-split wood and pulls it apart with his bare hands— so beautifully barbaric. A delicious shiver crawls down my spine and settles between my legs, making me ache in places that send a flush of warmth to my cheeks.

My hand sweeps across the coarse bristles of something, and I cut my gaze to a brush, its handle bound in a Bahari blue hairband. My blood curdles as I'm battered by thoughts of Cainon's hands in my hair, taming it into tight braids that made my scalp hurt.

*Avoid.*

I shake my head in sharp, jerky motions, trying to rattle the thoughts off their perch, flicking another hateful glance at my cupla. I try to tug it free again while scanning the collection of tools poked into small, hollowed-out stumps.

My eyes narrow on a chisel and hammer.

*Perhaps I can ... chip it loose?*

Finding an oily rag in one of the containers, I wrap it around the chisel's handle, set the sharp end against the cupla's chain, and curl my fingers around like a claw, keeping the chisel in place. I aim the hammer, stealing a quick glance at Rhordyn before I swing at the same time he does.

My feeble grip on the chisel slips, the sharp end slashing a gash in my wrist before clattering to the floor.

"Shit."

Wincing, I use the cloth to stem the blood, Cainon's cupla still firmly clamped around my wrist.

*Well, that was a waste of time.*

"What are you doing?"

I almost leap out of my skin, knocking the hammer onto the floor in a clatter. My cheeks burn as I turn to face Rhordyn in the doorway, stuffing my hands behind my back, heart pounding hard and fast.

He's all bulging muscles tailored to perfection, sweat running through the trail of dark hair that threads a line from his belly-button *down* ...

"Orlaith."

My eyes snap up, delving into his fathomless black pools.

I yearn to see the silver again. I don't know why he's hiding it from me.

"Nothing," I blurt, tightening my grip on the cloth. "Where are we?"

He walks forward, slowly.

Predatorily.

The hairs on the back of my neck lift.

"Abandoned cabin. I cleaned up while you were sleeping."

The words are crushed velvet, too deep and dark to be presented so quietly. And when fused with the way he's prowling toward me, I'm half certain my spine's about to give out.

He holds my eye contact until we're standing chest to chest, every breath erasing the space between us. Gently, he lifts his hand and reaches around the back of me.

My heart lurches, though I keep my face smooth.

Impassive.

I hold his shadowed gaze while he takes my fragile wrist in the crushing might of his large, calloused hand, except he's not crushing me at all. His grip is almost ... tender. Like I've imagined he cossets the coal when he's sketching.

For some reason, it makes the backs of my eyes sting.

I blink, but continue to hold his gaze, something in those inky depths screaming for me to *trust him*.

Problem is, I don't trust myself. Not now.

Not ever.

"I'll wait forever, Milaje."

The words are butter soft. Salt to my wound. When did he learn to handle sentences with such care? Why now?

*I'll wait forever ...*

The messed-up thing is, I believe him. And I can't stand this tension for another minute, let alone *forever*.

Slowly, and with my pulse raging in my ears, I drop the cloth and release my arm, allowing him to pull it between us, baring the wound in my wrist that's leaking a line of blood.

*Drip.*

*Drip.*

*Drip.*

The darkness in his eyes bleeds into the skin surrounding them, his canines sliding down so fast I get a chilling visual of how quickly he could rip into somebody's throat. He releases a rumbling sound so deep I feel it vibrate through my bones.

He looks at me in a way that breaks me down into tiny bits. "Did you do this on purpose?"

My breath hitches, heart thunders. All the softness has gone from his words—now sharp and hard like the axe he was wielding.

"What? No! I—"

His thumb brushes the side of my wrist where a bruise is blooming from all the times I tried to wriggle my hand free.

He frowns. "Milaje, you just unclip it."

*Fuck.*

Gently turning the cupla, his frown deepens. He touches the clasp, then pulls his finger back, revealing a stamp of burnt flesh.

He goes deadly still, his energy filling the room so fiercely I can hardly breathe.

"I— I got caught without it, and Cainon—"

My words clog my throat as I catch another glimpse of that deeper darkness in his eyes. The one that makes me feel like I'm being watched.

Hunted.

Like I'm being circled in slow, prowling strides I somehow haven't registered until this moment.

He wraps his hand around my wrist and crumbles my cupla into a scattering of pieces that fall to the floor like pebbles.

I gasp and shove back a step, looking at all the bits of blue and gold littering the floor as I tuck my hand against my chest and rub my bare wrist.

So beautifully *bare.*

I could cry, a feeling that quickly dissolves into confusion when I look up and see Rhordyn breathing deep and hard, his broad shoulders seeming to swell.

And his eyes …

They're black holes I'm certain I could fall into.

"Answer me this, Milaje." He cracks his neck, bunching his hands into fists, stretching them out. "Why would one walk *willingly* into a coupling ceremony with someone who soldered themself to one's wrist?"

My eyes widen as I stare at him, a tangle of words sitting on my slack tongue.

*How does he even know I made it to the ceremony?*

"You reek of his blood," he snips out, and I frown. "Your *palm,* Orlaith. In Bahari, part of their culture is to mix blood during their perverse coupling ceremonies."

My heart slams to a stop, gaze dropping to the strip of silk wrapped around my hand. I feel my eyes glaze, dazed snippets of the ceremony sifting to the surface:

*The sharp slice on my palm before Cainon took my hand, his slicked with something wet and warm.*

"Talk to me, Milaje."

I blink at him.

What does he want me to say? That I walked into that ceremony uncertain whether or not my plan would work? That I'm haunted by thoughts of what could have been had that doping fog not worked through my system in time for me to navigate the coupling? To have the wherewithal to coax Cainon into a poisonous kiss and prevent him from—

No.

Perhaps he wants me to tell him about how I almost choked to death on liquid bane? That all I could think about was that I was going to die a failure? That the little girl in the cell was going to die with unquenched hope in her heart, perhaps believing the filthy, vile words I wove for Cainon to earn me a second chance to set her free?

Perhaps he wants me to tell him I walked into Calah's feeding arena wearing tears of relief because I didn't want to continue living in a world where he didn't exist?

Or maybe he wants me to talk about how I ripped off my necklace on that pier and tried to kill Cainon? About how fantastically I failed to end the twisted, selfish man because I'm broken.

Cursed.

Because I leach all the *goodness* from the world but leave the ugly remains.

Does he want me to tell him that I looked at death and *laughed* because, in that moment, I truly believed Cainon was about to slay a monster just as worthy of death as himself?

*Avoid.*

I spin, moving toward the sink where I turn the faucet, the pipes groaning for a good few moments before water finally dribbles free. "I've got nothing to say," I murmur, filling my cupped hands. I splash my face, then run my wrist beneath the dribble, watching my blood swirl down the drain. "Do you want me to put any of this in a cup, or is it tainted now?"

I hate myself the moment the words leave my lips, but it's easier to attack than it is to defend.

"Don't deflect," he growls, and I slash a look at him over my shoulder. He's standing there with his arms crossed, staring at me from across the room. "There are things strangling you, and you're letting them."

I break our stare-off and rip the bind from my hand, toss it in the sink, then scrub the cut so hard it bleeds. "You've got no idea what you're talking about."

"Really?"

I shake my head, lathering my hand with a bar of soap.

"Every time you stuff something down, you tighten that noose," he grinds out, and I scrub deeper ... *deeper.* Watching more blood swirl down the drain. "Or maybe that's *exactly* what you want?"

*Avoid.*

I cup my trembling hands beneath the dribble of water I splash against my cheeks again. "You're wrong." I grab a cloth beside the sink and dig my face into it, scrubbing hard. "I'm perfectly fine."

My tone is firm.

Dismissive.

A full fucking *stop.*

His body aligns with my spine, and my heart bolts. Lowering the cloth, I see his hands gripping the sink either side of me, caging me in.

His lips skim my ear like a blow of winter wind, stealing my ability to think straight as shivers erupt down the side of my neck and across my bare shoulder, exposed by the gaping neckline of Rhordyn's oversized shirt. Feeling his eyes on me, I look up to meet his gaze in our reflection, the sun now sunk beneath the canopy, turning the windowpane into a perfectly reflective surface.

"Lie to me again," he murmurs, delivering the threat with such poised precision I feel it slide down my spine like an icy blade. "I *dare* you."

It's too much. Too heavy.

*Too intense.*

I close my eyes, cutting myself off, ignoring every cell in my body that's screaming for me to lean into him. For me to weave my hand up around the back of his neck and pull him down until our lips are a clash of fire and ice.

*Not mine*—I ruined our chances. I'll ruin him.

Again.

*Avoid.*

His cold hands settle around my upper arms, his voice too soft when he says, "You need to find a way to shed the weight of your damage, Orlaith. Or it will drag you under."

Then he leaves.

I buckle the moment the door snips shut, arms stretched up and clinging to the edge of the bench as I draw slow, steady breaths through my tightening throat. In through my nose, out through my mouth ...

*I'm already under.*

I open the door, his stare scraping across my skin the moment I exit the cabin. Avoiding his eyes, I pluck a path through the grass until I'm standing in the ring of firelight, looking up at the billowing plume of smoke rising to kiss the stars.

My heart is a wild, restless sprite caught in a cage ...

*You need to find a way to shed the weight of your damage.*

Feeling his icy perusal trace down my arm to the shears hanging from my hand, I drop my gaze.

He's sitting on one of the logs, elbows on his spread knees, hands clasped, watching me from beneath the thick, dark, coiled shelf of his hair—all roughly hewn perfection.

He's never appeared more real and reachable than he does right now.

And I've never felt further away.

"I need help with something."

He nods.

I chew my bottom lip. "You'll probably think it's silly ..."

"Try me," he says, voice thick. Like the words are spoken through molasses.

"Can you ..." I break his stare, looking down at the shears in my hand as a lump forms in the back of my throat that's hard to swallow past. "Can you cut my hair?"

The words hang in the air between us, like they're suspended on the end of strings. When I can't take the silence anymore—my cheeks so hot I'm certain they're blazing redder than the crackling embers—I see the tips of his boots kiss my toes.

I hadn't even noticed him stand.

He reaches down, easing the shears from my tight grip.

Clearing my throat, I step around him, lowering onto the log he was sitting on a moment ago and pushing my hair back from my shoulders. I brushed it inside, got all the tangles out until it was a sheet of golden silk, then vomited into the sink, Cainon's past words pinching bits of my breath until I felt like I was going to pass out.

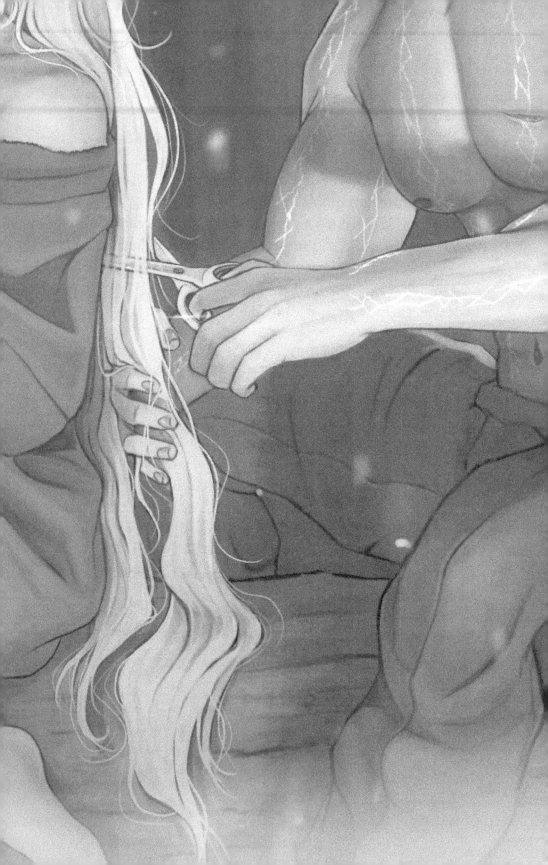

*You will never cut this, do you understand?*

I realized Rhordyn is right.

I'm not the same person I was. I have new scars and cracks in places that weren't there before. The soles of my feet are splintered from a field of thistles I sprinted through to get here.

I no longer enjoy weaving my fingers through the heavy lengths, or draw safety and satisfaction from it hanging around me like a shield. Instead, it reminds me of ugly things that made my skin crawl. Made me feel powerless and trapped. Like my voice had been snipped.

Like my body was no longer *mine*.

I hate it.

I want it gone.

Rhordyn crouches before me, and I dash a tear from my cheek, dropping my stare to the ground.

"How short?"

"I don't care."

He reaches forward, hooking his finger around a thick length of hair and pulling it over my shoulder so it's draped between us like a tether. "Are you sure?"

I nod, swatting another tear like it's an annoying bug that won't stop crawling down my cheek.

*Positive.*

"You don't look sure, Milaje."

"Do it," I rasp, and risk a glance at his eyes.

Silver.

Breathtakingly silver.

That single look plunders my soul and takes my breath away. Challenges me to hold it.

He lifts the shears and cuts.

A soft wave of relief splashes upon me, and I release a

shuddered sigh as a two-foot rope of hair flops limply in his hand.

"This okay?"

I nod, reaching up to pinch the shorter piece, rubbing my thumb back and forth across the severed ends ...

*This is perfect.*

"Keep going."

He sets the slack length on the ground and pulls another piece forward, snipping again, freeing me in quiet severs.

I look up into his eyes, but his brow is pinched, his gaze honed in concentration.

This massive, formidable, powerful man who can claw his way back to life with a talon through his chest ... he's cutting my hair, so utterly focused I think the sky could fall and he wouldn't even notice.

A smile tips my lips, another tear slipping down my cheek.

His gaze shifts, narrowing on my mouth, then up to my eyes, something flashing in the depths of his. "There she is," he whispers—the words so quiet I wonder if he meant to say them aloud.

If he even realizes he did.

He pushes to a stand and moves around the back of me while cool relief swirls inside my chest, soothing all the raw and ruined bits like a balm.

The blunt metal edge tickles my spine every time he opens the shears to capture another piece, kindling my skin with a burst of goosebumps as he cuts ... cuts ... taking healthy bites of my hair. Littering the grass with tainted twirls of gold.

I picture coils of thorny self-hatred withering in their place; each snipped strand a severed touch.

A loosened smile.

A purged lie.

Each tumbling tangle a weight lifted from my laden soul, pulling weeds of regret from my ribs, my heart.

He snips another heavy length free, and I feel it tumble down my back while another thorny vine wilts inside my chest, loosening my lungs.

My breath.

"I'm not very good at this."

I smile again. "I'm sure it's fine."

He moves around me, and I tuck the smile away before he can see it. Crouching, he frowns as he reaches behind the back of my neck, then pulls what's left of my hair forward, and I can tell he's trying to be gentle by the way he moves—like a giant cradling a mouse, careful not to squish it by accident.

"It's much shorter on the right," he murmurs. "If you hate it, I can even it up ..."

I see the unsaid words in his eyes. In the way he smooths the strands with a proud sort of fondness.

*He likes it.*

That alone makes me want to keep it this way.

"No, I love it." I comb my fingers through the sides, the left still long enough to reach my armpit. "I'm not changing a thing," I whisper. "Thank you."

He nods and sets the shears down, crouching by the stockpot to stir the stew. Oblivious to the fact that he just loosened one of the many chains bound around my chest.

Oblivious to the fact that I just fell even more in love with him.

We're two monsters in the dark, painful secrets lodged between us like dual-tipped spikes. I can't move any closer without hurting him, and I won't.

*Not again.*

# CHAPTER
*Rhordyn*
## 50

The stew bubbles and steams, flames licking the underside of the stockpot. I toss another piece of wood on the fire, sparks erupting.

Sitting on a log, elbows set on my knees, my gaze shifts to *her*—watching the flames, toying with a piece of grass.

My heart thumps high in my throat.

With less weight dragging them down, those loose waves frame her face in this fiercely wild way that gives her a cutting, exotic air.

Makes her look like a warrior.

I didn't tell her that I cut it shorter on one side because I thought it would frame the crystal roses growing like floral ghosts from that mark on her shoulder, mutated since I saw it last. Risen in places. Stretched farther across her chest and up the side of her neck. I certainly didn't tell her I counted the blooms on the beach before I resecured her necklace—*twelve*. Most the size of a pip, ranging to a cherry, and two the size of a mandarin.

Breathtaking. And so fucking haunting.

I doubt she's aware of her capabilities. That she has the power to wield her own light like the elders of her race—the ones who spilled from Mount Ether, and have since been hunted.

Slain.

Whether she's aware of it or not, her light's been seeping through the cracks in times of fear—similar to the raw emotion she must have felt when she hid herself from the Vruks all those years ago.

Those blooms tell me too much.

*Too little.*

They tell me the words she's biting back. The ones that keep choking her breath. The four severed nubs and the bruises on the back of her arm tell me she's got harmful tendencies she may or may not try to fall back upon.

Key word being *try.*

*Too much.*

*Too little.*

Her gaze flicks up, catching mine, a blush creeping over her cheeks that brings much needed color to her drawn complexion. She tucks the shorter side of her hair behind her ear and looks away, like she's afraid I'll see past her shields.

Little does she know, I'm already beneath them.

"What was that place I found earlier?" she asks, collecting her lopped hair and piling it behind the log she's seated on.

I clear my throat, reaching forward to stir the stew, hoping it smells alright. The moment she walked out that door, every sprig of herbs I'd stuffed into the pot lost their punch. I hope she never learns how bland the world really is.

If she does, I've failed her again.

"The Great Purge turned a large chunk of the continent to glass, but I'm beginning to wonder if the blast released a pocket of gas that has since blown out and forged that cavern. There was a well of illuminated water at its base that looked and smelled the same as the water in the bowl at Mount Ether. I saw a Vruk clawing out of the pool, like it had just been birthed."

Her eyes go wide like saucers. "So that cave is—"

"Constantly spawning Vruks, yes."

A small pause slips by. "And there was nobody down there ..." she pulls her bottom lip between her teeth and nibbles on it, "singing?"

"In the cavern?" I frown. "No. Why would there be?"

"Ignore me," she blurts, eyes churning with guarded thoughts. I'm about to press her on it when she says, "We need to go back and destroy it."

She's sitting straighter, like she wants to leap up and dart there right now. I'd love to get further inside that head and see exactly what she's thinking we could even do. Stuff the thing with logs? The Vruks would slash through them in a heartbeat.

"There's no point," I rumble, more concerned about the fact that there might be more openings *elsewhere*—perhaps where there aren't any moisture-suckling shadows to stem the flow. "It appears nothing is making it past the nest of Irilak."

"Not true. I saw a Vruk outside the walls of Parith."

I raise a brow. "Did you now?"

She nods. "It chased me. What if it came from there?"

Tilting my head to the side, I ask, "Did it look malnourished?"

"It was definitely *hungry*," she says, and a shadow slips over her eyes as she shivers, then shakes her head. "But no, not malnourished. It looked ... mighty. A beast in its prime. I didn't know they could get that big."

*She doesn't know a lot of things.*

"Well, all the Vruks in the cavern are being born into a world where dog eats dog. Those desperate enough to escape the pit of impending doom make the leap out into the gloom where they're swiftly disposed of. I doubt it came from there. If anything, that cavern is keeping a large pack of Irilak busy that would otherwise be preying on less favorable things. Like people."

She flinches, cutting me a harsh look, boasting those protective instincts that coax a certain part of me into a rumbling, ravenous stir. "They're not all like that ..."

*Yes, they are.*

I don't push it. Let her think the best of her little shadow friend. He won't hurt her, and everybody at the castle knows he won't move past my scent line. He won't hurt Baze because of the ring he wears—not that he's ever believed it or been willing to test the theory.

Orlaith feeds the thing, and I've never had the heart to tell her, but I top it up so it's not interested in preying on nearby village folk. An Irilak can't survive on a single mouse every few days, though I find it endearing that she believes otherwise.

I stir the stew again, lifting some of the meat to see it's beginning to pull apart.

"What happened to your chest?"

I raise a brow.

Her cheeks redden. "The marks where your tattoos used to be. N-not the ..."

She trails off as I look down at the wounds scribed across my skin, like somebody picked at the runes until the edges peeled up, allowing them to rip free like hangnails. Felt a bit like that when they came up, too, but on a much larger, more painful scale.

"Broke something," I say, turning my attention back to the stew.

*Now I just have to find a way to break the rest of them.*

"It looks painful."

I shrug.

Pain is watching her seed blink out, feeling it try to uproot from my soul in agonizing drags. Pain is feeling like every second is one second closer to losing her.

*Pain* is feeling like she couldn't give a fuck about being lost.

The marks are bug bites in comparison.

"It looks like it'll scar."

I lift my head, catching her gaze, flames bouncing off the lilac depths. "Perhaps I'm sick of hiding the scars?"

She doesn't last more than a second before she flicks her attention back to the fire. She could stab me through the heart again and it wouldn't hurt as much.

I stir the pot, feeling her warm, prickly perusal brush upon my chest in small, nipping increments, like she's stealing peeks. "Can I ... make a salve for it?"

I look up.

There's something in her eyes—the slightest speckle of

light that almost fucking breaks me. Like a star bursting to life.

It's not going to scar. Unlike the mark she made, the wounds will heal. Eventually. But I'll let her paint me in mashed-up herbs if it gets me another one of those glimmers.

Her cheeks are flushed again as she hurries on. "There are some herbs in the cabin. I think I saw some Prunella Vulgaris hanging by the door. It's really good for a lot of things. I know you're not really interested in this stuff, but I just thought ... well ..."

It's not that I'm not interested. Rai had similar interests—it's just easier not to look.

"Sure, Milaje. Knock yourself out."

Her eyes almost bug out of her head, and she bounds to her feet so fast you'd think her ass was on fire. "Prepare to have your mind blown. I'm going to make the best damn salve you've ever used."

Not difficult to achieve since I've never used one before.

I let the faintest smile free as she bolts toward the door, my shirt dangling around her thighs and draped off her slight shoulder. She disappears from sight, her scent blown away with a pushy breeze, and I'm instantly struck with the stew's busty aroma—hearty and packed full of botanical smells that make my mouth water.

I've heard her stomach rumbling. Mine's making the same sounds. Can't remember the last time I ate.

After some time, she comes dashing through the door with a wooden bowl tucked against her chest. "You're going to have to stop stirring the stew," she announces, settling on her knees before me.

I frown at the slurry of brown muck she drags her

fingers through, lifting them expectantly as she looks at me from beneath thick lashes.

Clearing my throat, I pull the spoon out and set the lid on top of the pot, lean back, and make room for her between my thighs. She begins painting my wounds like she's sweeping a paintbrush over my skin, nibbling her bottom lip in concentration.

I look away; focus on the fire. Picture myself in an ice bath, and pretend I'm not ready to combust at the vision of her.

The smell of her.

The feel of her *touching* me.

She has no idea of the power she wields. I'd crumble worlds just to see her smile.

"Shouldn't we be moving toward the Norse? Hitch a ride on a barge?" she asks, dragging her fingers through the goo again and painting up by my clavicle.

"Too much traffic. If we keep heading in this direction, we will eventually emerge near Quoth Point."

"Eventually," she echoes, pausing to look up at me from beneath her brows.

I shrug. "If it were the easy route, everybody would take it."

*And we absolutely wouldn't.*

She makes a soft humming sound and continues painting my wounds in slow, tender strokes, easing back to inspect her handiwork before wiping her fingers on the grass. "All done."

My chin drops to my chest. "Looks good."

She beams so bright it almost makes me reconsider my next action.

*Almost.*

I reach forward, pinching the knot on the bandage bound around her throat just as she's about to rock to her feet. She snaps her hand up and bands it around my wrist, wide eyes lit with a burst of wildfire.

"What are you doing?"

"Salving your wounds."

"I didn't agree to *salved wounds,*" she spits, yanking my wrist, grinding her teeth together in such a way I picture her canines breaking through.

My own punch down so fast the color leaches from her cheeks.

"And I don't want you dying of infection," I say, nice and slow. Steady. Betraying none of the wildness slashing at the underside of my skin. "Drop your hand. Now."

Her upper lip peels back as she rises higher on her knees, pushes her face close to mine, and *snarls*—making my heart rattle.

My pulse pumps hot and heavy, every cell in my body igniting as I thread my hand through her hair and gently tug, tipping her head. "Remember what I told you about that fire, Milaje." My gaze flicks to her lips. "This mouth is making promises that I doubt you have the intention of backing up."

She frowns, like she has no idea what I'm talking about.

Probably a good thing.

"Hand. Now."

She huffs out a sigh and loosens her grip. I pull my hand from her hair as she twists around so she's staring at the flames, then lumps on her ass on the ground between my wide-open thighs. Radiating enough anger to set fire to the

493

jungle, she tips her head, offering me access to the filthy bandage.

I grunt, brush her hair to the side, and begin untangling the bind, spicing the air with the smell of her blood. Though it's been over a day since I tasted her, there's not one part of me that hungers to sip at her with the smell of her pain so thick in the air. With visions of those severed nubs on her shoulder haunting me.

*I'd rather a bottled smile.*

Another unraveling twist of the bind, and I set bars of adamant around my insides. Not that it stops *him* from trying to thrash free the moment I reveal the extent of damage on the side of her throat.

My blood chills. The fire sputters, Orlaith's next breath blown out like a waft of smoke.

She's been torn at more than once—both deep enough to scar for life. One a flap of flesh hanging so loose I'm not sure how she's been managing without pain relief.

Any deeper and her throat would have been torn right out.

That *thing* inside me *slashes*, my veins igniting with electric shocks of power that pop against the binds still bound around my body. Like a storm cloud trapped beneath my skin, roiling.

Swelling.

"These were made by different mouths," I murmur, my voice laced with cold, bloody promises.

"The deeper one was a ... *man* called Calah," she rasps, and my heart skips a beat. "He's—"

"Dead. I took him down years ago."

She shakes her head, and there's a tremor to her voice as

she hurries on, "*Now* he is. Baze killed him in his burrow I discovered beneath an island in the bay. We rescued his prisoners. It's how I ended up on that pier. The rest got on the ship in time."

My eyes glaze.

Another failing of mine, and this one almost tore out her throat.

A heaviness rolls in across the sky, drops of rain splattering down from above, pinging off the bowls I'd brought out from inside.

Time liquidates.

Warmth settles on either side of my face. "Rhordyn ..."

Her voice tugs at me, and it takes me a moment to realize she's no longer sitting between my thighs but standing before me, drenched in rain now sheeting down, hands on my cheeks.

Shivering.

The fire is out. No light is left to illuminate her besides the sporadic bolts scribbling across the sky. But I don't need light to see her.

She glows within me like a fucking star.

"Where did you go?" she asks, and I swallow.

"I'm right here, Milaje." I reach around her, unhook the stockpot, then take her by the hand and lead her toward the cabin.

*Always.*

# CHAPTER
*Orlaith*
## 51

He slams the door shut behind us, water slopping beneath every hurried step as he pulls me through the cabin before dropping my hand. Bolts of lightning rattle the windowpane, illuminating glimpses of him setting the stockpot on the dining table; ripping open a cupboard; rooting around inside it while the chill bites all the way to my bones.

The storm rolled over and sponged up all the heat so fast I feel like I've jumped from Puddles straight into an icebox.

"Can you make another salve?" Rhordyn asks, rummaging through a chest on the floor, pulling out a candle and some gauze.

"S-sure," I stammer, teeth chattering as I drag my gaze along the bundles of herbs hanging from the ceiling.

He lights the candle and places it on the bench, along with the gauze, then proceeds to stack the stove with some twigs and husks from a basket beside it.

Gathering the herbs I need by the flashing lights from the storm and the candle's flickering flame, I pray I didn't accidentally grab something caustic. I saw some poison ivy up here somewhere—no idea why anyone would want to preserve that.

The last thing I need is a rash.

While Rhordyn tends to the fire, I shuck leaves off the sprigs and put them in a blue stone bowl with a splash of water, then grind it into a slurry with the pestle I found earlier. I just finish mashing it up when Rhordyn steps up behind me like a shifting mountain, snatching my breath as he shakes out a towel and drapes it around my shoulders.

I steal a backward glance at him as another bolt of lightning strikes, the cataclysmic look in his bold black eyes impaling me. So wild and unbalanced.

He's never looked so haunted—so *untethered*—like he's only a few heartbeats away from combusting.

He's a beautiful, monstrous enigma, and I would do *anything* to peek inside his head. To understand the darkness that toils behind his eyes.

"Thank you," I whisper, heart thumping hard and fast.

He pulls out a stool and sits, tugging me between his thighs with such commanding, unflinching poise that my lungs compact, the room so packed full of him it feels pointless to avoid his gaze.

He's everywhere.

All around me, pouring into my lungs in bursts of deep, frosty musk. He's the single element my heart is pumping through my veins in rapid beats.

Lifting the bowl of salve, he digs his fingers through the muck, tips my head to the side, and begins painting the wounds on my neck in a calm, composed manner—a contrast to the energy rolling off him. Goosebumps erupt down my neck, across my shoulder, his mighty presence such a pressure upon my chest that my knees threaten to give way.

In an attempt to anchor myself, I look out the window. ,

He binds the gauze around my throat, ties it off, then lifts my hand, inspecting the re-agitated wounds.

Another bolt of lightning, the resulting *boom* so loud the windowpane almost shudders free of its confines. A shudder I feel all the way to my core. My gaze shifts to Rhordyn's tattoos, and I notice the luminous pulse rippling through them is ...

*Erratic.*

Frowning, I raise my other hand while he paints my palm in salve, dragging the tips of my fingers across the pretty words like I'm writing them myself.

His skin pebbles beneath my touch.

"They're angry," I whisper, looking out the window again, noticing their turbulent dance is in sync with the feral beat of the storm outside.

"Yes."

Is the storm affecting him so greatly? Stirring him up and setting him on edge?

I continue tracing the script up the side of his neck, the uppermost one ending just below his carotid. I drag my finger back down again, following the hint of a line that weaves around his nipple.

"I wouldn't do that, Milaje."

His voice is a hoarse rumble.

"Why not?" I whisper, trailing a line down his sternum,

imagining my finger is the tip of a paintbrush. That he's a rock I'm swirling secrets upon.

"Because there's a very big part of me that wants to see for himself that you're okay," he bites out, like he's speaking through gritted teeth. "And if you keep touching me like that, I'm going to lose control."

I look up.

He's watching me like a hunter, his eyes cast in that deeper darkness that's as electrifying and unsettling as it is *thrilling*.

A big part of *me* wants to keep going. To find out what he means. The curious, stupid part that's utterly selfish.

*He can't be mine.*

I look at the scar on his chest—nesting amidst the savage remains of his shredded tattoos—then pull my hand away and tuck it behind my back.

*Not.*

*Mine.*

A deep rumble echoes from his chest, and he drops his gaze to my injured hand, using another roll of gauze to rebind it before he takes me by the upper arms, gently shifts me to the side, and stands.

"There's a woodshed out back," he says, removing a cloak from a wall hook. "I'll return soon, hopefully with some more dry wood."

He opens the door and goes, shutting it behind himself, and I pull my first full breath since we dashed in here. It shudders free as I'm reminded of all the reasons why I need to control myself. All the reasons I can't drop my walls and give in to this magnetism squeezing the space between us like a force of nature.

One blares louder than the rest ...

Apparently a talon through the heart is the only thing capable of killing Rhordyn, but I don't see him coming back from being sawed into scalding bits.

I loved my mother. I know I did.

*My darkness still ripped her apart.*

I pull Rhordyn's shirt up over my head and slop it on the ground, squeezing my hands into fists, releasing them. "*Not mine,*" I snarl, wiggling out of my pants before I wrap the towel around myself and secure it between my breasts.

Sighing, I ring the clothes out in the sink and drape them over a rack beside the stove.

The storm doesn't ease. If anything, it grows more restless every minute Rhordyn's gone—drumming against the roof, lashing the windowpanes, making the walls quake as though it's howling at me from all angles.

I lean over the sink and squeeze the excess water from my hair, glancing out the window as a flash of lightning ignites a huge, black shadow prowling around the treeline.

My heart leaps into my throat, pulse scattering. I stumble backward, falling onto my ass with a heavy *thump*.

I press my palm upon my chest and force myself to breathe—in through my nose, out through my mouth—drawing deep, soothing gulps of leather and ice.

*Breathe ...*

"Just my imagination," I mumble, scrubbing my face with my hands.

Shaking off the full-body shiver that has nothing to do with the cold, I stand, edging toward the window again, peeking out. Another flash of lightning, and all I see are trees reaching for bulbous clouds.

*Perhaps I'm going crazy.*

I turn my attention to the stockpot sitting on the table where Rhordyn set it down. I lift the lid and draw on the hearty, botanical scent, my stomach gurgling loud enough to wake a sleeping giant.

Not surprising since this will be my first meal in ... a *while.*

I rummage through a cupboard and find two bowls, spoons, cups, and a ladle—rinsing them, placing them on the table along with a jug of water and a small glass bunny I find tucked at the back. It's perched on its thumping feet, nibbling on a clover leaf, a hole drilled from its head all the way through the bottom, holding the remains of a spent candle I twist free.

Setting the bunny on the table, I reach for a clutch of purple blooms I've never seen before, hissing a breath when thistle thorns stab into my fingers. I frown at the flowers crowning the prickly stems as I suck off the small dots of red, then huff out a laugh.

Actually, it's quite fitting.

Dragging the stool over, I climb up, unravel the tie keeping the bouquet tethered to the ceiling, then leap down and—avoiding the stems—pop the dried blooms in the bunny vase, a smile gracing my lips.

*Cute.*

I place a bowl, spoon, and a cup on one side of the table, then pause, staring at the other bowl, a swirl of doubt clouding my enthusiasm. There's always been a place setting for him ... but he never eats.

Why would this time be any different?

I pick up the bowl, then hesitate, torn. My grumbling

stomach decides for me, and I shrug. He must be hungry, too, and if not …

*Nothing ventured, nothing gained.*

I arrange his setting opposite mine, place the ladle next to the stockpot, then step back, smiling at the little touch of brightness brought to this tiny room so full of restless energy and unsaid words. I draw a deep breath, blow it out, and drop into the seat facing the door, resting my chin on my clasped hands to wait.

And *wait*.

My stomach rumbles, the storm lashing against the walls so hard my imagination paints all sorts of monsters right outside the door. On the other side of the window, looking in.

What if *he's* just a figment of my imagination, and I'm sitting here waiting to have dinner with a ghost that's not coming back?

My chest tightens, gaze spearing to the note on the bedside barrel, sipping his beautifully scrawled words like I used to sip my caspun.

*Are you?*

*Am I going crazy?*

I squeeze my eyes shut, pop them open.

Do it again.

Again.

I don't wake in a gold-brushed room swathed in white sheets, shackled in a cupla with unfulfilled promises lodged in my chest like splinters. I'm still here—still breathing *his* scent.

*Still convinced this is too good to be true.*

The door shoves open, and my breath hitches as Rhordyn pours into the room like a storm cloud, stuffing into the too-small space, dwarfing everything, snatching all the air and holding it hostage.

But I don't need it. Not now.

I'd choose the vision of him—here and alive—over the breath in my lungs from now until the end of time.

The tightness eases from my chest, drawing my attention to a crack in my untended relief dome. To a single vine curling up in waving twists, stretching toward my heart like it's reaching for the sun.

I stuff it back down the hole and bog up the gap.

Rhordyn kicks the door shut, his arms laden with a pile of what I suppose is wood wrapped in the wet cloak like a big, knobbly parcel. Water dripping from his hair, clothes sodden, he shakes off his boots and makes his way into the room.

He looks at me, expression unreadable as his eyes dip, then lift again before drifting to the dinner table, his gaze scouring the settings. My heart beats me up from the inside as the entire world seems to still.

Even the storm seems to pause.

Slowly, he makes his way across the room, and there's something in the way he moves that I can't quite put my finger on, not as smooth and graceful as he usually is—like each step is a battle won. Stealing another glimpse at me, he settles the wood on the ground beside the stove.

Nausea riles through me, threatening to stem my appetite entirely.

*He hates it.*

*He's thinking of a way to let me down gently—like telling me he actually hates stew. That he only made so much because I looked really hungry.*

Seems like a Rhordyn thing to do.

Maybe he's a ghost, and he can't even eat ...

*Maybe I'm all alone in this room.*

He crouches before the stove, opens the hatch, and feeds the flames with several pieces of wood, the firelight caressing his beautifully sculpted face. Leaving the stove's hatch open, he stands, looking down on me.

My heart stills at the sight—his towering body framed by the roaring fire at his back.

I want nothing more than to sit with him. To enjoy the warmth and the sound of rain on the roof and the carefully prepared stew.

But what if he says no?

*Get it together, Orlaith. Been there, done that.*

*Lived to tell the tale.*

I scrape together every sapling of courage I can find in my overgrown insides, draw a deep breath, and ask, "Will you share a meal with me?"

"Always," he rumbles, the word almost knocking me off my seat. "If you're happy to serve me?"

*Serve* him?

All I've had to do this entire time to convince him to share a meal with me is ... *serve his food?*

Heat bursts in my belly, and I almost laugh, floundering through a long silence while I wrestle my delirium into some semblance of an answer, lathering more layers of light upon my trembling dome. "I'd love to. Do you want to get out of your wet clothes first?"

He swallows and nods, then moves through the room, grabs another towel off a wall shelf, and gets to work undoing his pants, easing them down—

Feeling something cold brush against the side of my face, I look at the window, and our gazes collide.

He's watching me through the reflection.

Watching me watch *him*.

*Undress.*

I suck a breath and look away, cheeks burning as I focus on the thistles and their sharp little spikes.

His footsteps pound the floorboards, making the hairs on the back of my neck lift as he brushes past so close I'm certain no more than a hair's breadth separates us. He settles into the seat I set for him, a blue towel tied around his middle.

I force my gaze on the thistles again.

*He's.*

*Not.*

*Mine.*

Raising the lid on the stockpot, I release a waft of steam, pouring the room full of the rich, hearty fragrance.

"Interesting choice of vase," he murmurs, and I glance at the bunny as I reach for his bowl.

"It's the cutest thing I've ever seen. And so realistic! Whoever crafted it is very talented."

He makes a choking sound that has me pausing with the ladle half dug into the stew.

"You okay?"

He nods, banging his fist against his chest real hard. "I'm fine. Please continue."

"Don't choke to death before we get to share our first meal."

"Been there, done that." He flashes me the faintest smile. Warm.

*Playful.*

"Lived to tell the tale."

My cheeks heat, and I lower my lashes.

I ladle some stew into his bowl, feeling his gaze trace the motion. "Is that enough?"

He shakes his head.

I lift a brow. "Hungry?"

"Always."

The word is growled with such a rich, rumbling cadence, all the blood in my body rushes between my legs, making *that* part of me throb so deeply it's almost too uncomfortable to sit still. Remembering what Rhordyn said about being able to smell my desire, I squeeze my thighs together and pray he's too hungry to notice anything other than the smell of the stew.

I ladle him another scoop, almost filling the bowl to the brim. I'm about to serve myself when he reaches for the spoon. "May I?"

"Serve me?"

He nods.

Apparently all my dreams are coming true—like this is one big, pretty picture my imagination conjured up with some fancy paintbrushes.

Clearing my throat, I let him take the ladle and fill my

bowl. He sets it before me—not too much, not too little. The exact amount I would have served myself.

Maybe I *did* serve it?

I internally slap myself.

*Stop that, Orlaith.*

"Thank you," I whisper, and he nods, picking up his spoon and skimming it across the surface of his steaming meal. Bringing it to his lips, he blows, then catches my gaze and takes the bite into his mouth.

A shiver ignites me from the inside out, and I draw a shuddered breath, watching him chew with a tender enthusiasm I never believed him capable of. His throat works as he swallows.

Holds my gaze.

I feel that look in my peaked nipples. Low in my belly, and in the warm throb between my legs that's threatening to undo me.

"Eat, Orlaith."

Eat. Yes. That's what I need to do. Focus on my meal. Not his deep, chesty sound of satisfaction, like this is the first meal he's ever consumed.

I jerk into action, scooping my own mouthful past my lips, groaning before I've even pulled the spoon free. Meat threads apart on my tongue, the rich, robust gravy perfectly seasoned with sage and rosemary and thyme and even a little garlic. My taste buds tingle as I chew, releasing more complexities.

I shake my head, swallowing, savoring the feel of it sliding down into me, heating my belly. "This is the best stew I've ever tasted," I say, the words half laughed, half choked. I'm not sure why I feel like crying over this single bite of stew, but here we are.

I look up to see him still watching me as he scoops another heap into his mouth, chewing.

Swallowing.

Such simple things, but it makes me feel like the wealthiest woman in the world. This might just be my favorite moment ever.

He finishes his bowl well before mine and politely asks for more, which I oblige. He pours me a glass of fresh, crisp water I guzzle back, wiping my mouth with the back of my arm.

He breaks my gaze to scrape his bowl clean, rumbling around the final meaty bite, and I realize I'm smiling again. Letting this moment fill me up in so many ways, like a thief stealing things I haven't earned.

Things I can't *afford*.

Looking inside, I find that pesky vine of relief has found another weak spot to split free of my dome, now twirling up my spine on a straight-shot to my heart. I rip it out at the roots, screw it up, and stuff it down the crack. I forge another dome and slam it atop the other, shoving it so flush against my sides I'm certain nothing else will escape.

Clearing my throat, I stack our empty bowls and stand, feeling Rhordyn's focus brush between my bare shoulder blades as I carry them to the sink. I turn the faucet, waiting for the pipes to groan into action so I can scrub the dishes clean.

He steps up beside me, nudging me out of the way just when the water dribbles free. "I'll clean up. You climb into bed."

Releasing a slow sigh, I spin, scanning the room ignited with the warm glow from the stove.

A stark realization dawns ...

"There's only one bed."

*Two of us.*

Rhordyn begins scrubbing the dishes. "Perfectly aware, Orlaith."

Panic nests in my throat, threatening to stunt the breath flowing in and out of my lungs.

There's not one part of me that doesn't want to share a bed with this man ... except my conscience.

"I'll take the armchair," I say, wandering toward it. "I'm smaller. And it's right by the fire, so I'll be nice and cozy."

"I don't plan on sleeping. You'll take the bed."

The words pack the room so full of mortar it leaves no space to wiggle.

*Guess I'm taking the bed, then.*

Chewing my lower lip, I look at the lumpy armchair that appears far too small for him ...

I find it hard to believe he doesn't intend on switching off—it's been a big day. But I'm not about to insist we share the bed. Not when I don't trust myself not to roll into his atmosphere while I'm sleeping. To do what I've been wanting to do since I saw him on the beach alive and well and whole.

Hug him.

*Love him.*

"Okay," I murmur, padding over to the bed and climbing in, nestling under the covers before I remove my towel and drop it onto the floor. Rearranging my pillows, I find a comfortable spot with my stare speared at the ceiling.

Rhordyn finishes cleaning up, the rain still hammering the windowpanes, though the lightning seems to have calmed. He moves through the room to stoke the fire and fill its belly with a lump of fresh wood, then settles into the chair, springs squeaking beneath his weight.

I draw a deep breath, release it slowly, scared to close my eyes for fear of waking up and realizing it was all a dream. That I'm still in Parith, pretending my heart belongs to another man. Or that I *did* wake on that beach, but Rhordyn's not here at all.

It's just me, alone with my demons and a ghost that haunts my broken heart.

I tip my head to the side, seeing if I can pick apart the illusion ...

He's *absolutely* too big for the chair, filling it so completely, arms crossed over his chest as he stares out the window, perhaps watching the rain splash against the panes.

He looks real—better than real.

This *feels* better than real.

Perhaps that's why I don't trust it. Like we're tucked in a bubble prone to pop.

My eyes snap to the ceiling again, and I rub my tightening chest, fingers brushing against my jewel. I lift it, peering into the fathomless blackness—the same inky tone as the gems on Baze's ring.

I pinch the latch Gunthar pieced back into place, rubbing it between my fingers, remembering that horrible day when I woke beneath a blazing tree wearing tattered scraps, surrounded by lumps of fried flesh.

By people I had *slain.*

I remember the way Zane's mother stared at me when she burst into the room, like she was looking into the eyes of a ghost. I remember the chill that seeped through my veins as she released an anguished sob.

"Someone recognized my ... fake skin," I whisper, focusing on a bundle of dried daisies hanging from the strings draped across the ceiling.

Little dead suns staring down at me.

The air tightens, like the room just packed full of something I can neither see nor comprehend.

"She took one look at my face and believed I was her daughter."

A question swells in my chest, becoming so big and restless it feels like my seams are splitting.

I slide my leg free of the blankets, feeling his cool stare drag along the length of bare thigh all the way to my hip and back down again, settling on the birthmark I tap with the tip of my finger.

My stupid curiosity lengthens her brittle throat.

Begs to be *bit*.

"How did a mother who put her child in the ground years ago know I had this birthmark on my leg?"

*Silence.*

I dare a peek at his eyes, catching his stare as he studies me with a hardness that makes every muscle in my body brace for the psychological impact of his response. Is he about to lie to me? Tell me I wouldn't understand? Perhaps he's thinking up a riddle to weave for me so I'm left stuck to all the sticky strings, trying to untangle myself?

A big part of me hopes that's exactly what he'll do. Lie to me.

*Push me further away.*

He draws a deep breath and rubs his scruffy jaw, then points to my necklace. "That jewel is steeped in the blood of Kvath."

My lungs compact.

*God of Death …*

My stunned mind cycles back to *Te Bruk o' Avalanste*, and I hear Kai's words as though he's right here, speaking to me:

*Kvath. God of Death. He can take on the many forms of the dead, and he made the Irilak with a piece of his shadow.*

My mind churns, gutters, chokes. I open my mouth, close it, carve my stare across the dried bouquets. "I thought you believed the Gods don't exist. You insinuated it right before you tossed that beautiful book in the flames like it was trash."

"Some of them *shouldn't* exist," he states with cold, brutal precision.

I swallow, chewing on his words like they're a piece of gristle.

Curiosity lifts another foot, edges her weight forward, sets it down a little closer.

"And how did you get his blood?"

"He gave it to me."

I suck the smallest gasp, head whipping to the side. He's staring at me with such intention I can't hold his gaze for more than two seconds before I break, stabbing my own back at the ceiling again.

Is that why Shay's drawn to me? The reason that pack of Irilak obeyed when I told them not to feast on the fallen sprites? Because I carry the blood of their Creator around my throat, dressed in the skin of a dead girl?

512

*He gave it to me ...*

The heavy, tangled statement weighs me down like a lump of lead plonked on my chest.

A tiredness seeps through my bones, mind, and heart, as if someone just slipped beneath my skin and blew out all the candle flames keeping me awake.

I roll to the side, facing the wall, giving him my back. Chastising my curiosity in the same ugly beat.

I've been wearing a dead girl's face all this time—Zane's *sister's.*

No wonder I was so drawn to him.

And I almost lost him, too. Just like I lost my brother.

I pull my knees close to my chest and wrap my arms around them tight.

*I shouldn't have asked.*

"Is that all you have?" His words rumble through the room.

I hug myself tighter.

"Yes," I say to the wall.

"Where have all your questions gone?"

I almost tell him they died with him. That I took a wrong turn, and now the road is dark and lonely with nothing but monsters decorating the shadows.

That I'm one of them.

I almost tell him I'm frightened to go to sleep, afraid he won't be here when I wake ...

But I don't.

"I'm tired, Rhordyn."

There's silence for so long I start to wonder if he's fallen asleep, but then he says, almost too soft for me to hear, "Goodnight, Orlaith."

# CHAPTER
*Rhordyn*
## 52

S he breathes soft and slow, still in the same position
she fell asleep in hours ago. She hasn't moved once.
Neither have I.

The storm continues to churn outside. Continues
to rip me apart from the inside, lashing in sync with my
splintered thoughts. I think of that glass bunny she used as
a vase—once soft and alive.

Now hard and dead.

She thinks she's the darkest shadow in the room, but
there is none darker than I. No monster that holds a candle
to the shit I've done.

She tucked into herself and put her back to her damage
like it'll all just go away. I've seen how that pans out. I
watched my sister die too many times not to smash down
Orlaith's walls.

Unapologetically.

I'm tempted to stalk over there and whip off the cover,

rip her out of bed, then back her against the wall. Tell her there's nowhere she can hide where I won't follow.

No hole she can crawl down that's too dark for me to *see*.

But she's naked under the covers, so I don't. There's a fine line between rage and feral fucking in the blood that runs thick through both our veins, and this cabin can't handle what I've got to throw at her.

The walls are too frail.

She wails, and her entire body jolts, arms flailing as she tips onto her back, face twisted.

Eyes still closed.

My heart slams against my ribs as she reaches for something I can't see, clawing at the air. She sobs, the sound so coarse and guttural I feel it slice through me like a serrated blade.

"Don't cry." She chokes. "*Don't cry. Don't cry. Don't—*"

I'm up and out of the chair, charging to the bed. Lightning pops and crackles to the tune of my hammering heart as I rip the blankets back and climb in next to her, hauling her against me.

She gasps awake, eyes wide and wild, cheeks stained with tears, her breaths turning short and sharp.

Strangled.

She wiggles around so our bodies are flush—a crush of soft and hard. She paws at me, weaving her legs through mine, tangling us together like her wisteria vine bound through the black stone of her balustrade.

Another bolt of lightning ignites her crumpled face as she drifts her hands up to my cheeks. "Let this not be a dream ..."

"I'm here. This is real. I'm not going anywhere."

A twisted sound rents from her as her body jerks, eyes so glazed I wonder if she's truly awake or caught somewhere in the middle. "I'm not okay," she whispers past shallow breaths, and the words alone could still my heart for good.

"I know …"

*Neither am I.*

Threading my hand behind her head, I tuck her into my chest that's shaking in time with the sky, resisting the urge to squeeze her more than her brittle bones can manage.

I don't want to hurt her. I want to fucking *mend* her.

I'm not the gentle man she needs. The sort she deserves. But I'm done playing a passive role in her life. I know where that road ends—heard it straight from Maars's mouth.

With her in the ground.

She believes she's expendable. That she owes the world, even though it's certainly never shown her the same liberties.

Just another war I need to wage. And *win*.

"Don't let me go," she whispers against my skin.

Against the scar she drew.

"Never."

I wrap my hand around her ribs so I can feel the peck of her heart, nudging her so deep into my neck I can gauge the rhythm of each tight breath until they become long, sleepy pulls that tug me into the depths with her.

My one. My only.

*Milaje.*

# CHAPTER 53

*Orlaith*

I pull from a sleep so quiet and still I don't want to wake. Don't want to slip off this warm slab of stone I'm wrapped around. That's rising and falling beneath me like it has real, working lungs, lulled by the slow, sludgy beat thumping against me.

*Thud-ump ...*

*Thud-ump ...*

*Thud-ump ...*

I nuzzle in, drawing myself full of leathery musk nipped with the smell of a frosty morning. A smell that paints itself all through my chest, filling me up—

*Rhordyn.*

My eyes snap open.

The window comes into focus first, the world beyond it crammed with the powdery brightness of morning, casting dim light through the cabin. I look to the chair Rhordyn was sitting in when I fell asleep and confirm that it is, indeed, empty.

My pulse whooshes in my ears as I register my nakedness. The blankets heaped on the ground.

The weight across my bare back.

Two heavy, *warm* arms bound around me. Arms belonging to the man *beneath* me—my legs tucked up and straddling his torso, head pressed firmly upon his beating heart. My hands are woven beneath his armpits, curled up his muscular back, my fingertips kissing his shoulder blades ...

Fuck—fuck—fuck—

Midnight memories pummel me: him dragging me flush with his rock-solid chest; me clawing at him, tangling us together; falling back asleep to the sound of his heart beating safely against me.

*It wasn't a dream. It was real.*

*He's here, in bed with me. Cuddling me. Letting me use him like a mattress.*

My dome bears a massive cleft straight through the middle, barely visible beneath everything that's spilled out of it—those raw, tender vines of relief I've been tucking and stuffing beneath the surface no longer vines but a *forest*.

They've used my spine as a ladder to weave around my ribs so tight there's no bone left in sight, then stitched my heart into a tidy lump that makes me feel so beautifully whole. They've smothered every other emotion in sight, sprouting thousands of little buds that look like they're just about to split their heads and bloom.

I squeeze my stinging eyes shut, releasing a slip of tears.

I thought my home was a castle sitting on the edge of a cliff, looking over a bay that's shaped like a monster bit the shore. I thought my home was a tower poked through the clouds, with my rocks and my paints and my plants. But I'd happily live right here for the rest of eternity and never feel another pang of homesickness. It's a realization that just makes more tears slip from my scrunched-up eyes.

Because this moment—this beautiful, perfect moment—is stolen.

*Not mine.*

His temperature snaps to cold so fast I gasp, wondering if I just imagined him warm in my half-asleep state.

*Must be it.*

I tune into his slow and steady breaths ...

I need to get up. To wiggle out of his hold before I do something stupid, like kiss him awake. Like reach back and take his hand, urge it farther down my spine, between—

*Get up, Orlaith.*

I open my eyes, lift my head the slightest amount, look straight into his silver eyes, and freeze.

My heart *whumps* into my stomach, a small, choked sound slipping free as I hold that paralyzing stare.

His hair is mussed from sleep, brows pinched, mouth serious, a tension strung between us so tight I'm certain it could shatter like splitting glass.

The world could combust right now and I wouldn't notice.

His throat works, and I whimper as his hand comes up to brush the tears from my cheek. I'm too drunk on the moment not to lean into his touch. To close my eyes and nuzzle his hand—stealing a sip of serenity because I'm greedy.

Happy.

*Bereft.*

Because I'm just about to let him go and blow him back to the wind.

I swallow, force myself to open my eyes. He doesn't stop me from sitting up, climbing off him. Doesn't shift a muscle until my feet kiss the floorboards.

His hand latches onto my wrist, and in a few swift motions he's sitting on the edge of the bed with me straddling his lap—forehead to forehead, breathing hot and heavy, his fingers delving into my hair that's a mess of wild, unruly waves around my face.

I can feel his manhood hard and heavy between us, resting against my belly.

I thread my hands through his beard so as to set some barrier between us ... partially. But also because I want to touch him.

Feel him.

*Love him.*

His body goes entirely still as I brush my lips against his, softer than the beat of a butterfly's wing. Because I'm a thief, stealing little trinkets, stashing them in my chest for when feast becomes famine. For when we're not stuffed into such a small space with too much of *him* and no room to breathe.

To think.

*To nurture my self-control.*

The storm in my stomach churns.

"I can't," I whisper pitifully, more tears slipping down my cheeks as he makes a rumbling sound, then feathers his lips along the edge of my jaw.

"*Speak* to me." The words patter against my pebbling skin, and his teeth dig in—a gentle nip that loosens the strings of my composure. A moan cuts into me as my head falls back, spine arching, my aching breasts pushing so far forward my nipples brush his chest, the blunt ends of my hair tickling between my shoulder blades as he ghosts his lips across my right clavicle.

He plants a kiss, and I can almost *feel* it brushing the petals of one of my blooms. Another is pressed beside it, like he's mapping a constellation with his mouth, hatching the next kiss upon my shoulder.

A smaller, softer one beside it.

Pleasure ripples through me like honey slugging through my veins, and I moan, swallowing a whimpered beg for him to do it again.

And again.

*For him to do it forever.*

His mouth journeys into the dip of my neck—tender.

Nudging.

My head tips to the side, and he blows an icy breath upon the stretched hollow, a shiver pebbling my skin.

I picture a senka bloom unraveling milky petals.

He drags his hand from my hair, down my spine, the frosty brush between my shoulder blades kindling my nerves.

My *want*.

He braces my back with his unflinching strength, giving me a perch to arch upon as he feathers more kisses across my clavicle.

I count each one, memorizing them.

Tucking them away.

*Ten ...*

*Eleven ...*

"Please."

*I didn't think he knew that word.*

He plants another kiss in unison with the heavy roll of my heart.

"I have nothing to say," I whisper, and he makes this deep, pained sound, his hand spearing up into my hair to cradle the back of my head. He presses our foreheads together so I'm looking into his silver orbs from beneath tear-stained lashes.

"Then *fight* me," he grits out from between clenched teeth. "Fucking *use* me if you have to."

There's a vulnerability in his eyes that breaks my fucking heart, a waiting silence shoving between us that seems to grow its own hungry pulse.

I used the man in the forest nymph lair. I will not *use* the man I love.

Delving my fingers through his thick locks, I blow a breath upon his lips, wishing I could tip forward.

Steal another taste.

"You deserve better than that …"

Than *me*.

Because I'm broken.

In pieces.

A tangled black vine that'll smother him to death.

His stare tracks over my face in catastrophic sweeps, darkening. "I don't. I deserve a lot of things but your respect isn't one of them."

"You don't understand," I whimper, my voice soft and fragile. Weak—just like my ability to battle the gravity bringing my mouth closer to his, thieving another brush of his lips. Another trinket I tuck away, cradling close to my heart. "My love will tear you *apart.*"

He digs his hand into the hair at the back of my head. "Then I'll die a happy man," he snarls, and crushes our lips together in a clash of desperate, wild abandon.

A deep, aching strike I fall upon the blade of.

*Willingly.*

I moan into his mouth, tugging at his hair as I tip his head to the side and stoke the kiss. Tasting him.

*Devouring* him.

More vines of tender relief cram into all my nooks and crannies until I can barely inflate my lungs, and my body grows loose like softening butter.

We tide together, a perfect meld of hunger and repose, our souls seeming to skim with the dig of our tongues and the pull of our lips. He rumbles into me, almost like a purr, making heat pool in my lower belly.

I grow greedy ... *ravenous.* Rock my hips.

*Just once.*

A zing of pleasure spears through me when that tender bundle of nerves brushes against his solid length, like an electric shock to the aching organ in my chest, reminding me of all my singed, jagged edges.

I break our kiss, resting my head on his shoulder, my breaths hard and heavy.

Heart thrashing.

*Breathe ...*

His arms move around me, lips skimming my temple, planting an icy kiss that ignites my skin in a flush of delicious goosebumps.

I open my eyes, seeing the wide, risen scar on his chest ...

A chill slips through my veins, dousing the throb between my legs.

I remember the feel of his blood on my hands; the way it felt when it dried and cracked.

I remember the way he kissed me on the head right before he slipped away.

I remember his final words that gave so much and took so little despite everything I'd just done to him.

*Don't cry.*

Guilt crashes over me. Ugly, selfish guilt—saturating the air, making it hard to breathe.

I can't control this *thing* inside.

*I ripped my own mother to bits.*

Not having him at all … it's worth much more than losing him again.

Setting one hand upon his scar, the other on his jaw, I look into silver eyes that reflect my flushed cheeks, tear-stained lashes, and the wild mess of my hair.

"Milaje—"

"This was a mistake."

His eyes shutter, a raw, angry sound boiling in the back of his throat.

"It can't happen again."

Drenched in the heady musk of our tangled scents, I unsaddle myself from his lap and take backward steps toward the clothing rack, willing him to stay.

*Don't make this harder than it already is.*

His canines lengthen. Ears sharpen. Eyes darken.

*Please—*

He stands, dwarfing me in both size and presence as he prowls forward—huge. Naked.

Beastly.

When he's so close I feel his static against my skin, he stops, grips my chin, and tips my head, his words a frost skimming my lips as he says, "I bow to no one, but I'll get down on my knees before the Gods and beg you to choose this. To *live*."

He plants a kiss on my forehead, and again, I picture him falling backward off a cliff—down into the frothy nether.

Dead.

"Get dressed," he murmurs against me, then grabs his pants off the rack and steps into them, pulling them up. "I'm taking you home." Snatching his sword, he makes for the door, thumping it shut behind himself.

I claw at my tightening throat, breaths turning short and sharp as I picture him in bits, reeking of scorched death ...

*Murderer.*

The vines that were so budding and hopeful turn yellow, brown, then *black*—breaking down into a blow of dust and inky seeds that clog my insides.

I carefully pick up those precious, hopeful seeds, tucking them through the split in my dome before plucking beads of luster, tenderly filling the jagged cleft as I crumple to the floor and weep.

# CHAPTER
*Orlaith*
## 54

Massaging my temples, I step over fallen fronds and fat, velvety vines that have woven paths through the soggy underbrush.

It began as a faint, insistent pecking between all the folds of my brain, a different kind of headache than the ones I've become accustomed to. Now it feels like a hammerbeak's making little holes in my skull to store its winter treats.

The clouds crackle overhead, strings of rain weaving through the canopy and pattering upon leaves that are round as dinner plates. They face the sky, seeking even the tiniest shaft of light that filters down through the oppressive foliage.

The rain's dribbled symphony is a welcome respite from the silence sitting heavily between us.

I peek over my shoulder, seeing Rhordyn four steps behind—sword in hand, his body a tower of rippling brawn.

Sooty gaze nailed to me.

I whip my head back around, cheeks heating, unable to

stop my mind from tumbling toward images of his mouth on my skin. Planting a tender trail of love that both lit me up and burned my blackened soul.

Clearing my throat, I brush a vine to the side as I step over a fallen log.

I tripped on a rock this morning and now Rhordyn refuses to take the lead—following with near-silent steps, unspeaking but for the odd stern instruction.

A broody shadow tethered to my wake.

Perhaps I should welcome the silence, but with his frosty gaze constantly pinned between my shoulder blades, and with the memory of his mouth on mine as our souls brushed against each other, the heavy patter of rain couldn't be more of a relief.

We reach a wall of vines, and he sets his hand on my shoulder, slashing a path through the squiggle of gnarly drapes in a few powerful strikes.

"Thank you," I say, stepping through the severed gash into yet another bushy, humid, tightly packed segment of the jungle.

*Fantastic.*

I readjust the sheath bound across my chest, the holster down my spine stuffed with the sword I took from the cabin. I stretch my shoulders, then my neck.

Get back to massaging my temples.

My foot hooks on a stone, and I lurch forward. Rhordyn's hand snakes around my middle so fast I don't register what's happening until I'm tugged against his hard chest—heaving breath, heart pounding. A flock of moths the size of my head launch off the surrounding tree trunks in a waggle of blue tones, swarming toward the jungle's canopy to resettle amongst the lofty trees.

"Brakenmoth," Rhordyn rumbles so close to my ear I feel the brush of his chilled lips devastating my nerves.

I swallow, loosening my grip on the dagger at my thigh. "Pretty."

"When threatened, they birth a stinger longer than your thumb, their venom potent enough to kill a child."

My blood chills. "I ... take back what I said."

"There are beasts that live in the gloom that have learned to hide from the Irilak," he mutters as the death moths shimmy their wings against their new resting spots, shifting their colors the slightest amount until they're one with the trees, vanishing before my eyes. "They're masters of camouflage and masking their scents." He looks at me, frowning. "The jungle is unpredictable, and your footsteps are getting sloppier by the second. Trip again and I'll carry you."

This headache has its claws dug so far into my skull that the thought of being carried is actually kind of nice, though I'll never admit that to him. There's not enough space in this dense jungle to escape the crippling tension strung between us as it is.

"Message received," I murmur, trying to wriggle out of his arm.

He tightens his grip, reaching up to grab one of the cupped leaves above my head. He eases it down until it's at my eye level, and I see the puddle of rain sitting in its deep hollow.

"Drink."

"I'm not thirsty."

In fact, my throat kind of aches, and the banana Rhordyn climbed a tree for a few hours ago isn't sitting too well inside me, despite being the best banana I've ever tasted—sweet like taffy threaded with notes of pineapple and melon.

"I can stand here all day," he says blandly, and I groan, lifting my hands to cradle his so I can gauge how much he tips the leaf.

Despite my reluctance, I welcome the crisp, luscious rainwater as it cools me from the inside out, nudging his hands when I've had my fill.

"Happy?" I ask, wiping my mouth.

He grunts, escorting the leaf back to its spot in our cramped confines.

Easing out of his hold, I continue forward, weaving around trees and an endless crumble of big, blue boulders threaded with veins of gold. So when I spot a black slab of stone peeking through a gap in the foliage, my heart stops.

"I can't believe it," I whisper, a bubble of hope swelling in my chest, the backs of my eyes burning as I dash through the trees.

*Are we almost at the border?*

*Is blue stone, humid heat, and slate foliage about to become fluffy grass, black rock, and ancient, gnarled trees with leaves the color of emeralds?*

I burst past the large dark slab into a blessed clearing four times the size of my room in Stony Stem. I count twelve flat stone spires punched through the circular perimeter, some clothed in silver vines of grayslades poking their heads toward the unsettled sky. There's a small, simple dwelling in the circle's center made from a bunch of logs all leaning against each other, meeting in the middle with a bind of vines keeping them in place—big enough to provide a night's shelter from the rain but not much else.

And the rain ... it's a treasure I swirl beneath, arms outstretched, face tipped to the sky. Drawing on air that's light and crisp.

For the first time since we set off this morning, I can *breathe*.

I stop, crouch, and thread my fingers into the thick, fluffy grass as Rhordyn stalks past me, poking his head inside the hut.

"How close are we to the border?" I ask, drawing a whiff of the sodden soil, digging my fingers deeper.

"Two days if we pick up our pace."

I groan into the grass.

*Not happening until I sleep this headache off.*

I lift my head, peeking at him from beneath my lashes. "Can we sleep here tonight?"

"There's still an hour before the sun goes down, and we haven't covered a lot of ground today. " He sweeps his gaze around the clearing, then looks at me over his shoulder, mouth a thin line as he slides his sword into his sheath and nods.

*Thank the Gods.*

My attention drifts past him to a huge, ancient-looking trumpet tree just beyond the ring of stones. It's in full bloom—little blue bell-shaped flowers littering the knobbly branches that stretch far and wide. A flush of tall, pale mushrooms sprout from one of the gnarled limbs about twelve feet off the ground.

Mushrooms I'm *boastfully* familiar with.

Dogwarth usually grows on shit, but it must thrive in this humid environment, and right now, it's the answer to all my brain-pecking, temple-aching problems.

I clamber up and sprint past Rhordyn, weaving between the stones as I unbuckle my sword and lean it against the base of the thick, wet trunk. I grip hold of a knot, set one foot against the sturdy surface, and haul myself up, moving from branch to branch.

Reaching a spot that's webbed in a shock of glassy veins, I frown, dragging my finger up the smooth lines, tracing them until they taper off ...

*Interesting.*

"One minute you want to stop for the night and the next you're climbing a tree?"

Rhordyn's baritone almost shocks me out of my skin.

"There's a patch of dogwarth up there," I say, stealing a peek of him at the tree's base. "Don't stand there, I might land on you."

He holds firm, folding his arms across his chest.

*Don't know why I bother sometimes.*

"If I fall—"

"We've spoken about this," he rumbles, and I pause, cutting him another glance.

*I won't determine your steps, Milaje. I'll even let you trip. But I refuse to let you fall.*

My cheeks heat, and I spear my attention back to the tree. Reaching a split in the trunk, I haul myself topside of the branch sprouting the patch of dogwarth. I push to a stand, and the branch wobbles beneath me, shaking some of the blue flowers loose and littering them upon Rhordyn's head.

I smile.

The line between his brow smooths.

I ease farther along the branch, past tufts of flowers, dropping onto my belly as I draw nearer to the mushrooms—a bigger, thicker branch arched over top of me like a doorframe.

I stretch my arm out and pluck one of the lofty stalks, pinch its root ball free, and give it a sniff, brows almost jumping off my face. I flick it away and hold the fleshy cup beneath a dribble of rain. "Well, that makes more sense," I murmur, stuffing the mushroom top in my mouth and chewing, moaning at the instant wash of relief. Like I just reached inside my skull and set a cool, numbing blanket over the bulge of pain.

*Sweet, sweet mercy.*

I narrow my attention on the remaining flush. On the smear of gooey black stuff that appears to have dripped down from above, saddling the branch like a streak of tar.

"What makes sense?"

I pluck another cap, rinse it off, and stuff it in my mouth, chewing through the dense, earthy flesh. "This stuff usually grows on crap," I say, swallowing. "I thought it was spawning up here due to the humidity, but no. It is, in fact, sprouting from a smear of shit."

Snapping off another large cup, I scope Rhordyn from my lofty perch, eyeing up my frowning target. "Catch."

I let go, certain it's going to hit him in the face, but his hand whips up in a blur, snatching it split seconds before it can pelt him in the eye. Lips straight, he gives me a stony look that tells me exactly how little he appreciates me throwing shit-spawned mushrooms at his face.

"Got it," he bites out, waving it at me. "Now get down."

"You're being very bossy for somebody twelve feet below me."

I look back to the cluster, eyeing up my next target. Doesn't hurt to have a healthy stockpile in my pocket for later. A few moments ago, my skull felt like a hammerbeak's cage, and I have no interest in feeling that way again while we're trundling through this muggy hell.

"Orlaith, I need you to come back down. Now."

I grasp another fat stem and snap it free. "What you need and what *I* need are two entirely different things," I say, dangling my ammunition over his head, aiming for my growling target.

I drop the mushroom, frowning when he steps to the side. Peering past me, he lets it fall to the ground rather than catch my shit-shroom like a gentleman.

I tsk. "That's not very nice. Let's try that again."

I'm plucking another stalk when a blow of wind shakes the branch, and I reach up to the one arched above me to steady myself.

It *moves* beneath my hand ...

I jerk back as a shrill hiss ignites my nerves. Stilling, skin tingling, my gaze slides up the thick, smooth branch.

Except it's not a branch at all.

A massive snake shudders, its brown and blue scales morphing into skin as black as the darkness coiled within my shadowy chasm. Faster than a flicked whip, its big, boxy head snaps around, red eyes blinking open, slitted pupils narrowed on me.

Heart hammering, I suck a sharp breath as the snake's long forked tongue slithers out, tasting the air.

My skin.

Its mouth cranks wide, exposing a sinewed cavern, two large, piercing sabers flexing down from its upper jaw.

My hand grips the hilt of my blade …

There's a whistling sound, and the snake's head slides off its wiggling body, a spray of blood splattering my face. I hug the tree as the thick, meaty length of its torso plunges past me, thudding to the forest floor in a squirming heap.

I look over my shoulder, and my heart fumbles over a foray of scattered beats.

Rhordyn's perched on the branch behind me like some fierce, mighty feline—teeth bared, ears sharp, his eyes an inky oblivion that shades the surrounding skin. He's wielding my plain silver sword that's slicked in blood, his beautifully barbaric body splashed in shades of red.

"They're *pack* basilisks," he snarls, slamming the sword into my hand. "And they're very territorial. Once their nest is disturbed, they swarm like a fucking plague." He leaps, landing so hard upon the ground vibrations travel up the tree.

Through my bones.

He rips his sword from its sheath. "*Stay there,*" he growls, leering up at me with wild eyes. Something thick and green as the grass slithers out of a nest of nearby shrubs, skin shuddering into a squirm of darkness. The serpent whips up, arching, maw cranked and fangs bared at Rhordyn's back.

Phantom hands seem to reach down from above and snatch my throat in a vice as he spins, cleaving his sword

534

through the basilisk's meaty neck so fast the entire motion is a blur of black and silver and richly tanned skin.

Of hissing, snarling might.

Silky plumes of blood spill across the grass.

The entire jungle seems to oscillate, and my surroundings unspool into a swarm of seething, slithering serpents that change color before my eyes, going from blues and browns and steely tones to a tangle of inky death—charging Rhordyn.

Lashing at him.

My throat tightens ...

*Tightens.*

Rhordyn moves too fast for me to trace; slashing, stabbing.

Slaying.

He's a tower of might, severing hissing heads with every cyclonic swipe of his sword, but the blackness keeps wriggling toward him. Piling around him.

*Smothering him.*

He's lost in a coiled knot of squirming bodies, and that invisible hand around my neck tightens so much I can barely catch a whistling breath.

Suddenly, I don't see snakes at all ...

I see my darkness erupting through splits in my skin, lashing out at the man I love. I see him in bits all over the ground, his singed flesh plagued with weeping boils, wide eyes unseeing.

Dead.

I see *me* standing over him with shadows staining my hands. With my face a twist of anguish as I claw at my chest, trying to delve a hole through my ribs and rip out the pain.

Time slows to a crawl.

That macabre death creature scurries over the edge of my internal chasm and untucks twiggy wings, legs bunched and tail dangling as it flaps my insides into such a rabid stir that every vine and crystal shard and speck of withered remains blows into a storm of toiling rage.

It tips its head and *screams*.

I drop my hold on the tree and fall toward a basilisk's head with a throat-blooding roar, impaling my sword into the crown of its skull—right between its eyes. Forcing the sharp tip past layers of leathery skin and bone before giving way to something soft.

The limp creature thuds to the ground, releasing my weapon with a wet squelch.

My sword becomes an extension of my arm as I hack through the throat of an arching beast, snipping its hiss— picturing another inky vine of scalding death decaying inside me.

Dying.

Another snarling whip of my arm, and I slash a creature straight through the head, cutting its face in two.

I turn on the writhing pile of coiled black bodies, certain I'm down in the depths of my internal chasm, stalking up to that sizzling darkness that does nothing but kill.

Kill.

*Kill.*

I raise my arms and drive the sword down, hacking at already mangled remains with savage blows that rake through my entire body.

Rhordyn punches free from the pile like a bloody ghoul rising from the dead, shoulders heaving, hands clawing, forging a path through the nest of black and blood—tossing chunks of carrion out of the way until he plants his feet on solid ground.

Still, I slash, slash, *slash*—mulching guts and gore with every frenzied strike, painting my face and arms and body in a lacquer of red.

But red is better than that sizzling black death.

*Red is better.*

*Red is better.*

*Red is—*

A weight settles on my shoulder.

I spin, snarling, the weapon in my hands colliding with Rhordyn's sword in a clang of clashing metal, the cross so violent I feel the strike rattle my bones, blood splashing off our blades, peppering his hard features.

I look into wide, inky eyes, to the reflection bouncing off their surface, and all I see is the face of a monster staring back.

*Everywhere she goes, death follows.*

*Everything she touches turns to ash.*

Suddenly, I don't see Rhordyn holding his sword at all ...

I see *me.*

My upper lip peels back as that creature continues to flap. Continues to scream up my throat, tilling up shards of emotion that rip me apart from the inside out.

I shake my head and laugh—a wild, untethered sound that kneels to the strings of my tangling insanity. "I hate you," I snarl.

A smack of lightning ignites the gloom, cleaving across that violet stare—so stark against the dark abyss.

"You do nothing but destroy everything you touch," I scream through the pummeling rain, blinking away a swell of tears. "Everything you *love*. The world would be so much better if you just *disappeared*."

"Orlaith—"

Yes.

*Her.*

I bare my teeth and *lunge*.

# CHAPTER

*Rhordyn*

# 55

I block her savage blow, the sound of metal on metal clashing through the jungle like the toll of a war bell. "You're a *monster*," she snarls, the battering rain rinsing the blood from her face and hair, her features ripped with the pure, undiluted *hate* she just threw at me.

"*Yours,* Orlaith."

Another swing, and she almost guts me, the tip of her sword whipping past my navel—so close a hiss of breath powers into me.

*Fuck.*

I block her next blow that cleaves straight for my throat, a snarl punching up from deep inside my chest. "That was close, Milaje."

"You killed her," she whimpers, hacking at me with a shot I block, breath catching.

My heart stills.

"Who, Orlaith? Who did I kill?"

"*Her!*" she screams, her voice an anguished lash.

Another hack at my abdomen, this one nicking my hip—a hairline graze too shallow to bleed.

Just.

But I'll take her sharpened blows until she's empty of them and then we'll start from scratch. Work out whatever it was that tipped the tide on her hatred back in my direction. If it's a never-ending cycle that goes on for all eternity, so fucking be it.

She spins, whirring, slashing at my legs. I leap back, so tuned into *her* I don't notice the basilisk carcass behind me until I'm stumbling over it, spine slamming against a tree. Her blade notches my throat, and she snarls, her warm breath assaulting my face.

I let my sword hang to the side.

Chest heaving, on her toes, she leans into me, sodden hair dripping the remains of bloody residue down her edges.

Brow buckling, I search her amethyst eyes.

She presses the blade deep enough that I feel my skin threatening to split, her eyes glazed, potent wrath staining the air. "And you're going to kill *him*, too." Her face crumbles, and I feel my heart mimic the motion. "You're going to try and take him from me again, aren't you?"

'*But I won't let you.*'

Her thoughts come to me like a toil of murky smoke blowing through my chest, and my frown deepens.

*Him ...*

"I hate you," she repeats, hissing the words through clenched teeth, and realization hits like a sledgehammer.

Her hate-filled barbs, her glazed eyes ...

*She's talking to herself.*

My ribs crunch around the heavy thump of understanding.

*The world would be so much better if you just disappeared ...*

I let my weapon fall to the ground, gripping her fist that's clenched around the pommel of hers. With my other hand, I seize the honed end of her sword.

Her gaze slides to the side, widening, upper lip trembling as wrath twists her beautiful face into a knot. I press, feeling the sharp slice into my palm, enriching the air with the smell of my blood. Thick.

Potent.

*Hers.*

Nostrils flaring, her brow buckles. She swallows, blinking the glaze from her eyes as they widen, lifting.

Looking right at me.

Terror flashes across those purple gemstones, shattering me to the core.

She stumbles back, her bloody sword thumping to the ground as she looks down at her quivering hands, stretching them, bunching them up. I stay leaning against the tree, breathing deep and hard, watching her sink into the depths—further and further away. Like a star falling from the sky in a tragic blaze of glitter and death.

*That's not for you, Milaje.*

"Before you put the talon through my chest, you told me you killed your mother."

Her head whips up, the roots of her seed squirming in my chest like I just prodded it with a stick.

Her eyes harden to flints, chin lifting. "I don't know what you're talking about."

"Don't lie to me," I whisper.

Her gaze fractures like crumbled glass, a faint whimper breaking free.

Her eyes plead for me not to look.

Mine wield the weight of an apology that will never be *enough* to lift the guilt ingrained in my soul.

"You didn't kill her."

I hear her heart skip a beat, something flashing in her stare that's gone too fast for me to track. "Wh-what do you mean?"

I look at the jewel hanging around her neck, back to her face, ripping at the grave inside my chest with bare and bloody hands. Knowing I'll probably never pull her back from what I'm about to say. A terrible truth I've held in my chest for far too long.

She'll never forgive me, but that's okay.

So long as she forgives herself.

"I used to purchase blood off your mother. Blood I'd use to build obsidian whelves like this one," I say dashing my hand at the stones.

Her gaze flicks at it, back to me.

"Places for people to find solace from the beasts plaguing the continent."

She frowns, shaking her head. "I don't—"

"I set her up in a house I thought was *safe*. But I was wrong."

*So fucking wrong.*

Tears puddle her eyes as she watches me—unblinking. Unbreathing.

"I found her that night bearing a wound from a Vruk."

*Save her, Rhordyn. Please.*

I'm trying …

"I-I don't understand—"

"I failed her. Failed to keep her *safe*. Then I put my sword through her heart."

A sound slips past Orlaith's lips—bruised and raw. She blinks, and tears shred down her cheeks, melding with the rain slicking my shirt to her trembling frame.

"I killed your mother, Orlaith. *Me.*"

# CHAPTER 56

*Orlaith*

I know the crushing weight of grief. It hammers you down until you're so flattened you hardly resemble yourself. You barely function, yet you're cursed to exist. Happy for people to walk all over you so long as it means you don't have to stand up and peer at your reflection in their eyes.

But if grief is crushing, this is the *opposite*.

It's the antidote.

*I didn't kill my mother.*

My face crumbles, eyes squeezing shut, chest shaking with the force of my silent sobs. I let that captive breath chafe my insides, tossed around by the relentless quake of my chest as I reach within and lift my dome.

Tip it to the side.

Observe in quiet wonder as the seeds of relief I'd tucked beneath take root, then sprout, curling around my ribs, climbing my vertebrae. Little buds swell, their skins splitting four ways, releasing clusters of butter-yellow petals—packing my insides with the color of sunshine. With comforting *warmth* and a fluttery blow of love.

Of *understanding*.

Heaving a shuddered exhale, I open my eyes, wounded by the bruised silver stare that's stuck to me. Looking at me like he's begging for punishment.

My heart splits.

*Guilt* ...

The festering wound you ignore until you're battleworn, teetering between life and death. Trying to lift yourself off the ground and find a reason to live again.

But he doesn't belong on that battlefield. He can't hold himself accountable for what unraveled that night.

I don't belong on that battlefield either.

My darkness didn't kill her ... It wasn't an all-consuming, uncontrollable beast. Meaning there is hope—beautiful, untethered *hope*.

"Thank you," I whisper, and Rhordyn's brow buckles.

*For showing my mother mercy in death so she didn't have to suffer ...*

*For unbolting me from this anchor of guilt ...*

"I'm not the monster I thought I was, and neither are you." There's a flash of confusion in his eyes as I move toward him with intention of my own.

*Unleashed.*

I push onto my tippy-toes, thread my hands up his chest, around his neck, fingers tangling with the hair on the back of his head as I crush my lips against his.

*Warm.*

*Blissfully warm.*

Yet his body is a statue, arms rigid at his sides. Even his chest is still, as though he can't bring himself to breathe.

I delve my fingers through his beard, tilt my head, and force his lips to part.

His energy shifts.

*Shatters.*

His arms bind around my body, tightening with each plunge of his tongue as he pours an agonized moan down my throat, into my chest. He pushes his hands through my hair, cupping my head and tugging us apart, forcing me to draw on air that's vastly inadequate because it hasn't come from *him.*

Brow buckled, he searches my eyes like he's hunting through my hoard of trinkets, then makes a pained sound. He steals my breath with a tender kiss that's deep and slow. That sinks into my soul and tastes every bruise. Every ache.

Every slice of pain.

Zings of pleasure pulse through me.

Greedily, I paw at his powerful form, tracing the exquisite expanse of his back, trailing my hands down, fingers delving past the waistband of his tight pants.

I want him to take me.

*Devour me.*

I want him to eat my soul and spit it out in a heap that can never be pieced together by anyone but him.

Another pained groan, and he grips my cheeks, tilting my head back to plant a kiss on my forehead. "Stop ..."

My gaze snaps up to meet his.

"Why?" I heave through battered breaths, his chest rising and falling at the same voracious pace.

"Because I'm about to rip into you so fast you'll cease to know where I end and you exist."

I whimper, my knees almost giving way as a hungry warmth thumps between my thighs. "What if I *want* that?" I dare to whisper.

Speaking my truth to the stars, wondering if they'll whisper back.

For a moment, *nothing*. Nothing but him and I as we compare our wounds through a single look.

"There's still so much you don't know, Orlaith."

"I don't care," I say earnestly.

*Nothing could change the way I feel.*

*For him.*

His eyes ignite, making me wonder if he saw my thoughts weave through the fabric of my soul.

I take a step back, slipping from his loosening grasp.

Another.

A tautness stretches between us, like perhaps he thinks I'm about to run from this.

From *us*.

My heart labors as I forge another backward step, swaying my hips a little.

Realization widens his eyes before they darken to a beautiful, devastating shade of oblivion. A deep rumble rattles the air but stays trapped inside his chest as his shoulders seem to swell, muscles expanding.

One glance at the bulge in his pants almost has me on my knees, and I realize he understands.

That he *sees*.

I'm not running *from* him ... I'm running *for* him.

"Milaje," he says, his voice a dusky roll that makes me feel both full and so *achingly* hollow.

I swallow.

Another backward step.

"Rhordyn ..."

"You don't understand the game you're playing."

A small smile hooks the corner of my mouth. "Teach me the rules?"

The tendons in his neck stretch as he draws his chest full of breath, then blows it out slowly. "If you run, I will chase."

His fists tighten, like he's picturing his hands snatching at my fleeing form, and a bolt of thrill thrums through my veins.

"I will catch you."

A shuddered inhale.

"Take you."

A wanting whimper.

"And there will be no turning back."

Another stolen step.

*Another.*

His upper lip peels back. "No more reckless *fucks.*"

The words are a shake of my soul. A question.

A seeking of confirmation.

I swallow thickly.

Cheeks heating, I take another backward step.

His sawing snarl pebbles my skin, canines slipping down so fast my breath catches.

"No more," I whisper, hearing his teeth grind.

His mighty chest inflates. Releasing through his nose,

he cracks his neck from side to side. "No more lies to hide your *hurt*," he growls, the words thicker than the last.

I hold his stare.

*Another backward step.*

His entire body locks up, as though he's putting all his strength into keeping his spine pinned to the tree.

Another bolt of thrill crackles through my veins, thrumming deep into my core, and a moan almost pries from my lips, my heart thumping so hard I feel it at the base of my throat.

"If you run, you're mine," he says, so deadly soft I barely catch it over the pattering rain.

I tilt my head to the side. "And if I don't?"

Silence. Even the storm seems to still its booming symphony while something toils in the depths of his eyes, rivulets of water traveling down his perfectly sculpted body. So barbarically beautiful my chest aches at the sight while other parts of me *hunger*.

He tips his head against the tree, looking at me from beneath lowered lashes. "Then I will tell you another truth so you can go back to hating me."

*Hate ...*

The love I have for this man has grown on a foundation of that four-letter word. He's seen so many of my ugly sides.

I've seen so many of his.

We're both bruised from the battle it took us to get here, but tall trees uproot in windstorms if the hole isn't dug deep enough to tether to the soil.

Love him today, hate him tomorrow. I'm not going anywhere.

I flick him a smile, turn on my heel, and *run*.

# CHAPTER 57

*Orlaith*

The rain stops as I sprint into the jungle's dense confines, pursued by silence. But my prickling skin and fraying nerves make me innately aware that he's chasing.

*Hunting.*

My lungs labor, heart pounding in rhythm with my feet, each hurried step strumming that raw, tender ache between my legs until every forward motion is a scarcely won victory.

I power around partially glassed trees half frozen in an eerie, see-through eternity, the other halves dead or bleached or crumbling. Rays of sunlight spear through translucent foliage, creating bright, glistening pockets in the gloom. Part of me wants to stop and marvel at the changing world around me, but my heart is pounding too hard. The throb in my core is too crippling.

*My monster's on my heels.*

Passing what looks like an entrance to a cave bored into

the edge of a hill, I risk a peek behind, unable to see him, but I feel his icy stare track across my face like a chilling prelude. Another bolt of pulse-scattering *thrill* erupts low in my belly and high in my chest, a moan whittling through my lips still stained in the taste of *him*.

Perfectly, beautifully *him*.

Heart in my throat, I loop around, then dash behind a massive fallen log that's half clothed in moss, tucking myself into a knot, heaving shuddered breaths. My gaze darts left and right, up and down, and I battle the urge to push my hand beneath the waistband of my pants. To press my fingers against the hungry ache.

Silence.

No slow patter of water still dribbling down from above. No crackle of thunder. Even the wind has stopped, the world around me so hollow of noise my breaths *saw,* my galloping heartbeat akin to the pound of hooves clopping against hard-packed soil.

*If I can hear it, so can he.*

Slowly, my breaths begin to tame. Still, the silence prevails, my skin prickling with baited anticipation, my pulse like a butterfly caught in the base of my throat as I continue to search left, right, up, down.

*Where is he?*

Frowning, I spin, rising onto my knees. Daring a peek over the log, I search the mangled jungle for any sign of—

A heavy thump behind me rattles my bones, and I gasp, whipping around, seeing *him*—a vision of corded muscle and fierce, regal beauty. All his veins have pushed to the surface; his tattoos so eerily still, no light flickers through the silver scrawl.

His eyes are the most catastrophic shade of black I've ever seen.

I scramble over the log in a flurry of unsteady movement, knees crumbling the moment I reach the other side.

He steps over it effortlessly, prowling after me as I scurry backward. Fanning a heat low in my belly that becomes unbearable, my nerves exposed to every sweep of his crippling gaze.

He looms above, casting me in a delicious slab of shadow.

My muscles lose strength, and I soften against the ground.

He drops to his knees, holding my stare as he reaches forward and unbuckles my sheath with slow, steady motions, setting it aside. He rips the buttons on my pants, easing the stubborn leather barrier down. My underwear yields to his slashing hand like they're nothing more than tissue paper, and my legs begin to part.

A raw, carnal invitation.

He makes a low rumbling sound, grips my thighs, and spreads them so wide there's nowhere for me to hide.

Bared.

*Vulnerable.*

He's right there, looking straight at me. Seeing the flushed, swollen evidence of my frantic need for him.

He sits perfectly still, releasing that rumbling sound with every deep exhale while his gaze hungers. While my core aches to be filled with his finger.

His tongue.

*Something.*

"Rhordyn. I *need* you ..."

*More than I need air in my lungs.*

His gaze cuts to mine, and he makes that sound again—almost a purr. So animalistic, betraying the words he's not saying.

It picks at the thread of my composure, leaving me so frayed I'm barely holding together.

I rock my hips. *"Rhor—"*

He drops his head between my thighs and plants his mouth on me, arms weaving around my legs as his tongue lashes through my folds—like a ravenous, feasting beast. A vortex of muscle-melting pleasure stirs, branches up into my center and down the inside of my thighs as I rock against his face, stomach clenched, peering over my heaving chest. Watching this big, barbaric man paw at my thighs while he rumbles through his meal, back muscles bulging, clawed fingers dimpling my skin.

There is nothing gentle about the way he's devouring me, every hot swirl of his tongue knotting me up until my entire body blazes with this tangled heat.

The rocking of my hips grows strength, and he sets a hand over my womb. Pins me down with silent command.

He flicks his thumb over that sensitive nub, kindling me, easing a finger inside. He pumps.

*Pumps.*

I whimper, tumbling, dissolving beneath him. My nails gouge into the dirt in a pathetic attempt to ground myself.

Still strumming that raw, exposed bundle of nerves, he replaces his finger with his tongue—digging deep.

I cry out, thighs trembling as he spreads my core, exposing more of me to his ravaging attention. Those dense rumbling sounds pour up into me, his tongue oscillating as it spears to a devastating beat while heat gathers.

Spreads.

*Peaks.*

My muscles clamp down as I *erupt,* spine curling, fingers tangling with his hair as he lifts his hand from my lower belly, releasing me.

I tug at the inky strands, wailing through the violent bolt of pleasure—wild and unleashed. I thrust against his face, softening with each roll of my hips until my muscles melt to buttery splendor.

He flattens his tongue against me, lapping, wringing out the last of my orgasm's fluttered heartbeat until I'm past the whittled end. Planting a kiss upon the inside of my thigh, he watches me from beneath the heavy fall of his lids, unraveling, breath blown out on a growl.

He rises, licking his lips. My legs still splayed before him.

I'm honey—warm and loose. Begging for something else.

Something *more.*

His hands drop to his pants, unbuttoning, and my heart lodges in my throat. I suck a shuddered gasp, eyes widening as he shucks them off, releasing his hard manhood—so thick and embossed in veins as pumped as the ones on his body.

A pearly bead leaks from the tip.

I moan, hungering at the sight of him, wondering what he would taste like. My hand threads down my body at the thought, fingers sliding through my slick folds, swirling around that bundle of nerves. Wanting.

*Needing.*

Watching every swirl, every dipping sweep, he makes

this raw, carnal sound. The tension between us grows tighter.

*Tighter.*

He moves, lifting me. Flipping me around effortlessly, my back flush with his heaving chest.

I reach—hands delving through his hair.

He binds me with his arm, nudging my head aside and laving at the sensitive skin below my ear as his hand eases between my legs, cupping me.

Holding me.

Then his fingers are coasting around my entrance. Spreading me. *In* me—thrusting.

*Stretching.*

Enriching me with a roll of slow, steady pumps.

My entire body tides with the motion, and I rock against him while he plants kisses upon my ear, easing his hand up under my shirt and brushing the tender peaks of my nipples.

My sensual moans bruise the atmosphere.

He rumbles as he tries to thread another finger in, strumming the strings of my already singing euphoria. "You're not ready for me, Milaje ..."

*Ahh—*

In a knee-jerk reaction, I manage to yank myself from his hold. From the thrusts of pleasure his fingers are devastating me with.

I clamber up to the tune of his sawing growl, spinning.

He's crouched on the ground where I left him—a sculpture of impeccably carved brawn, his eyes swirling shadows regarding me with crippling focus.

"Let me be the judge of that," I declare, walking

backward through the underbrush, watching him from beneath my lids.

He rumbles, fisting his thick length in slow pumps, the vision so raw and erotic my knees almost give way. "I'm not a regular man, Milaje. My body wasn't built to be broken. It was built to *break*."

I remember the way he handled my hair while he severed the heavy lengths, like a giant cradling a mouse.

That spark of thrill strikes me like a match, and I steal another backward step ...

"You're *fragile*. I don't want to hurt you."

"I decide what I can and cannot *handle*." I reach for the hem of my—*his* shirt and pull it over my head, letting it fall to the ground.

His chest inflates, this deep, abrasive sound grinding out of him as he devours me with his sweeping stare. He continues to work himself in long, white-knuckled strokes, and I raise my hands, threading my fingers through the damp tangles of my hair. "I want you inside my body."

His canines slide back down, the vision lashing me with a ripple of pleasure.

I don't want to hide—not with him. I want him to see that I'm here, achingly ready to take him.

Have him.

As *me*.

I want to feel him against a skin that's not covered in a layer of somebody else.

Skin that's *mine*.

Skin that's untouched—untainted by the hands and the *feel* of other men.

He lets out a warning growl as I reach for the chain

around my neck and unlatch the clasp, letting the necklace, gem, and conch fall to the ground with a clattering thump. My skin peels away, dissolving the final layer between us. Baring my *true* self.

My mark.

The flush of blooms weighing down my shoulder.

*So many* ...

Something lethal flashes in his eyes that would probably bring a spark of fear to my chest if I hadn't witnessed the way he so delicately handled my haircut. Instead, it feeds another wild blaze of pure electric *thrill*.

I'm playing with fire, I know I am, but I'm not leaving until I *burn*.

I lift my chin, brimming with fierce, primal confidence. "*My* body, Rhordyn."

*My.*

*Body.*

He stands—looking bigger than he ever has. Like this world is too small to smother the mighty essence of him erupting through the cracks of his stripped composure. So beautifully, boldly naked, carved to monstrous perfection.

I moan at the sight, coaxing him with another backward step.

He collects our clothes, my sheath, crushing them in his fist as he advances. Slow.

Predatory.

There's a challenge in my stare as I meet him stride for stride.

"Okay," he says carefully—*too* carefully.

Another step forward.

I thieve another back, watching him crouch and sweep

my necklace into the crushing might of his fist. "But if *anybody* sees you without this necklace on," he says, pushing to a stand, "I won't think twice before I put them down."

My heart thumps to a halt, the statement delivered with such cutthroat poise I feel the words sliding across my skin like a blade.

"So, what do you suggest, Milaje?" His head cants to the side. "Because those pretty blooms are out, and my tether is fraying by the second."

My heart vaults into my throat, cheeks heating.

*He called them pretty ...*

His deep voice cradled the word in such a beautiful way, I tuck the trinket beneath my ribs where I can love it forever.

I think of the cave a short sprint away—the one I passed during my dash through the jungle.

"Then I guess we find somewhere to hide together," I whisper, a smile kicking up the corner of my mouth at the ebony flame in his eyes.

I spin and *run*—faster than I ever have. So fast, the half-glassed trees smudge in my peripheral as I dodge and dip and leap.

It's no longer silent behind me.

It's *thunderous*.

# CHAPTER 58

*Orlaith*

I feel him nipping at my heels, breathing down the back of my neck. I can hear his pounding footsteps rattling the ground.

My frantic heart almost punches free of my ribs.

Rounding the small hill smothered in vines that have made this glassy wonderland their own, I find the sheltered cave tucked behind a large, glass-veined boulder.

I dash into the somewhat shadowed interior that's no bigger than my room in Stony Stem, clothed with a crunchy layer of dried leaves that must have blown in over the years. Jagged blades of sunshine cut through a handful of thin, translucent seams stretched across the ceiling, scribbling light across the ground.

I sweep my gaze around, spinning as darkness fills the entrance, like a broad shadow eclipsing the sun.

The moon.

Eclipsing my view of *anything* else.

The cavern packs full of his robust scent, almost bringing

me to my knees, the hunger in his starkly shadowed eyes making my heart pound harder.

My needy arousal is a wet smear between my thighs, still high on the thrill of the *chase*. Feeding off the restless energy thumping through my veins despite the empty ache of my core.

He drops to a crouch, setting my necklace, our clothes, and my sheath on the ground. Holding my stare, he pushes to stand.

I raise a brow in a silent *how did I do?*

He begins to circle me in slow, stalking strides. "Perfect, Milaje."

Pride fills my chest, but I don't move. Don't spin to keep his eye contact. Instead, I *relish* the way his gaze hungers over every inch of my naked body, smelting my bones.

"But we need to have a chat about giving your back to circling monsters."

"But you're *my* monster." I smile as he crosses before me, and I swear his breath stills. "You don't count."

He's behind me again, his attention dragging across the small of my back, and a tingle climbs my spine. "You wouldn't think that if you could see inside my head."

I think he'd be surprised.

He told me he'd rip the world apart if I tip my throat again, but I'd tip it to *him* in a heartbeat. Beg to be the sole benefactor of all that static energy rolling off him in waves.

Because I want to be caught.

Hungered over.

I want to be devoured so completely we're tangled for eternity.

*I want to do the same to him.*

561

He rumbles low, circling tighter.

*Tighter.*

"You're thinking very loud, Milaje ..."

My skin prickles, his baritone filling the cavern as completely as I want him to fill me.

He stalks into my line of sight, almost close enough to reach out and touch, our gazes colliding like a clash of fire and ice.

I lift a brow. "Then why is there still space between us?"

He launches—*hits*. Tangles us in a crush of lips and moans and lashing tongues and hot, fervid flesh.

Of desperate, wanting *need.*

His arms band around me, and he lifts, backing me against the smooth wall with my legs curled around him, his hands supporting my thighs with effortless strength, my core swollen and exposed.

Empty.

Too empty.

He breaks our kiss, pushing his forehead against mine. I hear him swallow, nudging my entrance, and even with me bared like this—so *open*—I understand his concern ...

*He's huge.*

My core contracts, anticipating.

Wanting.

*Hungering* for him to drive up and fill the aching hollow.

I rock my hips, dragging myself back and forth across his thick, silky tip. Feeding off the friction, shivering through a surge of need.

"Look at me, Milaje." I do, my heart a riot in my chest. "Tell me if you want me to stop."

*Why would I ever want that?*

"Of course."

His deep, throaty rumble fills the cavern. He drops me slower than the setting sun, and I gasp as he eases past my wet, pulsing entrance.

"See," I preen, restless around it, trying to shift my hips. "Told you I could manage."

"I've got a long way to go," he hisses out from between clenched teeth.

*Oh ...*

"More, *please,*" I rasp, threading my hands across his taut arms and shoulders, up the strained tendons in his neck and through his dense beard.

His chest expands, then releases, and he gently lowers me, sliding me onto him in perfect, stretching increments. Every gluttonous inch knots me up and unravels me, sweat gathering on my brow, between my breasts.

"Almost there," he rumbles, guiding me down until I'm brimming.

My upper gums throb as his thick, twitching length fills me so completely I'm straining at the seams. This primal sense of satisfaction swirls through my chest, warming my heart.

My soul.

"Are you okay?" he asks, brushing his lips against the sensitive skin just below my ear.

*So much better than okay.*

I nod through a groan and pull him close, tasting him with a deep, hungry kiss. Urging him to move with a shift of my hips.

He lifts me the slightest amount, then gently lowers me,

and my entire body ignites. I moan into his hungry mouth, urging him with another slow curl of my spine.

He lifts me again—higher this time.

Drops me down slowly.

I melt around him, little by little. Breath by breath. Slow shift by slow, aching shift as our hearts continue to pound in rapid unison.

"You're perfect," I whisper, feathering the words against his lower lip.

*"Perfectly yours."*

The words are accompanied by a low, rumbling growl that boils in his chest, vibrating through me. A smile steals across my face at the way it kindles my nerves. Makes me *burn.*

I plant a kiss upon his cheek.

His temple.

"I like it when you do that," I breathe close to his ear. The tension eases from his taut shoulders, like I'm taming a rabid beast.

He makes that sound again, lifting me higher, pausing just before his tip is free of my clenching core … sliding me back down with a deep, sensual roll of his hips.

A guttural moan crawls up my throat, and I throw my head back, another plunging thrust almost severing the threads of my self-control.

I look at him from beneath heavy lids as he draws out, then drives in hard enough to make my breasts bounce, stoking that flame. Unblinking, he watches me—like he's drinking from some well of life.

There's an edge to that look that unleashes something inside me. A wildness I don't want to tame.

This bludgeoning *throb* pounds to needy life in my gums, drilling into my canines, the roots of it stretching across the arch of my palate. Salivating, I swallow, tipping forward and flopping my head into his neck, feeling the tendons flex beneath my lips as he thrusts.

Thrusts.

*Thrusts.*

That *ache* turns to a sharp, splitting pain that has me crying out, buffering the sound by gently biting down on the taut stretch of his neck.

Something punches through my gums—

I'm suddenly empty, feet on the ground, pressed against the wall by his hand. He shoves back, and I crumple amongst the crunchy leaves—my gums still throbbing, twin fangs now dimpling my bottom lip.

Gasping for breath, I look up, seeing Rhordyn on the other side of the cavern, head down, fists bunched as he paces back and forth in heavy strides. Every muscle in his body pumped.

Beastly.

The sky rips the world apart outside, sheets of water visible through the archway to our darkening cavern.

He was so composed a second ago, so tame beneath my touch. Now he's wild.

*Unleashed.*

"What's wrong?"

"Put them away," he snarls, still pacing, tattoos lit with an erratic pulse in sync with the booming blasts cleaving the silence. "*Now.*"

"Put *what* away?"

"Your *canines,*" he barks. "I need them gone."

565

I frown.

*How the hell am I supposed to do that?*

I lift my hand, fingering the strange, sharp fangs still throbbing with the need to *bite*. Even pushing on them threads me full of moan-inducing pleasure.

He snarls again, shaking his head in jerky motions, refusing to look at me. Like he's battling a shadow of his own.

I give them another hard push, but it only splits me apart with a sharper spear of pleasure that almost bursts me in the most carnal way.

"I can't," I admit, the words mangled with my clotting emotion. My *confusion*. "I don't know how. This is the first time they've—"

"You can't bite me, Orlaith. You *can't*."

Is he worried I'm going to hurt him? That wasn't my intention. I wanted to *taste* him; wanted to feel his warmth gush across my tongue and slip down my throat.

*Still do.*

"I just— It felt *right*," I say, swallowing thickly, pressing against the foreign *things* again to relieve some of the tension—shooting another zing of rapture straight to my core.

Stirring me up.

I whimper, wishing he'd look at me. Step close to me.

*Touch me.*

"I know," he says, scrubbing his face with his hands. "It's not your fault, Milaje. But we can't do this. We have to stop."

I realize he's slipping away one prowled step at a time, and my heart dives.

I scramble up, moving forward.

His sharp snarl snaps through the space like the swing of a blade, and he moves so close to the wall he's almost shouldering it—still pacing back and forth.

Back and forth.

Gaze nailed to the ground.

A thought crosses my mind, filling me with a seed of hope.

I pause …

"What if I'm not facing you?" I suggest, lowering to my knees.

His stare whips sideways, paralyzing me with that dusky perusal. Again, I catch sight of that deeper entity staring back at me and shiver all the way to my bones.

I dig my hands through the foliage until they meet the stone beneath, pushing forward.

*Baring* myself.

He growls, and I watch from beneath my arm as he scents the air. Prowls around me, like some great beast circling his prey.

"Orlaith."

"Rhordyn."

"If I see you in this position before any other person, I'll kill them," he says, the words too soft to be so brutally honed—a chilling threat that lashes at my hot, throbbing core. "I'll eat their fucking entrails. Do you understand?"

I try to hide a smile. "I understand."

He begins rustling around in our pile of clothes. I think I hear the sound of my blade loosening before he crouches beside me. "Sit up."

Frowning, I do, perching on my folded legs. "Don't you like my idea?"

"I do, but watching your face is more than half the feast."

*Oh …*

"I want that, too," I whisper, settling into the realization that I'll have to be patient. Wait until my teeth slide back.

He presses something into my hand.

I glance down at the empty leather sheath he gifted me for my birthday—now laid across my palm. "I'm going to need you to do something, Milaje."

I tilt my head.

"What's this for?" I ask, looking past tangled, iridescent waves into his fathomless eyes.

"Your mouth," he says tenderly, and my heart thumps.

Hard.

*My mouth …*

"If we're going to continue, I need you to bite the sheath so you won't be tempted to bite *me*."

I salivate over his words, my stare glazing his thick, corded neck, canines throbbing with a deep, heady *want* as understanding dawns.

Swallowing, I bore my attention into his eyes again. "Okay," I whisper, handing it to him.

"Okay?"

I nod, opening my mouth.

Releasing a rumble, he brings the sheath to my lips, brushing it against my lower one before easing it between my teeth. "That's it," he murmurs. "Now, bite."

Holding his eye contact, I clamp down, sinking my canines into the leather stained with the smell and taste of *him*—exhaling a muffled moan when a wash of relief thrums between my legs and turns my body to butter.

My lids flutter, spine arching.

"Better?"

I nod, then chew so deep the hardy material is cushioning my canines from all angles, another mangled moan rupturing past the leather.

*So much better ...*

He produces a dense growl and plants a kiss on my head, then drops to his knees and lifts me. My legs wrap around the back of him as he braces my arched spine with his spread hand. "Set your feet on the ground and push yourself up."

I do, looking past my heaving breasts, down the slope of my navel, watching him rub the swollen tip of his manhood against my entrance in a trance of luscious swirls.

My hips buck, and I gasp, rocking against him. Wanting. *Needing.*

So exposed, open, sensitive.

"Fuck," he hisses, and I've never felt more *powerful.*

*Sexy.*

*Me.*

Another slow swirl, and he aims at my entrance again, swallowing. "Bite harder as you take me," he orders, voice raw.

I clamp down on the sheath, almost wailing in relief, giving in to the bend of my knees, bringing him inside myself one sliding inch at a time. I watch it all, relishing the stretch, hungering over the way he plunges up into me in devastating increments until I'm seated to the hilt— muscles tightening around his thick length.

My lashes sweep up, and I see that he's watching me with an all-consuming intensity, his chest heaving, sweat gathering on his temples, plastering inky curls to his forehead.

His gaze kisses my blooms. Traces the tangles of my hair. Climbs the thorns of my ears.

Settles in my eyes again.

"So beautiful," he rasps, his voice a crush of stone shards I swiftly steal.

Tuck away.

"You have no idea what you're doing to me." His words mimic my thoughts as he uses his hand on my spine to urge me closer, takes a healthy grip of my right hip, and presses his lips upon my forehead. "*No* idea."

I thread my hands around his neck. Tangle my fingers through his hair.

Certain my heart's about to burst.

My thighs burn as we move, soft and slow, then faster.

*Harder.*

I'm clay around him. Malleable.

*His.*

Absorbing each euphoric push and pull, I make raw, muffled sounds around the leather sheath. The strap slaps against us both, our bodies a synchronized tide of motion.

We move together.

*Work* together.

I arch my back, tilt my hips, exposing that tender bundle of nerves to our delicious friction, fanning my pleasure into a roaring flame.

Rhordyn pushes higher onto his knees and plants a hand on the ground behind me, draping me amongst the lush bed of crunchy leaves before he grips my thigh, lifting it the slightest amount.

Doused in the smell of nature, he drives our bodies together at such an angle that every thrust stokes a pallet of nerves deep inside my body. Plants hot bolts of pleasure in places I didn't know existed.

My thighs begin to quake, and I mewl, crawling up onto my elbows. Devouring the sight of his olive skin mottled with sweat. Of his powerful, well-defined muscles that shift and swell, his head tipped as he looks at me from beneath dark lashes.

My legs are wrapped around his tapered waist, his thick, velvety shaft plunging into me, dragging out.

*Driving back in.*

*Out again.*

The vision is so raw and carnal that muffled grunts escape me, and I chew the leather, spawning a gush of pleasure, my insides fluttering against his surging might.

I have no idea where the line is between us anymore. No idea if I'll ever feel whole again once he's no longer in me.

Feeling his gaze blaze across my face, I look up.

A smile touches his lips, and I almost combust as my heart threatens to punch a hole in my ribs.

I steal the smile. Stow it away.

*Mine.*

"*Yours,* Milaje."

His hand that was bracing my thigh spreads across my lower belly, a gentle pressure that takes each thrust to a blinding level of ecstasy. He thrums that sensitive nub between my legs with the pad of his thumb, and my entire body becomes a single exposed nerve—tightly wound and knotted to perfection.

Desperate to unravel.

*Flaming.*

His girth seems to swell inside me—becoming impossibly hard and heavy—and I whimper, spine arching, knowing I'm about to break.

Wanting him to break *with* me.

My arms buckle, and I fall back into the leaves as he surges forward, driving deep. Planting his forehead against mine. He threads his hand up into my hair, pouring treasured exhales upon my face—an intensity in his gaze that collects every one of my heartstrings and *tugs.*

"Bite for me, Milaje." His stare plows deeper, until I'm certain he's cradling my soul as he razes my body with claiming rolls of his hips. "Bite as hard as you fucking can."

I clamp down, gorging on the taste of leather and the smell of *him*, a bolt of ecstasy flaring across my palate.

He tips my head, nuzzles my ear, and plows deep, rumbling a single shattering word ...

"*Come.*"

My body locks, decadent waves of pleasure rippling through me, spearing down my spine and powering into my molten core. Fraying my nerves one by one until I'm a messy tangle of taut limbs and clamping muscles.

Bound over me in a knot of charging might, Rhordyn releases a thunderous roar—his thick length pulsing, painting my womb in hot spurts as he pounds into me hard and fast.

I'm blind and quaking from the inside out, toes curled, breath caught in the back of my throat. Half convinced I'll never recover from the volcanic blows of euphoria coursing through my system.

I claw at him, coming apart at a cellular level.

Recrystallizing around him.

He strikes every ounce of ecstasy from my quivering body until I can breathe again.

*Move* again.

Thrusts slowing, his head drops down to my neck, and he plants a gentle, nudging kiss above my bandage, casting goosebumps across my shoulder.

My muscles melt, lids growing heavy, a sound of deeply seated relish blooming up my throat. My canines sink back up into my gums with an aching tug, and I remove the sheath, tossing it to the side.

I pull his face to mine and press our lips together, inhaling his tapering heaves.

He rocks onto his back, taking me with him, and we thump amongst the dried and crumpled foliage. I nuzzle his chest, still holding him inside my body as he brushes my hair aside and plants a kiss on the tip of my thorned ear. Another farther down.

Another.

My eyes sweep shut, lulled by his rumbling breaths and the delicate tingles ghosting down the side of my neck ...

I want to be like this forever—with leaves in my hair, surrounded by nature, full of *him*. Smelling like both of us. So perfectly melded.

So *right*.

I feel warm and safe and whole in his arms, my throat thickening with a deep sense of *belonging*. Like our souls just collided in a burst of light and the blackness between stars, and we built our *own* sky to nestle amidst.

Fawning over buttery blooms of relief growing through my belly, my core, I drift—

He twitches inside me, his heavy manhood stiffening. *Kindling* me into a restless flame that rocks my hips despite my utter lack of energy.

He produces a throaty laugh, packed full of amusement, and it's the most beautiful sound I've ever heard. Swiftly stolen by my thieving hands and tucked somewhere safe.

I crush some of my lustrous beads and build a crystal chest beneath my ribs, then tuck his laugh in the hollow— along with the rest of my precious trinkets.

He blows a warm breath against one of my blooms, ruffling the swirl of petals, then nuzzles into my neck. "We can't sleep like this, Milaje. I won't be able to let you rest."

He presses a kiss to my budding smile, and I nod dozily, then groan through my displeasure when he grips my hips with his strong hands and pulls from my raw, tender core. Hating the sudden emptiness.

But then he maneuvers my body so my head is planted atop his heart, and the hard thump of it pounding against my ear fills me just the same.

I bunch my legs up either side of him and thread my hands beneath his armpits, fingers curling around his barreling shoulders. The tips of his fingers paint secrets atop my flush of blooms as I drift into a balmy sleep …

*Home.*

# CHAPTER
### *Rhordyn*
## 59

The sun sank, then rose, and is now halfway across the sky outside—the blades of light shafting down in bold lines, like a luminous cage I'd happily stay trapped in forever.

Orlaith releases a contented sigh, clinging to me the same way she has all night and half the day, reminding me of the way krah sleep; but upside down and hanging from their tails.

I'd forgotten what it felt like to truly *rest*. But over the past two nights, she's given me more uninterrupted sleep than I've had since before Rai fell. This right here—it tames every bristled cell. Smooths every scar.

Stifles every curdled scream.

I pull a leaf from her hair and brush my hand across her flushed cheek dusted with a constellation of luminous freckles I've counted then recounted while I've watched her sleep.

I smile.

She's everything light, bright, and beautiful to my hard, coarse darkness, her ivory skin such a stark contrast to the tone of mine.

Sweeping the blunt end of an iridescent wave from her eyes, I run the pad of my thumb along the sharp tips of her thorns.

She shudders. I'd think it from my touch, except her teeth begin to chatter.

I notice the fine sheen of sweat upon her brow and the skin above her paling upper lip.

My blood ices.

I spread my hand across her spine—unnaturally warm— and give her a gentle shake. "Orlaith?"

She mumbles something incoherent and digs her face deeper into my chest, shuddering again.

Shaking the cage of the *thing* trapped beneath my ribs.

"*Orlaith*," I growl, threading my hand up through her hair and giving it a firm tug, pulling her head back, her mouth popping open the slightest amount. "Open your eyes. *Now.*"

"Stop yelling," she mumbles, her words a garbled slur. "You can get the same message across without raising your voice."

"Then open your fucking eyes."

She groans, prying them open, revealing the whites shot through with a burst of red.

My heart stills.

Some of the light has sponged from her crystalline irises despite the blades of sun that have been carving across her back all morning.

"You're not well."

"I'm fine," she slurs, closing her eyes, trying to nestle against me again. My grip on her hair doesn't waver, and she makes a frustrated grunting sound as she tries to tug her head forward. "I've got a headache that I need to sleep off. So if you'll just—"

"It's midday. You've been sleeping all night and half the day." Her eyes drag open, pupils tightening on me. "You have a fever. You're sick."

A line forms between her brows, gaze drifting to her right hand. Her eyes widen slightly before they whip back to me.

"I'm fine," she blurts.

Too fucking quickly.

*I thought we were over this.*

I push into a sitting position, reaching around her with my right arm, holding her wide, wild gaze as I wrap my hand around her wrist and give it a tug. She digs the tips of her fingers into my shoulder, and my eyes flare.

"You don't want to play this game with me." Outside, the sky darkens, dulling the shards of sunlight splitting down into the cavern. "Not right now."

A look of pained resolution crosses her face as she mutters a curse beneath her breath and loosens her grip on my shoulder, allowing me to wrangle her arm free. She leans back a little, and I coax her hand between us, eyes narrowing on the red welt that's forming on her knuckle.

I frown, inspecting it closely. "Did you get bitten by something?"

"Probably," she murmurs, but there's hesitation in her voice, her attention locked on the sore.

I grip her chin and lift her face, forcing her to meet my stare. "I'm only dealing in absolutes. Yes or no."

She chews her lip a moment, then shakes her head. Something niggles at me I can't quite put my finger on ... but then I home in on the bitter, biting scent seeping from her pores.

*Guilt.*

My blood ices as a thought slits my mind, leaving a bloody gash. Her cheeks pale, like she can see the question brewing like a fucking Blight boil.

"Did you climb the wall, Orlaith?"

Silence. Not even a breath.

I draw my chest full of air, blow it out slowly, though it does nothing to soften the sharp slashes shredding through my guts.

Splintering my bones.

"The one I told you not to go over. Did you climb the fucking wall?"

She winces, looking like she wants to curl into herself and hide.

Slowly, she nods.

My canines slide down, every muscle in my body tensing as my skin threatens to split. The sky rips open, spilling a torrent of rain that roars at the cavern's tight entrance, the silver scripture on my skin digging its fucking spikes in.

I bet the stars had a laugh last night while I slept with her upon me, certain I'd found a way to be with her while skirting the stones. Feeling true happiness for the first time in over a thousand years.

I bet they had a *real good laugh* knowing the seeds were already planted—that they'd already made their move.

"Maybe I did get bitten by something?" she blurts as I shift my body. "*Maybe—*"

I tuck her against the wall, then grab her necklace and set it into her hand. "Speak into that shell, Milaje. Call Kai. He might be able to help."

If he can heal a wound on her leg, he can heal her fucking disease from the outside in.

Or at least try.

"I'll be right back." I stalk toward the exit, snatching my pants; halfway out when she calls my name. I stall, looking over my shoulder at her—arms bound around her legs, tears puddling her lower lids, lips sapped of all their hue. She itches at the boil, bursting it.

This bludgeoning pain in my chest feels worse than death.

"Where are you going?" she whispers, her scent screaming the words she's not saying.

*She's scared.*

Of me, the storm, or the wound on her hand, I don't know. But there's only one thing that matters now.

That we find a way to veer the course of this brewing tragedy.

"To get our swords. Tell Kai we'll meet him by the cliff at Lotton Cove. That if he's not there by sundown, I'll skin him alive."

Her eyes widen as I spin on my heel and leave.

# CHAPTER

*Orlaith*

# 60

Rhordyn charges through the jungle so fast the world is a nauseating smear, forcing me to tuck my face against his flickering tattoos and squeeze my eyes shut, raindrops splatting my fervid skin like icy bolts. A pattered relief to the fire in my veins.

I slip between layers of consciousness.

Dropping away …

… Coming to.

The jungle's colors have gone from blues and browns and steely shades to a much darker smudge of it all.

*Is the sun beginning to set? Are we getting closer?*

Nervous bubbles explode in my chest at the thought of seeing my best friend for the first time in over a month; guilt, shame, confusion, and fear a volley of fisted blows to my ribs.

*I don't want him seeing me like this …*

I just want to hide. Curl up and sleep. Rhordyn should

take me back to the cavern where we can ride out the week together, cloistered away from the world.

Enjoy the time we have.

It always felt stolen, anyway. Like a dream. A precious trinket that was doomed to rust in my chest.

Now I understand why.

The constant bumping wreaks havoc on my bladder, making me groan into Rhordyn's chest. "Stop, please ..."

His feet slam to a halt so fast I almost spontaneously vomit, looking up into his sooty eyes. "I need a bush break."

*That might turn into a spew break.*

Not even breathing hard, he sets me on the ground, snatching me around the waist when my legs give way.

"I'm fine," I tell him. "Just ... displacement." Though I do wonder why the ground is tipping. Bulging, like it doesn't know which shape it wants to be.

My teeth chatter despite the fact that my blood is lava, my fake skin feeling tighter than ever.

Fingers tangling with my necklace, I yank gently. "Can I take off my—"

"Definitely not."

*Bit rude. He didn't even take time to consider it.*

I sigh, wondering if he would be opposed to me shedding a *different* layer, like my pants or my to—

"Your clothes stay on."

*Didn't realize I even said that out loud.*

"Can't I just leave them off after I go? I swear I'll put them back on before we reach Kai's tongue ..."

I hope for a laugh. At the very least, a *smile*.

A happy trinket for me to cling to.

But all I get is silence—taut, tangible silence that only succeeds in making me feel like he's slipping away, too.

I tip my head to the side, looking up at him through the sodden lengths of my hair, missing the feel of his lips on mine. Of his breath pouring into my lungs.

Filling me up.

"I don't want to die crushed beneath the weight of your silent anger ..."

His eyes darken further. "You're not dying," he snarls, the thick, feral words pummeling me.

Weighing me down.

I know all about denial; have drunk from its poisonous well too many times to count. But I don't want to argue. Not now.

Not again.

"Okay." I offer him a soft smile that seems to make his eyes harden, like he can see the lie I'm buttering all over my face. But it feels better than sadness. Regret.

Fear.

"I'm going to relieve myself," I murmur, easing his arm from where it's still bound around my waist. "Don't watch."

"Don't go far," he rumbles, and I wave, meandering across the unsteady terrain. I itch the back of my hand, certain there's something grubbing beneath the skin.

The trees continue to darken, stretching like inky limbs. Reaching for me.

Finding a nice, cozy shrub, I squat and do my business, re-button my pants, then begin to wander back.

A distant twang makes my ears twitch.

I look up in time to see Rhordyn—a charging blur barreling for me. I don't get a chance to brace before I'm tackled to the ground so hard and fast all the breath is punched from my lungs.

There's a thudding sound as something impales the tree not two feet away, and I look up, heart in my throat.

An arrow with a gray fletching wobbles to a still in the trunk. Perfectly level with where my heart would have been a split second ago.

"Did somebody just *shoot* at me?"

Rhordyn snarls, rears back, and crushes me against his chest. I'm lifted, cradled as he bolts through the forest, cutting a zigzag path, dodging an invisible threat while my heart beats me up.

Everything becomes a blur of rain and darkening foliage and booming, ground-crackling sounds that shaft into my tender skull and threaten to split me. The constant change of direction makes my guts tip, flip, and squirm.

I swallow the retching urge inching up my throat, cheeks tingling, hearing more of those thudding sounds.

Too close.

Too many.

I try to tip my head back to glance behind us, but Rhordyn's violent, air-splitting growl makes me reconsider.

We near a clearing, and I glimpse gray tents through the trees, armored soldiers spilling from their flaps, yelling at each other.

Swarming.

The spears and swords they wield are a dull silver—the iron weapons I saw being forged in Cainon's personal armory.

"Fuck," Rhordyn hisses, charging on. There's the whistling of more arrows splitting the air. The pound of them thudding into trees. His entire chest jerks, and his soft, grunting sound *screams* at me.

*He's hit …*

I look up into his inky eyes, at the darkness smudged into the skin surrounding them, wild panic notching its noose around my throat.

"Rhor—"

Another thud snatches my breath … *Another* … His face twitching with each horrific, puncturing blow, though his feet continue to pound the earth. The next thud sounds like it lands farther down his body, and he stumbles a step.

My heart and guts plummet as he snarls, regains his teeth-gritted composure, and carries on.

My throat tightens.

A head pokes out over the edge of my internal chasm, inky eyes blinking. That *creature* scurries out, tail flicking in its wake. Wings folded back, it uses my spine as a ladder, chased by that slithering slur of darkness that weaves up the insides of my skin and *slices* for release—the tapered tips honed into razor blades that *hack*.

*Hack.*

*Hack.*

My head fills with so much pressure I'm certain my skull's going to split as we break through the jungle's fringe, coming to a grassy plateau that stretches beneath the weeping sky, then falls away, melding with the distant sound of crashing waves.

*A cliff.*

Rhordyn doesn't stop running, though his steps are slower now, every breath strained.

Another meaty thud—louder this time. I feel that sound

in my chest as he pitches forward, almost losing me in his stumble, something sharp poking through his shoulder and snatching my ability to breathe.

A large, pronged arrowhead.

That creature wraps its claws around my ribs, tips upside down, stretches its twiggy wings, and starts to *flap*—tilling up crystal debris and vines, shredding those buttery blooms. It stretches its neck, opens its maw, and *screams* as a wildness surges through my veins, one barbed word bouncing around inside my chest like a thorny ball.

*Protect.*

*Protect.*

*Protect.*

"Put me down."

He regains his footing, heaving breath, forcing us forward with another churn of unsteady steps—like he didn't even hear me. He snarls through elongated canines, his face a rabid twist of wrath and pain.

"Rhordyn, I said *put me down!*"

No response.

No loosening of his arms.

That darkness continues to bludgeon my brain as I look over his shoulder to where the steep wall of the jungle meets the grassy plateau, gray-armored guards spilling through gaps between the trees.

*Gray Guards.*

Another whistling sound has my heart in my throat—a long, thick arrow cleaving the air at the speed of a lightning strike. I feel the moment it thumps into Rhordyn's back, like someone just shoved their hand down my throat and mulched my heart in their clenched fist.

He lurches, time stretching.

The ground comes at us too fast.

Too slow.

Flung forward, I collide with the hard-packed earth, my lungs slamming into a state of paralysis. Mouth gaping, I try to move.

Breathe.

I look down my body to where Rhordyn's crouched, snarling. The tattoos on his forearm pulse with a light that makes my eyes ache, and he heaves it back, makes a fist, then punches the ground—boring a crater into the soil that makes the world jolt.

The hairs on the backs of my arms lift, the air singeing with a shock of ... *something*.

Something I've felt before.

*On the pier.*

There's a deafening *boom*, a blinding flash of light, and a punch of lightning rips down from the sky; a forked spear of silver threaded with a fracture of black. Everything rocks beneath us, and I'm battered by a cataclysmic *crack* that battles the ringing in my ears.

My gaze homes on the jagged cleft of glass now zigzagged through the ground, up through two soldiers paused midstep.

Their bows lifted, notched arrows pointed in our direction. Both glass statues bar a finger here, a nose and cheek there, the bits of remaining flesh weeping lines of blood that *drip*.

*Drip.*

*Drip.*

He ... *killed* them.

*He turned them to glass.*

The creature in my chest continues to squawk and flap and scream as I look at Rhordyn, and my breath catches.

Heart stills.

He's hunched over my legs, head down, blood bubbling from his lips. His arms bend, dropping him lower, and I see he's saddled with arrows both short and tall, thin and thick. Glossy lines of red leak from each gory puncture wound, dribbling.

My creature shreds at my ribs with its bramble claws, slashing so hard I think it might break through, darkness threatening to slit my skull.

More guards spill from the jungle, others retreating to the fringe, screaming orders, forming a line that moves in unison as they raise armed longbows, pointing them skyward. *"Volley!"* someone bellows over the thrashing storm.

Rhordyn groans, crawling forward. Covering me.

*Entirely.*

He lifts his head, locking eyes with mine as a cloud of arrows darken the rumbling sky. The aching muscle in my chest pinches, itchy pops flaring across my shoulder.

Up the side of my neck.

*"No!"*

My pained cry whittles between us, and he holds my stare as the arrows rain upon him.

I see each piercing sting in the twitch of his face muscles. Feel each brutal impale in the short, jagged puffs of breath upon my cheeks. Hear each sickening thud plowing through flesh and muscle and bone as he's ripped apart in punctured increments.

For me.

My guts twist, heartstrings snap, tears slip free as his blood falls like rain. His eyes glaze, and he pulls a bubbling gasp, head falling between his bulging shoulders.

His right arm buckles slightly.

Something thuds so deep into my upper arm I feel it pierce through the other side, striking me with a blaze of pain. I cry out, curling the limb against my chest.

Rhordyn's head snaps up, and he looks at me in a way that chills me to the bone as his nostrils flare once ... twice ... gaze flicking to the arrow protruding from my arm. His beautiful, powerful, *broken* body jerks, and his chest swells to the tune of cracking, crunching, popping bones.

"*What's ...*"

*What's happening?*

He loosens our sheaths from where they're strapped against his chest. Both swords thump to the ground before he reaches behind his back, snaps a few arrows, and tosses them aside like pesky twigs. Planting his forehead against mine, he closes his eyes.

The breath he pours over me is *charged.*

"He won't hurt you ..." he pleads, his voice gravel. Unfathomably robust and ...

*Unfamiliar.*

"Wh-what do you mean?" I lift my good hand to his cheek, flinching when his jaw pops out of place beneath my touch.

My breath snags, hand dropping to my hammering chest as he opens his eyes, but they're not his eyes at all. They're ghastly globes enriched with a shade of darkness that looks like it was hewn from somewhere not of this world. This close up, I see distant galaxies caught in the gloomy confines, certain I'm tumbling through the fathomless ether, trapped beneath the crushing might of my own insignificance.

This close up, I realize how small I am. How fragile.

A single speck of light.

Yet he's looking at me like I'm the sun he orbits.

Rhordyn's lips part with a distorted howl, the skin on his face shredding, making room for his expanding maw packed full of sharp, gnashing teeth, his canines growing longer than my forearm.

Time slams to a still, the rain like strips of string suspended around us as I watch. Horrified.

*Hypnotized.*

His face changes shape. Becomes big and boxy, sprouting a pelt of black fur that softens his thickening neck with a dense, regal mane and clothes his bulging shoulders and swelling back. There's the sharp sound of his pants ripping, shreds of black material fluttering on the swirling wind.

Fear lacerates me with talon-tipped strikes, immobilizing my body.

My mind.

His body expands to mighty proportions until it's no longer a man huddled over me like a shield, but a *beast*— dwarfing me in his catastrophic presence. A massive, black Vruk, just like the one I saw outside of Parith.

*The one that ate the men I burned.*

*Rhordyn's—*

*He's—*

Wild, unruly emotions mulch my flesh, masticating my bones as my mind trips over itself. Tries to regain footing.

Trips again.

*The monster you know is safer than the monster you don't* ...

My breath puffs free, and I try to flatten myself against the grass as the beast drops closer, sniffing at me through a wide, dog-like nose that's black and wet. He digs his stumpy muzzle into the crook of my neck, and my entire body shudders, icy fear paralyzing my lungs.

My spine.

He draws several short whuffs, then lifts his head as a deep growl vibrates from his big, furry chest to mine. He shakes his body, the remaining arrows flying around him like water shook from a dog, before his head whips around, attention boring on the Gray Guards stumbling over each other.

Pointing.

The beast turns, dashes a fluffy tail across my face, and *roars*.

The Gray Guards are no longer shooting. They're *running*.

*Screaming.*

The beast pounces, talons punching from his paws. He charges toward the trees in long, ground-shaking strides, disappearing.

My darkness slithers back into the chasm, and I realize my creature is no longer screaming; bound in its wings, tail coiled around one of my ribs. It hangs, face tucked into its puffed plumage as I scramble to my feet.

Sobbing through winced half breaths, I stumble over a series of backward steps, moving toward the smashing sounds of the ocean at my back, not wanting to take my stare off the tree line. With my injured arm tucked close to my chest, I glance at the hole Rhordyn punched in the ground. At the vein of glass that forks toward the two soldiers eternally running.

He told me there were things I still didn't know, but this ...

*I wasn't expecting this.*

The fever continues to squish through my veins in hot pumps, my heart and head and body battling entirely different wars as I shuffle toward the thump of crashing waves. Piercing screams and agonized cries come to me on a whip of wind before they're snipped brutally fast, and that chilling, thunderous roar battles the howl of the storm. Rattles my heart.

He's out there ... killing them.

Ripping them apart.

I remember the way he ate the men my power dismantled, crunching through them like a ravenous beast, and another shudder shakes my bones.

My heel edges over the sharp fall of the cliff, and my heart leaps into my throat. I lurch forward— away from the edge—knees crumbling. Wincing from the bolt of pain that splits my arm as I plant both hands firmly on the ground, blood dribbling.

I try to pull out the arrow, screaming when the tug burns through the wound like a fiery poker.

Dropping my bloody, trembling hand, I glance over my shoulder to a churning torrent of waves thrashing against the sheer blue-stone cliff, the water dull and gray bar the white, frothy swirls.

There are no more shrill screams ripping through the stormy haze. No more sadistic, ground-shuddering roars.

It's just me, the rain, the crackling sky, and the heavy pound in my ears.

The hairs on the backs of my arms lift, and in my peripheral, a black smudge pushes free of the jungle. A hoarse sob bursts up my throat at the sight of the beast prowling toward me in slow, stalking strides, low on his haunches, maw splashed in so much blood it's dribbling from the slick fur at his chin. His leathery, frost-kissed scent comes to me, melded with the coppery tang of his slain victims.

"Don't come any closer," I say, shoving to a stand, and his lips pull back as he releases a grating rumble that ripples through me.

The talons retract from his blood-slicked paws, and he drops so close to the ground his belly brushes the grass, his unnerving eyes paving across me like icy blades.

He comes within an arm's length, one crawled motion at a time, every shift of his body making his meaty muscles ripple and swell.

So much power. So much might.

*So much death.*

"Please," I whisper, raising my good hand between us, not even sure he can understand me. "Please stop ..."

The beast whines, dropping his chin upon the ground, like he's trying to make himself smaller. Less frightening.

Impossible when his sable eyes are hammering me into a quivering pulp.

There's a shrill *crack*, and my eyes widen, heart tripping.

Fissures claw toward me from that glassy crater, carving

off a giant half-moon chunk of the cliff that captures me perfectly.

*Terribly.*

I have a split second to take in the flash of raw, primal agony in the beast's eyes before the ground beneath me plummets to the tune of his aching lament, his paws whipping out to snatch at thin air. Wind tears at my body.

I plunge hard and fast, my mind dunking into its own inky void as the ocean bellows beneath me, swallowing me in its monstrous maw.

# CHAPTER
## Orlaith
# 61

Cool drops of water scatter upon my blazing skin, luring me from my smokescreen sleep. I heave a strangled breath, the salty smell of the ocean filling my lungs.

Subtle *taps* puff against me like little blows of air ...

Familiar.

*Impossible.*

I drag my eyes open, seeing a smudge of white hair and deeply tanned flesh. Seeing piles of sparkly things that bounce piercing shards of light that hurt my squishy brain.

A groan bubbles up my throat as I scan my blurry surroundings, trying to hone my vision, panic clawing at my lungs. Shredding them.

Tightening a noose around my throat.

"Where—"

"It's okay, Treasure. It's okay ..."

*Kai ...*

Sobbing, I squeeze my eyes shut.

"I've got you. You're safe."

*I'm not.*

"I have to remove the bolt, Treasure. I need to snap it first, then pull it out."

A deep throbbing pain penetrates my senses, and I shift my hazy gaze to my arm, mind barreling back to visions of *him* saddled in arrows.

He was crouched over me, bleeding.

Faltering.

*Protecting.*

I whimper, releasing a string of tears as I squeeze my eyes shut.

"Are you ready?"

*No.*

"Yes," I whisper, giving a tight nod.

He takes my arm and gently lays it across my chest, a stab of fiery pain searing through me. There's a snapping sound, a devastating ricochet, and a scream bludgeons up my throat when the shaft slides free, grating past bruised and tender bone.

My body convulses in muscle-munching pain as I tumble toward a pall of sleepy darkness ... hoping this is a nightmare. That I'll wake in a cavern wrapped around *him*—high on the smell and the feel and the ache of *us*.

Loving us.

*Hoping ...*

Blinking my eyes open, I take in the damp, salty smell of my smudged surroundings, shot through with a cold bolt of disappointment.

*It wasn't a nightmare …*

I didn't wake in a nest of crunchy leaves curled around the man I love, tending buttery blooms of relief and a bursting heart. Instead, my entire body is one big *hurt*. Even the simple task of moving my lids hurts so much I want to weep.

An agonizing slug of lava blazes through my veins, my arm cropped across my chest—alight with a fiery itch, as though grubs are gnawing at the underside of my skin, tearing off chunks of flesh. I feel that same gluttonous grubbing in my lungs, like the meat is being consumed in gobbled bites.

I cough and sputter, tasting blood and the rancid tang of sour milk, certain every muscle in my body is being kneaded, stretched, or snapped.

Exhaustion gores its thumbs into my eyes, threatening to burst them. Heavy lures tug at my lids, and I choke through another gargled breath that feels like the beginning of the end …

My head flops to the side, lids growing heavier.

*Heavier.*

Through the haze of my vision, I see a deeply tanned man with white hair emerging from behind a pile of sparkly things.

*He looks like Kai.*

*He can't be Kai.*

"Treasure, you're awake …"

The lures tugging at my lids win the war, and I tumble back into an inky sleep that wraps me in its black, leathery wings.

This is real. I'm dying—the end beneath my feet, waiting

to open its maw and *chomp*. To weigh the heavy regret in my heart, then spit me out as dust.

And all I want is *him*.

*TAP. TAP. TAP. TAP. TAP. TAP. TAP. TAP.*

I release a groan that jerks my chest into a foray of violent coughs, panic crushing its hands around my ribs—certain I'm drowning from the inside out. Deep, wet hacks shred my lungs, and I tip my head to the side, retching the blood that bubbles up with each soggy heave.

"That's it, Treasure. Get it up ..."

Fire seeps from my pores. Drips off me in rivulets that do nothing to quell this raging inferno.

The spasm abates, panic loosening as my head flops. I draw a rattling breath and squint into a pair of emerald eyes.

*Kai ...*

"I'm s-so sorry," I rasp, not wanting to die without him knowing the weight of my regret, hacking through another round of chest-cleaving coughs as I try to scrub the masticating lava grubs from my leg.

My arm.

"No, Treasure ... Don't be sorry." He cups my cheek with a warm hand I nuzzle against, then wail at the pain, feeling as if my skin is sliding off the bone. "*Fuck*."

My wail turns into a wet, rancid cough, and I arch to the side in an agonizing roll, retching curdled, lumpy stuff that tastes like my rotted insides coming away in chunks.

"I failed you from the *start*."

*I don't know what he means.*

*But it doesn't matter—not anymore.*

I'm bereft at the thought as I vomit another lumpy mouthful into a bowl I can barely make out. A premature death has always felt imminent, like a shadow slithering around me. Watching me.

Ticking down my days.

But the look in that Vruk's big, inky eyes as the world crumbled beneath me will haunt me to the end. Like I punched my fist through his chest and ripped out his heart, clutching it in my bloody hand as I fell.

Kai tilts me back and tips my head to the side. There's a swishing sound before something slippery, cold, and wet is laid upon the searing hurt that feels as though it spans half my cheek.

I reach up, try to peel it off, but Kai gently eases my hand away.

"It will help, Treasure. You must leave it on."

*I wish he'd score his fingers across the hurt instead. Tear out the things that are gnawing at me.*

*TAP. TAP. TAP. TAP. TAP. TAP. TAP. TAP.*

The sound splits my skull, and I groan.

"Shh-shh-shh … It's okay, Treasure. You're doing *so* well. We're going to get you through this. I just need you to hold on a bit longer, okay? Keep being strong," he says, patting the sore, its sizzling roots wiggling down into my skull.

My jaw.

Much like the hungry welt on my hand. My foot.

Everything hurts, and the world's shaking to the beat

of that *tapping*—the cavern, the water lapping at the treasured shore made of sparkly things that tinkle.

*I must be in Kai's trove ...*

I wish I could see it properly. Appreciate it. Tell him how beautiful it is and fawn over all of his pretty, precious keepsakes.

I shut my eyes, my vision useless anyway—a grub in each one, munching on my corneas, grating their teeth around my pupils.

Distorting things.

*TAP. TAP. TAP. TAP. TAP. TAP. TAP. TAP. TAP. TAP. TAP. TAP. TAP. TAP.*

"That *sound*," I gurgle, feeling it peck at my skull with each incessant *tap*.

Kai snarls as inky claws grip my consciousness, crushing it in their tightening fists.

# CHAPTER
*Kai*
## 62

This time when she opens her eyes, a gurgled scream rips up her throat as she reaches for the ceiling, her violet irises gobbled up by blown pupils.

*"Kai? Are you—"* Wheezing through short, bubbling breaths, she searches the space around me. I can tell by the erratic wobble of her eyes that she's lost her sight.

'*Let out. Let out. Let out.*'

I ignore Zyke's screeching pleas and grip Orlaith's seaweed-bound hand. Do what little I can to tether her by planting a kiss on the inside of her wrist—right where her rapid pulse picks at me. Too fast.

Too violent.

Zyke becomes a manic, thrashing swirl in my chest, whipping against my ribs with his slashing tail.

"Treasure ..."

Her lips tremble, face crumbling. She lifts her other hand and blindly pats my chest. "You're here ..."

My heart cracks.

I should have been *there*.

And *now*—

I scan her war-stricken body, recalling the wounds I discovered when she first came to us:

Deep cuts in her palms.

An arrow through her arm.

Bite wounds on her neck ...

All healed, then replaced by boil upon boil upon fucking *boil*.

I pull a strip of seaweed from a slurry of spit and seawater and dress another wound as Zyke releases a whining lament. "I'm here, Treasure."

*I'm finally here.*

*TAP. TAP. TAP. TAP. TAP. TAP. TAP. TAP.*

I sweep the beads of sweat from her brow, stealing a glance at the ceiling while that fucking *tap* continues to ricochet all the way down to my trove.

It's bold. Relentless.

It hasn't stopped for hours.

Days.

I'm not even sure anymore.

All I know is that *he* did this to her.

*Rhordyn.*

He's a land beast. He should have *protected* her.

If she dies, I'm going to murder him. Let Zykanth masticate him into blood and guts and gore, then spit the residue into all five seas so his cells will never bind themselves together again.

Not in this lifetime. Maybe if the world implodes, then rekindles again in the form of another.

I use a clamshell to collect a dribble of fresh water from

the split in the smooth, black-stone wall, then bring it to her chapped lips, coaxing her head up. She drinks, and I feel a sense of relief, until she tips to the side and retches it straight back up again—now tinged with blood.

"It's okay, Treasure." I rub her back while she heaves. "You're okay ..."

A filthy lie I'll never forgive myself for. She's not okay.

*Not at all.*

Her frail, infected body buckles to the tune of her retching, and a heaviness sloshes upon my chest.

*TAP. TAP. TAP. TAP. TAP. TAP. TAP. TAP. TAP. TAP. TAP. TAP.*

Zykanth whips against my ribs so hard I loosen a hissed breath. *'Free Zykanth. Eat violent man and steal stick. Angry man pay for hurting treasured one.'*

Orlaith falls back against the pelt of damp seaweed, head rocking side to side as she whimpers. "That sound—"

"I know, Treasure."

*I fucking know.*

If she asks to be rid of it, I'll set Zykanth free. Let him swim up there and silence Rhordyn for good.

Orlaith tries to scratch her weepy, boil-riddled skin, then whimpers and screws her face up when she realizes her hands are useless—bandaged in flat ropes of weed. She kept tearing at her skin, encouraging more sores to spawn.

I lift her, pull her close to my chest, rocking her gently.

Giving her hush sounds.

I think it's been longer than five days since she plummeted into Zykanth's open maw when she fell from the cliff, and she's only gotten worse.

I *failed* her.

She whimpers, reaching skyward again when the tapping somehow grows louder.

More abrupt.

"Rhordyn ..."

Zykanth growls so loud the water lapping at our treasured shore ripples, sound waves ricocheting off the curved ceiling. A few coins even tinkle down the slope of our coin mound.

I brush a tangle of hair back from her face. "No, Treasure. It's Kai—"

"I need him," she rasps, setting her hand on my face as she tries to look at me. "I *need*—"

Her body spasms with another coughing, spluttering heave, and my upper lip trembles.

I steal a glance at the ceiling. In the direction of that shellhead with the stick. But then I train my attention back on Orlaith and see a look in those unseeing eyes that mimics a pain I feel in my chest at the absence of my vicious one ...

Zykanth stops his slithering stir, tapping at Orlaith's edges. *'Treasured one* want *angry man? Treasured one must have sick heart like sick skin.'*

"I don't think that's it," I whisper aloud as her eyes roll backward, her body going limp.

Lifeless.

If it weren't for the quiet tap of her heart, I'd almost believe ...

Swallowing thickly, I gently lower her to the pelt, planting a kiss on her blazing forehead. Hating myself for not being able to save her.

Zyke lets out another long lament.

My heart grows heavy, wetness glazing my cheeks as I

look to the fucking ceiling again, knowing exactly where I would want to be if I were drawing my last breath …

With Vicious.

'*Bad idea. Zykanth not agree to bad idea.*'

'We'll let him have her,' I tell Zyke, my tone as firm as my resolve.

*Let her die with him.*

*Let him see what he's done. How much he failed her, too.*

Zykanth stills, listens …

'Once she's gone, you can kill him.'

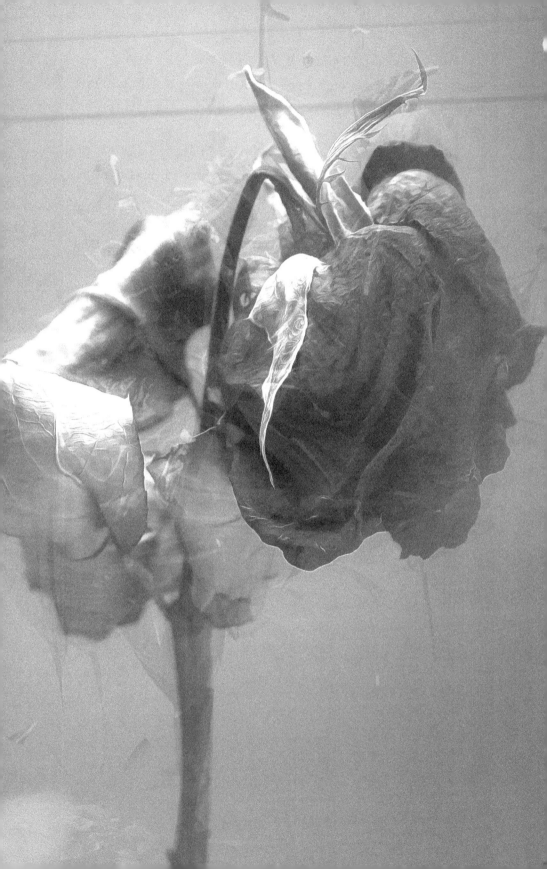

# CHAPTER
*Rhordyn*

## 63

The slate sea rages beneath the howling wind and battering rain, the midday sun hidden behind a churn of cyclonic clouds as I strike the metal pole against the stones over, and over, and over.

Her seed is a sputtering star, roots tugging from where it's anchored to my ribs and the pit of my soul—a violent upheaval threatening with each agonizing pull. I picture an ancient tree being ripped from the soil in devastating increments, my claws punched deep into the precious cargo. A failing anchor.

*She's dying.*

I strike the stones, again, again, *again*—roaring to the wind and the fucking rain.

Roaring to the sky and the sea.

*Myself.*

My beast is a restless shadow slashing at my insides. Desperate to rip through my skin and make it right.

She fell just like Rai fell, and I can't stop seeing it.

*Reliving* it.

The ocean balloons with an eruption of angry bubbles, and I heave a guttural breath. That invisible pulse *thumps* against me with violent blows as I toss the stick and fall to my knees upon the black serrated rocks.

Water gushes aside like parting curtains, revealing a huge, blocky head half the size of a ship, dressed in silver scales. Big green serpentine eyes blink open from beneath a shelf of mossy-colored shards, narrowing on me.

Plumes of steam shoot from flared nostrils, and the beast makes this deep, groaning sound akin to a creaking ship. The water oscillates, his long, slithering mass churning beneath the waves, dishing flashes of fins and frills.

"*Give her to me!*" The plea scrapes my throat raw. "*Please!*"

I've never begged. Not once. But I'll stay on my knees until I feel that flame sputter out.

Then ...

I'll rip the world to shreds.

Another haunting rumble agitates the water while my arms hang loosely at my sides. Pathetic and useless.

*So fucking useless.*

My animal hacks at a rib, *swiping.*

My bones ache, begging to crunch, jaw popping out of place as my skin threatens to split.

Those green eyes harden with lethal promise, and he plows a few feet closer to the rocks, maw cranking, exposing rows of serrated teeth. Curled in the center of his plump tongue, wearing strips of frayed cloth and binds of seaweed ...

*Her.*

My heart plummets.

Her skin is pocked with raw, weepy craters and bulging pink boils, some with pale heads that look like they're about to burst. Her bladed shoulder is hunched around her frailness, hip bones jutting, sharpened peaks. Like the disease has feasted on her from the inside out.

Made a meal out of her.

"Bite down and I'll glass your fucking insides," I growl, leaping over a shred of pearly sabers and into the pink, sinuous cavern that reeks of fish guts, landing on his fleshy tongue. "I'm here, Milaje," I whisper against Orlaith's temple as I swoop her into my arms. Her body is limp and cold.

*Too* cold.

I jump out of the drake's maw and into the howling wind, sprinting over sharp rocks that slice into my feet while *he* continues to rage against my ribs—hacking.

Slashing.

I power around the bay, the roaring waves stretching up the shore, as though reaching for me. I blast up the steep, irregular stairs cut into the black cliff face, not looking back until I'm halfway up—the swiftest glance.

He's still there, green eyes pinned to me while his huge, serpentine body roils beneath the surface.

I don't pretend to not know why.

I *know* why.

He's considering all the ways he wants to chew me up and spit me out because he thinks her life is about to end.

In a way, he's right.

Cresting the top of the stairs, I see a slack-faced Mersi holding the door open, her eyes wide, all the color sapped from her cheeks. Rain plasters her ruddy hair to her face, her apron snapping in the wind.

Her hand lifts to her mouth as her auburn stare grazes Orlaith's body.

Her face.

"Oh, my girl ..."

"*Get back,*" I roar, and she shifts out of the way.

I charge past, and Mersi's hurried, shuffled footsteps chase my thundering ones as the door thuds shut, snipping the howling sounds of the storm. Bundled in my arms, Orlaith's slow, rattling breaths fuel my rage.

My self-*disgust.*

"She could still overcome this on her own, Rhordyn ..."

Mersi's words are an aching plea but pebbles to my iron shield as I barrel around a corner so fast the flames of a wall sconce flicker. "That chance is dwindling by the hour. I will not *gamble* her life."

"The disease peaks at day five. She could still survive—"

I spin, forcing Mersi to stop four steps back, her stare running over Orlaith's disease-ravaged body flopped in my arms like a corpse. "Does she *look* like she's going to survive?"

My words boom in unison with a slash of lightning that strikes close enough to rattle a nearby window.

Mersi's features soften as she sighs, a deep sadness in her eyes. "You know, I saw the moment she fell in love with you."

Her words scour that part of me already raw and bleeding.

Swallowing, I spin on my heel, and charge down the hall again, her footsteps chasing me.

"She was in the garden just over a year ago, planting one of her rose bushes while I helped her mulch the others. Do you remember?"

I snarl, letting the beast inside me loosen some of his rage into the sawing sound tossed behind me as I race around a corner. Down a flight of stairs.

*Yes.*

"You came storming over while her hands were still dug in the dirt and told her you were holding a small fete. That she needed to see what the world had to offer so she knew what she was missing by hiding behind her Safety Line."

I turn a corner. Plow down another short flight of stairs. "What's your fucking point, Mersi?"

"She dodged the statement, as expected. Pretended you didn't say a thing. Asked if you liked her rose bush. And you told her—"

"*I like everything you plant,*" I grit out between clenched teeth, remembering the light that kindled in her eyes. The light I ignored.

*Chastised myself for.*

"You planted a spark in her, then left it to simmer until she was so sick with unrequited love that she accepted the cupla of another male. You've been nothing but *devoid* to that girl, Rhordyn. And now she's dying of a sickness that could have been prevented had you only been *honest* with her."

Her words are arrows—the iron type that burns going through skin and muscle and leaves me weak at the knees.

She's right, of course. A shame I'll wear for the rest of my life.

In working so hard to avoid this very situation, I drove it into existence.

"And though it pains my heart to say it ... I must. If you're doing *this* out of duty or self-service, let her *rest*, Rhordyn."

My heart stills in unison with my feet, the sconce beside me wavering.

Slowly, I turn.

Mersi stops several feet away, the flashing storm outside igniting her twisted face stained with tears.

"If you don't *love* her," she pleads, the words a strangled sob, "then *let her rest*."

My blood chills so fast all four candles in the sconce sputter out, my animal a statue inside me.

Watching.

"Your first mistake was assuming a measly four-letter word could encapsulate the way I feel for her," I say, tilting my head to the side, slicing Mersi with a stare I hope she feels all the way to her bones. "Your second was assuming I'll *ever* let her go. Make a third and we're done."

There's a moment of taut stillness.

Mersi's cheeks swell, a smile breaking across her face, reaching her eyes. Confused, I frown, watching her loosen the knot of her apron strings.

Taking it off.

She bunches it in her hands and swats a tear from her cheek. "Then she doesn't need me anymore," she says, peering up at me through glassy eyes, a fresh smile welling, though it stems a little when she looks at Orlaith. "Give her a kiss for me. Tell her a measly four-letter word cannot encapsulate the way I feel about her, and that I'll be over to share tea when she's well."

My frown deepens.

She nears me, and I give her my back, standing stiff as she passes—not wanting to risk contact between them, though she still sets her hand between my shoulder blades and whispers, "If you hurt my girl again, I'll find a way to spike your stew with senna."

I kick the door open, storm into my room, and set Orlaith on the bed, her body flopping against the mattress in a way that threatens to shred my skin.

Set *him* free.

"Milaje ..."

I brush my hand across her sweat-dappled brow.

She makes a gurgling sound that breaks my chest, then opens her eyes, pupils so blown there's nothing left of the violet. Her stare rolls around, like she's searching, her breaths beginning to saw. Faster.

*Faster.*

"*Rhordyn?*" she rasps, reaching—

I capture her seaweed-bound hand, planting it against my cheek. "I'm here, Milaje. You're safe."

Her brow buckles, eyes squeezing shut.

I bracket her face with my hands—soft enough that she can hopefully sense me there without agitating her wounds—and imagine she can see me. That she's whole, healthy, smiling and not broken in my bed.

"Is this a dream?"

"No," I say past my thickening throat.

*It's a nightmare.*

I scent her blossoming relief, and she sobs through another wet breath, nuzzling against my hand. Crying out a sharp wail of pain that makes me want to crush this fucking world in my fist.

"I'm s-sorry ..."

*So am I.*

Her other hand lifts, her face a twist of agony as she blindly reaches for my chest, setting her palm atop my heart.

Her features soften the slightest amount.

"I don't want to go," she whispers, her tone growing a spine of ... *determination.* "I need you to know I want to stay right here forever. With you."

I frown. "You're not going anywhere."

For some reason, she cries harder. Her body jerks, and she coughs—deep, wet barks that make my binds chew.

She comes up for tired, gurgled breaths. "But it— It *hurts ...*"

Those words crackle through my splitting heart.

My beast swipes at my ribs as fat tears slip down her cheeks. "I ... I want the hurt to end, Rhordyn. *Please.*"

*Please?*

"I ... want to spend my last breath kissing you."

My heart stops.

*She's passing me goodbye notes like she thinks I'm going to put a fucking sword through her chest and end her suffering.*

The realization sinks its teeth into the obsidian vault stashed beside her dimming seed. A chest stacked full of wounds that will never heal—too painful to even think about.

As soon as this moment ends, I'll stuff this one in there, too.

"Okay, Milaje." I press the whisper of a kiss to her head, vibrating with self-hate. "I'm going to stop the pain, okay?"

Her relieved sob shreds me.

"I'm sorry," I say, squeezing my eyes shut.

So fucking sorry she didn't get a chance to flourish. That I let her believe I hated her rather than myself. That she'll probably never look at me without seeing the mutts that sealed her mother's fate.

That she's about to be tethered to the face of her nightmares.

Most of all, I'm sorry she'll never understand why I couldn't—*can't* give her the choice she deserves. Not if I can avoid it. There's no reality where I'll freely offer her the weight of her fallen species. Of the entire *world*. There's no reality where she wouldn't allow herself to fall upon that blade.

*None.*

I lean back as a comforted smile touches her lips, her chin wobbling, lids drifting shut, more tears slipping free. "I'll b-be a flower in your garden."

*Never.*

I growl past lengthening canines, then sink my teeth into my bottom lip, swirling a gush of blood through my mouth before I gently cup her face.

Press my lips to hers.

She whimpers into me as I spear my tongue deep,

lacing her with a thousand sorrys. A thousand pleas for forgiveness.

*It'll never be enough.*

I drop my hand to her throat and gently massage her wounded skin, counting the seconds before she finally swallows, knowing they're her final moments of freedom. That from this day on, she won't be able to go a day without *relying* on me; her biggest, most lethal weakness.

A tender vulnerability, constantly ticking down.

I'm buying us moments, sidestepping fate, only to tether it to our heels where it'll snap at us with every forward step for the rest of our lives. But like a starving thief, I'll take those stolen moments and devour each one until there's nothing left to steal.

She sucks a shuddered gasp, and then she's deepening the kiss with the force of a wildfire, pulling my face closer. Swallowing.

*Breathing.*

Spine arching, she moans through the wash of pure, untainted ecstasy I feel pulsing through our building bond as my blood muddies her system, brushing away her lone existence. Planting a malignant, parasitic seed deep inside her chest.

A seed I can sense just like I can her warm, blossoming presence whenever she enters a room, or her sweeping gaze no matter the distance between us.

A seed I *worship*—a direct link that allows me to gush her full of strength and life.

A seed that brings us closer in every way but the one that truly matters …

Her acceptance of me.

Of *us*.

Her body grows limp, and I pull back, heaving choked breaths, clawing at my chest. Seeing her lips smudged in my blood as she draws sleepy breaths.

"I'm sorry," I whisper again, planting another kiss upon her temple—right beside a shrinking wound that churns my heart.

Because it's *working*.

Rebuilding her from the inside out, piecing her together with every thud of her racing heart.

I lean farther back, scrubbing my face, threading my fingers through my hair and gripping tight. My shoulders curl, the weight of my decision compounding …

There's a very good chance that when she wakes, she's going to hate me more than she *ever* has.

And it might just ruin me.

# CHAPTER 64

*Orlaith*

*The frail boy in the cell has dusky eyes, and the roots of his iridescent hair have started to darken.*
*His light is fading.*
*His skin is broken.*
*He's wet himself.*
*He cries for somebody he calls Lord ...*
I would like to kill them all over again.

*Drift ...*

*I throw a blanket over the portrait and hide it in a room where I don't have to look at everything I lost.*
*I'll never paint in color again.*

*Drift ...*

*There's fear in her wide eyes as she looks at me, hunting for a mark made by the blade she just swung. The seed*

*beneath my ribs thumps in acknowledgement to her hand
upon my chest—directly above it.*
*I'm tumbling. Feeling things. Fighting them before fate sets
its eyes on her.*
*Snips her breath.*
They can't have her.

D r i f t . . .

*I'm in a cold room only lit by a shard of light that shoots
down from far above, bathing the glass sculpture of a man
and a woman—forever embracing.*
*Forever choosing not to stay.*
*I don't know why I've come here ...*
*It always hurts.*

D r i f t . . .

*I'm proud. Bereft.*
Petrified.
*Surrounded by her colors and scent, I watch a ship sail
away—the smell of her blood, fear, and heartache still
thick on the back of my throat.*
*She almost drowned trying to escape me, because I didn't
talk. Again.*
*Always.*
*Why did I lock that door? My unsaid words might slit her
throat. Burn her at the stake. Cut off her ears.*
*I'll only have myself to blame.*

D r i f t . . .

*Her hand is around me, working me.*
*Greedy, I fall into her carnal attention, gorging on her*
*scraps like an animal.*
*I hate myself for it.*
What I really want is her heart.

D r i f t . . .

*There's a hole in my chest, and I want to tell her it's okay.*
*Because it is.*
*I deserve to wear her hurt.*
*Her hate.*
*But for the first time in my life, I have so many words to*
*say ... and now I can't catch breath to speak them.*

D r i f t . . .

*She's kneeling on a bed of white pillows, her lips a dark*
*shade of red. Another man lays her down, and she lets him.*
*"Kiss me."*
*I can see the lie in her gold-dusted eyes.*
*His hands are on her. Now his lips.*
*I'm murderous.*
Powerless.
*This mouth won't scream my words—*

D r i f t . . .

*I'm looking into the amethyst eyes of someone who fills my*
*chest entirely, her hand on my cheek, regret in her watery*
*gaze.*

*My heart breaks even before she calls it a mistake.*

*D r i f t . . .*

*She's walking across a branch above my head while blue flowers rain. She looks down, and my world tunnels as she smiles.*
*It's the most beautiful thing I've ever seen, and it's all for me.*

*D r i f t . . .*

*I'm inside her, and I never want to leave.*
*She runs her hands across my shoulders and kisses me like I'm fragile. Like she's not scared of me.*
*For the first time in my life, I don't feel like a monster.*
*This is all that matters. Us.*
*The world can fuck itself.*
*Fate will never find her.*

*D r i f t . . .*

*My beast pops the man's skull between his teeth, brains spattering the back of his throat.*
*He's certain that if he wears the blood of her enemies, she will see how much he loves her.*
*That she will accept him.*
*I wish it were that easy.*

*D r i f t . . .*

*She's falling, and we're powerless. There's no balance in this moment.*
*There's only pain.*

## D r i f t ...

*A* gasp cuts into me, flushing my lungs with the smell of leather and a crisp winter morning.
*Him.*

His essence is alive in the warm air that's cradling me, in his scent infusing me with every breath. He's in my *chest*—like he slipped his fingers between my ribs and tilled a void deep in the matter of my soul, filled it with a black, velvety seed that's curled its robust roots around the delicate bones.

It feels so *right* inside me, like a missing piece sown into place, thumping with its own steady heartbeat ... strong and mighty.

*Anchoring* me.

*Is this a dream, too?*

Confusion powers my heart into a thundering roar.

I open my eyes and look around.

*Black sheets tucked over me like a shield.*

*Clean, black, untorn shirt that swims on me.*

*Black walls.*

*Black.*

*Black.*

*Black.*

The color sinks into my soul like the sun on my skin.

*Castle Noir ...*

I breathe big, clear, *beautiful* breaths as I look at my arms, stretching them out. Tipping them both ways.

*No boils.*

The scars on my palms are gone, and my hands fly to my neck—blissfully smooth.

*No bite wounds ...*

*How—*

Deep rumbling sounds come to me, and my gaze bolts around the ungarnished walls.

A familiar window looks out onto a stormy night sky, and my pulse churns, stare halting on the easel that boasts an unfinished sketch I've seen before—resting hands that seem so at ease. Blinking back prickling emotions, I look to the fireplace glowing with a scattering of pulsing embers casting the room in a warm, red glow. I suck a gasp, heart stilling at the monstrous mound of black fur, huge paws, and wide, unblinking eyes nesting before it.

Looking at me.

I'm pelted with a vision of Rhordyn's flesh splitting, sprouting an inky pelt that was soon splashed in blood. Echoes of his pained lament impale me, tears puddling my lower lids.

Dripping down my cheeks.

Another smooth rolling sound vibrates through my chest, his placid gaze fixed.

His ears prick forward as I sit up so I can get a better look.

Scraps of material litter the floor surrounding him— as though he took control so fast Rhordyn had no time to remove his pants. Those big, glossy eyes trace me as I wiggle toward the side of the bed and set my feet on the cold stone floor, heart pounding.

Another deep rumble fills the room. Fills my chest—like

he's pouring the sound straight through my ribs; almost a purr that sprouts me full of a strong sense of ...

*Safety.*

I remember the funny dream I had that feels like a nuzzling truth, getting comfortable amidst the ashy gloom. A dream where a blood-lusting beast was part of me, sewn into my seams. It was crunching through bones. Pitted with this raw, archaic belief that the blood I drew equated the love I had for ... *someone.*

I remember the crippling sense of inadequacy as I watched that someone fall.

*Me.*

The dreams ... They're like trinkets of truth passed to me. Trinkets I tuck away to examine later.

I edge forward in slow, cautious steps, Rhordyn's shirt swimming around me, brushing against my thighs. The beast stays bound around himself, the tip of his long, fluffy tail flicking side to side.

Rusty firelight warms my prickling skin as I draw close enough that his deep, rumbling breaths dapple my bare legs, fluttering the shirt's hem. Stilling, I lower to my knees, peering straight into those fathomless globes.

"You—"

My voice chimes like a honey-sewn song, and my hand slaps upon my throat.

*Why do I sound so strange? Where has my rasp gone? Did that heal too?*

A shadow looms over me before something soft sweeps against my cheek, and I realize with a start that it's his tail—making shivers burst across the side of my neck.

It brushes across my chin, back up my cheek. Repeats in a slow, gentle stroke.

A foreign feeling pumps through my chest, my ribs, and vibrates down my spine. Makes me feel warm and snuggly. *Comforted.*

Like a soft hug for my heart.

Another swish of his tail, almost like a paintbrush gliding across my cheek, and I smile, deciding I like it very much.

Deciding I'm more and more certain he's *not* going to eat me.

I shuffle forward until I'm tucked before his big, wet nose, my eyes level with his ebony globes that reflect my messy hair and flushed cheeks. "You protected me," I whisper, lifting my hand, and his tail pauses mid-swish as I edge it forward—slow.

Measured.

The beast whuffs through flared nostrils, blowing the blunt ends of my hair off my shoulders as I lower my hand into the dip between his eyes and rub his soft, sleek fur.

He releases a rumbling purr that suggests he's enjoying the attention, and the faintest smile kicks up the corner of my mouth.

That seed in my chest *throbs.*

I think of Rhordyn—tucked somewhere inside the beast—and my heart lurches.

*Can he see me?*

*Hear me?*

I wonder what he's thinking. Feeling.

How he's going to react when I ask him the questions bubbling inside my chest.

"I need to see him," I whisper.

There's a long, tense silence.

Another tail brush to the cheek.

Another.

A stern, firmly rooted sense of *stubborn* pulses through me, mimicking the look in the beast's eyes.

*I don't think he wants to let him out.*

I give him another rub, this time behind his twitching ear, and he tips his head, nuzzling into the action. Lids lowering.

*He likes that spot.*

I keep going until every breath is a deep, sawing purr, then pull my hand away and shuffle back.

He blows out a short whuff, eyes snapping open, his massive paw easing across the stone and nudging against my thigh once.

Twice.

I shake my head. "No more ear scratches until I see him. *Please ...*"

He blinks at me.

Again.

With a groan, he eases onto his haunches like a shifting mountain.

The popping crunch of breaking bones curdles my blood, and I scramble to my feet, heart in my throat as midnight fur begins to recede. That thick, black mane curls into a scruffy head of hair, monstrous torso compounding, limbs refining until olive skin stretches across a broad, beautiful back.

Arms.

Legs.

Until *he* is crouched before me, on his knees, head bowed between his bare, powerful shoulders while he heaves sawing breaths. The silver scrawls on his skin pulse in rhythm with the seed inside my chest—so slow and strong compared to my thundering thoughts and the rapid fire of my hammering heart.

Vines of relief sprout through my insides, twisting around that seed.

Nuzzling it.

Bursting buttery blooms.

I reach forward, brushing my hand across his cheek.

He shudders.

Slowly, he lifts his head, and there's such raw vulnerability in his silver-stung stare that fresh tears slip down my cheeks.

He watches them fall, swallowing. With a deep inhale, he lifts both arms—an invitation that cups my heart and settles it in the safe spot behind his much stronger ribs.

I step forward, wrapping my arms around his neck, whimpering when he crushes me against his body, his hand spreading across my shoulder blades. He nuzzles into me as his chest inflates with an uneven breath, and more of those internal blooms burst, turning my insides into a sea of tiny suns.

*Home.*

I pull a shaken breath, intoxicating myself with his leathery scent. My tongue begins to tingle, and I become primitively aware of the *thump* of his heart, a familiar ache spreading up the arch of my palate, down into my canines ...

A taste flashes through my memory: thick, robust, silky warmth spilling down my throat, quenching my pain.

*Him.*

I swallow, wanting.

Needing.

"You fed me your blood," I whisper—so loud against his silence.

I almost choke on the sharp scent of *guilt* that floods the room.

"Yes."

His voice is black velvet, swathing me in its richness.

I dig my face farther into his hair, one hand at the back of his head, the other stretched across his shoulders—fingers swirling over his skin like silent whispers.

"Why?"

"Because I refuse to live in a world where you don't exist."

My heart cracks, the words passed to me so gently despite the rough timbre abrading my pebbling flesh. Glazing my eyes with another sheen of tears.

"It saved me."

Not a question. I can feel his strength thrumming through my veins like liquid stone.

Another thick, thirsty swallow.

Another silent whisper—this one closer to his spine.

"Yes ..."

"I'm healed, so why am I still ..." I clear my throat, cheeks burning, "*hungry* for you?"

He pushes his head deeper into my chest.

A long, agonizing pause before his baritone rumbles through my mind like a boulder battling against the walls of my skull: *'From now on, you'll need my blood daily. Or you'll wither. Go slowly mad. If you go long enough without it ... you'll die.'*

I choke on the heavy punch of his crippling admission, passed to me in such a deeply personal way that I can still feel their echo settling into the folds of my brain.

*The Safe ...*

*The goblet ...*

*The single drop of blood ...*

Suddenly, it all makes such explosive sense.

My knees buckle, but he holds me up, his hands scaling my back, pulling me to him. A lone word thrums through me, emerging from the epicenter of that seed tucked amongst my ribs.

It pounds into my heart.

My soul.

Blazes through me like a falling star, leaving a raw, gaping slash of *confusion*.

*Mate.*

I know, without a doubt, that I've never thought a truth so pure.

Tears carve down my cheeks as he swallows, tightening his arms. Subtle confirmation that squeezes my heart just as much.

A hazy memory comes to me, nudging, then prodding.

Shoving for attention.

*The two of us near my rose garden,* his *words cutting into me like the jagged edge of a serrated blade ...*

I draw a ragged breath, hold it, blow it out slow. "*Mates, Orlaith, are a fairy tale,*" I whisper.

He stiffens.

I mine a few tender vines of courage, bind them around my heart, and continue. "*A tragedy painted with the pretty face of a happily ever after, but at its core, it's still a fucking tragedy.*"

*Silence ...*

I pull away.

He looks up, the shadow of something unreadable passing across his chiseled features.

Drawing a steadying breath, I focus on his swirling silver eyes that seem to plead with me—like he knows exactly what I'm about to ask.

"Why are we a tragedy, Rhordyn?"

# EPILOGUE

*Rhordyn*

There's a stillness about this place, like even the wind's afraid to stir the tidal lake of Athandon. To reach across the water and brush the steep, gray volcano that lords from the lake's epicenter.

*Mount Ether.*

Dead animals litter the shore—horses, krah, a number of dune cats. Having sipped the water that holds a malignant truth, they didn't make it far before their bodies changed from the inside out.

Turned to stone.

The volcano excretes toxic minerals that spike the lake—a natural form of taxidermy that most creatures don't see coming; too desperate for a drink to heed the eerie warning signs.

Breathing thick, putrid air that smells of sulfur, I pace back and forth while I wait for the stepping stones to appear.

The only safe way across to Mount Ether.

The still water reflects the world like a mirror despite

the slow, silent drop of the water level. There are no ripples. No gentle laps at the shore.

Nobody knows where the water goes when it lowers. There's no outlet. Like the ground breathes it all the way in, then flushes it out again once every sun cycle. Sometimes it happens fast, other times slow—a risky journey for only the truly desperate and devoted.

I'm far from devoted.

The stones begin to surface—seven hundred and twenty-two of them poking above the glossy, noxious water. I don't bother waiting for them to peak before knotting the stirrups high on Eyzar's saddle, lifting the struggling hoof-strung goat off the back of him, and smacking him on the ass.

"*Go home!*"

With a toss of his head, he turns and gallops across the slate planes, perhaps sensing my agitation. I hate sending him off on his own, but from here, the road is too dangerous.

I heft the goat upon my shoulders to the tune of Eyzar's retreat and the bleating drone of the goat as I leap from the powdery gray shore onto the first rock.

The crystal-clear water allows a perfect view of fallen men, women, and creatures of all casts scattered across the lake's floor like stone statues, reaching for daylight with stretched fingers and vacant, stony stares. Those who came seeking Maars but didn't make it all the way across the path in time.

Victims of the tidal rise.

I shiver despite the warm, fat goat around my shoulders,

every fitted struggle threatening to throw me off balance as I leap from stone to stone, its bleating cries grating me.

I jump onto the far shore and charge up stairs shrouded in mist. My thighs burn by the time I step onto the volcano's crown, battered by the sound of my deep breaths and the distant *tap, tap, tap*. A sound that pitches into my spine.

Makes my guts cramp.

I follow it, finding Maars hunched at the base of one of the stone monoliths protruding from the mountain's crown, a dark, twisted shadow tucked within a gray hooded cloak that's frayed at the hem. A wiggling thread of black scripture is bound around his arm, squealing every time he bangs more of its length into the slate with a smack of his iron hammer.

Pausing mid-swing, Maars tips his face to the sky and draws a long breath through flared nostrils.

His head whips in my direction, exposing the face hidden within the cavern of his hood: smooth, unlike the skin on his hands. His eye sockets are empty bar a scoop of skin, though it doesn't stop you from feeling *seen*. As though he's hunting the beat in your heart like the animal he's become.

"Maars."

"Rhordyn, Rhordyn, far from home. Nice of the beast to finally roam."

I grunt, then flip the goat off my shoulders and release the binds around its hooves. It tips onto its side and scrambles up, then runs—wild eyed—straight toward the awaiting predator.

Maars releases a skin-scuttling snarl, leaving his

squirming ribbon of scripture half hanging from the wall as he drops his hammer and leaps upon the goat.

He bares his serrated maw, then rips into the soft flesh of the animal's throat. A plume of blood spills across its snowy fur. Maars holds—pinning the creature down until it gives a final, sputtering jerk, its mouth dropping open, tongue flopped out the side.

Maars pulls back, panting, producing a ravaged smile that's all bloody, pin-teethed horror, using his iron-tipped fingernails to cleave open the animal's chest cavity. He plows his hand into the hole until he's elbow deep, fishing around.

*Fucking hell.*

"I see your table manners have improved."

His responding laugh is manic and curdled as he rips the heart free, holding the steaming organ in his clawed hand. He bites into the round flesh, ripping off a chunk he gnaws in greedy, ravenous chews, blood dribbling down his chin and arm. "Yum like a plum," he says around a mouthful of masticated gore.

"I'm glad you approve."

He turns his attention on me, ripping into the organ again, stuffing his cheeks full of steaming, wet flesh. "Questions, questions don't ask themselves," he says through a bulging bite.

My nerves rattle.

I clear my throat and cast my stare on the stone beside me, its toothed tip high in the sky. Chest tight, I study the chiseled depths of countless prophecies—half filled with a thick, black substance.

Though some are not.

In some, the blackness has whittled away, leaving plain, gutless scriptures. Not many, but *some*. A handful.

*Hope.*

Crouching, I find the writings that are carved into my heart just as much as they're carved into this fucking stone and jab my finger at Orlaith's morbid life map. "This," I growl. "Has this changed?"

Another bite. More unsightly chewing while my patience frays.

He swallows a gulp so large I can see the mound of it working down his lanky throat as he tips his head to the side. "The more you know, the more you woe. Be happy you're not chained to the truth as I, Rhordyn. Ignorance is a gift."

"*Has. It. Changed?*" I snarl past the monstrous-size fangs punching through my gums.

Maars goes as still as one of the many statues littering the lakeside. "No."

The word is a nail hammered deep into my soul.

"And no matter how much you distance yourself or try to wrestle fate in your favor, *her* you will not savor. The world will keep trying to kill her until you're forced to seal the bond, cradling borrowed months before the final lines draw their fangs. Matters will be taken out of your hands."

I'm certain he just shoved his iron-tipped fingers into my chest and tore out my heart. Like it's *mine* he's now sinking his teeth into—feasting on.

I fall to my knees, suddenly starved for air, my vision stirring like the mist that muddies the mountain.

"You know, those words called to me like they wanted to be free," he says through the sloshy sounds of his chewing.

*Hasn't. Fucking. Changed.*

I slam my hands against the stone to steady myself while my beast rages inside, tipping his head to gnaw at my ribs with his back molars. I close my eyes and heave through rumbling breaths as I work to regain my composure.

"I went down to the bowl with my fishing pole, and the wee thing just *flicked* out of the water and wrapped around my arm like an eel. It never wiggled in pain as I chiseled it into the rock. Never screamed. It just slipped into its stony grave like it was too tired to misbehave. Only once before have one of my scriptures acted that way, and you know how that came to play. Decay and dismay."

I look over my swelling shoulder into the hollow sockets of his soulless eyes. See a fresh wave of hunger igniting his blood-splashed features.

"With you diving into my bowl after your sister, then being spat out like a trout on the shore bearing Kvath's prized sword, *Endagh Ath Mahn,*" he says, boasting that haunting smile again.

*The Sword of End.*

I swallow, forcing the slur of bile back down into my gut as I bunch my hands into fists, knuckles grating against stone.

Maars tips his head to the other side, clicking his tongue. "Wonder, wonder, I often do. How did *you* end up with such a ... *spectacular* weapon?"

I say nothing, content on letting silence hang while I growl through thick breaths, trying to keep my skin from splitting.

Joints from popping.

Maars makes a low humming sound. "It caused quite a

shake, you know." He points to the darkening sky with his chisel. "I felt it from below. In my bones. A rattle I've felt again … *recently*."

My brows collide. "The sword is useless to me now. I am bound. I am no *threat* to any of them." Besides—they spawned a perfect *defense* right in my path.

The markings around Maars's throat flicker as he opens his mouth, though all that comes out is a bloody, hacked splat. Snarling, he reaches into the cowl of his hood and massages his neck. "We are equals," he sneers. "If you are ever in need of an end, you have a friend. Perhaps, one day, you will crave it as I do, and we can do each other a great deed of service."

I ignore his rambles, looking at her prophecy again, hissing breaths through clenched teeth. Though I delight in the idea of putting the beast to rest and ending the plague of this fucking place, his fallen misery is not my priority.

*She is.*

"Tell me which one of you threaded our fates together," I demand through a rusty growl.

"Who do you think?" Maars laughs—a wild, twisted sound that consists only of the sharpest notes, bloodied spittle flinging from the wide gaps between his sharpened teeth. "Jakar does like his punishments, and fall in line the others do. Puppets, puppets *burn them all*," he hisses with bitterness.

I turn, looking at the monster nesting by my slain sacrifice.

"You can't coax a serpent with a warm, fresh meal, then expect it not to appeal." He brings the half-eaten heart to his nose and draws a deep sniff. "Do you think it was a mere *accident* that you were there that night? That you nearly put your talon through her chest to make it right?"

My nails dig into the feverish flesh of my palms. "*Explain.*"

"Shan't. Can't." He flicks a bloody hand toward the sky. "Just that every thread is specifically woven because *he* feeds off the suffering of weeds. It's why your father's fall was such a loss. He balanced Jakar's insanity, but that balance has turned to calamity. *Gone.*"

*So fucking gone.*

I feel it in my bones, making them creak and groan from the skewed pressure. Felt it kneeling on my chest like a mountain the moment I was born.

"Take the Bahari High Master, for example—a sample," Maars continues.

I still.

Listen.

"Calah's son supports the stones almost as much as the Shulák do; will never know that the Blight he's wielded into a shield around his city took his mate at the tender age of less than two. Nobody is safe in this place of chafed hate and lost faith. Jakar plays the world in ghastly tunes for his own sick enjoyment, but you already know that," he says, plucking a vein from the heart and slurping it like a mouse's tail as he waggles absent brows. "It's written all over your skin. His win."

I look away, down toward the crater lake.

"Why *her?*"

He makes that humming sound again. Guts squirming, I watch him pluck another vein free, wrapping it around his finger before sucking it off the tip. "You believe you are the catalyst. I can neither confirm nor deny. I have fished for the answer, but all I could pull up was the poor, decapitated head of a once frolicking scripture. Like somebody reached into my bowl and slaughtered the poor soul."

My heart plummets so fast it feels like the world's tipping.

Further proof to support my swelling theory. But it's just that—a theory. It's certainly not one I'll ever voice, stashed away in an obsidian vault tucked inside my chest, right next to her precious, glowing seed.

Stuffed away with other things I'll never think of again.

"Let me give you one more truth I managed to tuck away for this very special day," he says, and I whip my gaze at him, eyes narrowing. "Since you finally graced me with your presence again."

"What's the catch?"

He sets the fleshy remnants of the heart back in the goat's gaping chest cavity and slurps the blood off his fingers. "In return, you will bear in mind that of which I yearn. Should you ever want to … *spend* the swords blow and leave the world behind."

I frown, wondering when he got so desperate to die.

My insides curdle as he tips his head, his cowl shrugging back to reveal his bald scalp. He threads his entire knobbly hand into his wide-open mouth, then reaches down his throat until he's almost elbow deep. He *pulls,* making choked sounds, and his bloody hand re-emerges, clenched around a long, fleshy ribbon of wiggling, black scripture.

He yanks the squealing prophecy free, then tosses it on the ground by my feet where it hisses slithered words:

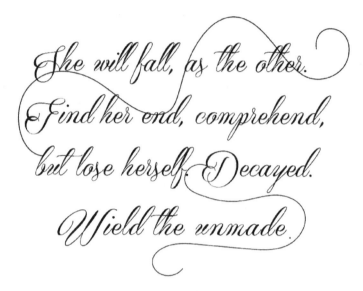

*She will fall, as the other.*
*Find her end, comprehend,*
*but lose herself. Decayed.*
*Wield the unmade.*

It withers into a mangled ball while Maars coughs and sputters, wiping a dribble of black blood from his milky lips.

I replay the words in my head, frowning.

*Hinging.*

"Did you catch the last line?"

"You weren't listening?" I can feel his disapproving leer even though he has no eyes. "The poor thing perished without cherish. You should have been paying closer attention."

Blocking him out, I chew on the echo of hissed words—tasting them. Trying to release the deeper notes.

Wield the unmade ... *I'm sure that's what it said at the end.*

Spinning, I crouch and place my hand on her prophecy. Trace it with the tip of my finger as I mutter the words in my head for the millionth time:

*Light will bloom from sky and soil,
skin tarnished by the brand of death.
Watch her grow, twist and sow, Smother her while
she sleeps or catch the lethal grace. A bond will
soon embrace. Strengthened by lover's well,
separate ... befell. Weakened, the strike must land.
Or fall to Shadow's hand. The world
will fall to Shadow's hand.*

"You want my advice, concise?"

"No."

I've never wanted his silence more in my entire life.

"Stop fighting it," he offers anyway. "Happiness tastes much *sweeter* when it's short lived. Let her drink you, roots will sink through. Take your precious little time and enjoy it like a rhyme—sublime. Then *gone*. You can't save her without forsaking the world, bound man." He points to the darkening sky, a single star hatching red. The first that pocks into existence every night. "Nobody can."

I steal a glance at the ruddy star, then at the withered prophecy on the ground, back to the one on the stone. I push to a stand and stalk toward the stairs, taking them two at a time.

*We'll see about that.*

# THANK YOU

Thank you for reading To Flame a Wild Flower!
I hope you've enjoyed the journey so far.

As a lot of you know, this story first came to me
in a dream, and it hasn't let me go since. I'd planned the
entire series before I wrote a single word—
it just *spoke* to me.

The *Characters*.

The *World*.

The *Relationships*.

This book healed my heart, and I hope some of you felt
the same. I finally got to release some secrets and give the
characters a chance to stretch their roots into the soil.

To anchor themselves.

I know I said this after To Bleed a Crystal Bloom
and To Snap a Silver Stem, but there really
is still SO much story left to tell …

**The board has only just been set.**

Again, thank you for reading!

## —SARAH

# ᴀCKNOWLEDGMENTS

I wouldn't have been able to publish this book without the help of my incredible team and the unending support of my family.

My babies—thank you for being so patient while Mummy wrote her book. Thank you for the jokes and loves and hugs. The Editor & The Quill—Chinah, how did I get lucky enough to have you in my life?

Thank you for everything you poured into this story. As always.

Thank you for your friendship, your mastery, your attention to detail. Thank you for digging so deep and for the late nights and early mornings. You go above and beyond with every book I write, and I'm so lucky to have you in my life.

Mum—thank you for putting your life on hold to be there for me throughout the months leading up to every release. Thank you for all the heartbeats you poured into helping me polish this story, and for plucking me out of the ashes more than once, dusting me off, blowing fire back into me, and telling me to keep going.

Philippa—thank you for always being there for me. For your endless support and smiles and positivity. Thank you for making sure our family still functions during the pre-release months when I stop existing.

I never have enough words to say how thankful I am.

Lauren—what can I say? You came in like a firefly and lit up the dark shroud I'd tucked myself amongst.

Thank you for reading my words, for your thoughtful critiques, and for not being afraid to speak your mind. You helped this story become the best version of itself, and for that I'll be forever grateful.

Lois—thank you for taking the time to read the proof version of this book. Your enthusiasm towards the story gave me strength in the hours when I needed it the most.

Forever grateful.

Angelique—as always, thank you for the hours you put into reading my draft. For your sage insight, and for being a such a strong presence throughout the process.

Brittani—thank you for your friendship, your laughs, your listening ear, your attention to detail. Thank you for always being there for me right up until the end.
Love you so much.

Raven—thank you for your endless words of encouragement. For always being there and telling me to keep going. Thank you for your friendship and for the endless deep belly laughs that always pick me up. Love you to the moon and back, and I can't wait to be back in the sprint room with you again.

Josh—my love. Thank you for supporting me, for loving me, and for always believing in me. You're amazing, and I'm so lucky to be doing life with you.

A.T. Cover Designs—Aubrey, thank you for the stunning covers. For pouring so much heart and soul into every single one of my graphics, and for bringing this story to life visually. You are incredibly talented, and I'm constantly blown away by everything you do!

And of course, thank you to my incredible readers—the Bloomers—who spur me on every single day. I see the hours you put into your artwork, theories, and loving the book, and it breathes life into me. I can't wait to bring you more words!

Sarah. Xo

# About the Author

Born in New Zealand, Sarah now lives on the Gold Coast with her husband and three young children. When she's not reading or tapping away at her keyboard, she's spending time with her friends and family, her plants, and enjoying trips away in the snow.

Sarah has been writing since she was small, but has only recently begun sharing her stories with the world. She can be found on all the major social media platforms if you want to keep up to date with her releases.